Happy Birthday, Dad

Love,
Melissa, Doug &
Katie
1994

THE BEST FROM FANTASY & SCIENCE FICTION

A 40th Anniversary Anthology

T H E   B E S T   F R O M

Fantasy
&
Science Fiction

A 40th ANNIVERSARY ANTHOLOGY

Edited by
Edward L. Ferman

St. Martin's Press
New York

To my mother, Ruth Ferman, for her 80th year

CONTENTS

Preface *Edward L. Ferman*		xi
Introduction *Harlan Ellison*		xiii
The Cat Hotel *Fritz Leiber*		1
Slow Birds *Ian Watson*		17
Judgment Call *John Kessel*		44
The Aliens Who Knew, I Mean, <u>Everything</u> *George Alec Effinger*		62
The God Machine *Damon Knight*		78
Understanding Human Behavior *Thomas M. Disch*		82
A Rarebit of Magic *John Morressy*		105
In Midst of Life *James Tiptree, Jr.*		119
Surviving *Judith Moffett*		139
Cage 37 *Wayne Wightman*		174
While You're Up *Avram Davidson*		212
Eidolons *Harlan Ellison*		215
Face Value *Karen Joy Fowler*		230

Buffalo Gals, Won't You Come Out Tonight
Ursula K. Le Guin   243

The Boy Who Plaited Manes   *Nancy Springer*   272

Out of All Them Bright Stars   *Nancy Kress*   285

Salvador   *Lucius Shepard*   293

State of the Art   *Robert Charles Wilson*   312

Black Air   *Kim Stanley Robinson*   322

Uncle Tuggs   *Michael Shea*   349

*   *   *

PREFACE

This is the twenty-fifth volume in *The Best from Fantasy & Science Fiction* series and, except for one theme anthology (*The Best Horror Stories from The Magazine of Fantasy & Science Fiction*, St. Martin's, 1988), it is the first collection from the magazine to appear since 1982.

Thus my problem in putting together this book was finding room for all the stories I wanted to include from this longer-than-usual period of 1982 to 1988. There was no perfect solution; the best we could do was to publish a bigger book, and this was accomplished. We offer in this volume twenty stories rather than the usual dozen or so.

The series began in 1952, when founding editors Anthony Boucher and J. Francis McComas edited a collection of top stories from the first three years of publication. This first *Best from F&SF* included stories by Cleve Cartmill, L. Sprague de Camp, Martin Gardner, Richard Matheson, Robert Arthur, and others.

This was, in fact, rather an early SF anthology, since the species didn't exist until the 1940s, and the series quickly became a frequent feature on the SF publishing landscape. The 2nd through the 8th in the series were edited by Boucher; 9–11 by his successor, Robert P. Mills; 12–14 by Avram Davidson; and 15–24 by me.

This book also celebrates 40 years of publication. In looking back,

I'm aware of only a few changes in *F&SF* (for instance, we use hardly any reprints these days) and am struck by the similarities to the early issues and the vision of the founding editors. There remain no taboos at *F&SF*, except for trite ideas and bad writing. There remains a commitment to publishing new writers—you will find several in this book, along with many famous names—and a commitment to publishing quality SF and fantasy that is the equal of any fiction published anywhere.

—Edward L. Ferman

* * *

INTRODUCTION

Harlan Ellison

Just toss that stack of stuff on the floor; sit down, make yourself comfortable. It's good to see you. When you called and said you wanted to drop by, I thought you were coming to bust my chops about missing another deadline. I mean, it's so seldom we actually get to *see* each other these days. I write the column, send it in, chat with Ed or Audrey—"Will you make it by the tenth?" "Yes, I'll have the column to you without fail, trust me on this." "Are you sure?" "Yes, I'm certain, don't worry about it." Like that. So there's been a long time between. Just sitting down and talking. So tell me, Eff, how the hell you keeping?

I'll say this for you, you're not showing your age. Turning forty doesn't seem to have had any effect on you. Looking good.

But then, I'm still fifteen years older than you. We're both getting on. I was fifteen when you were born, did you know that? Now you're forty, and I'm fifty-four. That's a long time to be friends, Eff. Lot of hot type in the slag bucket.

Did I ever tell you how tough it was for me to start selling to you? No? You mean, in all these years, we've never reminisced about that? You're kidding; I can't believe it.

Well, it *was* tough. Now that I've had so many stories in your pages, and that "Special Harlan Ellison Issue" back in July of 1977, and the column for the last—what is it?—four, five years, I'll bet you've forgotten that I never actually appeared in you till August '62. Your first issue was fall 1949, and I was submitting to Tony Boucher and Mick McComas as early as 1951. And not only was I rejected regularly by *them* (but always with a nice, if brief, encouraging note), but when Bob Mills became the editor in 1958, and I'd been writing professionally for three years at that point, even *he* turned down everything I submitted. And he was my *agent!* It didn't happen for you and me till Avram took over. And he bought "Paulie Charmed the Sleeping Woman" for that August '62 issue.

Do you remember that issue, Eff?

What a killer!

It led off with Fritz's "The Secret Songs" and included Dean McLaughlin's "The Voyage Which is Ended" and Horace Gold's "What Price Wings?" and jeezus what a batch of names on that table of contents: Gordy Dickson, Ted Cogswell, J.T. McIntosh, Randy Garrett, Avram doing books, Isaac with the science column, a Feghoot by Reg as "Grendel Briarton" and quite a lot more. To be in such company! I glowed for a month.

What? Oh, you remember the infamous "false sale," do you? Yeah (he said bitterly), I remember it, too. That was one of the most embarrassing practical jokes ever played on me. I like to die, as we used to say in Ohio, which was where I was living when it happened. Refresh your memory? Sure. But please don't pay any attention to the grimace of pain as I recount.

Well, what happened—as best I can remember—was this:

It was early in 1952. Along about March, if I recall correctly. I'd been doing this fanzine called *Dimensions* (or maybe it was still called *Science Fantasy Bulletin*, I don't know) and was involved with Cleveland fandom, and I was writing these dumb little SF stories and sending them out, and getting them bounced right back at me. Usually with a printed rejection slip from *Argosy* and *Blue Book* and *New World Writing* and *Colliers*, or from the SF specialty magazines. The only difference was, I'd met a lot of the editors who were working in those days—Bea Mahaffey at *Other Worlds*, Bill Hamling at *Imagination*, John Campbell at *Astounding*—it hadn't become *Analog* yet, I guess—and they were all very kind to me, bouncing the stuff (which was pretty sophomoric), but always encouraging me with a handwritten comment on the printed form. For instance . . .

Fantasy and Science Fiction

Sep 14 51

```
Harlan Ellison    THE BEER CAMPAIGN
     Sorry, but-

nice idea...but once you've stated it,
that's all.  You haven't developed it
into a story.
```

The Editors

That was one of Tony's. It kept me going, I'll tell you. Boy, did I revere that man! To sell a story to Tony Boucher was one of the most important things in my life. I knew, even then, even as a high school kid, that having *Anthony Boucher* accept a story would be the imprimatur that would validate all the dreams I had that I could be a writer worth reading.

So out would go these idiot stories, and back would come these idiot stories with printed rejection slips or little notes saying try again; and it went on all through 1951 and 1952.

And then, one day, I got a letter from Tony saying that he really liked a short thing I'd sent, titled "Monkey Business." (If I recall correctly. A piece of correspondence from that period, from another editor, rejecting a couple of other yarns, contains a comment "Glad to hear of your success with *The World of Roger 1132.* And I rejected it, tsk

tsk. I hang my head in shame." It gives me pause. But since the only "success" I'd had at that point was with "Monkey Business," I guess it'll have to wait till some archivist figures it out before the mystery is solved.)

Anyhow, the letter from Tony said it was a sale, it was a nifty little yarn, and that a check would be coming along shortly.

Well, I just died and went to heaven. Like the teenaged fool that I was, I ran around proclaiming that I'd "hit" *F&SF*. It sure as hell was the envy of all the other fans who'd been trying to break into the pros. Silverberg was dumbfounded. He had been writing and submitting, too, and he didn't sell his first story till two years later . . . so I was something of a celebrity in fandom. And it made the rounds, and everyone was startled and some were pleased and some said I was making it up.

And no check ever arrived.

And when someone checked with Tony Boucher, he was utterly unaware of any such purchase. He made it clear that no, *F&SF* had not bought a story from me, and when he compared the letter (which I had to mail to him in the flesh, in those pre-Xerox days) with one of his own, he was forced to tell me that the initials signed to the missive were a forgery.

Someone had gotten hold of a piece of *F&SF* stationery and had sent the bogus acceptance letter "to put Ellison in his place." It was all a nasty joke.

I died and went to The Hell of Unending Embarrassment.

The story never came back. I don't even have a copy in my files. Lost forever. Not that it matters much, I suppose. It probably wasn't a very good story to begin with. And I never found out who'd pulled the gag, though Dean Grennell once told me that he'd managed to cop some *F&SF* notepaper (and I have, in my files, a photo of a bogus *F&SF* note he sent me as a gag) and it wasn't that hard to do. What? Oh, no, hell no, it wasn't Dean who'd done it to me. We were, and remain, friends, and I know he wouldn't have been so cruel. He was, and is, one of the kindest men I've ever known. But if *he* could get his hands on some of that notepaper, well, I guess others could have, as well. It was a mean trick to pull on a kid so hungry to break into print, and it was one of the earliest manifestations I experienced of that nasty streak that runs through fandom. And I was a laughingstock in SF circles . . . not the last time *that's* happened, I'm sorry to admit.

Does it still bother me? Yeah, I guess it does. Because I was this highly verbal, hyperactive kid, dazzled by the wonders of the genre, and all the glamorous writers in it, I ran around like a loon, making an obnoxious pest of myself. I suppose the only reason no one snuffed me was that I was obviously well-meaning, no matter how annoying; and I guess longtime friends like Bob Bloch and Cliff Simak and Isaac saw some potential in me; and they kept the Visigoths from rending me. Not that I was smart enough to assist them much. But that phoney *F&SF* acceptance letter was an ugly stunt and, yeah, even now, more than a quarter century later, I get wistfully morose about what a jackass I was made to appear.

But you can imagine, Eff, how intent I was to "justify" myself. And the only way to do that, was to sell to you.

Then Tony died, and that was the end of that.

And when my own agent couldn't find merit in my work, for the venue I most hungered to reach, it produced a sense of awful ambivalence. Why was it that I could sell hundreds of yarns to *other* magazines, some of them more prestigious, most of them better paying . . . but couldn't crack the pages of *F&SF*? If I'm any good at all, I thought, why the hell can't I get into *F&SF*?

So then, Avram came in as editor, and he bought "Paulie . . ." (which I never thought was all that hotcha-cha a piece of work) and I had sold to *F&SF*. And I don't think I placed anything with you again till the special two hundredth issue, which was January of 1968—one of the stories from *Partners in Wonder*, a collaboration with Sheckley. Terrific story, but I always had the feeling it sold because Bob's name was on it. That one was bought by Ed Ferman. He was in charge by '68, if you recall. (It may be that I'd had a book review or two between '62 and '68, but of stories there were none.)

And then, later that year, in October, Ed published "Try a Dull Knife," which was pretty experimental; and he got back a lot of good comment, and that started the honeymoon.

So Ed bought "The Deathbird" and "The Place with No Name" and dozens of others. And a bunch of them won awards. And on and on through the years. Till I started the film column, which has been some kind of weird exercise, let me tell you; and now Ed wants me to write an introduction for the 40th anniversary anthology.

And I've got to tell you, Eff, I haven't the faintest damned idea what I can write.

It's hard, kiddo. I *grew up* with *F&SF*. I mean, can you imagine what it was like to be intense and smart and absolutely no-price socially as a kid in Cleveland, back in 1950; to love reading SF and fantasy but to be bewildered by hard science and to know you just can't write like that, yet hunger to tell stories in the genre? And then to read *F&SF*, where the accent was on strong literary values! To be exposed to a range of great writing beyond merely those who wrote SF—Oliver La Farge, Wakefield, Dickens, Jack Finney, Leslie Charteris, Robert Graves . . . my god, how the list goes on. Tony and Mick were so well read, so awesomely *urbane,* just sampling the work of the great masters of literature in those pages of the early issues made me dizzy with disbelief at how ignorant I was, how presumptuous I was to think I could be a writer without having read all of these astonishing talents. So I went at it. Every time I'd come across someone like Lord Dunsany or Robert Nathan, Ben Ray Redman or Saki, I'd ravage the school library or the public library, and read everything I could cram into my head.

Eff, I've got to be honest about this. I think, as much as anything, I learned how to write from the college of *F&SF*, that special reading course Tony and Mick proffered along with a feast of good stories.

So what am I to write about, for this 40th anniversary thing Ed has in mind? How do I relate the history of a magazine that published Chad Oliver and Chuck Beaumont and Dick Matheson and Ted Sturgeon and Ward Moore and Sheck and all the others, who were blazing new paths *every month!*? How do I express my anger at stick-up-the-ass volumes like *Best American Short Stories* or the annual O. Henry Awards that have totally ignored these forty years of your existence? Look back at the last forty years of those annual "best" collections, and see if you can find a dozen stories out of the hundreds they've selected as "the best" each year, that compare even remotely to The Best that *F&SF* has published. It's miserable, is what it is!

See, I don't want to get mawkish, Eff. I don't want to do one of those phoney flag-waving routines about how special and how wonderful and how influential and blah blah blah. We had enough of that crap with Dukakis and Bush.

And I don't want to spin out some dull literary history that will bore those who've been through it, and stun those who'll be coming to F&SF through the pages of this book. And to be honest, it's always so damned *personal*. If I were to bore the readers with that "false acceptance" story, would it amount to anything? Would they understand that for forty years this magazine has been a lot more than just a newsstand periodical of tall tales? Would they understand that this magazine, you big Eff you, that it's been a standard-bearer for exemplary writing in a time and in a nation where slovenly thinking and inept storytelling have become the norms? Is there some way to get that across without sounding like a city hall pol beating the drum for a hack alderman?

I don't think so, Eff. I don't think I'm the guy to do this. I think it ought to fall to someone like Sprague or Ayjay, or maybe even Isaac. They're a lot more serious about such things.

It's okay for the two of us to sit here and *schmooz*, but it's something else to write an introduction to forty years of brilliant literary production.

So I think I'll just tell Ed I can't do it. No, it's nice of you to say that, and I think you're cute, too, kiddo; but I'm going to call Ed in the morning and just beg off.

I've made up my mind.

So.

Remember the time Ed and Audrey . . . what's that? You want to know *what*? How the hell should I know why Ferman keeps running that slug-line on your table of contents—*Including Venture Science Fiction*—when the magazine folded almost twenty years ago. Maybe he's got some outstanding subscriptions. Maybe it's got something to do with keeping rights to the title. How'm *I* supposed to know? Ferman's beyond my understanding altogether. I mean, how rational can a guy be who keeps publishing *my* stuff, even when they threaten to burn down his house?

You figure out why he asked *me* to write his introduction, and I'll figure out why *Venture Science Fiction*.

And would you mind not hogging the chips 'n' dip.

It's nice having an incipient old fart like you visiting, but I've got to tell you, there is a lack of dignity with all that guacamole dripping on your cover.

So, as I was saying: remember the time Ed and Audrey . . .

The Cat Hotel

✻   ✻   ✻

Fritz Leiber

No SF writer has won more awards than Grand Master Fritz Leiber, and few have his range and variety. Among his many enthusiasms are cats, but cat lover or not, you are sure to be delighted by this tale about the adventures of two curious pets and their mistress.

✻   ✻   ✻

FROM the cool patch of floor by the kitchen door Gummitch, an orange cat of endless curiosity and great patience, watched the younger and slenderer gray cat Psycho stand motionless over their water dish, peering down at her reflection. The day was hot, but she did not drink.

Although they were not related, Gummitch felt a big-brotherly concern for Psycho. He wondered if she were studying the mirror world or even considering oversetting the dish to create a water-sculpture as he'd done on occasion.

Or if something sinister were at work.

Kitty-Come-Here, their featherbrained mistress, known to humans as Helen Hunter, stopped in the dining room doorway, a small slender woman in a thin flowered dress carrying a furled green parasol and a small white handbag.

"I've called a taxi, Gummitch," she informed him, "to take me to the Concordia Convalescent Hospital to make polite inquiry of my beloved widowed mother-in-law as to how her broken hip is mending, and sweet worried noises. Though truly it is the great Harry Hunter's place to do that." She sniffed. "Don't you think, Gummitch, his business trips have come most conveniently since the catastrophe? I leave you in charge of the house. Please don't go out and pick a fight with the Mad Eunuch, it's much too sultry. Ah, there's the buzzer. Psycho, if you can stop admiring yourself for a moment and listen to me, be a good kitling and do everything that Gummitch tells you to, bar bedroom stuff. Now good-bye, chaps."

Gummitch himself rather wished that Old Horsemeat were here, not to pay dutiful filial visits, but to consult with about Psycho. Except that of late his strange parent-god had been imbibing rather too freely of the second of the two wondrous and terrible evil-tasting human beverages—not mind-quickening coffee, which had the power almost (but not quite, alas) to gift brutes with human speech, but insidious sometimes-burning alcohol, the mocker and jester—and as a result was not to be trusted as much as formerly.

Kitty-Come-Here, the ginger cat had to admit, was showing flashes of unaccustomed thoughtfulness and reliability—though not many or very bright, he hastened to add. Still and all, beneath her solemn kitteny playfulness, there did seem to be something new, serious and mysteriously sad, growing by fits and starts under the bobbed black hair of the little lady who had come to Old Horsemeat (to use his words) from over the Shortwaved Ocean, in contradistinction to the Pacific.

The cat heard the front door close.

Somewhat later, at Concordia, Helen Hunter backed smiling and cooing out of Mrs. Hobart Hunter's single dim ground-floor room rather more hurriedly than she'd planned so as not, at all costs, to hear the deep sob she suddenly *knew* was going to burst convulsively from behind the bravely composed face and tightly pressed, serenely smiling lips of the cologne-scented old lady supine in the narrow high bed. For if she did hear it, she'd have to go back and do all her clucking, Harry-excusing work over again, and she as suddenly knew she simply couldn't *bear* that. Panic touched her, and in its unreasoning grip she backed rather faster and farther than she'd intended—all the way into the equally dim double room across the hall.

Gaining some control of herself, she turned around rapidly, surveyed the three beds and three old women crowding the room, and was momentarily shocked moveless and speechless, the contrast with what she had been visiting was so positively scaly.

Her mother-in-law had been tucked in neatly (of course she had a broken hip), while these creatures sprawled all which ways in their nightgowns (after all, it *was* warm) on top of their covers and pillows with all sorts of resultant untidy, immodest, even obscene disclosures.

In the single room there were a few neatly arranged objects on the bedside table and nothing whatever on the top sheet save Mrs. Hobart Hunter's pale flaccid arms extended decorously down her sides. Here all three beds and tabletops were littered with a jumble of soiled crumpled tissues, hair-holding combs and brushes, candy boxes, lunch remnants, paper cups, photographs, books, papers, and magazines, mostly astrology.

Harry's mother had been recently washed and neatly groomed, smelled of cologne.

These women had elf-locked or straggly flying hair, what there was of it, smeared lipstick, were smudged with dirt, looked greasy. They had a variety of odors about them. Really, they stank.

The first old woman had scrawny legs, a chunky pot-bellied body, and a little screwed-up face with squinting eyes and a button nose that would have looked scowly-angry except her small mouth was smiling.

The second old woman was fat like a little bumpy mountain with immense hips, droopy jowls, and large peering pop-eyes.

The third old woman was skinny as death itself, had a blotched pallor all over, a curving beak of a nose, and no chin to speak of. An empty brass cage hung beside her bed.

Helen took in all this in three rapid snapshots, as it were. A couple more seconds and she might have recovered her poise, but just then the first old woman asked with a chuckle, "Lose your way, dearie?"

"Something frighten you, chickie?" the third old woman chimed like a cracked bell.

"Well, you certainly aren't my niece Andrea," the second old woman observed in a voice like suet.

"No, I don't believe I am," Helen started to say inanely and broke off midway, flustered.

"My, what a lovely green parasol," the third old woman continued.

"And what lovely bobbed hair. You do look cool," the first old woman added enviously.

"You look nice enough to eat," the second old lady concluded in her flannel tones.

"Oh, do please excuse me," Helen began and then turned and ran out before she garbled anything more or yielded to the impulse to respond to the last remark with "Is *that* what made you so fat, you dirty old cannibal?"

In her hurry she turned the wrong way in the hall, and rather than repass Mrs. Hobart Hunter's door and risk hearing snuffles, she left the Concordia by the way of the door to the concrete-surfaced "patio" surrounded on three sides by a tall hedge, which was simply the backyard of the one-story convalescent hospital and figured as an airing spot for the mostly elderly patients.

It was empty now, save for a few white tables and chairs in need of a paint job, and very hot. Helen unfurled her parasol and departed by the one exit available if you didn't want to go back through the Concordia, a two-foot gap in the back hedge—she had to tip her parasol to get through.

She emerged in an untidy, unpaved alley with garbage cans. From the newspapers scattered around them the words "Korea," "239 Communists," "McCarthy," and "Rosenbergs" leaped up, reminding her of how Harry had said to Gummitch, "We live in a witch-hunt age, you hear me, cat? They got the diplomats and movie actors. They'll be after writers next, writers and cats. Remember how the Inquisition got after you along with the witches? Maybe the FBI will come for you and me at the same time."

Across the alley was another tall hedge with a matching gap in it, through which she could see a wedge of very green lawn that looked much more attractive than the littered sandy alley, so she pressed on through, tipping her parasol again and noting that the way underfoot was somewhat worn, as if these back exits were in regular use.

The gap was in a back corner of the property she entered. Straight ahead of her, the intensely green lawn stretched to the next street and was so thick and springy underfoot she was reminded of her native England.

There emerged into view a neat two-story wooden Victorian house whose gleaming white paint put the Concordia to shame. By its back door there was parked a shining white motor scooter with a white box fixed behind its sheepskin saddle. A narrow walk of pale gravel led from it close around the house to the next street.

Just next to Helen at the back of the property was a large area enclosed by a neat mesh-wire fence several feet higher than the hedge. Inside it were more lawn, three graceful low trees, some tidy bushes, two flower beds, and a low summer house (it looked) white as the main building with a white scrollwork sign over its open door that read, in much-serifed black letters, "Wicks Cat Hotel."

As she strolled wonderingly forward around the enclosure, Helen congratulated herself that her green parasol and flowered dress suited her very well to this handsome environment. Thank goodness, she told herself, she'd washed her hair and taken a shower just before coming out.

Coming around in front of the enclosure, where there was a latched door in the mesh, she surveyed it more closely, at once spotting a tranquil Himalayan on a tiny platform in one of the low trees and two strolling lilac-point Siamese slender as fashion models. The longer she looked, the more cats she saw ensconced in the bushes, sniffing the flowers, and wandering in and out of the little building, all of them elegant and well behaved, a few rather plain tabbies among the aristocracy, which included a blue Persian, a crinkly coated dark silver Rex, and a Havana brown who positively flamed. She said aloud softly, "Oh, Gummitch, if you could see this. A positive cat heaven!"

"Some persons do voice that reaction. But who is Gummitch, pray?"

Helen turned to face a trim woman her own age, two inches taller, fully as slender, but a degree sturdier than herself. A straw blonde, she wore her hair cropped and white slacks and Nehru jacket at once medical, military, and chic. Her right eye was deep blue, the other brown.

"He's my cat," Helen said eagerly, and when the other did not at once respond volunteered, "I'm Helen Hunter."

"Wendy Wicks," the other responded, extending her hand. "I'm the proprietor. Do I rightly discern in your speech a British accent with the lilt of Wales?"

Nodding, Helen countered, "And I a Scots?"

"Truly enough, though I come from the Lakes. Which makes us fellow countrymen," the other said approvingly, adding an extra squeeze to their handshake. "Would you care to look inside?" She unlatched the mesh door. Helen furled her parasol.

The guests of the Wicks Hotel took no notice of them. Inside the low white building the two women stood comfortably enough, though Helen noted Harry would have had to stoop here. It was all one room lined with about sixty comfortably large cages in three tiers, each with its rug, water and food dish, and cat-box. The floor was occupied only by some hassocks, a climbing frame, and an imposing gray Tudor castle of stout cardboard with numerous cat-size windows and doors.

Helen echoed herself with, "A cat paradise!"

Wendy ended her little talk with, "Some of our guests are quite long-term, while their mistresses go to New York or London for the plays, or on extended ocean cruises," and gave Helen a hotel card on which her first name was spelled "Wendele," had the initials "D.V.M" behind, and there was the subscript "hospital facilities available."

Wendy said, "The next time you're out of town, Gummitch might enjoy our hospitality. That is, unless he's an unneutered male."

"He is," Helen informed her. "My husband, Harry, has very fixed ideas upon that point—"

"I know," the other interposed with a touch of venom, "men are apt to entertain such barbarous notions."

"—and so do I, I was going to say," Helen concluded bravely.

Wendy caught her hand and squeezed it, saying with a disarming smile, "There are, of course, my dear, good arguments, aside from patristic ones, to be made for that position. Even the Amazons had to make compromises. Why, I've taken toms myself in the hospital. Come, let me show you that."

Helen followed her out of the hotel and its grounds up to the back door of the Victorian house. As they passed the motor scooter Wendy touched it, saying, "Our ambulance," then, as she opened the white door beyond, "The Wicks Cat Hospital! No other species accepted!"

Inside was a spotless veterinary examination—and, Helen supposed, emergency room—everything cat-sized and -adapted. Suspended on brass wires from points along the skull, spine, and tail was the complete skeleton of a cat, which struck her as rather grisly. A large 1953 calendar on the wall featured phases of the moon.

Wendy said, "Wait a minute and I'll show you our isolation ward for infectious cases. I'll call you," and she pushed through one of the two inner doors.

Helen peeked after her in time to see her draw a black curtain in front of three cages like those in the hotel, then drew back a little guiltily.

"Come in," Wendy called and when Helen had complied pointed out three glass-fronted large white boxes against the wall opposite the three curtained cages.

"Our isolation cubicles," she explained. "They have their own ventilation system."

Two of the boxes were empty. The other held a young seal-point Siamese, who peered out at them bright-eyed enough.

"I detected a mild respiratory infection in this one of our guests," Wendy explained, "and am treating it with antibiotics. She'll probably return to the hotel tomorrow." The phone in the examination room rang. "Excuse me," she said.

Alone, after a few seconds Helen yielded to curiosity. She crossed the room and started to lift a corner of the black curtain.

"Mrs. Hunter!" the other called from the doorway, "do you realize that cats are subject to certain diseases in which their eyes become temporarily hypersensitive to light? You might have permanently injured one of our patients."

"I'm sorry, I didn't know," Helen said, backing off.

"I think you had best leave," the other went on in a gruff doctor voice, and as she escorted a flurried Helen through the other inside door of the examination room through a long old-fashioned parlor with a large fireplace, continued formidably, "In the past, Mrs. Hunter, persons have gained entry to these premises under false pretences with the intention of kidnapping valuable cats to hold for ransom and for even worse purposes!" Her mismatched eyes flashed coldly.

"You surely don't think that I—" Helen began, more apologetic than indignant.

"No, I suppose not, I guess," Wendy replied with sudden and surprising return to her earlier amiability, "but after all, Helen, I have showed you everything here, and I'm sure that we both have other things to do." She led Helen into a front hall with a wide staircase leading to the second story. Then, as she let her out the front door, where a brass plate read "Wicks Cat Hospital," she gave Helen's hand a final squeeze and said with a smile, "Come back for another visit, dear, anytime you wish. Only remember that I'm another lone Britisher in an alien land and a profession dominated by arrogant males, so I have become overly sensitive and suspicious."

Hastening home by bus, Helen's feelings were mixed. She still felt drawn to Wendy. Such a strong, handsome, competent girl with a really beautiful face if you made allowance (if that were needed) for slightly overlarge upper center incisors and rather long large ears, though growing close to the skull, and of course the intriguing blue-brown eye pair. Why, it was years and years since she'd noticed so much about a person she'd met only once. Am I becoming infatuated? she asked herself with a silent giggle.

But then, on the other hand, the veterinary's sudden exaggerated hostility and the rather shivery details of the cat skeleton and black curtain. What had been behind that, anyway? The light-sensitive story was surely a blind because the light in the "isolation ward" had been on when the doctor'd first gone in and drawn the curtain.

And yet at the same time the whole place had reminded her so much and so nostalgically of England—the lawn, the house and cat motel, the woman herself—half-awakening deep-buried memories of all sorts, some of them, Helen felt sure, very strange.

When she left the bus, the day, though more sultry than ever, had darkened, and when she stuck her key in her own front door, she heard a low rumble of thunder.

Gummitch was waiting inside, uttering a "Mrrp-Mrrp!" in which there was more alarm and indignation than greeting. He ran halfway up the stairs and then paused to look back over his shoulder. Heart sinking, Helen followed him to the upstairs bathroom, where Psycho lay curled motionless in the pale green washbowl as though it was a cat sarcophagus. The young cat seemed only half-conscious; her eyes were filmed, her short gray fur was rough, her nose hot.

Helen carried her downstairs to the phone and dialed the number on the card given her by Wendy, who answered on the third ring, listened to Helen's rapid description, and said only, "Don't do anything. I'll be there."

Waiting would have been easier for Helen if she'd been told to do something. She opened the front door to the gathering dark and low growling thunder. She asked, "Whatever happened, Gummitch? Did Psycho go out and eat something?" But the orangy cat answered only, "Mrrp-Mrrp!" Finally she called a taxi.

As if that had been the proper charm to hurry events, there was a purring "put-put" from down the street. Going to the door with Gummitch close beside her, she saw that the approaching storm had banished twilight and brought on instant night, into which the pale shape of the hospital scooter and rider came like the ghost of a modern centaur. It nosed into the driveway, then rode diagonally across the lawn to park at the foot of the front steps.

Wendy was now wearing additionally a white cap with rather long visor, and she stripped off white gauntlets as she came up the steps, carefully took Psycho into her arms, and briefly examined her.

"She's very sick and must be taken to the hospital at once and given treatment," she pronounced. "I'll have a full report for you tomorrow morning. Don't worry too much: she's a young cat and I believe we've caught it in time. Her chances of complete recovery are very good." All this while carrying Psycho down the steps, gently laying her in the box behind the saddle, which opened at a touch, and getting astride the vehicle, having thrust her gauntlets in the top of her slacks.

"Good-bye, chaps," she called as she drove off carefully at an even pace.

It all happened so fast that Helen, who'd hurried down the steps with Gummitch after her, couldn't think what to call back. But now as they both watched the white scooter disappear down the dark street, she said, "Oh, Gummitch, what have we done to Psycho?"

"Warra warra," the cat replied, concerned and somewhat angry. He hadn't liked the cat doctor's looks, and he also believed that his own close presence was in any case something essential to Psycho's safety and recovery.

Thunder rumbled, closer now.

A taxicab drew up. Its driver got out and, seeing Helen, opened the rear door and came a few steps up the walk.

She arrived at a quick decision, called to him, "I'll just get my bag and wrap; be with you in a second," and ran up the steps into the house, thinking Gummitch had run back ahead of her; cars often had that effect on him.

But the cat had other ideas. He'd circled off sideways into the darkness, made a craftily wide circle through some bushes, and sneaked into the cab when the driver wasn't looking.

Inside he did not spring on the seat, but instead crouched in the dark far corner of the floor. He did not intend the investigations he had in mind to be thwarted. And indeed when Kitty-Come-Here got in, she was so busy giving the driver instructions as to where the Wicks Cat Hospital was, and so agitated generally, that she actually didn't notice him. She slung her light coat on the seat beside her, and it trailed over, further concealing him.

Gummitch congratulated himself on his sagacity. What doesn't move in the shadows, isn't seen. Old Horsemeat had more than once recited to him Eliot's poem about McCavity, the mystery cat modeled on Professor Moriarty, and if there were a Moriarty, there had to be a cat Sherlock Holmes, didn't there?

When the cab drew up at the newly repainted old white house with the brass plate beside the door and Kitty-Come-Here got out, saying to the driver, "Please wait for me," Gummitch slid out right behind her and immediately ducked under the vehicle, preparatory to beginning another of his wide circles. Geometric evasiveness, that's one more of my methods, he told himself.

Helen mounted to the open porch and pushed the buzzer, and when it wasn't answered quickly, plied the brass knocker, too. But when the door was finally opened, it was by an unsmiling and doctor-faced Wendy, who did not move aside to let her in.

"It's past visiting hours," she said coldly. "Really, Helen, I know you're concerned about your cat, but you mustn't become hysterical. You can't see Psycho now in any case; she's in isolation."

"But you didn't even tell me what's wrong with her," Helen protested.

"Very well. Your cat is suffering from epidemic feline enteritis, the most widespread and dangerous cat plague of them all, one for which early immunization is a necessary precaution observed by all half-way informed owners. But you never had shots for her, did you? No, I thought not. Perhaps your husband doesn't believe in that, either."

Gummitch watched the two from the next to the top step of the stairs to the porch, only his narrowed eyes showing over. When the cat doctor was in the midst of her condescending and reproachful lecture, he flowed up onto the porch and along it to the second window from the door, which was open wide at the bottom, and softly looped through, hugging the wall and sill, into the dim large room beyond.

Outside, the cat doctor continued, "What treatment is she getting? I injected serum and water in proper quantity, gave by mouth a chemical agent I've had good results with, and disposed her comfortably in an isolation cubicle, where she is getting *rest*, which is something even veterinary doctors require and get on rare occasions, and you no doubt could do with yourself. Please do not call before 9 A.M. tomorrow. Good night, dear Helen." And she closed the door.

After a moment of staring at it with both fists clenched, Helen returned to her cab, disconsolate and fuming delicately. The driver asked her, "Excuse me, lady, but did you have a cat with you in there when we came over?"

"Certainly not!" she replied impatiently. "Why do you ask?"

"I don't know," the driver responded warily. "I just thought. . . ." His voice trailed off.

I shouldn't have been so short with him, she told herself. Natural of him to suppose that when you go to a cat hospital you take a cat. Probably thought I had it wrapped in my coat or something.

Nevertheless, the matter worried her a little. Now she wouldn't feel easy until she'd seen Gummitch. But when she did, at least she could speak out her mind to him, relieve her injured feelings a little. Oh, that wicked (but so dashing) doctor woman!

In the Wicks Cat Hospital living room, Gummitch had immediately found a good hiding place under an easy chair against a wall, from which he could survey the whole room, study the black carpet with its curious designs in white lines, and wait until things settled down before beginning his detective work—see which way the cat doctor was going to jump, you might put it.

After shutting the door on Helen, she came rapidly through the living room (Gummitch saw only her trousered legs footed with white oxfords) and went through the swinging door at its back end. Outside, thunder crackled. The storm was definitely getting nearer.

After enough time for Gummitch to go into a half-doze, the cat doctor returned, setting the swinging door wide open, he was happy to see, though he could have managed it himself, he was confident, as well as many knobs and some latches.

She moved more thoughtfully this time, going to one of the bookcases and selecting a volume to take with her, before exiting to the front hall, leaving dimmed lights behind her everywhere. He heard her going upstairs.

Helen was in a quandary. She'd paid off the taxi driver, tipping him generously to make up for her shortness with him, but when she'd gone into the house there'd been no Gummitch to greet her and hear what she thought of the doctor woman. He might have gone out through the cat door, of course, on some business of his own, but wouldn't he have waited to ask her about Psycho? Had the taxi driver really seen a cat? Despite Wendy's warning she dialed again the number on the card, but this time got only an answering service which could just take messages to give the doctor when and if she called in. Outside, thunder boomed. Helen didn't like being all alone in the house.

Back in the living room of the cat hospital, the cat-detective still bided his time under the easy chair. After another period of waiting, during which there were faint footsteps overhead that finally ceased—the cat doctor's and someone else's, still lighter but thumpy ones—Gummitch ventured out and unhurriedly made his way toward the back of the room, frequently pausing to sniff. Outside, the crackling came more often, and suddenly he heard the patter, then the pelting of swift-breaking rain, and from the window behind him felt a breath of chilly storm-breeze.

The white-line pattern on the black carpet was a curious one of triangles and triskelions and swastikas, and just in front of the cold, empty but practical fireplace and with one of its five points aimed straight at it, a huge empty star. There welled up in his mind a murky racial memory of an even wider hearth with a huge fire blazing in it and naked women standing before it in a pentacle and rubbing into each other's bodies an ointment that had a not altogether unpleasing acrid odor.

Gummitch glided into the examination room, saw the hanging cat skeleton, hissed under his breath, then sprang to the table before it, and gave it an experimental pat. The little bones rattled softly and the skull swung a bit, as if to see who its disturber was.

He next entered the isolation ward, the door of which was also set open. Perhaps because of the soft purr of their ventilation system, his gaze fixed at once on the three glass-fronted isolation cubicles, and he leaped lightly to the shelf in front of them.

In the cubicle Psycho lay on her side with eyes closed and ears drooped. He couldn't repress a mew of excitement, then, with his muzzle pressed against the glass, mewed softly twice more and rapped the pane lightly with a paw. She did not stir.

The young Siamese in the next cubicle was making motions at him, but Gummitch ignored her, continuing to study Psycho. He could discern her gray chest rise and fall a little, regularly, while her fur looked a little brighter than it had in the pale green washbowl, he thought— or hoped.

He reminded himself then that he was a detective in enemy territory and couldn't afford to give way for long to dumb dutifulness. With an effort he tore his gaze away from Psycho's window, turned to survey the rest of the isolation ward, and saw for the first time the three now uncurtained wire cages against the opposite wall.

The fur on his back rose and his tail thickened.

In the first cage was a little old dog with squinched-up face and beady eyes that glared at him continuously, a black Pekinese.

In the second cage was an animal of the same shape as the little green frogs he'd seen hopping around in the spring. Only this one was bigger and fatter, with warts. And it didn't hop, but just crouched slumpingly and fixed upon him its large cold, cold eyes. It was the same color as the dog.

On a low perch in the third cage was a rather large bird which Gummitch knew to be a parrot because the Mad Eunuch's owner kept a bright green one with a big yellow beak. But this one was mangy and ancient-looking and malevolent-eyed, while its wickedly curving beak pointed straight at him. Both its beak and its ragged feather coat were inky black.

The little dog coughed hackingly, and thunder crashed outside as if the heavens were riven, while the great glare of lightning that simultaneously shone through the open doorway called Gummitch's attention to a fourth ebon beast just now hopped there and regarding him with an intelligence that seemed greater and more evil than that of the others.

It was an animal that Gummitch had never seen before, but

thought because of its overlarge front top teeth must be related to squirrels, one of whom had terrified him in kittenhood when they'd first seen each other close from opposite sides of a window. And it had long, tall ears. Gummitch could only imagine it to be a deformed giant tailless squirrel, the product of mad science or vile sorcery.

Now it turned and, as lightning flared again and thunder crashed, hopped—to report, Gummitch was suddenly sure, to the cat doctor. The fearless cat-detective reached an instant decision and leaped down and raced after. The monstrous beast crossed the living room in four long hops, but Gummitch could readily match that speed, he found. In the front hall at the foot of the stairs, the beast turned at bay, making mewling sounds. Gummitch advanced on it stiff-legged and back arched, involuntarily letting out a loud and most undetectivelike caterwaul.

Then he saw beyond it the cat doctor coming down the stairs. She was stark naked, bore in her hand a long yellowish knife with a red hilt, and glared at him, the lips of her small mouth parted in a snarl that revealed her large front teeth.

He retreated to the living room. She came after, her knife advanced before her, followed by the black hopping giant squirrel-monster. Gummitch cast one longing look at the open window, but then remembered his responsibilities. To the accompaniment of the storm's hammer blows and flashes, he raced twice around the room to baffle them, then darted through the examination room back into the isolation ward. They came after him relentlessly. From atop Psycho's cubicle he caterwauled defiance. They came up to it.

But then the storm's final and climatic thunder-crash and dazzling lightning-flare revealed to all three of them a new figure framed in the doorway, a rather small person wearing a dripping yellow oilskin and a deep-brimmed sou'wester.

It was Kitty-Come-Here, and she cried out, "Gummitch! I knew I'd find you here!"

Gummitch's fur relaxed a little. Wendy shoved the knife under some papers on the table beside her. The black squirrel-monster mewled innocently.

Kitty-Come-Here eyed the three of them in turn, taking her time about it, and then her gaze went on to the three occupants of the wire cages. At last she cried out comprehendingly, "Wendy, you are a *witch*.

And that black rabbit there is your familiar. And although you claim this is a hospital for cats only, you've been treating or boarding the *familiars* of those three dreadful old women (all witches, of course; you probably have a whole coven!) in the Concordia in the room opposite my mother-in-law's. The resemblances are all unmistakable and prove my case. And when there's no outsider to see, you go around naked— "sky-clad" is your witch expression for that, isn't it? And you were chasing Gummitch and trying to do something to him, weren't you?"

Wendy reached a lab smock from a hook on the wall and shoul-dered into it leisurely. "Why, I never heard a more ridiculous set of ideas in my whole life," she said guilelessly. "It's true I sometimes bend the hospital's only-one-species rule a little, and it wouldn't do to ad-vertise that to the mistresses of our guests. And I have a pet hare; drop a curtsy, dear Bunnykins! Cats are wonderful, but one needs a break from them when one sees them all the time. And I do occasionally doctor or board pets of patients in the Concordia, both apt to be elderly for obvious reasons. Any psychologist will tell you, dear Helen, that people, especially elderly ones, grow to resemble their pets, or else select them with that point unconsciously in mind. I habitually sleep raw, and tonight when Bunnykins and I discovered loose in the hospital what we took to be a stray tom bent on rapine (how could I know he was your Gummitch, dear?), we were seeking to eject him, that is all. There, does that answer your questions?"

"I don't think so," Helen said stoutly. "Why are all these animals *black*, I want to know? And what were you hiding when I came in?"

"I have a deep professional interest in melanism," Wendy told her. "And by the by, how *did* you get in?"

"When no one answered the door, I climbed through the open window, and now I'm glad I did! You still haven't told me—"

A joyous meow! from Gummitch interrupted this interchange. He was looking in Psycho's window. The young grey cat lifted her head a little and opened her eyes, which were no longer filmed with sickness, but bright with cat intelligence. She was smiling at Gummitch and them all. Though obviously still very weak and quite haggard-looking, she was clearly on the road to recovery.

This most happy occurrence rather put an end to serious accu-sations of witchcraft and other ill-feeling, and when Wendy insisted on serving them tea in a pot with an English Union Jack on it, with milk to go with it and seedcake, and with a saucer of milk for Gummitch, peace was fully sealed. Gummitch drank a third of his milk to please Kitty-Come-Here, though keeping a most wary eye on the cat doctor and Bunnykins, who appeared to resent that name, the cat judged, though continuing to act the innocent fool.

Afterward, going home by taxi, Helen told Gummitch, "I still think she may be a witch, you know, but a rather nice one, just being kind to some dirty old sister witches—ugh, old as *Macbeth!*—and their sick animals. And she did have to admit you were most well-behaved, Gummitch, for a tom. I think that's a lot, coming from her. And you *did* uncover the whole thing, whatever it was, you know, you clever, sneaky cat. You broke through her British reticence, all right. She'd have played snob-doctor all night, otherwise. And did you notice, Gummitch, she had the slimmest and most stalwart body and the darlingest little breasts, almost as small as mine. I'm sure we're leaving Psycho in very good hands. But how should we tell Old Horsemeat about all this, Gummitch, when he comes back from his business revels? Not everything, I think, though of course he'd love it all for one of his stories."

Gummitch decided she was still pretty featherbrained.

Slow Birds

*　　*　　*

Ian Watson

Ian Watson is one of F&SF's most versatile contributors, equally at home with contemporary fantasy, horror, or the most inventive SF. Here is an example of the latter—a story that describes an Earth that is slowly being "glassed" over by the mysterious engines of destruction known as slow birds. At the same time, it is a stirring family drama that spans generations.

*　　*　　*

IT was Mayday, and the skate-sailing festival that year was being held at Tuckerton.

By late morning, after the umpires had been out on the glass plain setting red flags around the circuit, cumulous clouds began to fill a previously blue sky, promising ideal conditions for the afternoon's sport. No rain; so that the glass wouldn't be an inch deep in water as last year at Atherton. No dazzling glare to blind the spectators, as the year before that at Buckby. And a breeze verging on brisk without ever becoming fierce: perfect to speed the competitors' sails along without lifting people off their feet and tumbling them, as four years previously at Edgewood when a couple of broken ankles and numerous bruises had been sustained.

After the contest there would be a pig roast; or rather the succulent fruits thereof, for the pig had been turning slowly on its spit these past thirty-six hours. And there would be kegs of Old Codger Ale to be cracked. But right now Jason Babbidge's mind was mainly occupied with checking out his glass-skates and his fine crocus-yellow hand-sail.

As high as a tall man, and of best old silk, only patched in a couple of places, the sail's fore-spar of flexible ash was bent into a bow belly by a strong hemp cord. Jason plucked this thoughtfully like a harpist, testing the tension. Already a fair number of racers were out on the glass, showing off their paces to applause. Tuckerton folk mostly, they were—acting as if they owned the glass hereabouts and knew it more intimately than any visitors could. Not that it was in any way different from the same glass over Atherton way.

Jason's younger brother Daniel whistled appreciatively as a Tuckerton man carrying purple silk executed perfect circles at speed, his sail shivering as he tacked.

"Just look at him, Jay!"

"What, Bob Marchant? He took a pratfall last year. Where's the use in working up a sweat before the whistle blows?"

By now a couple of sisters from Buckby were out too with matching black sails, skating figure-eights around each other, risking collision by a hair's breadth.

"Go on, Jay," urged young Daniel. "Show 'em."

Contestants from the other villages were starting to flood on to the glass as well, but Jason noticed how Max Tarnover was standing not so far away, merely observing these antics with a wise smile. Master Tarnover of Tuckerton, last year's victor at Atherton despite the drenching spray. . . . Taking his cue from this, and going one better, Jason ignored events on the glass and surveyed the crowds instead.

He noticed Uncle John Babbidge chatting intently to an Edgewood man over where the silver band was playing; which was hardly the quietest place to talk, so perhaps they were doing business. Meanwhile on the green beyond the band the children of five villages buzzed like flies from hoop-la to skittles to bran tub, to apples in buckets of water. And those grown-ups who weren't intent on the band or the practice runs or on something else, such as gossip, besieged the craft and produce stalls. There must be going on for a thousand people at the festival, and the village beyond looked deserted. Rugs and benches and half-barrels had even been set out near the edge of the glass for the old folk of Tuckerton.

As the band lowered their instruments for a breather after finishing *The Floral Dance*, a bleat of panic cut across the chatter of many voices. A farmer had just vaulted into a tiny sheep-pen where a lamb almost as large as its shorn, protesting dam was ducking beneath her to suckle and hide. Laughing, the farmer hauled it out and hoisted it by its neck and back legs to guess its weight, and maybe win a prize.

And now Jason's mother was threading her way through the crowd, chewing the remnants of a pasty.

"Best of luck, son!" She grinned.

"I've told you, Mum," protested Jason. "It's bad luck to say 'good luck'."

"Oh, luck yourself! What's luck, anyway?" She prodded her Adam's apple as if to press the last piece of meat and potatoes on its way down, though really she was indicating that her throat was bare of any charm or amulet.

"I suppose I'd better make a move." Kicking off his sandals, Jason sat to lace up his skates. With a helping hand from Daniel he rose and stood knock-kneed, blades cutting into the turf while the boy hoisted the sail across his shoulders. Jason gripped the leather straps on the bow-string and the spine-spar.

"Okay." He waggled the sail this way and that. "Let's go, then. I won't blow away."

But just as he was about to proceed down on to the glass, out upon the glass less than a hundred yards away a slow bird appeared.

It materialized directly in front of one of the Buckby sisters. Unable to veer, she had no choice but to throw herself backwards. Crying out in frustration, and perhaps hurt by her fall, she skidded underneath the slow bird, sledging supine upon her now snapped and crumpled sail. . . .

They were called slow birds because they flew through the air—at the stately pace of three feet per minute.

They looked a little like birds, too, though only a little. Their tubular metal bodies were rounded at the head and tapering to a finned point at the tail, with two stubby wings midway. Yet these wings could hardly have anything to do with suspending their bulk in the air; the girth of a bird was that of a horse, and its length twice that of a man lying full length. Perhaps those wings controlled orientation or trim.

In colour they were a silvery grey; though this was only the colour of their outer skin, made of a soft metal like lead. Quarter of an inch beneath this coating their inner skins were black and stiff as steel. The noses of the birds were all scored with at least a few scrape marks due to encounters with obstacles down the years; slow birds always kept the same height above ground—underbelly level with a man's shoulders —and they would bank to avoid substantial buildings or mature trees, but any frailer obstructions they would push on through. Hence the individual patterns of scratches. However, a far easier way of telling them apart was by the graffiti carved on so many of their flanks: initials entwined in hearts, dates, place names, fragments of messages. These amply confirmed how very many slow birds there must be in all— something of which people could not otherwise have been totally convinced. For no one could keep track of a single slow bird. After each one had appeared—over hill, down dale, in the middle of a pasture or half way along a village street—it would fly onward slowly for any length of time between an hour and a day, covering any distance between a few score yards and a full mile. And vanish again. To reappear somewhere else unpredictably: far away or close by, maybe long afterwards or maybe soon.

Usually a bird would vanish, to reappear again.

Not always, though. Half a dozen times a year, within the confines of this particular island country, a slow bird would reach its journey's end.

It would destroy itself, and all the terrain around it for a radius of two and a half miles, fusing the landscape instantly into a sheet of glass. A flat, circular sheet of glass. A polarised, limited zone of annihilation. Scant yards beyond its rim a person might escape unharmed, only being deafened and dazzled temporarily.

Hitherto no slow bird had been known to explode so as to overlap an earlier sheet of glass. Consequently many towns and villages clung close to the borders of what had already been destroyed, and news of a fresh glass plain would cause farms and settlements to spring up there. Even so, the bulk of people still kept fatalistically to the old historic towns. They assumed that a slow bird wouldn't explode in their midst during their own lifetimes. And if it did, what would they know of it?

Unless the glass happened merely to bisect a town—in which case, once the weeping and mourning was over, the remaining citizenry could relax and feel secure.

True, in the long term the whole country from coast to coast and from north to south would be a solid sheet of glass. Or perhaps it would merely be a checkerboard, of circles touching circles: a glass mosaic. With what in between? Patches of desert dust, if the climate dried up due to reflections from the glass. Or floodwater, swampland. But that day was still far distant: a hundred years away, two hundred, three. So people didn't worry too much. They had been used to this all their lives long, and their parents before them. Perhaps one day the slow birds would stop coming. And going. And exploding. Just as they had first started, once. Certainly the situation was no different, by all accounts, anywhere else in the world. Only the seas were clear of slow birds. So maybe the human race would have to take to rafts one day. Though by then, with what would they build them? Meanwhile, people got by; and most had long ago given up asking why. For there was no answer.

The girl's sister helped her rise. No bones broken, it seemed. Only an injury to dignity; and to her sail.

The other skaters had all coasted to a halt and were staring resentfully at the bird in their midst. Its belly and sides were almost bare of graffiti; seeing this, a number of youths hastened on to the glass, clutching penknives, rusty nails and such. But an umpire waved them back angrily.

"Shoo! Be off with you!" His gaze seemed to alight on Jason, and for a fatuous moment Jason imagined that it was himself to whom the umpire was about to appeal; but the man called, "Master Tarnover!" instead, and Max Tarnover duck-waddled past then glided out over the glass, to confer.

Presently the umpire cupped his hands. "We're delaying the start for half an hour," he bellowed. "Fair's fair: young lady ought to have a chance to fix her sail, seeing as it wasn't her fault."

Jason noted a small crinkle of amusement on Tarnover's face; for now either the other competitors would have to carry on prancing around tiring themselves with extra practice which none of them needed, or else troop off the glass for a recess and lose some psychological edge. In fact almost everyone opted for a break and some refreshments.

"Luck indeed!" snorted Mrs. Babbidge, as Max Tarnover clumped back their way.

Tarnover paused by Jason. "Frankly I'd say her sail's a wreck," he confided. "But what can you do? The Buckby lot would have been bitching on otherwise. 'Oh, she could have won. If she'd had ten minutes to fix it.' Bloody hunk of metal in the way." Tarnover ran a lordly eye over Jason's sail. "What price skill, then?"

Daniel Babbidge regarded Tarnover with a mixture of hero worship and hostile partisanship on his brother's behalf. Jason himself only nodded and said, "Fair enough." He wasn't certain whether Tarnover was acting generously—or with patronizing arrogance. Or did this word in his ear mean that Tarnover actually saw Jason as a valid rival for the silver punch-bowl this year round?

Obviously young Daniel did not regard Jason's response as adequate. He piped up: "So where do *you* think the birds go, Master Tarnover, when they aren't here?"

A good question: quite unanswerable, but Max Tarnover would probably feel obliged to offer an answer if only to maintain his pose of worldly wisdom. Jason warmed to his brother, while Mrs. Babbidge, catching on, cuffed the boy softly.

"Now don't you go wasting Master Tarnover's time. Happen he hasn't given it a moment's thought, all his born days."

"Oh, but I have," Tarnover said.

"Well?" the boy insisted.

"Well . . . maybe they don't go anywhere at all."

Mrs. Babbidge chuckled, and Tarnover flushed.

"What I mean is, maybe they just stop being in one place then suddenly they're in the next place."

"If only you could skate like that!" Jason laughed. "Bit slow, though . . . Everyone would still pass you by at the last moment."

"They must go somewhere," young Dan said doggedly. "Maybe it's somewhere we can't see. Another sort of place, with other people. Maybe it's them that builds the birds."

"Look, freckleface, the birds don't come from Russ, or 'Merica, or anywhere else. So where's this other place?"

"Maybe it's right here, only we can't see it."

"And maybe pigs have wings." Tarnover looked about to march

towards the cider and perry stall; but Mrs. Babbidge interposed herself smartly.

"Oh, as to that, I'm sure our sow Betsey couldn't fly, wings or no wings. Just hanging in the air like that, and so heavy."

"Weighed a bird recently, have you?"

"They look heavy, Master Tarnover."

Tarnover couldn't quite push his way past Mrs. Babbidge, not with his sail impeding him. He contented himself with staring past her, and muttering, "If we've nothing sensible to say about them, in my opinion it's better to shut up."

"But it isn't better," protested Daniel. "They're blowing the world up. Bit by bit. As though they're at war with us."

Jason felt humorously inventive. "Maybe that's it. Maybe these other people of Dan's are at war with us—only they forgot to mention it. And when they've glassed us all, they'll move in for the holidays. And skate happily for ever more."

"Damn long war, if that's so," growled Tarnover. "Been going on over a century now."

"Maybe that's why the birds fly so slowly," said Daniel. "What if a year to us is like an hour to those people? That's why the birds don't fall. They don't have time to."

Tarnover's expression was almost savage. "And what if the birds come only to punish us for our sins? What if they're simply a miraculous proof—"

"—that the Lord cares about us? And one day He'll forgive us? Oh goodness," and Mrs. Babbidge beamed, "surely you aren't one of *them*? A bright lad like you. Me, I don't even put candles in the window or tie knots in the bedsheets anymore to keep the birds away." She ruffled her younger son's mop of red hair. "Everyone dies sooner or later, Dan. You'll get used to it, when you're properly grown up. When it's time to die, it's time to die."

Tarnover looked furiously put out; though young Daniel also seemed distressed in a different way.

"And when you're thirsty, it's time for a drink!" Spying an opening, and his opportunity, Tarnover sidled quickly around Mrs. Babbidge and strode off. She chuckled as she watched him go.

"That's put a kink in his sail!"

*   *   *

Forty-one other contestants, besides Jason and Tarnover, gathered between the starting flags. Though not the girl who had fallen; despite all
best efforts she was out of the race, and sat morosely watching.

Then the Tuckerton umpire blew his whistle, and they were off.

The course was in the shape of a long bloomer loaf. First, it
curved gently along the edge of the glass for three quarters of a mile,
then bent sharply around in a half circle on to the straight, returning
towards Tuckerton. At the end of the straight, another sharp half circle
brought it back to the starting—and finishing—line. Three circuits
in all were to be skate-sailed before the victory whistle blew. Much
more than this, and the lag between leaders and stragglers could lead
to confusion.

By the first turn Jason was ahead of the rest of the field, and all
his practice since last year was paying off. His skates raced over the
glass. The breeze thrust him convincingly. As he rounded the end of
the loaf, swinging his sail to a new pitch, he noted Max Tarnover
hanging back in fourth place. Determined to increase his lead, Jason
leaned so close to the flag on the entry to the straight that he almost
tipped it. Compensating, he came poorly on to the straight, losing a
few yards. By the time Jason swept over the finishing line for the first
time, to cheers from Atherton villagers, Tarnover was in third position;
though he was making no very strenuous effort to overhaul, Jason
realised that Tarnover was simply letting him act as pacemaker.

But a skate-sailing race wasn't the same as a foot-race, where a
pacemaker was generally bound to drop back eventually. Jason pressed
on. Yet by the second crossing of the line Tarnover was ten yards behind,
moving without apparent effort as though he and his sail and the wind
and the glass were one. Noting Jason's glance, Tarnover grinned and
put on a small burst of speed to push the front-runner to even greater
efforts. And as he entered on the final circuit Jason also noted the
progress of the slow bird, off to his left, now midway between the long
curve and the straight, heading in the general direction of Edgewood.
Even the laggards ought to clear the final straight before the thing got
in their way, he calculated.

This brief distraction was a mistake: Tarnover was even closer
behind him now, his sail pitched at an angle which must have made

his wrists ache. Already he was drifting aside to overhaul Jason. And at this moment Jason grasped how he could win: by letting Tarnover think that he was pushing Jason beyond his capacity—so that Tarnover would be fooled into overexerting himself too soon.

"Can't catch me!" Jason called into the wind, guessing that Tarnover would misread this as braggadocio and assume that Jason wasn't really thinking ahead. At the same time Jason slackened his own pace slightly, hoping that his rival would fail to notice, since this was at odds with his own boast. Pretending to look panicked, he let Tarnover overtake—and saw how Tarnover continued to grip his sail strenuously even though he was actually moving a little slower than before. Without realizing it, Tarnover had his angle wrong; he was using unnecessary wrist action.

Tarnover was in the lead now. Immediately all psychological pressure lifted from Jason. With ease and grace he stayed a few yards behind, just where he could benefit from the 'eye' of air in Tarnover's wake. And thus he remained till half way down the final straight, feeling like a kestrel hanging in the sky with a mere twitch of its wings before swooping.

He held back; held back. Then suddenly changing the cant of his sail he did swoop—into the lead again.

It was a mistake. It had been a mistake all along. For as Jason sailed past, Tarnover actually laughed. Jerking his brown and orange silk to an easier, more efficient pitch, Tarnover began to pump his legs, skating like a demon. Already he was ahead again. By five yards. By ten. And entering the final curve.

As Jason tried to catch up in the brief time remaining, he knew how he had been fooled; though the knowledge came too late. So cleverly had Tarnover fixed Jason's mind on the stance of the sails, by holding his own in such a way—a way, too, which deliberately created that convenient eye of air—that Jason had quite neglected the contribution of his legs and skates, taking this for granted, failing to monitor it from moment to moment. It only took moments to recover and begin pumping his own legs too, but those few moments were fatal. Jason crossed the finish line one yard behind last year's victor; who was this year's victor too.

As he slid to a halt, bitter with chagrin, Jason was well aware that it was up to him to be gracious in defeat rather than let Tarnover seize that advantage, too.

He called out, loud enough for everyone to hear: "Magnificent, Max! Splendid skating! You really caught me on the hop there."

Tarnover smiled for the benefit of all onlookers.

"What a noisy family you Babbidges are," he said softly; and skated off to be presented with the silver punch-bowl again.

Much later that afternoon, replete with roast pork and awash with Old Codger Ale, Jason was waving an empty beer mug about as he talked to Bob Marchant in the midst of a noisy crowd. Bob, who had fallen so spectacularly the year before. Maybe that was why he had skated diffidently today and been one of the laggards.

The sky was heavily overcast, and daylight too was failing. Soon the homeward trek would have to start.

One of Jason's drinking and skating partners from Atherton, Sam Partridge, thrust his way through.

"Jay! That brother of yours: he's out on the glass. He's scrambled up on the back of the bird. He's riding it."

"What?"

Jason sobered rapidly, and followed Partridge with Bob Marchant tagging along behind.

Sure enough, a couple of hundred yards away in the gloaming Daniel was perched astride the slow bird. His red hair was unmistakable. By now a lot of other people were beginning to take notice and point him out. There were some ragged cheers, and a few angry protests.

Jason clutched Partridge's arm. "Somebody must have helped him up. Who was it?"

"Haven't the foggiest. That boy needs a good walloping."

"Daniel Babbidge!" Mrs. Babbidge was calling nearby. She too had seen. Cautiously she advanced on to the glass, wary of losing her balance.

Jason and company were soon at her side. "It's all right, Mum," he assured her. "I'll fetch the little . . . perisher."

Courteously Bob Marchant offered his arm and escorted Mrs. Babbidge back on the rough ground again. Jason and Partridge stepped flat-foot out across the vitrified surface accompanied by at least a dozen curious spectators.

"Did anyone spot who helped him up?" Jason demanded of them. No one admitted it.

When the group was a good twenty yards from the bird, everyone but Jason halted. Pressing on alone, Jason pitched his voice so that only the boy would hear.

"Slide off," he ordered grimly. "I'll catch you. Right monkey you've made of your mother and me."

"No," whispered Daniel. He clung tight, hands splayed like suckers, knees pressed to the flanks of the bird as though he was a jockey. "I'm going to see where it goes."

"Goes? Hell, I'm not going to waste time arguing. Get down!" Jason gripped an ankle and tugged, but this action only served to pull him up against the bird. Beside Dan's foot a heart with the entwined initials 'ZB' and 'EF' was carved. Turning away, Jason shouted, "Give me a hand, you lot! Come on someone, bunk me up!"

Nobody volunteered, not even Partridge.

"It won't bite you! There's no harm in touching it. Any kid knows that." Angrily he flat-footed back towards them. "Damn it all, Sam."

So now Partridge did shuffle forward, and a couple of other men too. But then they halted, gaping. Their expression puzzled Jason momentarily—till Sam Partridge gestured; till Jason swung round.

The air behind was empty.

The slow bird had departed suddenly. Taking its rider with it.

Half an hour later only the visitors from Atherton and their hosts remained on Tuckerton green. The Buckby, Edgewood and Hopperton contingents had set off for home. Uncle John was still consoling a snivelling Mrs. Babbidge. Most faces in the surrounding crowd looked sympathetic, though there was a certain air of resentment, too, among some Tuckerton folk that a boy's prank had cast this black shadow over their Mayday festival.

Jason glared wildly around the onlookers. "Did nobody see who helped my brother up?" he cried. "Couldn't very well have got up himself, could he? Where's Max Tarnover? Where is he?"

"You aren't accusing Master Tarnover, by any chance?" growled a beefy farmer with a large wart on his cheek. "Sour grapes, Master Babbidge! Sour grapes is what that sounds like, and we don't like the taste of those here."

"Where is he, dammit?"

Uncle John laid a hand on his nephew's arm. "Jason, lad. Hush. This isn't helping your Mum."

But then the crowd parted, and Tarnover sauntered through, still holding the silver punch-bowl he had won.

"Well, Master Babbidge?" he enquired. "I hear you want a word with me."

"Did you see who helped my brother onto that bird? Well, did you?"

"I didn't see," replied Tarnover coolly.

It had been the wrong question, as Jason at once realized. For if Tarnover had done the deed himself, how could he possibly have watched himself do it?

"Then did you—"

"Hey up," objected the same farmer. "You've asked him, and you've had his answer."

"And I imagine your brother has had his answer too," said Tarnover. "I hope he's well satisfied with it. Naturally I offer my heartfelt sympathies to Mrs. Babbidge. If indeed the boy *has* come to any harm. Can't be sure of that, though, can we?"

"Course we can't!"

Jason tensed, and Uncle John tightened his grip on him. "No, lad. There's no use."

It was a sad and quiet long walk homeward that evening for the three remaining Babbidges, though a fair few Atherton folk behind sang blithely and tipsily, nonetheless. Occasionally Jason looked around for Sam Partridge, but Sam Partridge seemed to be successfully avoiding them.

The next day, May the Second, Mrs. Babbidge rallied and declared it to be a "sorting out" day; which meant a day for handling all Daniel's clothes and storybooks and old toys lovingly before setting them to one side out of sight. Jason himself she packed off to his job at the sawmill, with a flea in his ear for hanging around her like a whipped hound.

And as Jason worked at trimming planks that day the same shamed, angry frustrated thoughts skated round and round a single circuit in his head:

'In my book he's a murderer. . . . You don't give a baby a knife to play with. He was cool as a cucumber afterwards. Not shocked, no. Smug. . . .'

Yet what could be done about it? The bird might have hung around for hours more. Except that it hadn't. . . .

Set out on a quest to find Daniel? But how? And where? Birds dodged around. Here, there and everywhere. No rhyme or reason to it. So what a useless quest that would be!

A quest to prove that Dan was alive. And if he were alive, then Tarnover hadn't killed him.

'In my book he's a murderer. . . .' Jason's thoughts churned on impotently. It was like skating with both feet tied together.

Three days later a slow bird was sighted out Edgewood way. Jim Mitchum, the Edgewood thatcher, actually sought Jason out at the sawmill to bring him the news. He'd been coming over to do a job, anyway.

No doubt his visit was an act of kindness, but it filled Jason with guilt quite as much as it boosted his morale. For now he was compelled to go and see for himself, when obviously there was nothing whatever to discover. Downing tools, he hurried home to collect his skates and sail, and sped over the glass to Edgewood.

The bird was still there; but it was a different bird. There was no carved heart with the love-tangled initials 'ZB' and 'EF'.

And four days after that, mention came from Buckby of a bird spotted a few miles west of the village on the main road to Harborough. This time Jason borrowed a horse and rode. But the mention had come late; the bird had flown on a day earlier. Still, he felt obliged to search the area of the sighting for a fallen body or some other sign.

And the week after that a bird vanished only a mile from Atherton itself; this one vanished even as Jason arrived on the scene. . . .

Then one night Jason went down to the Wheatsheaf. It was several weeks, in fact, since he had last been in the alehouse; now he meant to get drunk, at the long bar under the horse brasses.

Sam Partridge, Ned Darrow and Frank Yardley were there boozing; and an hour or so later Ned Darrow was offering beery advice.

"Look, Jay, where's the use in you dashing off every time someone spots a ruddy bird? Keep that up and you'll make a ruddy fool of yourself. And what if a bird pops up in Tuckerton? Bound to happen sooner or later. Going to rush off there too, are you, with your tongue hanging out?"

"All this time you're taking off work," said Frank Yardley. "You'll end up losing the job. Get on living is my advice."

"Don't know about that," said Sam Partridge unexpectedly. "Does seem to me as man ought to get his own back. Supposing Tarnover did do the dirty on the Babbidges—"

"What's there to suppose about it?" Jason broke in angrily.

"Easy on, Jay. I was going to say as Babbidges are Atherton people. So he did the dirty on us all, right?"

"Thanks to some people being a bit slow in their help."

Sam flushed. "Now don't you start attacking everyone right and left. No one's perfect. Just remember who your real friends are, that's all."

"Oh, I'll remember, never fear."

Frank inclined an empty glass from side to side. "Right. Whose round is it?"

One thing led to another, and Jason had a thick head the next morning.

In the evening Ned banged on the Babbidge door.

"Bird on the glass, Sam says to tell you," he announced. "How about going for a spin to see it?"

"I seem to recall last night you said I was wasting my time."

"Ay, running around all over the country. But this is just for a spin. Nice evening, like. Mind, if you don't want to bother. . . . Then we can all have a few jars in the Wheatsheaf afterwards."

The lads must really have missed him over the past few weeks. Quickly Jason collected his skates and sail.

"But what about your supper?" asked his mother. "Sheep's head broth."

"Oh, it'll keep, won't it? I might as well have a pasty or two in the Wheatsheaf."

"Happen it's better you get out and enjoy yourself," she said. "I'm quite content. I've got things to mend."

Twenty minutes later Jason, Sam, and Ned were skimming over the glass two miles out. The sky was crimson with banks of stratus, and a river of gold ran clear along the horizon: foul weather tomorrow, but a glory this evening. The glassy expanse flowed with red and gold reflections: a lake of blood, fire, and molten metal. They did not at first spot the other solitary sail-skater, nor he them, till they were quite close to the slow bird.

Sam noticed first. "Who's that, then?"

The other sail was brown and orange. Jason recognized it easily. "It's Tarnover!"

"Now's your chance to find out, then," said Ned.

"Do you mean that?"

Ned grinned. "Why not? Could be fun. Let's take him."

Pumping their legs, the three sail-skaters sped apart to outflank Tarnover—who spied them and began to turn. All too sharply, though. Or else he may have run into a slick of water on the glass. To Jason's joy Max Tarnover, champion of the five villages, skidded.

They caught him. This done, it didn't take the strength of an ox to stop a skater from going anywhere else, however much he kicked and struggled. But Jason hit Tarnover on the jaw, knocking him senseless.

"What the hell you do that for?" asked Sam, easing Tarnover's fall on the glass.

"How else do we get him up on the bird?"

Sam stared at Jason, then nodded slowly.

It hardly proved the easiest operation to hoist a limp and heavy body on to a slowly moving object whilst standing on a slippery surface; but after removing their skates they succeeded. Before too long Tarnover lay sprawled atop, legs dangling. Quickly with his pocket knife Jason cut the hemp cord from Tarnover's sail and bound his ankles together, running the tether tightly underneath the bird.

Presently Tarnover awoke, and struggled groggily erect. He groaned, rocked sideways, recovered his balance.

"Babbidge . . . Partridge, Ned Darrow . . . ? What the hell are you up to?"

Jason planted hands on hips. "Oh, we're just playing a little prank, same as you did on my brother Dan. Who's missing now; maybe forever, thanks to you."

"I never—"

"Admit it, then we might cut you down."

"And happen we mightn't," said Ned. "Not till the Wheatsheaf closes. But look on the bright side: happen we might."

Tarnover's legs twitched as he tested the bonds. He winced. "I honestly meant your brother no harm."

Sam smirked. "Nor do we mean you any. Ain't our fault if a bird decides to fly off. Anyway, only been here an hour or so. Could easily be here all night. Right, lads?"

"Right," said Ned. "And I'm thirsty. Race you? Last ones buys?"

"He's admitted he did it," said Jason. "You heard him."

"Look, I'm honestly very sorry if—"

"Shut up," said Sam. "You can stew for a while, seeing as how you've made the Babbidges stew. You can think about how sorry you really are." Partridge hoisted his sail.

It was not exactly how Jason had envisioned his revenge. This seemed like an anti-climax. Yet, to Tarnover no doubt it was serious enough. The champion was sweating slightly . . . Jason hoisted his sail, too. Presently the men skated away . . . to halt by unspoken agreement a quarter of a mile away. They stared back at Tarnover's little silhouette upon his metal steed.

"Now if it was me," observed Sam, "I'd shuffle myself along till I fell off the front . . . Rub you a bit raw, but that's how to do it."

"No need to come back, really," said Ned. "Hey, what's he trying?"

The silhouette had ducked. Perhaps Tarnover had panicked and wasn't thinking clearly, but it *looked* as if he was trying to lean over far enough to unfasten the knot beneath, or free one of his ankles. Suddenly the distant figure inverted itself. It swung right round the bird, and Tarnover's head and chest were hanging upside down, his arms flapping. Or perhaps Tarnover had hoped the cord would snap under his full weight; but snap it did not. And once he was stuck in that position there was no way he could recover himself upright again, or do anything about inching along to the front of the bird.

Ned whistled. "He's messed himself up now, and no mistake. He's ruddy crucified himself."

Jason hesitated before saying it: "Maybe we ought to go back? I mean, a man can die hanging upside down too long . . . Can't he?" Suddenly the whole episode seemed unclean, unsatisfactory.

"Go back?" Sam Partridge fairly snarled at him. "You were the big mouth last night. And whose idea was it to tie him on the bird? You wanted him taught a lesson, and he's being taught one. We're only trying to oblige you, Jay."

"Yes, I appreciate that."

"You made enough fuss about it. He isn't going to wilt like a bunch of flowers in the time it takes us to swallow a couple of pints."

And so they skated on, back to the Wheatsheaf in Atherton.

At ten thirty, somewhat the worse for wear, the three men spilled out of the alehouse into Sheaf Street. A quarter moon was dodging from rift to rift in the cloudy sky, shedding little light.

"I'm for bed," said Sam. "Let the sod wriggle his way off."

"And who cares if he don't?" said Ned. "That way, nobody'll know. Who wants an enemy for life? Do you, Jay? This way you can get on with things. Happen Tarnover'll bring your brother back from wherever it is." Shouldering his sail and swinging his skates, Ned wandered off up Sheaf Street.

"But," said Jason. He felt as though he had blundered into a midden. There was a reek of sordidness about what had taken place. The memory of Tarnover hanging upside-down had tarnished him.

"But what?" said Sam.

Jason made a show of yawning. "Nothing. See you." And he set off homeward.

But as soon as he was out of sight of Sam he slipped down through Butcher's Row in the direction of the glass alone. It was dark out there with no stars and only an occasional hint of moonlight, yet the breeze was steady and there was nothing to trip over on the glass. The bird wouldn't have moved more than a hundred yards. Jason made good speed.

The slow bird was still there. But Tarnover wasn't with it; its belly was barren of any hanged man.

As Jason skated to a halt, to look closer, figures arose in the darkness from where they had been lying flat upon the glass, covered by their sails. Six figures. Eight. Nine. All had lurked within two or three hundred yards of the bird, though not too close—nor any in the direction of Atherton. They had left a wide corridor open; which now they closed.

As the Tuckerton men moved in on him, Jason stood still, knowing that he had no chance.

Max Tarnover skated up, accompanied by that same beefy farmer with the wart.

"I did come back for you," began Jason.

The farmer spoke, but not to Jason. "Did he now? That's big of him. Could have saved his time, what with Tim Earnshaw happening along—when Master Tarnover was gone a long time. So what's to be done with him, eh?"

"Tit for tat, I'd say," said another voice.

"Let him go and look for his kid brother," offered a third. "Instead of sending other folk on his errands. What a nerve."

Tarnover himself said nothing; he just stood in the night silently.

So, presently, Jason was raised on to the back of the bird and his feet were tied tightly under it. But his wrists were bound together too, and for good measure the cord was linked through his belt.

Within a few minutes all the skaters had sped away towards Tuckerton.

Jason sat. Remembering Sam's words he tried to inch forward, but with both hands fastened to his waist this proved impossible; he couldn't gain purchase. Besides, he was scared of losing his balance as Tarnover had.

He sat and thought of his mother. Maybe she would grow alarmed when he didn't come home. Maybe she would go out and rouse Uncle John. . . . And maybe she had gone to bed already.

But maybe she would wake in the night and glance into his room and send help. With fierce concentration he tried to project thoughts and images of himself at her, two miles away.

An hour wore on, then two; or so he supposed from the moving of the moon-crescent. He wished he could slump forward and sleep. That might be best; then he wouldn't know anything. He still felt drunk enough to pass out, even with his face pressed against metal. But he might easily slide to one side or the other in his sleep.

How could his mother survive a double loss? It seemed as though a curse had descended on the Babbidge family. But of course that curse had a human name; and the name was Max Tarnover. So for a while Jason damned him, and imagined retribution by all the villagers of

Atherton. A bloody feud. Cottages burnt. Perhaps a rape. Deaths even. No Mayday festival ever again.

But would Sam and Ned speak up? And would Atherton folk be sufficiently incensed, sufficiently willing to destroy the harmony of the five villages in a world where other things were so unsure? Particularly as some less than sympathetic souls might say that Jason, Sam, and Ned had started it all.

Jason was so involved in imagining a future feud between Atherton and Tuckerton that he almost forgot he was astride a slow bird. There was no sense of motion, no feeling of going anywhere. When he recollected where he was, it actually came as a shock.

He was riding a bird.

But for how long?

It had been around, what, six hours now? A bird could stay for a whole day. In which case he had another eighteen hours left to be rescued in. Or if it only stayed for half a day, that would take him through to morning. Just.

He found himself wondering what was underneath the metal skin of the bird. Something which could turn five miles of landscape into a sheet of glass, certainly. But other things too. Things that let it ignore gravity. Things that let it dodge in and out of existence. A brain of some kind, even?

"Can you hear me, bird?" he asked it. Maybe no one had ever spoken to a slow bird before.

The slow bird did not answer.

Maybe it couldn't, but maybe it could hear him, even so. Maybe it could obey orders.

"Don't disappear with me on your back," he told it. "Stay here. Keep on flying just like this."

But since it was doing just that already, he had no idea whether it was obeying him or not.

"Land, bird. Settle down onto the glass. Lie still."

It did not. He felt stupid. He knew nothing at all about the bird. Nobody did. Yet somewhere, someone knew. Unless the slow birds did indeed come from God, as miracles, to punish. To make men God-fearing. But why should a God want to be feared? Unless God was insane, in which case the birds might well come from Him.

They were something irrational, something from elsewhere, something which couldn't be understood by their victims any more than an ant colony understood the gardener's boot, exposing the white eggs to the sun and the sparrows.

Maybe something had entered the seas from elsewhere the previous century, something that didn't like land dwellers. Any of them. People or sheep, birds or worms or plants . . . It didn't seem likely. Salt water would rust steel, but for the first time in his life Jason thought about it intently.

"Bird, what are you? Why are you here?"

Why, he thought, is anything here? Why is there a world and sky and stars? Why shouldn't there simply be nothing for ever and ever?

Perhaps that was the nature of death: nothing for ever and ever. And one's life was like a slow bird. Appearing then vanishing, with nothing before and nothing after.

An immeasurable period of time later, dawn began to streak the sky behind him, washing it from black to grey. The greyness advanced slowly overhead as thick clouds filtered the light of the rising but hidden sun. Soon there was enough illumination to see clear all around. It must be five o'clock. Or six. But the grey glass remained blankly empty.

Who am I? wondered Jason, calm and still. Why am I conscious of a world? Why do people have minds, and think thoughts? For the first time in his life he felt that he was really thinking—and thinking had no outcome. It led nowhere.

He was, he realized, preparing himself to die. Just as all the land would die, piece by piece, fused into glass. Then no one would think thoughts any more, so that it wouldn't matter if a certain Jason Babbidge had ceased thinking at half past six one morning late in May. After all, the same thing happened every night when you went to sleep, didn't it? You stopped thinking. Perhaps everything would be purer and cleaner afterwards. Less untidy, less fretful: a pure ball of glass. In fact, not fretful at all, even if all the stars in the sky crashed into each other, even if the earth was swallowed by the sun. Silence, forever: once there was no one about to hear.

Maybe this was the message of the slow birds. Yet people only carved their initials upon them. And hearts. And the names of places which had been vitrified in a flash; or else which were going to be.

I'm becoming a philosopher, thought Jason in wonder.

He must have shifted into some hyperconscious state of mind: full of lucid clarity, though without immediate awareness of his surroundings. For he was not fully aware that help had arrived until the cord binding his ankles was cut and his right foot thrust up abruptly, toppling him off the other side of the bird into waiting arms.

Sam Partridge, Ned Darrow, Frank Yardley, and Uncle John, and Brian Sefton from the sawmill—who ducked under the bird brandishing a knife, and cut the other cord to free his wrists.

They retreated quickly from the bird, pulling Jason with them. He resisted feebly. He stretched an arm towards the bird.

"It's all right, lad," Uncle John soothed him.

"No, I want *to go*," he protested.

"Eh?"

At that moment the slow bird, having hung around long enough, vanished; and Jason stared at where it had been, speechless.

In the end his friends and uncle had to lead him away from that featureless spot on the glass, as though he was an idiot. Someone touched by imbecility.

But Jason did not long remain speechless.

Presently he began to teach. Or preach. One or the other. And people listened; at first in Atherton, then in other places too.

He had learned wisdom from the slow bird, people said of him. He had communed with the bird during that night's vigil on the glass.

His doctrine of nothingness and silence spread, taking root in fertile soil, where there was soil remaining rather than glass—which was in most places, still. A paradox, perhaps: how eloquently he spoke—about being silent! But in so doing he seemed to make the silence of the glass lakes sing; and to this people listened with a new ear.

Jason traveled throughout the whole island. And this was another paradox, for what he taught was a kind of passivity, a blissful waiting for a death that was more than merely personal, a death which was also the death of the sun and stars and of all existence, a cosmic death which transfigured individual mortality. And sometimes he even sat on the back of a bird that happened by, to speak to a crowd—as though chancing fate or daring, begging, the bird to take him away. But he never sat for more than an hour, then he would scramble down, trembling but quietly radiant. So besides being known as 'The Silent Prophet,' he was also known as 'The Man who rides the Slow Birds.'

On balance, it could have been said that he worked great psychological good for the communities that survived; and his words even spread overseas. His mother died proud of him—so he thought—though there was always an element of wistful reserve in her attitude. . . .

Many years later, when Jason Babbidge was approaching sixty, and still no bird had ever borne him away, he settled back in Atherton in his old home—to which pilgrims of silence would come, bringing prosperity to the village and particularly to the Wheatsheaf, managed now by the daughter of the previous landlord.

And every Mayday the skate-sailing festival was still held, but now always on the glass at Atherton. No longer was it a race and a competition; since in the end the race of life could not be won. Instead it had become a pageant, a glass ballet, a re-enactment of the events of many years ago—a passion play performed by the four remaining villages. Tuckerton and all its folk had been glassed ten years before by a bird which destroyed itself so that the circle of annihilation exactly touched that edge of the glass where Tuckerton had stood till then.

One morning, the day before the festival, a knock sounded on Jason's door. His housekeeper, Martha Prestidge, was out shopping in the village; so Jason answered.

A boy stood there. With red hair, and freckles.

For a moment Jason did not recognize the boy. But then he saw that it was Daniel. Daniel, unchanged. Or maybe grown up a little. Maybe a year older.

"Dan . . . ?"

The boy surveyed Jason bemusedly: his balding crown, his sagging girth, his now spindly legs, and the heavy stick with a stylised bird's head on which he leaned, gripping it with a liver-spotted hand.

"Jay," he said after a moment, "I've come back."

"Back? But . . ."

"I know what the birds are now! They *are* weapons. Missiles. Tens and hundreds of thousands of them. There's a war going on. But it's like a game as well: a board game run by machines. Machines that

think. It's only been going on for a few days in their time. The missiles
shunt to and fro through time to get to their destination. But they can't
shunt in the time of that world, because of cause and effect. So here's
where they do their shunting. In our world. The other possibility-
world."

"This is nonsense. I won't listen."

"But you must, Jay! It can be stopped for us before it's too late. I
know how. Both sides can interfere with each other's missiles and
explode them out of sight—that's here—if they can find them fast
enough. But the war over there's completely out of control. There's a
winning pattern to it, but this only matters to the machines any longer,
and they're buried away underground. They build the birds at a huge
rate with material from the Earth's crust, and launch them into other-
time automatically."

"Stop it, Dan."

"I fell off the bird over there—but I fell into a lake, so I wasn't
killed, only hurt. There are still some pockets of land left, around the
Bases. They patched me up, the people there. They're finished, in
another few hours of their time—though it's dozens of years to us. I
brought them great hope, because it meant that all life isn't finished.
Just theirs. Life can go on. What we have to do is build a machine
that will stop their machines finding the slow birds over here. By making
interference in the air. There are waves. Like waves of light, but you
can't see them."

"You're raving."

"Then the birds will still shunt here. But harmlessly. Without
glassing us. And in a hundred years time, or a few hundred, they'll
even stop coming at all, because the winning pattern will be all worked
out by then. One of the war machines will give up, because it lost the
game. Oh I know it ought to be able to give up right now! But there's
an element of the irrational programmed into the machines' brains too;
so they don't give up too soon. When they do, everyone will be long
dead there on land—and some surviving people think the war machines
will start glassing the ocean floor as a final strategy before they're
through. But we can build an air-wave-maker. They've locked the
knowledge in my brain. It'll take us a few years to mine the right metals
and tool up and provide a power source. . . ." Young Daniel ran out
of breath briefly. He gasped. "They had a prototype slow bird. They

sat me on it and sent me into other-time again. They managed to guide
it. It emerged just ten miles from here. So I walked home."

"Prototype? Air-waves? Power source? What are these?"

"I can tell you."

"Those are just words. Fanciful babble. Oh for this babble of the
world to still itself!"

"Just give me time, and I'll—"

"Time? You desire time? The mad ticking of men's minds instead
of the great pure void of eternal silence? You reject acceptance? You
want us to swarm forever aimlessly, deafening ourselves with our noisy
chatter?"

"Look . . . I suppose you've had a long, tough life, Jay. Maybe I
shouldn't have come here first."

"Oh, but you should indeed, my impetuous fool of a brother. And
I do not believe my life has been ill-spent."

Daniel tapped his forehead. "It's all in here. But I'd better get it
down on paper. Make copies and spread it around—just in case Atherton gets glassed. Then somebody else will know how to build the
transmitter. And life can go on. Over there they think maybe the human
race is the only life in the whole universe. So we have a duty to go on
existing. Only, the others have destroyed themselves arguing about
which way to exist. But we've still got time enough. We can build ships
to sail through space to the stars. I know a bit about that too. I tell you,
my visit brought them real joy in their last hours, to know this was all
still possible after all."

"Oh, Dan." And Jason groaned. Patriach-like, he raised his staff
and brought it crashing down on Daniel's skull.

He had imagined that he mightn't really notice the blood amidst
Daniel's bright red hair. But he did.

The boy's body slumped in the doorway. With an effort Jason
dragged it inside, then with an even greater effort up the oak stairs to
the attic where Martha Prestidge hardly ever went. The corpse might
begin to smell after a while, but it could be wrapped up in old blankets
and such.

However, the return of his housekeeper down below distracted
Jason. Leaving the body on the floor he hastened out, turning the key
in the lock and pocketing it.

It had become the custom to invite selected guests back to the

Babbidge house following the Mayday festivities; so Martha Prestidge would be busy all the rest of the day cleaning and cooking and setting the house to rights. As was the way of housekeepers she hinted that Jason would get under her feet; so off he walked down to the glass and out onto its perfect flatness to stand and meditate. Villagers and visitors spying the lone figure out there nodded gladly. Their prophet was at peace, presiding over their lives. And over their deaths.

The skate-sailing masque, the passion play, was enacted as brightly and gracefully as ever the next day.

It was May the Third before Jason could bring himself to go up to the attic again, carrying sacking and cord. He unlocked the door.

But apart from a dark stain of dried blood the floorboards were bare. There was only the usual jumble stacked around the walls. The room was empty of any corpse. And the window was open.

So he hadn't killed Daniel after all. The boy had recovered from the blow. Wild emotions stirred in Jason, disturbing his usual composure. He stared out of the window as though he might discover the boy lying below on the cobbles. But of Daniel there was no sign. He searched around Atherton, like a haunted man, asking no questions but looking everywhere piercingly. Finding no clue, he ordered a horse and cart to take him to Edgewood. From there he traveled all around the glass, through Buckby and Hopperton; and now he asked wherever he went, "Have you seen a boy with red hair?" The villagers told each other that Jason Babbidge had had another vision.

As well he might have, for within the year from far away news began to spread of a new teacher, with a new message. This new teacher was only a youth, but he had also ridden a slow bird—much farther than the Silent Prophet had ever ridden one.

However, it seemed that this young teacher was somewhat flawed, since he couldn't remember all the details of his message, of what he had been told to say. Sometimes he would beat his head with his fists in frustration, till it seemed that blood would flow. Yet perversely this touch of theatre appealed to some restless, troublesome streak in his audiences. They believed him because they saw his anguish, and it mirrored their own suppressed anxieties.

Jason Babbidge spoke zealously to oppose the rebellious new ideas, exhausting himself. All the philosophical beauty he had brought into the dying world seemed to hang in the balance; and reluctantly he called for a 'crusade' against the new teacher, to defend his own dream of Submission.

Two years later, he might well have wished to call his words back, for their consequence was that people were tramping across the countryside in between the zones of annihilation armed with pitchforks and billhooks, cleavers and sickles. Villages were burnt; many hundreds were massacred; and there were rapes—all of which seemed to recall an earlier nightmare of Jason's from before the time of his revelation.

In the third year of this seemingly endless skirmish between the Pacificists and the Survivalists Jason died, feeling bitter beneath his cloak of serenity; and by way of burial his body was roped to a slow bird. Loyal mourners accompanied the bird in silent procession until it vanished hours later. A short while after that, quite suddenly at the Battle of Ashton Glass, it was all over, with victory for the Survivalists led by their young red-haired champion, who it was noted bore a striking resemblance to old Jason Babbidge, so that it almost seemed as though two basic principles of existence had been at contest in the world: two aspects of the selfsame being, two faces of one man.

Fifty years after that, by which time a full third of the land was glass and the climate was worsening, the Survival College in Ashton at last invented the promised machine; and from then on slow birds continued to appear and fly and disappear as before, but now none of them exploded.

And a hundred years after that all the slow birds vanished from the Earth. Somewhere, a war was over, logically and finally.

But by then, from an Earth four fifths of whose land surface was desert or swamp—in between necklaces of barren shining glass—the first starship would arise into orbit.

It would be called *Slow Bird*. For it would fly to the stars, slowly. Slowly in human terms; two generations it would take. But that was comparatively fast.

A second starship would follow it; called *Daniel*.

Though after that massive and exhausting effort, there would be no more starships. The remaining human race would settle down to cultivate what remained of their garden in amongst the dunes and floods and acres of glass. Whether either starship would find a new home as habitable even as the partly glassed Earth, would be merely an article of faith.

On his deathbed, eighty years of age, in Ashton College lay Daniel who had never admitted to a family name.

The room was almost indecently overcrowded, though well if warmly ventilated by a wind whipping over Ashton Glass, and bright-lit by the silvery blaze reflecting from that vitrified expanse.

The dying old man on the bed beneath a single silken sheet was like a bird himself now: shrivelled with thin bones, a beak of a nose, beady eyes and a rooster's comb of red hair on his head.

He raised a frail hand as if to summon those closest, even closer. Actually it was to touch the old wound in his skull which had begun to ache fiercely of late as though it was about to burst open or cave in, unlocking the door of memory—notwithstanding that no one now needed the key hidden there, since his Collegians had discovered it independently, given the knowledge that it existed.

Faces leaned over him: confident, dedicated faces.

"They've stopped exploding, then?" he asked, forgetfully.

"Yes, yes, years ago!" they assured him.

"And the stars—?"

"We'll build the ships. We'll discover how."

His hand sank back on to the sheet. "Call one of them—"

"Yes?"

"*Daniel*. Will you?"

They promised him this.

"That way . . . my spirit . . ."

"Yes?"

". . . will fly . . ."

"Yes?"

". . . into the silence of space."

This slightly puzzled the witnesses of his death; for they could not know that Daniel's last thought was that, when the day of the launching came, he and his brother might at last be reconciled.

Judgment Call

*   *   *

John Kessel

*John Kessel has been an occasional but distinguished contributor to
F&SF over the years, with stories such as "Another Orphan," "Freedom
Beach," and the strong story you are about to read. "Judgment Call"
is about a minor league baseball player, and while it may not be precisely
a baseball story, it is concerned with things that make baseball fascinating: averages, statistics, luck . . .*

*   *   *

BOTTOM of the first, no score, Dutch on first, Simonetti on
second, two outs. In the bar afterward, Sandy replayed it in his
head.

Sandy had faced this Louisville pitcher maybe twice before. He
had a decent fastball and a good curve, enough so he'd gotten Sandy
out more than his share. And Sandy was in a slump (three for eighteen
in the last five games), and the count was one and two; and the Louisville
catcher was riding him. The ump was real quiet, but Sandy knew he
was just waiting to throw his old rabbit punch to signal the big K—fist
punching the air, but it might as well be Sandy's gut. It was hot. His
legs felt rubbery.

Old War Memorial was quiet. There weren't more than fifteen

hundred people there, tops; Louisville was leading the American Association, and the Bisons were dead last. The steel struts holding up the roof in right were ranked in the distance like the trees of the North Carolina pine forest where he grew up, lost in the haze and shadows of the top rows where nobody ever sat. The sky was overcast, and a heavy wind from the lake snapped the flag out in left center, but it was very hot for Buffalo, even for June. People were saying the climate was changing: it was the ozone layer, the Japs, the UFOs, the end of the world. Some off-duty cop or sanitation worker with a red face was ragging him from the stands. Sandy would have liked to deck him, but he had to ignore it because the pitcher was crouched over shaking off signals. He went into his stretch.

Then something happened: suddenly Sandy knew, he just knew he could hit this guy. The pitcher figured he had Sandy plugged—curveball, curveball, outside corner and low, then high and tight with the fastball to keep him from leaning—but it hit Sandy like a line drive between the eyes that he had the *pitcher* plugged, he *knew* where the next pitch was going to be. And there it was, fastball inside corner; and he turned on it; and *bye-bye, baby*! That sweet crack of the ash. Sandy watched it sail out over the left field fence; saw the pitcher, head down, kick dirt from the mound—sorry, guy; could be you won't see the majors as soon as you thought—and jogged around the bases feeling so *good*. He was going to live forever. He was going to get laid every night.

That was just his first at bat. In the bottom of the sixth, he made a shoestring catch in right center, and in the second and the seventh, he threw out runners trying to go from first to third. At the plate he went four for five, bringing his average up to a tantalizing .299. And number five was an infield bounce that Sandy was sure he'd beat out, but the wop ump at first called him out. A judgment call. The pud-knocker. But it was still the best game Sandy had ever played.

And Aronsen, the Sox general manager, was in town to take a look at the Bisons in the hope of finding somebody they could bring up to help them after the bad start they'd had. After the game he came by in the locker room. He glanced at Sandy's postgame blood panel. Sandy played it cool: he was at least 0.6 under the limit on DMD, not even on scale for steroids. Sandy should get ready right away, Aronsen told him, to catch the morning train to Chicago. They were sending

Estivez down and bringing him up. They were going to give him a chance to fill the hole in right field. Yessir, Sandy said, polite, eager.

Lordy, lordy—yes sir, he'd thought as he walked down Best with Dutch and Leon toward the Main Street tramway—good-bye, War Memorial. The hulk of the stadium, the exact color of a Down East dirt farmer's tobacco-stained teeth, loomed above them, the Art Deco globes that topped its corners covered with pigeon shit. Atop the corroded limestone wall that ran along the street was a chain-link fence, rusted brown, and atop the fence glistened new coils of barbed wire. The barbed wire was supposed to keep vagrants from living in the stadium. It made the place look like a prison.

Now it was a few hours later, and Sandy was having a drink with Dutch and Leon at the Ground Zerp on Delaware. He'd already stopped by a machine and withdrawn the entire six hundred dollars in his account, had called up the rental office and told them he was leaving and they could rent the place because he wasn't coming back. Chalk up one for his side. Sandy paid for the first round. He had it figured: you paid for the first stiff one, you didn't hesitate a bit, and the others would remember that much better than how slow you were on the second or third: so if you played it right, you came out ahead on drinks when the evening was done. Even when you didn't, you got the rep with the regulars at the bar of being a generous kind of guy. Sure enough, Dutch had paid for the second round and Leon for the third, and then some fans came by and got the next two. So Sandy was way ahead. His day. Only one thing was needed to make it complete.

"You lucky sonofabitch," Dutch shouted over the din of the talk and the flatscreen behind the bar. "You haven't played that well in a month. The Killer decides to go crazy on the day that Aronsen's in town."

There was more than kidding in Dutch's voice. "That's when it pays to look your best," Sandy said.

Dutch stared at the screen, where a faggot VJ with a wig and ruffles and lace cuffs was counting down the Top 100 videos of the twentieth century. Most of them were from the past two years. "Wouldn't do me any good," Dutch said. "They've got two first basemen ahead of me. I could hit .350 and I wouldn't get a shot at the majors."

"Playin' the wrong position, man," said Leon. His high eyebrows gave him a perpetually innocent expression.

Dutch didn't have the glove to play anywhere else but first. Sandy felt a little sorry for Dutch, who had wrecked his chances with HGH. At eighteen he had been a pretty hot prospect, a first baseman who could hit for average and field O.K. But he didn't have any power, so he'd taken the hormone in order to beef up. He'd beefed up, all right—going to six five, 230—but his reflexes got shot to hell in the process. Now he could hit twenty home runs in triple-A ball, but he struck out too much and his fielding was mediocre and he was slow as an ox. And the American League had abandoned the DH rule just about the time Dutch went off the drug.

It was a sad story. But Sandy got tired of his bitching, too. A real friend didn't bitch at you when you got called up. "You ought to work on the glove," he said.

A glint of hate showed in Dutch's face for a second, then he said, "I got to piss," and headed for the men's room.

"Sometimes he gets to me," Sandy said.

Leon lazily watched the women in the room, leaning his back against the bar, elbows resting on the edge, his big, gnarled catcher's hands hanging loosely from his wrists. On the screen behind him, a naked girl was bouncing up and down on a pink neon pogo stick. Sandy couldn't tell if she was real or vidsynthed.

"Got to admit, Killer, you ain't been playin' that good lately," Leon said over his shoulder. They called Sandy "The Killer" because of the number of double plays he hit into: Killer as in rally killer. "You been clutched out. Been tryin' too hard."

Now it was Leon, too. Leon had grown up in Fayetteville, not ten miles from Sandy's dad's farm, but Sandy would not have hung around with Leon back there. Leon was ten years older, his father was a noncom at Fort Bragg, and he was the wrong color. Sandy always felt like blacks were keeping secrets that he would just as soon not know.

Sandy finished his bourbon and ordered another. "You don't win without trying."

Leon just nodded. "Look at that talent there." He pointed his chin toward a table in the corner.

At the table, alone, sat a woman. He wondered how she had got there without him noticing her: she had microshort blonde hair and a pale oval face with a pointed chin. Blue lips. Her dark eyelashes were long enough so that he could see them from the bar. But what got him was her body. Even from across the room, Sandy could tell she was major league material. She wore a tight blue dress and was drinking something pale, on the rocks.

She looked over at them and calmly locked glances with Sandy. Something strange happened then. He had a feeling of vertigo, and then was overwhelmed by a vivid memory, a flashback to something that had happened to him long before.

It's the end of the summer of your junior year of high school, and you're calling Jocelyn from the parking lot of the Dairy King out near Highway 95. Brutal heat. Tapping your car keys impatiently on the dented metal shelf below the phone. Jocelyn is going to Atlantic Beach with Sid Phillips, and she hasn't even told you. Five rings, six. You had to get the news from Trudy Jackson and act like you knew all about it when it was like you'd been kneed in the groin.

An answer. "Hello?"

"Miz James, this is Sandy Ellison. Can I talk to Jocelyn?"

"Just a minute." Another wait. The sun burns the back of your neck.

"Hello." Jocelyn's voice sounds nervous.

The anger explodes in your chest. "What the fuck do you think you're doing?"

A semi blasts by on Highway 95, kicking up a cloud of dust and gravel. You turn your back to the road and hold your hand over your other ear.

"What are you talking about?"

"You better not fuck with me, Jocelyn. I won't take it."

"Slow down, Sandy. I—"

"If you go to the beach with him, it's over." You try to make it sound like a threat instead of a plea.

At first, Jocelyn doesn't answer. Then she says, "You always were a jerk." She hangs up.

You stand there with the receiver in your hand. It feels hot and greasy. The dial tone mocks you. Then Jeff Baxter and Jack Stubbs drive in Jeff's Trans-Am, and the three of you cruise out to the lake and drink three six-packs. "Bitch," you call her. "Fucking bitch."

The woman was still staring at him. She didn't look at all like Jocelyn. Sandy broke eye contact. He realized that Dutch had come

back, had been back for a while while Sandy was spaced-out. Fucking
Jocelyn.

Sandy made a decision. "One hundred says I boost her tonight."

Leon regarded him coolly. Dutch snorted. "Gonna pull down your
batting average, boy."

"Definitely a tough chance," Leon said.

"You think so? It's my day. We'll see who's trying too hard, Leon."

"You got a bet."

Sandy pulled the wad of bills out his shirt pocket and laid two
fifties on the bar. "You hold it, Dutch. I'll get it back tomorrow when
I pick up my gear." Dutch stuffed the redbucks into his shirt pocket.
Sandy picked up his drink and went over to the table. The woman
watched him the whole way. Up close she was even more spectacular.
"Hey," he said.

"Hello. It's about time. I've been waiting for you."

He pulled out a chair and sat down. "Sure you have."

"I never lie." Her smile was a dare. "How much is riding on this?"

He couldn't tell whether she was hostile or just a tease. Well, he
could go with the pitch. "One hundred," Sandy said. "That's a week's
pay in triple-A."

"What is triple-A?" Her husky voice had some trace of accent to
it—Hispanic?

"Baseball. My name is Sandy Ellison. I play for the Bisons."

She sipped her drink. Her ears were small and flat against her
head. The shortness of her hair made her head seem large and her
violet eyes enormous. He would die if he didn't have her that night.
"Are you a good player?" she asked.

"I just got called up to the majors. Monday night I'll be starting
for Chicago."

"You are a lucky man."

Luck again. The way she said it made Sandy think for a moment
he was being set up: Leon and Dutch and all that talk about luck. But
Dutch was too dumb to pull some elaborate practical joke. Leon was
smart enough, but he wasn't mean enough. Still, it would be a good
idea to stay on his guard. "Not luck; skill."

"Oh, skill. I thought you were lucky."

"How come I've never seen you here before?"

"I'm from out of town."

"I figured as much. Where?"

"Lexington."

Sandy ran his finger around the rim of his glass. "Kentucky? We just played Louisville. You follow the Cards on their road trips?"

"Road trips?"

"The game we played today was against the Louisville Cardinals. They're in town on a road trip."

"What a coincidence." Again the smile. "I'm on a road trip, too. But I'm not following this baseball team. I came to Buffalo for another reason, and I'm leaving tomorrow."

"It's a good town to be leaving. You help me celebrate, and I'll help you."

"That's why I'm here."

Right. Sandy glanced over at the bar. Leon and Dutch were talking to a couple of women. On the flatscreen was a newsflash about the microwave deluge in Arizona. Shots of househubs at the supermarket wearing their aluminized suits. He turned back to the woman and smiled. "Run that by me again."

The woman gazed at him calmly over her high cheekbones. "Come on, Sandy. Read my lips. This is your lucky day, and I'm here to celebrate it with you. A skillful man like you must understand what that means."

"Did Leon put you up to this? If he did, the bet's off."

"Leon is one of those two men at the bar? I don't know him. If I were to guess, I would guess that he is the black man. I'd also guess that you proposed the bet to him, not he to you. Am I right?"

"I made the bet."

"You see. My lucky guess. Well, if you made the bet with Leon, then it's unlikely that Leon hired me to trick you. It is unlikely for other reasons, too."

This was the weirdest pickup talk Sandy had ever heard. "Why do I get the feeling there's a proposition coming?"

"Don't tell me you didn't expect a proposition to pass between us sometime during this conversation."

"For sure. But I expected to be making it."

"Go ahead."

Sandy studied her. "You northern girls are different."

"I'm not from the North."

"Then you're from a different part of the South than I grew up in."

"It takes all kinds. May I ask you a question?"

"Sure."

"Why the bet?"

"I just wanted to make it interesting."

"I'm not interesting enough unless there's money riding on me?"

Riding on her. Sandy smiled. The woman smiled back. "I just like to raise the stakes," he said. "But the bet is between me and them, to prove a point. It has nothing to do with you."

"You're not very flattering."

"That's not what I meant."

"Yes. We can make it even more interesting. You think you can please me?"

Sandy finished his bourbon. "If you can be pleased."

"Good. So let's make it very interesting." She opened her clutch purse and tilted it toward him. She reached inside and held something so that Sandy could see it. A glint of metal. It was a straight razor.

"If you don't please me, I get to hurt you. Just a little."

Sandy stared at her. "Are you kidding?"

She stared back. Her look was steady.

"Maybe you're not as good as you tell me. Maybe you'll need to have some luck."

She had to be teasing. Sandy considered the odds. Even if she wasn't, he thought he could handle her. Sandy stood up. "It's a deal."

She didn't move. "You're sure you want to try this?"

"I know what I want when I see it."

"You already know enough to make a decision?"

He came around to her side of the table. "Let's go," he said. She closed her purse and led him toward the door. Sandy winked at Leon as they passed the bar; Leon's face looked as surprised and skeptical as ever. The girl's hips, swaying as she walked ahead of him, pulled him along the way the smell of food in the dumpster by the concession stand drew the retirees living in the cardboard boxes on Jefferson Avenue.

Once in the street he slipped an arm around her waist and nudged her over to the side of the building. Her perfume was dizzying. "What's your name?" he asked her.

"Judith," she said.

"Judith." It sounded so old-fashioned. There was a Judith in the Bible, he thought. But he never paid attention in Bible Class.

He kissed her. He had to force his tongue between her lips. Then she bit it, lightly. Her mouth was strong and wet. She moved her hips against him.

You are twelve. You're sitting in the Beulah Land Baptist Church with your mother. She must be thirty-five or so, a pretty woman with blonde hair, putting on a little weight. Your father doesn't go to church. Lately your mother has been going more often and reading from the Bible after supper.

Some of your classmates, including Carrie Ford and Sue Harvey, are being baptized that Sunday. The two girls ride the bus with you, and Carrie has the biggest tits in the seventh grade.

The choir sings a hymn while the Reverend Mr. Foster takes the girls into the side room; and when the song is done, the curtains in front of the baptismal font open and there stand the minister and Carrie, waist-deep in the water. Carrie is wearing a blue robe, trying nervously not to smile. Behind them is a painting of the lush green valley of the Promised Land, and the shining City on the Hill. The strong light from the spot above them makes Carrie's golden hair shine, too.

The Reverend Mr. Foster puts his hand on Carrie's shoulder, lifts his other hand toward heaven, and calls on the Lord.

"Do you renounce Satan and all his ways?" he asks Carrie.

"Yes," she says, looking holy. She crosses her hands at the wrists, palms in, and folds her hands over those tits, as if to hold them in.

The Minister touches the back of her neck. She jumps a bit, and you know she didn't expect that, but then lets him duck her head beneath the surface of the water. He holds her down for a long time, making sure she knows who's boss. You like that. The Minister says the words of the baptism and pulls her up again.

Carrie gasps and sputters. She lifts her hands to push the hair away from her eyes. The robe clings to her chest. You can see everything. As she tries to catch her breath, you feel yourself getting an erection.

You put your hand on your lap and try to make the erection go away, but the mere contact with your pants leg makes you get even harder. You can't help it; your dick has run away with you. You turn red and shift uncomfortably in the pew, and your mother looks at you. She sees your hand on your lap.

"Sandy!" she hisses. A woman in front of you looks around.

Your mother tries to ignore you. The curtains close. You wish you were dead. At the same time you want to get up, go to the side room, and watch Carrie Ford take off her wet robe and towel herself dry.

He felt the warmth of Judith's lips on his, her arms around his neck. He pushed away from her, staring. This was no time for some drug flashback. After a moment he placed his hands on either side of her head against the wall and leaned toward her. She bit her lower lip. He had an erection after all. Whether it was because of the memory or Judith, he couldn't tell; he couldn't tell; he felt the embarrassment and guilt that had burned in him at the church. He felt mad. "Listen," he said. "Let's go to my place."

"Whatever you like." They walked down the block to the tram station. Sandy lived in one of the luxury condos that had been built on the Erie Basin before the market crash. He had an expensive view across the lake. It was even more high-rent now that the Sunbelters were moving North to escape the drought.

They got off downtown and walked up River Street to the apartment; he inserted his ID card and punched in the security code. The lock snapped open, and Sandy ushered her in.

The place was wasted on Judith. She walked through his living room, the moon through the skylight throwing triangular shadows against the cathedral ceiling and walls, and thumbed on the bedroom light as if she had been there before. When he followed her, he found her standing just inside the door. She began to unbutton his shirt. He felt hot. He tried to undress her, but she pushed his hands away, pushed him backward until he fell awkwardly onto the water bed. She stood above him. The expression on her face was very grave.

She knelt on the undulating bed and rested her hands on his chest. He fumbled on the headboard shelf for the amyl nitrite. She pushed his hand away, took one of the caps, and broke it under his nose. His heart slammed against his ribs as if it would leap out of his chest; the air he breathed was hot and dry, and the tightness of the crotch of his jeans was agony. Eventually she helped him with that, but not before she had spent what seemed like an eternity making it worse.

The sight of her naked almost made him come right then. But she knew how to control that. She seemed to know everything in his mind before he knew it himself; she responded or didn't respond as he needed, precisely, kindly. She became everything that he wanted. She took him to the brink again and again, stopped just short, brought him back. She seemed hooked into the sources of his desire: his pain, his fear, his hope all translated into the simple, slow motions of her sex and his. He forgot to worry about whether he was pleasing her. He forgot who he was. For an hour he forgot everything.

It was dark. Sandy lay just on the edge of sleep with his eyelids sliding closed and the distant sound of a siren in the air. The siren faded.

"You're beautiful, Sandy," Judith said. "I may not cut you after all."

Sandy felt so groggy he could hardly think. "Nobody cuts The Killer," he mumbled, and laughed. He rolled onto his stomach. The bed undulated; he felt dizzy.

"Such a wonderful body. Such a hard dick."

She slid her hand down his backbone, and as she did, all the muscles of his back relaxed, as if it were a twisted cord that she was unwinding. It was almost a dream. In the back part of his mind was a tiny alarm, like the siren that had passed into another part of the city.

"Now," said Judith, "I want to tell you a story."

"Sure."

Lightly stroking his back, Judith said, "This is the story of Yancey Camera."

"Funny name." He felt so sleepy.

"It is. To begin with, Yancey Camera was a young man of great promise and trustful good nature. Would you believe me if I told you that he was as handsome as the leading man in a black-and-white movie? He was that handsome, and was as smart as he was handsome, and was as rich as he was smart. His dick was as reliable as his credit rating. He was a lucky young man.

"But Yancey did not believe in luck. Oh, he gave lip service to luck; when people said, 'Yancey, you're a lucky boy,' he said, 'Yes, I guess I am.' But when he thought about it, he understood that when they told him how lucky he was, they were really saying that he did not deserve his good fortune; had done nothing to earn it; and, in a more rationally ordered universe, he would not be handsome, smart, or rich, and his dick would be no more reliable than any other man's. Yancey came to realize that when people commented on his luck, they were really expressing their envy, and he immediately suspected those people. This lack of trust enabled him to spot more than a few phonies, for there was a large degree of truth in Yancey Camera's analysis.

"The problem was that as time went on and Yancey saw how much venality was concealed by people's talk of luck, he forgot that he had not initially done anything to earn the good looks, intellect, wealth, and hard dick that he possessed. In other words, Sandy, he came to disbelieve in luck. He thought that a man of his skills could control every situation. He forgot about the second law of thermodynamics, which tells us that we all lose, and that those times when we win are merely local statistical deviations in a universal progress from a state of lower to a state of higher entropy. Yancey's own luck was just such a local deviation. As time passed and Yancey's good fortune continued, he began ultimately to think that he was beyond the reach of the second law of thermodynamics."

Forget the alarm; forget the razor. The second law of sexual dynamics. First you screw her, then she talks. Sandy thought about the instant he had hit the home run, the feel of the bat in his hands, the contact with the ball so pure and sweet he knew it was out of the park even before he had finished following through.

"This is a sin that the Fates call hubris," Judith said, "and as soon as they realized the extent of Yancey Camera's error, they set about to rectify the situation. Now, there are several ways in which such an imbalance can be restored. It can be done in stages, or it can be done in one sudden, enormous stroke.

"And here my story divides: in one version of the story, Yancey Camera marries a beautiful young woman, fathers four sons, and opens an automobile dealership. Unfortunately, because Yancey's home is built on the site of a chemical waste dump, one of his boys is born with spina bifida and is confined to a wheelchair. The child dies at the age of twelve. One of his other boys is unable to compete in school and becomes a behavior problem. A third is brilliant but commits suicide at the age of fourteen when his girlfriend goes to the beach with another boy. Under the pressure of these disappointments, Yancey's wife becomes a shrill harridan. She gets fat and drinks and embarrasses him at parties. Yancey gets fat, too, and loses his hair. He is left with the consolation of his auto dealership, but then there is a war in the Middle East in which the oil fields are destroyed with atomic weapons.

Suddenly there is no more oil. Yancey goes bankrupt. A number of other things happen that I will not tell you about. Suffice it to say that by the end of this version of the story, Yancey has lost his good looks, his money, and finally his fine mind, which becomes unhinged by the pressures of his misfortune. In the end he loses his hard dick, too, and dies cursing his bad luck. For in the end he is certain that bad luck, and not his own behavior, is responsible for his destruction. And he is right."

"That's too bad."

"That is too bad, isn't it?" Judith lifted the hair from the back of his neck with the tips of her fingers. It tickled.

"The other version of the story, Sandy, is even more interesting. Yancey Camera grows older, and success follows success in his life. He marries a beautiful young woman who does not get fat, and fathers four completely healthy and well-adjusted sons. He becomes a successful lawyer and enters politics. He wins every election he enters. Eventually he becomes the President of the Entire Country. As president he visits every state capital. Everywhere he goes the people of the nation gather to meet him, and when Yancey departs, he leaves two groups of citizens behind. The first group goes home saying, 'What a fortunate people we are to have such a handsome, smart, and wealthy president.' Others say, 'What a smart, handsome, and wealthy people we are to have elected such a handsome, smart, and wealthy leader.' What a skilled nation, they tell themselves, they must be. Like their president, they assume that their gifts are not the result of good luck but of their inherent virtue. Therefore, all who point out this good luck must be jealous. And so the Fates or the second law of thermodynamics deal with Yancey's nation as they dealt with Yancey in the other version of this story. In their arrogance, Yancey Camera and his people, in the effort to maintain an oil supply for their automobiles, provoke a war that destroys all life on earth, including the lives, good looks, wealth, and hard dicks of all the citizens of that country, lucky and unlucky. The end.

"What do you think of that, Sandy?"

Sandy was on the verge of sleep. "I think you're hung up on dicks," he mumbled, smiling to himself. "All you women."

"Could be," Judith whispered. Her breath was warm on his ear. He fell asleep.

He woke with a start. She was no longer lying beside him. How

could he have let down his guard so easily? She could have ripped him
off—or worse. Where had he put the cash from the bank? He rolled
over and reached for his pants on the floor beside the bed, then poked
his index finger into the hip pocket. It was empty. He felt an adrenal
surge, lurched out of bed, and began to haul on his pants. He was
hopping toward the hallway, tugging on his zipper, when he saw her
through the open bathroom door.

She turned toward him. The light behind her was on. Her face
was totally in shadow, and her voice, when she spoke, was even huskier
than the voice he had heard before.

"Did you find it?" she asked.

He felt afraid. "Find what?"

"Your money."

Then he remembered he had stuck the crisp bills, fresh from the
machine, into the button-flap pocket of his shirt. He ran back to the
bed, found the shirt on the floor, and fumbled at it. The money was
there.

When he turned back to her, she was standing over him. She
reached down and touched his face.

You're fifteen. You are sitting at the chipped Formica table in the
kitchen of the run-down farmhouse, sweating in the ninety-degree heat,
eating a peanut butter sandwich and drinking a glass of sweet tea. The
air is damp and hot as a fever compress. Through the patched screen
door, you can see the porch; the dusty, red-clay yard; and a corner of
the tobacco field, vivid green, running down toward the even darker line
of trees along the bend of the Cape Fear that marks the edge of the farm.
The air is full of the sweet smell of the tobacco. Even the sandwich tastes
of it.

You're wearing your high school baseball uniform. Your spikes and
glove—a Dale Murphy autograph—rest on the broken yellow vinyl of
the only other serviceable kitchen chair. You're starting in right today,
at two o'clock, in the first round of the Cumberland County champi-
onships, and afterward you're going out for pizza with Jocelyn. Your
heart is pulling you away from the farm; your thoughts fly through a
jumble of images; Jocelyn's fine blonde hair, the green of the infield grass,
the brightly painted ads on the outfield fence, the way the chalk lines
glow blinding white in the summer sun, the smell of Jocelyn's shoulders
when you bury your face in the nape of her neck. If you never have to

suffer through another summer swamped under the sickly sweet smell of tobacco, it will be all right with you.

You finish eating and are washing out the glass and plate in the sink, when you hear your father's boots on the porch and the screen door slams behind him. You ignore the old man. He comes over to the counter, opens the cupboard, and takes out the bottle of sour mash bourbon and a drinking glass. Less than an inch is left in the bottom of the bottle. He curses and pours the bourbon into the glass, then drinks it off without putting down the bottle. He sighs heavily and leans against the counter.

You dry your hands quickly and get your glove and spikes.

"Where you going?" your father asks, as if the uniform and equipment are not enough.

"We got a game today."

He looks at you. His eyes are set in a network of wrinkles that come from squinting against the sun. Mr. Witt, the high school coach, has the same wrinkles around his eyes, but his are from playing outfield when he was with Atlanta. And Mr. Witt's eyes are not red.

Your father doesn't say anything. He takes off his billed cap and wipes his forearm across his brow. He turns and reaches into the sugar canister he keeps in the cupboard next to his bottles. You try to leave, but are stopped by his voice again. "Where's the sugar bowl money?"

"I don't know."

His voice is heavy, slow. "There was another twelve dollars in here. What did you do with it?"

You stand in the door, helpless. "I didn't touch your money."

"Liar. What did you do with it!"

Pure hatred flares in you. "I didn't take your fucking money, you old drunk!"

You slam out the screen door and stalk over to the beat-up Maverick that you worked nights and weekends saving up to buy. You grind the gearshift into first, let the engine roar through the rotten muffler, spin the tires on the dirt in the yard. In the side mirror you see the old man standing on the porch shouting at you. But you can't hear what he's shouting, and the image shakes crazily as you bounce up the rutted drive.

Sandy flinched. He was crouched in his apartment, and the woman was standing over him. He still shook with anger at his father's accusation, still sweated from the heat; he could still smell the tobacco baking in the sun. How he hated the old man and his suspicion. For the first time in years, he felt the vivid contempt he'd had then for the smallness that made his father that way.

He backed away from Judith, shaking. She reached out and touched him again.

You're in this same bedroom, leaning half out of a bed where you've just gotten your ashes hauled better than you have in your entire life, in order to stick your finger into a pocket to see whether you've been robbed. On the day that you made the majors, on the day that you played better than you have in your entire life, on the day you played better than, in truth, you know you are really able to play. Sticking your finger into your pants pocket like a half-wit sticking his finger up his ass because it feels so good. A pitiful loser. Just like your father.

Sandy jerked away from her. He scrambled toward the bed, suddenly terrified. His knees were so weak he couldn't pull himself into the bed.

"What's the matter, Sandy?" She stepped toward him.

"Don't touch me!"

"You don't like my touch?"

"You're going to kill me." He said it quietly, amazed; and as he spoke, he realized it was true.

She moved closer. "That remains to be seen, Sandy."

"Don't touch me again! Please!"

"Why not?"

Cowering, he looked up at her, trying to make out her face in the darkness. It wasn't fair. But then something welled up in him, and he knew it *was* fair, and that was almost more than he could stand. "I'm sorry," he said.

She knelt beside him, wrapped her arms around him, and said nothing.

After a while he stopped crying. He wiped his eyes and nose with the corner of the bed sheet, ashamed. He sat on the edge of the bed, back to her. "I'm sorry," he said.

"Yes," she said. Then he saw that in her other hand, the one she had not touched him with, she held the straight razor. She had been holding it all the time.

"I didn't realize I might be hurting your feelings," he said.

"You can't hurt my feelings." There was no emotion in her voice.

There was nothing. Looking at her face was like looking at an empty room.

"Don't worry," she said, folding the blade back into the handle. "I won't hurt you."

It was a blind voice. Sandy shuddered. She leaned toward him. Her body was excruciatingly beautiful, yet he stumbled back from the bed, grabbing for his shirt, as if the pants weren't enough, as if it were January and he was lost on the lakefront in a blizzard.

"You don't have to be afraid," she said. "Come to bed."

He stood there, indecisive. He had to get out of there. She was insane—fuck insane; she wasn't even human. He looked into her cold face. It was not dead. It was like the real woman was in another place and this body was a receiver over which she was bringing him a message from a far distance—from another country, from across the galaxy. If he left now, he would be okay, he knew. But something that might have happened to him would not happen, and in order to find out what that was, he would have to take a big chance. He looked up at the moon through the skylight. The clouds passed steadily across it, making it look like it was moving. The moon didn't move that fast; it moved so slowly that you couldn't tell, except Sandy knew that in five minutes the angle of the shadows on the wall and chair and bed would be all different. The room would be changed.

She was still in bed. Sandy came back, dropped the shirt, took off his pants, and got in beside her. Her skin was very smooth.

The clock read 8:45; he would have to hurry. He felt good. He got his bags out of the closet and began to pack. Halfway through, he stopped to get the shirt he had left on the floor. He picked it up and shoved it into his laundry bag, then remembered the cash and pulled it out again. She had left him fifteen dollars. One ten, five ones.

He pushed the shirt down into the bottom of the bag and finished packing. He called a cab and rode over to War Memorial.

On the Hitachi in the cab, he watched the morning news, hoping to get the baseball scores. Nothing. The Reverend Mr. Gilray declares the Abomination of Desolation has begun, the Judgment is at hand. Reports the Israelis have used tactical nukes in the Djibouti civil war. Three teenagers spot another UFO at Chestnut Ridge.

When he got to the park, Sandy tipped the cabbie a redbuck and went directly to the locker room and cleaned out his locker. He was hoping to avoid Leon or Dutch, but just as he was getting ready to leave, Dutch showed up to take some hitting before the Sunday afternoon game.

"Looks like I underrated you, sport. Just like on the field." He hauled out his wallet and began to get the bills.

"Keep it," Sandy said.

"Huh?" Dutch, surprised, looked like a vanilla imitation of Leon's perpetual innocence.

"Leon won the bet."

Dutch snickered. "She got wise to you, huh?"

Sandy zipped his bag shut and picked up his glove and bats. He smiled. "You could say that. I got to go—cab's waiting. Wish me luck."

"Thought you didn't need luck."

"Goes to show you what I know. Say good-bye to Leon for me, O.K.?" He shook Dutch's hand and left.

The Aliens Who Knew, I Mean, Everything

* * *

George Alec Effinger

George Alec Effinger's novels include The Wolves of Memory, What
Entropy Means to Me, *and* When Gravity Fails. *Among his many
contributions to F&SF are those rarest of birds, the successful SF comedy.
The story below is a superior example. When he sent it, Mr. Effinger
observed that aliens are usually presented in only two lights: either saintly
E.T. types, or ugly things that want to eat us. There are other possibilities, of course . . .*

* * *

I WAS sitting at my desk, reading a report on the brown pelican
situation, when the secretary of state burst in. "Mr. President," he
said, his eyes wide, "the aliens are here!" Just like that. "The aliens
are here!" As if I had any idea what to do about them.

"I see," I said. I learned early in my first term that "I see" was
one of the safest and most useful comments I could possibly make in
any situation. When I said, "I see," it indicated that I had digested the
news and was waiting intelligently and calmly for further data. That
knocked the ball back into my advisers' court. I looked at the secretary
of state expectantly. I was all prepared with my next utterance, in the
event that he had nothing further to add. My next utterance would be,

"Well?" That would indicate that I was on top of the problem, but that I couldn't be expected to make an executive decision without sufficient information, and that he should have known better than to burst into the Oval Office unless he had that information. That's why we had protocol; that's why we had proper channels; that's why I had advisers. The voters out there didn't want me to make decisions without sufficient information. If the secretary didn't have anything more to tell me, he shouldn't have burst in in the first place. I looked at him awhile longer. "Well?" I asked at last.

"That's about all we have at the moment," he said uncomfortably. I looked at him sternly for a few seconds, scoring a couple of points while he stood there all flustered. I turned back to the pelican report, dismissing him. I certainly wasn't going to get all flustered. I could think of only one president in recent memory who was ever flustered in office, and we all know what happened to him. As the secretary of state closed the door to my office behind him, I smiled. The aliens were probably going to be a bitch of a problem eventually, but it wasn't my problem yet. I had a little time.

But I found that I couldn't really keep my mind on the pelican question. Even the president of the United States has *some* imagination, and if the secretary of state was correct, I was going to have to confront these aliens pretty damn soon. I'd read stories about aliens when I was a kid, I'd seen all sorts of aliens in movies and television, but these were the first aliens who'd actually stopped by for a chat. Well, I wasn't going to be the first American president to make a fool of himself in front of visitors from another world. I was going to be briefed. I telephoned the secretary of defense. "We must have some contingency plans drawn up for this," I told him. "We have plans for every other possible situation." This was true; the Defense Department has scenarios for such bizarre events as the rise of an imperialist fascist regime in Liechtenstein or the spontaneous depletion of all the world's selenium.

"Just a second, Mr. President," said the secretary. I could hear him muttering to someone else. I held the phone and stared out the window. There were crowds of people running around hysterically out there. Probably because of the aliens. "Mr. President?" came the voice of the secretary of defense. "I have one of the aliens here, and he suggests that we use the same plan that President Eisenhower used."

I closed my eyes and sighed. I hated it when they said stuff like that. I wanted information, and they told me these things knowing that I would have to ask four or five more questions just to understand the answer to the first one. "You have an alien with you?" I said in a pleasant enough voice.

"Yes, sir. They prefer not to be called 'aliens.' He tells me he's a 'nuhp.' "

"Thank you, Luis. Tell me, why do you have an al—Why do you have a nuhp and I don't?"

Luis muttered the question to his nuhp. "He says it's because they wanted to go through proper channels. They learned about all that from President Eisenhower."

"Very good, Luis." This was going to take all day, I could see that; and I had a photo session with Mick Jagger's granddaughter. "My second question, Luis, is what the hell does he mean by 'the same plan that President Eisenhower used'?"

Another muffled consultation. "He says that this isn't the first time that the nuhp have landed on Earth. A scout ship with two nuhp aboard landed at Edwards Air Force Base in 1954. The two nuhp met with President Eisenhower. It was apparently a very cordial occasion, and President Eisenhower impressed the nuhp as a warm and sincere old gentleman. They've been planning to return to Earth ever since, but they've been very busy, what with one thing and another. President Eisenhower requested that the nuhp not reveal themselves to the people of Earth in general, until our government decided how to control the inevitable hysteria. My guess is that the government never got around to that, and when the nuhp departed, the matter was studied and then shelved. As the years passed, few people were even aware that the first meeting ever occurred. The nuhp have returned now in great numbers, expecting that we'd have prepared the populace by now. It's not their fault that we haven't. They just sort of took it for granted that they'd be welcome."

"Uh-huh," I said. That was my usual utterance when I didn't know what the hell else to say. "Assure them that they are, indeed, welcome. I don't suppose the study they did during the Eisenhower administration was ever completed. I don't suppose there really is a plan to break the news to the public."

"Unfortunately, Mr. President, that seems to be the case."

"Uh-huh," That's Republicans for you, I thought. "Ask your nuhp something for me, Luis. Ask him if he knows what they told Eisenhower. They must be full of outer-space wisdom. Maybe they have some ideas about how we should deal with this."

There was yet another pause. "Mr. President, he says all they discussed with Mr. Eisenhower was his golf game. They helped to correct his putting stroke. But they are definitely full of wisdom. They know all sorts of things. My nuhp—that is, his name is Hurv—anyway, he says that they'd be happy to give you some advice."

"Tell him that I'm grateful, Luis. Can they have someone meet with me in, say, half an hour?"

"There are three nuhp on their way to the Oval Office at this moment. One of them is the leader of their expedition, and one of the others is the commander of their mother ship."

"Mother ship?" I asked.

"You haven't seen it? It's tethered on the Mall. They're real sorry about what they did to the Washington Monument. They say they can take care of it tomorrow."

I just shuddered and hung up the phone. I called my secretary. "There are going to be three—"

"They're here now, Mr. President."

I sighed. "Send them in." And that's how I met the nuhp. Just as President Eisenhower had.

They were handsome people. Likable, too. They smiled and shook hands and suggested that photographs be taken of the historic moment, so we called in the media; and then I had to sort of wing the most important diplomatic meeting of my entire political career. I welcomed the nuhp to Earth. "Welcome to Earth," I said, "and welcome to the United States."

"Thank you," said the nuhp I would come to know as Pleen. "We're glad to be here."

"How long do you plan to be with us?" I hated myself when I said that, in front of the Associated Press and UPI and all the network news people. I sounded like a room clerk at a Holiday Inn.

"We don't know, exactly," said Pleen. "We don't have to be back to work until a week from Monday."

"Uh-huh," I said. Then I just posed for pictures and kept my mouth shut. I wasn't going to say or do another goddamn thing until my advisors showed up and started advising.

* * *

Well, of course, the people panicked. Pleen told me to expect that, but I had figured it out for myself. We've seen too many movies about visitors from space. Sometimes they come with a message of peace and universal brotherhood and just the inside information mankind has been needing for thousands of years. More often, though, the aliens come to enslave and murder us because the visual effects are better, and so when the nuhp arrived, everyone was all prepared to hate them. People didn't trust their good looks. People were suspicious of their nice manners and their quietly tasteful clothing. When the nuhp offered to solve all our problems for us, we all said, sure, solve our problems—*but at what cost?*

That first week, Pleen and I spent a lot of time together, just getting to know one another and trying to understand what the other one wanted. I invited him and Commander Toag and the other nuhp bigwigs to a reception at the White House. We had a church choir from Alabama singing gospel music, and a high school band from Michigan playing a medley of favorite collegiate fight songs, and talented clones of the original stars nostalgically re-creating the Steve and Eydie Experience, and an improvisational comedy troupe from Los Angeles or someplace, and the New York Philharmonic under the baton of a twelve-year-old girl genius. They played Beethoven's Ninth Symphony in an attempt to impress the nuhp with how marvelous Earth culture was.

Pleen enjoyed it all very much. "Men are as varied in their expressions of joy as we nuhp," he said, applauding vigorously. "We are all very fond of human music. We think Beethoven composed some of the most beautiful melodies we've ever heard, anywhere in our galactic travels."

I smiled. "I'm sure we are all pleased to hear that," I said.

"Although the Ninth Symphony is certainly not the best of his work."

I faltered in my clapping. "Excuse me?" I said.

Pleen gave me a gracious smile. "It is well known among us that Beethoven's finest composition is his Piano Concerto No. 5 in E-flat major."

I let out my breath. "Of course, that's a matter of opinion. Perhaps the standards of the nuhp—"

"Oh, no," Pleen hastened to assure me, "taste does not enter into it at all. The Concerto No. 5 is Beethoven's best, according to very rigorous and definite critical principles. And even that lovely piece is by no means the best music ever produced by mankind."

I felt just a trifle annoyed. What could this nuhp, who came from some weirdo planet God alone knows how far away, from some society with not the slightest connection to our heritage and culture, what could this nuhp know of what Beethoven's Ninth Symphony aroused in our human souls? "Tell me, then, Pleen," I said in my ominously soft voice, "what *is* the best human musical composition?"

"The score from the motion picture *Ben-Hur*, by Miklos Rózsa," he said simply. What could I do but nod my head in silence? It wasn't worth starting an interplanetary incident over.

So from fear our reaction to the nuhp changed to distrust. We kept waiting for them to reveal their real selves; we waited for the pleasant masks to slip off and show us the true nightmarish faces we all suspected lurked beneath. The nuhp did not go home a week from Monday, after all. They liked Earth, and they liked us. They decided to stay a little longer. We told them about ourselves and our centuries of trouble; and they mentioned, in an offhand nuhp way, that they could take care of a few little things, make some small adjustments, and life would be a whole lot better for everybody on Earth. They didn't want anything in return. They wanted to give us these things in gratitude for our hospitality: for letting them park their mother ship on the Mall and for all the free refills of coffee they were getting all around the world. We hesitated, but our vanity and our greed won out. "Go ahead," we said, "make our deserts bloom. Go ahead, end war and poverty and disease. Show us twenty exciting new things to do with leftovers. Call us when you're done."

The fear changed to distrust, but soon the distrust changed to hope. The nuhp made the deserts bloom, all right. They asked for four months. We were perfectly willing to let them have all the time they needed. They put a tall fence all around the Namib and wouldn't let anyone in to watch what they were doing. Four months later, they had a big cocktail party and invited the whole world to see what they'd accomplished. I sent the secretary of state as my personal representative. He brought back some wonderful slides: the vast desert had been turned into a botanical miracle. There were miles and miles of flowering plants now, instead of the monotonous dead sand and gravel sea. Of course, the immense garden contained nothing but hollyhocks, many millions of hollyhocks. I mentioned to Pleen that the people of Earth had been hoping for a little more in the way of variety, and something just a trifle more practical, too.

"What do you mean, 'practical'?" he asked.

"You know," I said, "food."

"Don't worry about food," said Pleen. "We're going to take care of hunger pretty soon."

"Good, good. But hollyhocks?"

"What's wrong with hollyhocks?"

"Nothing," I admitted.

"Hollyhocks are the single prettiest flower grown on Earth."

"Some people like orchids," I said. "Some people like roses."

"No," said Pleen firmly. "Hollyhocks are it. I wouldn't kid you."

So we thanked the nuhp for a Namibia full of hollyhocks and stopped them before they did the same thing to the Sahara, the Mojave, and the Gobi.

On the whole, everyone began to like the nuhp, although they took just a little getting used to. They had very definite opinions about everything, and they wouldn't admit that what they had were *opinions*. To hear a nuhp talk, he had a direct line to some categorical imperative that spelled everything out in terms that were unflinchingly black and white. Hollyhocks were the best flowers. Alexander Dumas was the greatest novelist. Powder blue was the prettiest color. Melancholy was the most ennobling emotion. *Grand Hotel* was the finest movie. The best car ever built was the 1956 Chevy Bel Air, but it had to be aqua and white. And there just wasn't room for discussion: the nuhp made these pronouncements with the force of divine revelation.

I asked Pleen once about the American presidency. I asked him who the Nuhp thought was the best president in our history. I felt sort of like the Wicked Queen in "Snow White." Mirror, mirror, on the wall. I didn't really believe Pleen would tell me that I was the best president, but my heart pounded while I waited for his answer; you never know, right? To tell the truth, I expected him to say Washington, Lincoln, Roosevelt, or Akiwara. His answer surprised me: James K. Polk.

"Polk?" I asked. I wasn't even sure I could recognize Polk's portrait.

"He's not the most familiar," said Pleen, "but he was an honest if unexciting president. He fought the Mexican War and added a great amount of territory to the United States. He saw every bit of his platform become law. He was a good, hardworking man who deserves a better reputation."

"What about Thomas Jefferson?" I asked.

Pleen just shrugged. "He was O.K., too, but he was no James Polk."

My wife, the First Lady, became very good friends with the wife of Commander Toag, whose name was Doim. They often went shopping together, and Doim would make suggestions to the First Lady about fashion and hair care. Doim told my wife which rooms in the White House needed redecoration, and which charities were worthy of official support. It was Doim who negotiated the First Lady's recording contract, and it was Doim who introduced her to the Philadelphia cheese steak, one of the nuhp's favorite treats (although they asserted that the best cuisine on Earth was Tex-Mex).

One day, Doim and my wife were having lunch. They sat at a small table in a chic Washington restaurant, with a couple of dozen Secret Service people and nuhp security agents disguised elsewhere among the patrons. "I've noticed that there seem to be more nuhp here in Washington every week," said the First Lady.

"Yes," said Doim, "new mother ships arrive daily. We think Earth is one of the most pleasant planets we've ever visited."

"We're glad to have you, of course," said my wife, "and it seems that our people have gotten over their initial fears."

"The hollyhocks did the trick," said Doim.

"I guess so. How many nuhp are there on Earth now?"

"About five or six million, I'd say."

The First Lady was startled. "I didn't think it would be that many."

Doim laughed. "We're not just here in America, you know. We're all over. We really like Earth. Although, of course, Earth isn't absolutely the best planet. Our own home, Nupworld, is still Number One; but Earth would certainly be on any Top Ten list."

"Uh-huh." (My wife has learned many important oratorical tricks from me.)

"That's why we're so glad to help you beautify and modernize your world."

"The hollyhocks were nice," said the First Lady. "But when are you going to tackle the really vital questions?"

"Don't worry about that," said Doim, turning her attention to her cottage cheese salad.

"When are you going to take care of world hunger?"

"Pretty soon. Don't worry."

"Urban blight?"

"Pretty soon."

"Man's inhumanity to man?"

Doim gave my wife an impatient look. "We haven't even been here for six months yet. What do you want, miracles? We've already done more than your husband accomplished in his entire first term."

"Hollyhocks," muttered the First Lady.

"I heard that," said Doim. "The rest of the universe absolutely *adores* hollyhocks. We can't help it if humans have no taste."

They finished their lunch in silence, and my wife came back to the White House fuming.

That same week, one of my advisers showed me a letter that had been sent by a young man in New Mexico. Several nuhp had moved into a condo next door to him and had begun advising him about the best investment possibilities (urban respiratory spas), the best fabrics and colors to wear to show off his coloring, the best holo system on the market (the Esmeraldas F-64 with hex-phased Libertad screens and a Ruy Challenger argon solipsizer), the best place to watch sunsets (the revolving restaurant on top of the Weyerhauser Building in Yellowstone City), the best wines to go with everything (too numerous to mention —send SASE for list), and which of the two women he was dating to marry (Candi Marie Esterhazy). "Mr. President," said the bewildered young man, "I realize that we must be gracious hosts to our benefactors from space, but I am having some difficulty keeping my temper. The nuhp are certainly knowledgeable and willing to share the benefits of their wisdom, but they don't even wait to be asked. If they were people, regular human beings who lived next door, I would have punched their lights out by now. Please advise. And hurry: they are taking me downtown next Friday to pick out an engagement ring and new living room furniture. I don't even *want* new living room furniture!"

Luis, my secretary of defense, talked to Hurv about the ultimate goals of the nuhp. "We don't have any goals," he said. "We're just taking it easy."

"Then why did you come to Earth?" asked Luis.

"Why do you go bowling?"

"I don't go bowling."

"You should," said Hurv. "Bowling is the most enjoyable thing a person can do."

"What about sex?"

"Bowling *is* sex. Bowling is a symbolic form of intercourse, except you don't have to bother about the feelings of some other person. Bowling is sex without guilt. Bowling is what people have wanted down through all the millennia: sex without the slightest responsibility. It's the very distillation of the essence of sex. Bowling is sex without fear and shame."

"Bowling is sex without pleasure," said Luis.

There was a brief silence. "You mean," said Hurv, "that when you put that ball right into the pocket and see those pins explode off the alley, you don't have an orgasm?"

"Nope," said Luis.

"That's your problem, then. I can't help you there, you'll have to see some kind of therapist. It's obvious this subject embarrasses you. Let's talk about something else."

"Fine with me," said Luis moodily. "When are we going to receive the real benefits of your technological superiority? When are you going to unlock the final secrets of the atom? When are you going to free mankind from drudgery?"

"What do you mean, 'technological superiority'?" asked Hurv.

"There must be scientific wonders beyond our imagining aboard your mother ships."

"Not so's you'd notice. We're not even so advanced as you people here on Earth. We've learned all sorts of wonderful things since we've been here."

"What?" Luis couldn't imagine what Hurv was trying to say.

"We don't have anything like your astonishing bubble memories or silicon chips. We never invented anything comparable to the transistor, even. You know why the mother ships are so big?"

"My God."

"That's right," said Hurv, "vacuum tubes. All our spacecraft operate on vacuum tubes. They take up a hell of a lot of space. And they burn out. Do you know how long it takes to find the goddamn tube when it burns out? Remember how people used to take bags of vacuum tubes from their television sets down to the drugstore to use the tube tester? Think of doing that with something the size of our mother ships. And we can't just zip off into space when we feel like it. We have to let a mother ship warm up first. You have to turn the key and let the thing warm up for a couple of minutes, *then* you can zip off into space. It's a goddamn pain in the neck."

"I don't understand," said Luis, stunned. "If your technology is so primitive, how did you come here? If we're so far ahead of you, we should have discovered your planet, instead of the other way around."

Hurv gave a gentle laugh. "Don't pat yourself on the back, Luis. Just because your electronics are better than ours, you aren't necessarily superior in any way. Look, imagine that you humans are a man in Los Angeles with a brand-new Trujillo and we are a nuhp in New York with a beat-up old Ford. The two fellows start driving toward St. Louis. Now, the guy in the Trujillo is doing 120 on the interstates, and the guy in the Ford is putting along at 55; but the human in the Trujillo stops in Vegas and puts all of his gas money down the hole of a blackjack table, and the determined little nuhp cruises along for days until at last he reaches his goal. It's all a matter of superior intellect and the will to succeed. Your people talk a lot about going to the stars, but you just keep putting your money into other projects, like war and popular music and international athletic events and resurrecting the fashions of previous decades. If you wanted to go into space, you would have."

"But we *do* want to go."

"Then we'll help you. We'll give you the secrets. And you can explain your electronics to our engineers, and together we'll build wonderful new mother ships that will open the universe to both humans and nuhp."

Luis let out his breath. "Sounds good to me," he said.

Everyone agreed that this looked better than hollyhocks. We all hoped that we could keep from kicking their collective asses long enough to collect on that promise.

* * *

When I was in college, my roommate in my sophomore year was a tall, skinny guy named Barry Rintz. Barry had wild, wavy black hair and a sharp face that looked like a handsome, normal face that had been sat on and folded in the middle. He squinted a lot, not because he had any defect in his eyesight, but because he wanted to give the impression that he was constantly evaluating the world. This was true. Barry could tell you the actual and market values of any object you happened to come across.

We had a double date one football weekend with two girls from another college in the same city. Before the game, we met the girls and took them to the university's art museum, which was pretty large and owned an impressive collection. My date, a pretty elementary ed. major named Brigid, and I wandered from gallery to gallery, remarking that our tastes in art were very similar. We both liked the Impressionists, and we both liked Surrealism. There were a couple of little Renoirs that we admired for almost half an hour, and then we made a lot of silly sophomoric jokes about what was happening in the Magritte and Dali and de Chirico paintings.

Barry and his date, Dixie, ran across us by accident as all four of us passed through the sculpture gallery. "There's a terrific Seurat down there," Brigid told her girlfriend.

"Seurat," Barry said. There was a lot of amused disbelief in his voice.

"I like Seurat," said Dixie.

"Well, of course," said Barry, "there's nothing really *wrong* with Seurat."

"What do you mean by that?"

"Do you know F. E. Church?" he asked.

"Who?" I said.

"Come here." He practically dragged us to a gallery of American paintings. F. E. Church was a remarkable American landscape painter (1826–1900) who achieved an astonishing and lovely luminance in his works. "Look at that light!" cried Barry. "Look at that space! Look at that air!"

Brigid glanced at Dixie. "Look at that air?" she whispered.

It was a fine painting and we all said so, but Barry was insistent.

F. E. Church was the greatest artist in American history, and one of the best the world has ever known. "I'd put him right up there with Van Dyck and Canaletto."

"Canaletto?" said Dixie. "The one who did all those pictures of Venice?"

"Those skies!" murmured Barry ecstatically. He wore the drunken expression of the satisfied voluptuary.

"Some people like paintings of puppies or naked women," I offered. "Barry likes light and air."

We left the museum and had lunch. Barry told us which things on the menu were worth ordering, and which things were an abomination. He made us all drink an obscure imported beer from Ecuador. To Barry, the world was divided up into masterpieces and abominations. It made life so much simpler for him, except that he never understood why his friends could never tell one from the other.

At the football game, Barry compared our school's quarterback to Y. A. Tittle. He compared the other team's punter to Ngoc Van Vinh. He compared the halftime show to the Ohio State band's Script Ohio formation. Before the end of the third quarter, it was very obvious to me that Barry was going to have absolutely no luck at all with Dixie. Before the clock ran out in the fourth quarter, Brigid and I had made whispered plans to dump the other two as soon as possible and sneak away by ourselves. Dixie would probably find an excuse to ride the bus back to her dorm before suppertime. Barry, as usual, would spend the evening in our room, reading *The Making of the President 1996*.

On other occasions Barry would lecture me about subjects as diverse as American literature (the best poet was Edwin Arlington Robinson, the best novelist James T. Farrell), animals (the only correct pet was the golden retriever), clothing (in anything other than a navy blue jacket and gray slacks a man was just asking for trouble), and even hobbies (Barry collected military decorations of czarist Imperial Russia, he wouldn't talk to me for days after I told him my father collected barbed wire).

Barry was a wealth of information. He was the campus arbiter of good taste. Everyone knew that Barry was the man to ask.

But no one ever did. We all hated his guts. I moved out of our dorm room before the end of the fall semester. Shunned, lonely, and bitter Barry Rintz wound up as a guidance counselor in a high school in Ames, Iowa. The job was absolutely perfect for him; few people are so lucky in finding a career. If I didn't know better, I might have believed that Barry was the original advance spy for the nuhp.

When the nuhp had been on Earth for a full year, they gave us the gift of interstellar travel. It was surprisingly inexpensive. The nuhp explained their propulsion system, which was cheap and safe and adaptable to all sorts of other earthbound applications. The revelations opened up an entirely new area of scientific speculation. Then the nuhp taught us their navigational methods, and about the "shortcuts" they had discovered in space. People called them space warps, although technically speaking, the shortcuts had nothing to do with Einsteinian theory or curved space or anything like that. Not many humans understood what the nuhp were talking about, but that didn't make very much difference. The nuhp didn't understand the shortcuts, either; they just used them. The matter was presented to us like a Thanksgiving turkey on a platter. We bypassed the whole business of cautious scientific experimentation and leaped right into commercial exploitation. Mitsubishi of La Paz and Martin Marietta used nuhp schematics to begin construction of three luxury passenger ships, each capable of transporting a thousand tourists anywhere in our galaxy. Although man had yet to set foot on the moons of Jupiter, certain selected travel agencies began booking passage for a grand tour of the dozen nearest inhabited worlds.

Yes, it seemed that space was teeming with life, humanoid life on planets circling half the G-type stars in the heavens. "We've been trying to communicate with extraterrestrial intelligence for decades," complained one Soviet scientist. "Why haven't they responded?"

A friendly nuhp merely shrugged "Everybody's trying to communicate out there," he said. "Your messages are like Publishers Clearing House mail to them." At first, that was a blow to our racial pride, but we got over it. As soon as we joined the interstellar community, they'd begin to take us more seriously. And the nuhp had made that possible.

We were grateful to the nuhp, but that didn't make them any easier to live with. They were still insufferable. As my second term as president came to an end, Pleen began to advise me about my future career.

"Don't write a book," he told me (after I had already written the first two hundred pages of *A President Remembers*). "If you want to be an elder statesman, fine; but keep a low profile and wait for the people to come to you."

"What am I supposed to do with my time, then?" I asked.

"Choose a new career," Pleen said. "You're not all that old. Lots of people do it. Have you considered starting a mail-order business? You can operate it from your home. Or go back to school and take courses in some subject that's always interested you. Or become active in church or civic projects. Find a new hobby: raising hollyhocks or collecting military decorations."

"Pleen," I begged, "just leave me alone."

He seemed hurt. "Sure, if that's what you want." I regretted my harsh words.

All over the country, all over the world, everyone was having the same trouble with the nuhp. It seemed that so many of them had come to Earth, every human had his own personal nuhp to make endless suggestions. There hadn't been so much tension in the world since the 1992 Miss Universe contest, when the most votes went to No Award.

That's why it didn't surprise me very much when the first of our own mother ships returned from its 28-day voyage among the stars with only 276 of its 1,000 passengers still aboard. The other 724 had remained behind on one lush, exciting, exotic, friendly world or another. These planets had one thing in common: they were all populated by charming, warm, intelligent, humanlike people who had left their own home worlds after being discovered by the nuhp. Many races lived together in peace and harmony on these planets, in spacious cities newly built to house the fed-up expatriates. Perhaps these alien races had experienced the same internal jealousies and hatreds we human beings had known for so long, but no more. Coming together from many planets throughout our galaxy, these various peoples dwelt contentedly beside each other, united by a single common feeling: their dislike for the nuhp.

Within a year of the launching of our first interstellar ship, the population of Earth had declined by 0.5 percent. Within two years, the population had fallen by almost 14 million. The nuhp were too sincere and too eager and too sympathetic to fight with. That didn't make them any less tedious. Rather than make a scene, most people just up and left. There were plenty of really lovely worlds to visit, and it didn't cost very much, and the opportunities in space were unlimited. Many people who were frustrated and disappointed on Earth were able to build new and fulfilling lives for themselves on planets that, until the nuhp arrived, we didn't even know existed.

The nuhp knew this would happen. It had already happened dozens, hundreds of times in the past, wherever their mother ships touched down. They had made promises to us and they had kept them, although we couldn't have guessed just how things would turn out.

Our cities were no longer decaying warrens imprisoning the impoverished masses. The few people who remained behind could pick and choose among the best housing. Landlords were forced to reduce rents and keep properties in perfect repair just to attract tenants.

Hunger was ended when the ratio of consumers to food producers dropped drastically. Within ten years, the population of Earth was cut in half, and was still falling.

For the same reason, poverty began to disappear. There were plenty of jobs for everyone. When it became apparent that the nuhp weren't going to compete for those jobs, there were more opportunities than people to take advantage of them.

Discrimination and prejudice vanished almost overnight. Everyone cooperated to keep things running smoothly despite the large-scale emigration. The good life was available to everyone, and so resentments melted away. Then, too, whatever enmity people still felt could be focused solely on the nuhp; the nuhp didn't mind, either. They were oblivious to it all.

I am now the mayor and postmaster of the small human community of New Dallas, here on Thir, the fourth planet of a star known in our old catalog as Struve 2398. The various alien races we encountered here call the star by another name, which translates into "God's Pineal." All the aliens here are extremely helpful and charitable, and there are few nuhp.

All through the galaxy, the nuhp are considered the messengers of peace. Their mission is to travel from planet to planet, bringing reconciliation, prosperity, and true civilization. There isn't an intelligent race in the galaxy that doesn't love the nuhp. We all recognize what they've done and what they've given us.

But if the nuhp started moving in down the block, we'd be packed and on our way somewhere else by morning.

The God Machine

* * *

Damon Knight

Damon Knight has long been one of SF's best regarded novelists, critics, and editors, but F&SF readers know him through his superior short stories, beginning with "Not With A Bang," a short piece that appeared in our second issue in 1950 and eventually became a classic. "The God Machine" is a very short story about the ultimate merger: between electronics and religion.

* * *

NOT a good morning. Bunny is on the rampage again. Three people in the Art Department are out with AIDS. Heavy smog. At ten o'clock Terry is called in to Olly's office. Terry is the creative director. Olly is the president. Handlebar mustache, striped T-shirt, Adidas. Beside Olly's desk sits a little man with a suitcase in his lap. Plastic suitcase. Undistinguished haircut.

"Terry," says Olly, "I want you to meet Bill Sonntag. He's here to show us the marketing miracle of 1985. The client is Universal Electric. They want a presentation for a thirty-mil all media campaign starting in September."

"What is the product, Bill?" Terry inquires.

"It's, like, God in a box," says Bill.

"How's that for a slogan?" asks Olly, popping a pill. "Not bad, eh, Terry?"

"Terrific, just terrific, Olly. What does it do?"

"I'm going to let Bill explain that. Take him back to your office —and Terry, lock your door."

They go to Terry's office. Terry moves a teddy bear to make room for Bill to sit down. "What is your position with U.E., Bill?" he asks.

"I'm not with them, I'm the inventor. One of the inventors. They sent me because nobody else seems to be able to explain it."

Terry nods several times. "Excuse me." He takes two aspirin. "Well, so it's God in a box? What does that mean, exactly?"

"O.K.," says Bill. "The basic idea is, is that God is immanent in certain objects—like, for instance, the best example is the ark of the covenant. I don't know if you're familiar with the story of Uzzah, in the Second Book of Samuel?"

"Remind me."

"Maybe I better start farther back? See, the ark was like a box made of wood, about four feet by two by two. It was supposed to have the tablets of the law in it—you know, the ones that God gave to Moses."

"Oh, yeah."

"You saw the movie, right? O.K., that makes it a little easier. Well, the story goes, they're moving the ark in a cart, and this Uzzah sees it's about to tip over, so he puts his hand on it, like to steady it? And he gets a charge of something that kills him."

"This box is something that kills people, Bill?" Terry asks. He takes two more aspirin.

"No, no, that's only if you get too big a jolt. Like electricity? Anyway, what got us thinking, it says in the Bible the ark was covered inside and out with gold. Now there could be two reasons for that. One, gold is a precious metal, O.K.?"

"You're right there, Bill. What's the other reason?"

"The other reason is—" Bill leans forward confidentially—"gold is a good conductor. Not just a good conductor, a *great* conductor. So we said, What if there *is* something in holy objects that could be electronically enhanced, or, you know, throttled down if it's too strong? The first thing we tried was a really old set of the scrolls, the Torah. Bingo. Furthermore, we found out you can transfer this power by leaving your holy object in a lead-lined container with some other object. For a relic, like a piece of bone, say we use bone. Lamb is the best."

"That's unbelievable, Bill."

"I know. That's the problem. All I can do is, is I can let you try yourself. May I ask what your religion is, Terry?"

"I'm a Presbyterian."

"O.K, you get the Protestant model. For that, we had to go to old Bibles—we bought a Gutenberg, and maybe you think that didn't cost. We found out later the Wycliffe is just as good." Bill is taking a small black box out of the suitcase. He lays it on the desk, and Terry looks at it. On the left is a dial, and on the right, inset in the box, a disk of some off-white material. Bill plugs it in; a red light comes on.

"Now what you do is, is you just relax and put your fingers on this ceramic plate, and then slowly turn up the gain. This is a low-immanence circuit, so you don't have to worry. Go ahead."

Terry does as he is told. The ceramic plate is cool and slick under his fingers. He turns the dial with his other hand. "I don't feel a thing."

"You got it all the way up? That's funny." Bill pulls the box toward him. "Let's try the theometer." He takes a bright little instrument from among the ballpoint pens in his shirt pocket, lays it across the ceramic plate. The digital readout stays at "0".

"Dead," says Bill. He opens the case and peers inside. "O.K., here's the trouble—it blew a resistor." He pulls out a little cylinder and shows it to Terry. In the box, nestled among wires and ugly electrical parts, is a Gideon Bible.

"This is a prototype," Bill says. "Still a few bugs in it. The production model will have all printed circuits." He gropes in his suitcase, finds another resistor and puts it in, closes the case. "Try it again."

Terry puts his fingers on the ceramic plate, turns the dial up. Almost at once, a feeling of indescribable peace comes over him. He no longer cares about Bill's haircut or Olly's T-shirts. The throbbing at the back of his head goes away.

"See? See?" says Bill, exposing his mediocre dentistry.

Bill leaves the machine with Terry. Terry calls in Lori and Reggie and swears them to silence. Over the next three days, they rough out a campaign. It is terrific. The client is impressed. Terry gets a bonus.

The fall campaign is a success. "HOLINEX for instant tranquility—the peace that passes understanding at the touch of a button, in the privacy of your own home!" Hospitals buy the professional model at $1,795. Psychiatrists buy it. The home models retail for $695 plus tax. People line up for it in department stores. It comes in Protestant, Catholic, Orthodox, and Reformed versions. For the overseas market, Buddhist, Muslim, and Hindu versions are on the drawing boards.

Church and synagogue attendance zooms, then nosedives, until pastors begin allowing worshipers to bring their Holinexes. An enterprising minister in the East Village announces plans to build them into the backs of pews. Labor unrest is down. Gross national product is up.

Bunny is happy. Olly is happy. Terry is not happy. There are persistent rumors that Bill's partner, the other inventor, is confined to a mental institution, where he performs miracles of healing but has to be anchored to a bed to keep him from floating away. Yesterday, the day before Christmas, Terry saw a black man levitating up the stairway of the IRT at Fiftieth Street. A week ago he found himself speaking in Japanese, a language he does not know, to a Puerto Rican waiter in a restaurant. For the past several days, Terry has been bleeding slightly from the palms of his hands. This morning, when he left the apartment, his wife asked him, "When will you be home?"

"Verily, I know not," Terry answered.

Now he is up on the parapet of the agency building, looking down at Third Avenue, from which the strains of "Away in a Manger" arise. He knows that in a moment he will spread his arms and step off. Will he fly?

Understanding Human Behavior

A Romance of the Rocky Mountains

* * *

Thomas M. Disch

Thomas M. Disch is one of the rare writers who is comfortable in both the SF field and in mainstream literary fiction and whose work is highly regarded in both worlds. Among his stories for F&SF *are "On Wings of Song" and "The Brave Little Toaster." "Understanding Human Behavior" is about having a second chance at life, a fairly familiar SF idea, but there is nothing old-hat in this fresh and ironic vision, in which Richard Roe, an empty page waiting to be filled, comes to Boulder, Colorado to work, hike, and look for a purpose in life.*

* * *

1

HE would wake up each morning with a consciousness clear as the Boulder sky, a sense of being on the same wave length exactly as the sunlight. Innocence, bland dreams, a healthy appetite—these were glories that issued directly from his having been erased. Of course there were some corresponding disadvantages. His job, monitoring the terminals of a drive-in convenience center, could get pretty dull, especially on days when no one drove in for an hour or so at a stretch, and even at the busiest times it didn't provide much opportunity for human contact. He envied the waitresses in restaurants and the drivers of buses their chance to say hello to real live customers.

Away from work it was different; he didn't feel the same hunger for socializing. That, in fact, was the major disadvantage of having no past life, no established preferences, no identity in the usual sense of a history to attach his name to—he just didn't *want* anything very much.

Not that he was bored or depressed or anything like that. The world was all new to him and full of surprises: the strangeness of anchovies; the beauty of old songs in their blurry Muzak versions at the Stop-and-Shop; the feel of a new shirt or a March day. These sensations were not wholly unfamiliar, nor was his mind a *tabula rasa*. His use of the language and his motor skills were all intact; also what the psychologists at Delphi Institute called generic recognition. But none of the occasions of newness *reminded* him of any earlier experience, some first time or best time or worst time that he'd survived. His only set of memories of a personal and non-generic character were those he'd brought from the halfway house in Delphi, Indiana. But such fine memories they were —so fragile, so distinct, so privileged. If only (he often wished) he could have lived out his life in the sanctuary of Delphi, among men and women like himself, all newly summoned to another life and responsive to the wonders and beauties around them. But, no, for reasons he could not understand, the world insisted on being organized otherwise. An erasee was allowed six months at the Institute, and then he was despatched to wherever he or the computer decided, where he would have to live like everyone else, either alone or in a family (though the Institute advised everyone to be wary at first of establishing primary ties), in a small room or a cramped house or a dormitory ship in some tropical lagoon. Unless you were fairly rich or very lucky, your clothes, furniture, and suchlike appurtenances were liable to be rough, shabby, makeshift. The food most people ate was an incitement to infantile gluttony, a slop of sugars, starches and chemically enhanced flavors. It would have been difficult to live among such people and to seem to share their values except so few of them ever questioned the reasonableness of their arrangements. Those who did, if they had the money, would probably opt, eventually, to have their identities erased, since it was clear, just looking around, that erasees seemed to strike the right intuitive balance between being aware and keeping calm.

He lived now in a condo on the northwest edge of the city, a room and a half with unlimited off-peak power access. The rent was modest (so was his salary), but his equity in the condo was large enough to suggest that his pre-erasure income had been up there in the top percentiles.

He wondered, as all erasees do, why he'd decided to wipe out his past. His life had gone sour, that much was sure, but how and why were questions that could never be answered. The Institute saw to that. A shipwrecked marriage was the commonest reason statistically, closely followed by business reverses. At least that was what people put down on their questionnaires when they applied to the Institute. Somehow he doubted those reasons were the real ones. People who'd never been erased seemed oddly unable to account for their behavior. Even to themselves they would tell the unlikeliest tales about what they were doing and why. Then they'd spend a large part of their social life exposing each other's impostures and laughing at them. A sense of humor they called it. He was glad he didn't have one, yet.

Most of his free time he spent making friends with his body. In his first weeks at the halfway house he'd lazed about, ate too much junk food, and started going rapidly to seed. Erasees are not allowed to leave their new selves an inheritance of obesity or addiction, but often the body one wakes up in is the hasty contrivance of a crash diet. The mouth does not lose its appetites, nor the metabolism its rate, just because the mind has had memories whited out. Fortunately he'd dug in his heels, and by the time he had to bid farewell to Delphi's communal dining room he'd lost the pounds he'd put on and eight more besides.

Since then, fitness had been his religion. He bicycled to work, to Stop-and-Shop, and all about Denver, exploring its uniformities. He hiked and climbed on weekends. He jogged. Once a week, at a Y, he played volleyball for two hours, just as though he'd never left the Institute. He also kept up the other sport he'd had to learn at Delphi, which was karate. Except for the volleyball, he stuck to the more solitary forms of exercise, because on the whole he wasn't interested in forming relationships. The lecturers at the halfway house had said this was perfectly natural and nothing to worry about. He shouldn't socialize until he felt hungry for more society than his job and his living arrangements naturally provided. So far that hunger had not produced a single pang. Maybe he was what the Institute called a natural integer. If so, that seemed an all-right fate.

What he did miss, consciously and sometimes achingly, was a purpose. In common with most fledgling erasees, there was nothing he *believed* in—no religion, no political idea, no ambition to become famous for doing something better than somebody else. Money was about the only purpose he could think of, and even that was not a compelling purpose. He didn't lust after more and more and more of it in the classical Faustian go-getter way.

His room and a half looked out across the tops of a small plantation of spruces to the highway that climbed the long southwestward incline into the Rockies. Each car that hummed along the road was like a vector-quantity of human desire, a quantum of teleological purpose. He might have been mistaken. The people driving those cars might be just as uncertain of their ultimate destinations as he was, but seeing them whiz by in their primary colors, he found that hard to believe. Anyone who was prepared to bear the expense of a car surely had somewhere he wanted to get to or something he wanted to do more intensely than *he* could imagine, up here on his three-foot slab of balcony.

He didn't have a telephone or a TV. He didn't read newspapers or magazines, and the only books he ever looked at were some old textbooks on geology he'd bought at a garage sale in Denver. He didn't go to movies. The ability to suspend disbelief in something that had never happened was one he'd lost when he was erased, assuming he'd ever had it. A lot of the time he couldn't suspend his disbelief in the real people around him, all their pushing and pulling, their weird fears and whopping lies, their endless urges to control other people's behavior, like the vegetarian cashier at the Stop-and-Shop or the manager at the convenience center. The lectures and demonstrations at the halfway house had laid out the basics, but without explaining any of it. Like harried parents the Institute's staff had said, "Do this," and "Don't do that," and he'd not been in a position to argue. He did as he was bid, and his behavior fit as naturally as an old suit.

His name—the name by which he'd christened his new self before erasure—was Richard Roe, and that seemed to fit too.

--------------------------------- **2** ---------------------------------

At the end of September, three months after coming to Boulder, Richard signed up for a course in *Consumership: Theory and Practice* at the Naropa Adult Education Center. There were twelve other students in the class, all with the dewy, slightly vulnerable look of recent erasure. They sat in their folding chairs, reading or just blank, waiting for the teacher, who arrived ten minutes late, out of breath and gasping apologies. Professor Astor. While she was still collecting punch cards and handing out flimsy xeroxes of their reading list, she started lecturing to them. Before she could get his card (he'd chosen a seat in the farthest row back), she was distracted by the need to list on the blackboard the three reasons that people wear clothing, which are:

1. Utility,
2. Communication, and
3. Self-Concept.

Utility was obvious and didn't need going into, while Self-Concept was really a sub-category of Communication, a kind of closed-circuit transmission between oneself and a mirror.

"Now, to illustrate the three basic aspects of Communication, I have some slides." She sat down behind the A/V console at the front of the room and fussed with the buttons anxiously, muttering encouragements to herself. Since the question was there in the air, he wondered what her black dress was supposed to be communicating. It was a wooly, baggy, practical dress sprinkled with dandruff and gathered loosely about the middle by a wide belt of cracked patent leather. The spirit of garage sales hovered about it. "There!" she said.

But the slide that flashed on the screen was a chart illustrating cuts of beef. "Damn," she said, "that's next week. Well, it doesn't matter. I'll write it on the board."

When she stood up and turned around, it seemed clear that one of the utilitarian functions of her dress was to disguise or obfuscate some twenty-plus pounds of excess baggage. A jumble of thin bracelets jingled as she wrote on the board:

1. Desire,
2. Admiration,
3. Solidarity.

"There," she said, laying down the chalk and swinging round to face them, setting the heavy waves of black hair to swaying pendulously, "It's as simple as red, white, and blue. These are the three types of response people try to elicit from others by the clothes they wear. Blue, of course, would represent solidarity. Policemen wear blue. French workingmen have always worn a blinding blue. And then there's the universal uniform of blue denim. It's a cool color and tends to make those who wear it recede into the background. They vanish into the blue, so to speak.

"Then white." She took a blank piece of paper from her desk and held it up as a sample of whiteness. "White is for white-collar workers, the starched white shirt wearable only for a single day being a timeless symbol of conspicuous consumption. I wish the slide projector worked for this: I have a portrait by Hals of a man wearing one of those immense Dutch collars, and you couldn't begin to imagine the work-hours that must have gone into washing and ironing the damned thing. The money. Basically that's what our second category is about. There's a book by Thorstein Veblen on the reading list that explains it all. Admittedly there are qualities other than solvency and success we may be called upon to *admire* in what people wear: good taste, a sense of paradox or wit, even courage, as when one walks through a dangerous neighborhood without the camouflage of denim. But good taste usually boils down to money: the good taste of petroleum-derived polyesters as against—" She smiled and ran her hand across the piled cloth of her dress. "—the *bad* taste of wool. Wit, likewise, is usually the wit of combining contradictory class-recognition signals in the same costume—an evening gown, say, trimmed with Purina patches. You should all be aware, as consumers, that the chief purpose of spending a lot of money on what you wear is to proclaim your allegiance to money *per se*, and to a career devoted to earning it, or, in the case of diamond rings, the promise to keep one's husband activated. Though in this case we begin to impinge on the realm of desire."

To all of which he gave about as much credence as he gave to actors in ads. Like most theories it made the world seem more, not less, complicated. Ho-hum, thought he, as he doodled a crisp doodle of a many-faceted diamond. But then, as she expounded her ideas about Desire, he grew uneasy, then embarrassed, and finally teed-off.

"Red," she said, reading from her deck of three-by-fives, "is the color of desire. Love is always like a red, red rose. It lies a-bleeding like a beautiful steak in a supermarket. To wear red is to declare oneself ready for action, especially if the color is worn below the waist."

There he sat in the back row in his red shorts and red sneakers thinking angry red thoughts. He refused to believe it was a coincidence. He was wearing red shorts because he'd bicycled here, a five-mile ride, not because he wanted to semaphore his instant availability to the world at large. He waited till she'd moved off the subject of Desire, then left the classroom as inconspicuously as possible. In the Bursar's Office he considered the other Wednesday-night possibilities, mostly workshops in posture or poetry or suchlike. Only one—*A Survey of Crime in 20th Century America*—offered any promise of explaining people's behavior. So that was the one he signed up for.

The next day instead of going to work he went out to New Focus and watched hang-gliders. The most amazing of them was a crippled woman who arrived in a canvas sling. Rochelle Rockefeller's exploits had made her so famous that even Richard knew about her, not only on account of her flying but because she was one of the founding mothers of New Focus and had been involved in sizable altercations with the state police. The two women who carried her down from New Focus in the sling busied themselves with straps and buckles and then, at Rochelle's nod, launched her off the side of the cliff. She rose, motor-assisted, on the updraught and waved to her daughter, who sat watching on the edge of the cliff. The girl waved back. Then the girl went off by herself to the picnic table area where two rag dolls awaited her atop one of the tables.

He walked over to the table and asked if she minded if he shared the bench with her.

She shook her head and then in a rather dutiful tone introduced her dolls. The older was Ms. Chillywiggles, the younger was Ms. Sillygiggles. They were married. "And *my* name is Rochelle, the same as my mother. What's yours?"

"Richard Roe."

"Did you bring any *food?*"

"No. Sorry."

"Oh, well, we'll just have to pretend. Here's some tuna fish, and here's some cake." She doled out the imaginary food with perfunctory mime to her dolls, and then with exaggerated delicacy she held up—what was it?—something for him.

"Open your mouth and close your eyes," she insisted.

He did, and felt her fingers on his tongue.

"What was that?" he asked, afterward.

"Holy Communion. Did you like it?"

"Mm."

"Are you a Catholic?"

"No, unless that just made me one."

"*We* are. We believe in God the Father Almighty and *everything.* Ms. Chillywiggles was even in a *convent* before she got married. Weren't you?" Ms. Chillywiggles nodded her large wobbly head.

Finding the subject uncomfortable, he changed it. "Look at your mother up there now. Wow."

Rochelle sighed and for a moment, to be polite, glanced up to where her mother was soaring, hundreds of feet above.

"It's incredible, her flying like that."

"That's what everyone says. But you don't need your leg muscles for a hang-glider, just your arms. And her arms are very strong."

"I'll bet."

"*Some* day we're going to go to Denver and see the dolls' Pope."

"Really. I didn't know dolls had a Pope."

"They do."

"Will you look at her now!"

"I don't like to, it makes me sick. I didn't want to come today, but no one would look after me. They were all *building.* So I had to."

"It doesn't make you want to fly someday, seeing her up there like that?"

"No. Some day she's going to kill herself. She knows it, too. That's how she had her accident, you know. She wasn't always in a wheel-chair."

"Yes, I've heard that."

"What's so awful for *me* is to think she won't ever be able to receive the Last Sacrament."

The sun glowed through the red nylon wings of the glider, but even Professor Astor would have had a hard time making that fit her theory. Desire! Why not just Amazement?

"If she does kill herself," Rochelle continued dispassionately, *"we'll* be sent to an orphanage. In Denver, I hope. And Ms. Chillywiggles will be able to do missionary work among the dolls there. Do you have any dolls?"

He shook his head.

"I suppose you think dolls are only for *girls.* That's a very old prejudice, however. Dolls are for anyone who *likes* them."

"I may have had dolls when I was younger. I don't know."

"Oh. Were you erased?"

He nodded.

"So was my mother. But I was only a baby then. So I don't remember any more about her than she does. What I think is she must have committed some really terrible sin, and it tortured her so much she decided to be erased. Do you ever go in to Denver?"

"Sometimes."

Ms. Sillygiggles whispered something in Ms. Chillywiggles' ear, who evidently did not agree with the suggestion. Rochelle looked cast down. "Damn," she said.

"What's wrong?"

"Oh, nothing. Ms. Sillygiggles was hoping *you'd* be able to take them to Denver to see the dolls' Pope, but Ms. Chillywiggles put her foot down and said Absolutely Not. You're a stranger: we shouldn't even be talking to you."

He nodded, for it seemed quite true. He had no business coming out to New Focus at all.

"I should be going," he said.

Ms. Sillygiggles got to her feet and executed an awkward curtsey. Rochelle said it had been nice to make his acquaintance. Ms. Chillywiggles sat on the wooden step and said nothing.

It seemed to him, as he walked down the stony path to where he'd locked his bicycle to a rack, that everyone in the world was crazy, that craziness was synonymous with the human condition. But then he could see, through a break in the close-ranked spruces, the arc of a glider's flight—not Rochelle Rockefeller's, this one had blue wings—and his spirits soared with the sheer music of it. He understood, in a moment of crystalline levelheadedness, that it didn't make a speck of difference if people were insane. Or if he was, for that matter. Sane and insane were just stages of the great struggle going on everywhere all the time: across the valley, for instance, where the pines were fighting their way up the sides of the facing mountain, hurling the grenades of their cones into the thin soil, pressing their slow advantage, enduring the decimations of the lightning, aspiring (insanely, no doubt) toward the forever unreachable fastness of the summit.

When he got to the road his lungs were heaving, his feet hurt, and his knees were not to be reasoned with (he should not have been running along such a path), but his head was once again solidly fixed on his shoulders. When he called his boss at the Denver Central Office to apologize for absconding, he wasn't fired or even penalized. His boss, who was usually such a tyrannosaurus, said everyone had days when they weren't themselves, and that it was all right, so long as they were few and far between. He even offered some Valiums, which Richard said no-thank-you to.

3

At Naropa the next Wednesday, the lecturer, a black man in a spotless white polyester suit, lectured about Ruth Snyder and Judd Gray, who, in 1927, had killed Ruth's husband Albert in a more than usually stupid fashion. He'd chosen this case, he said, because it represented the lowest common denominator of the crime of passion and would therefore serve to set in perspective the mystery and romance of last week's assassinations, which Richard had missed. First they watched a scene from an old comedy based on the murder, and then the lecturer read aloud a section of the autobiography Judd Gray had written in Sing Sing while waiting to be electrocuted:

> I was a morally sound, sober, God-fearing chap, working
> and saving to make Isabel my wife and establish a home. I met
> plenty of girls—at home and on the road, in trains and hotels.
> I could, I thought, place every type: the nice girl who flirts, the
> nice girl who doesn't, the brazen out-and-out streetwalker I was
> warned against. I was no sensualist, I studied no modern cults,
> thought nothing about inhibitions and repressions. Never read

Rabelais in my life. Average, yes—just one of those Americans Mencken loves to laugh at. Even belonged to a club—the Club of Corset Salesmen of the Empire State—clean-cut competitors meeting and shaking hands—and liking it.

There was something in the tone of Judd Gray's voice, so plain, so accepting, that made Richard feel not exactly a kinship, more a sense of being similarly puzzled and potentially out of control. Maybe it was just the book's title that got to him—*Doomed Ship*. He wondered, not for the first time, whether he might not be among the fifteen percent of erasees whose past has been removed by judicial fiat rather than by choice. He could, almost, imagine himself outside the Snyder bedroom in Queens Village, getting steadily more soused as he waited for Albert to go to sleep so that then he could sneak in there and brain him with the sash weight in his sweaty hand. All for the love of Ruth Snyder, as played by Carol Burnett. He couldn't, however, see himself as a more dignified sort of criminal—a racketeer or an assassin or the leader of a cult—for he lacked the strength of character and the conviction that those roles would have required, and he'd probably lacked it equally in the life that had been erased.

After the class he decided he'd tempt Fate and went to the cafeteria, where Fate immediately succumbed to the temptation and brought Professor Astor of *Consumership: Theory and Practice* to his table with a slice of viscid, bright cherry cheesecake. "May I join you?" she asked him.

"Sure. I was just going anyhow."

"I like your suit," she said. This close she seemed younger, or perhaps it was her dress that made that difference. Instead of last week's black wool bag she was wearing a dull blue double-knit with a scarf sprinkled with blurry off-red roses. One glance and anyone would have felt sorry for her.

His suit was the same dull blue. He'd bought it yesterday at the Stop-and-Shop, where the salesman had tried to convince him not to buy it. With it he wore a wrinkled Wrinkle-Proof shirt and a tie with wide stripes of gray and ocher. "Thanks," he said.

"It's very '70s. You're an erasee, aren't you?"

"Mm."

"I can always tell another. I am too. With a name like Lady Astor

I'd have to be, wouldn't I? I hope I didn't offend you by anything I said last week."

"No, certainly not."

"It wasn't directed at you personally. I just read what it said in my notes, which were taken, all of them, practically verbatim from *The Colors of the Flag.* We teachers are all cheats that way, didn't you know? There's nothing we can tell you that you won't find expressed better in a book. But of course learning, in that sense, isn't the reason for coming here."

"No? What is then?"

"Oh, it's for meeting people. For playing new roles. For taking sides. For crying out loud."

"What?"

"That's an old expression—for crying out loud. From the '40s, I think. Actually your suit is more '40s than '70s. The '40s were *sincere* about being drab; the '70s played games."

"Isn't there anything that's just here and now, without all these built-in meanings?"

She poised her fork over the gleaming cheesecake. "Well," she said thoughtfully, then paused for a first taste of her dessert. "Mnyes, sort of. After you left last week, someone in the class asked if there wasn't a way one could be just anonymous. And what I said—" She took another bite of cheesecake. "—was that to my mind—" She swallowed. "—anonymity would come under the heading of solidarity, and solidarity is always solidarity *with* something—an idea, a group. Even the group of people who don't want to have anything to do with anyone else—even they're a *group.* In fact, they're probably among the largest."

"I'm amazed," he said, counterattacking on sheer irresistible impulse, "that you, a supposed expert on consumerism, can eat junk like the junk you're eating. The sugar makes you fat and gives you cancer, the dye causes cancer too and I don't know what else, and there's something in the milk powder that I just heard about that's lethal. What's the point of being erased if afterwards you lead a life as stupid as everybody else's?"

"Right," she said. She picked up a paper plate from an abandoned tray and with a decisive rap of her fist squashed the wedge of cheesecake flat. "No more! Never again!"

He looked at the goo and crumbs splattered across the table, as well as on her scarf (there was a glob on his tie too, but he didn't notice that), and then at her face, a study in astonishment, as though the cheesecake had exploded autonomously. He started to laugh, and then, as though given permission, she did too.

They stayed on, talking, in the cafeteria until it closed, first about Naropa, then about the weather. This was his first experience of the approach of winter, and he surprised himself at the way he waxed eloquent. He marveled at how the aspens had gone golden all at once, as though every tree on a single mountain were activated by one switch and when that switch was thrown, bingo, it was autumn; the way, day by day, the light dwindled as his half of the world tilted away from the sun; the way the heat had come on in his condo without warning and baked the poor coleus living on top of the radiator; the misery of bicycling in the so much colder rain; and what was most amazing, the calmness of everyone in the face of what looked to him like an unqualified catastrophe. Lady Astor made a few observations of her own, but mostly she just listened, smitten with his innocence. Her own erasure had taken place so long ago—she was evasive as to exactly when—that the world had no such major surprises in store for her. As the chairs were being turned upside down onto the tabletops, he made a vague semi-enthusiastic commitment to hike up to New Focus some mutually convenient Sunday morning, to which end they exchanged addresses and phone numbers. (He had to give his number at work.) Why? It must have been the demolition of that cheesecake, the blissful feeling, so long lost to him, of muscular laughter, as though a window had been opened in a stuffy room and a wind had rushed in, turning the curtains into sails and bringing strange smells from the mountains outside.

In the middle of November the company re-assigned him to the central office in downtown Denver, where he was assistant Traffic Manager for the entire Rocky Mountain division. Nothing in his work at the convenience center had seemed to point in this direction, but as soon as he scanned the programs involved, it was all there in his head and fingers, lingering on like the immutable melody of $1 + 1 = 2$.

The one element of the job that wasn't second nature was the increased human contact, which went on some days nonstop. Hi there,

Dick, what do you think of this and what do you think of that, did you see the game last night, what's your opinion of the crisis, and would you *please* speak to Lloyd about the time he's spending in the john. Lloyd, when spoken to, insisted he worked just as hard in the john as in the office and said he'd cut down his time on the stool as soon as they allowed him to smoke at his desk. This seemed reasonable to Richard but not to the manager, who started to scream at him, calling him a zombie and a zeroid, and said he was fired. Instead, to nobody's great surprise, it was the manager who got the axe. So, after just two weeks of grooming, Richard was the new Traffic Manager with an office all his own with its own view of other gigantic office buildings and a staff of thirty-two, if you counted temps and part-timers.

To celebrate he went out and had the famous hundred-dollar dinner at the Old Millionaire Steak Ranch with Lloyd, now the assistant Traffic Manager, with not his own office but at least a steel partition on one side of his desk and the right, thereby, to carcinogenate his lungs from punch-in to punch-out. Lloyd, it turned out, after a second Old Millionaire martini, lived up at New Focus and was one of the original members of the Boulder branch of the cult.

"No kidding," said Richard, reverently slicing into his sirloin. "So why are you working down here in the city? You can't commute to New Focus. Not this time of year."

"Money, why else. Half my salary, maybe more now, goes into the Corporation. We can't live for free, and there sure as hell isn't any money to be earned building a damned pyramid."

"So why do you build pyramids?"

"Come on, Dick. You know I can't answer that."

"I don't mean you as a group. I mean you personally. You must have *some* kind of reason for what you're doing."

Lloyd sighed long-sufferingly. "Listen, you've been up there, you've seen us cutting the blocks and fitting them in place. What's to explain? The beauty of the thing is that no one asks anyone else *why* we're doing what we're doing. Ever. That's Rule Number One. Remember that if you ever think of joining."

"Okay, then tell me this—why would I *want* to join?"

"Dick, you're hopeless. What did I just *say* to you? Enjoy your steak, why don't you? Do I ask why you want to throw away two hundred dollars on a dinner that can last, at the longest, a couple hours? No, I just enjoy it. It's beautiful."

"Mmn, I'm enjoying it. But still I can't keep from wondering."

"Wonder all you like—just don't ask."

4

With the increased social inputs at work he had gradually tapered off on his visits to Naropa. Winter sealed him into a more circumscribed routine of apartment, job, and gym, as mounds of snow covered the known surfaces of Boulder like a divine amnesia. On weekends he would sit like a bear in a cave, knitting tubes of various dimensions and looking out the window and not quite listening to the purr of KMMN playing olden goldens in flattened-out, long-breathed renditions that corresponded in a semi-conscious way to the forms of the snow as it drifted and stormed and lifted up past the window in endless unraveling banners.

He had not forgotten his promise to Lady Astor, but a trip to New Focus was no longer feasible. Even with skis and a lift assisting, it would have been an overnight undertaking. He phoned twice and explained this to her answering machine. In reply she left a message—"That's okay."—at the convenience center, which got forwarded to the central office a week later. His first impression, that Destiny had introduced them with some purpose in mind, was beginning to diminish when one Saturday morning on the bus going to the gym he saw a street sign he'd never noticed before, Follet Avenue, and remembered that that was the street she lived on. He yanked the cord, got off, and walked back over unshoveled sidewalks to the corner of 34th and Follet, already regretting his impulse: 15 blocks to go, and then he might not find her home. It was 8 degrees below.

In the course of those 15 blocks the neighborhood dwindled from dowdy to stark. She lived in a two-story clapboard shopfront that looked like an illustration of the year daubed in black paint over the entrance: 1972. The shopwindows were covered with plywood, the plywood painted by some schizophrenic kindergarten with nightmarish murals, and the faded murals peered out forlornly from a lattice of obscene graffiti, desolation overlaying desolation.

He rang her bell and, when that produced no result, he knocked.

She came to the door wrapped in a blanket, hair in a tangle, bleary and haggard.

"Oh, it's you. I thought it might be you." Then, before he could apologize or offer to leave: "Well, you might as well come in. Leave your overshoes in the hall."

She had the downstairs half of the building, behind the boarded-up windows, which were sealed, on this side, with strips of carpet padding. A coal stove on a brick platform gave off a parsimonious warmth. With a creaking of springs Lady Astor returned to bed. "You can sit there," she said, gesturing to a chair covered with clothes. When he did, its prolapsed bottom sank under him like the seat of a rowboat. At once a scrawny tabby darted from one of the shadowy corners of the room (the only light came from a small unboarded window at the back) and sprang into his lap. It nuzzled his hand, demanding a caress.

While he stumbled through the necessary explanations (how he happened to be passing, why he hadn't visited before), she sipped vodka from a coffee cup. He assumed it was vodka, since a vodka bottle, half-empty and uncapped, stood on the cash register that served as a bedside table. Most of the shop-fittings had been left *in situ*: a glass counter, full of dishes and cookware; shelves bearing a jumble of shoes, books, ceramic pots, and antique, probably defunct electric appliances. A bas-relief Santa of molded plastic was affixed to the wall behind the bed, its relevance belied by layers of greasy dust. The room's cluttered oddity combated its aura of poverty and demoralization, but not enough: he felt stricken. This was another First in the category of emotions, and he didn't know what to call it. Not simply dismay; not guilt; not pity; not indignation (though how could anyone be drunk at ten o'clock on a Saturday morning!); not even awe for the spirit that could endure such dismalness and still appear at Naropa every Wednesday evening, looking more or less normative, to lecture on the theory and practice of (of all things) Consumership. All these elements and maybe others were fuddled together in what he felt.

"Do you want a drink?" she asked, and before he could answer: "Don't think it's polite to say yes. There's not much left. I started at six o'clock, but you have to understand I don't *usually* do this. But today seemed special. I thought, why not? Anyhow why am I making excuses. I didn't invite you, you appeared at the door. I knew you would, eventually." She smiled, not pleasantly, and poured half the remaining vodka into her coffee cup. "You like this place?"

"It's big," he said lamely.

"And dark. And gloomy. And a mess. I was going to get the windows put back in, when I took the lease last summer. But that costs. And for winter this is warmer. Anyhow if I did try to make it a shop I don't know what I'd sell. Junk. I *used* to throw pots. What *didn't* I used to do. I did a book of poetry based on the Tarot (which is how I latched onto the job at Naropa). I framed pictures. And now I lecture, which is to say I read books and talk about them to people like you too lazy to read books on their own. And once, long ago, I was even a housewife, would you believe that." This time her smile was positively lethal. There seemed to be some secret message behind what she was saying that he couldn't uncode.

He sneezed.

"Are you allergic to cats?"

He shook his head. "Not that I know of."

"I'll bet you are."

He looked at her with puzzlement, then at the cat curled in his lap. The cat's warmth had penetrated through the denim and warmed his crotch pleasantly.

"God damn it," she said, wiping a purely hypothetical tear from the corner of her bleary eye. "Why'd you have to pick this morning? Why couldn't you have phoned? You were always like that. You schmuck."

"What?"

"Schmuck," she repeated. And then, when he just went on staring: "Well, it makes no difference. I would have had to tell you eventually. I just wanted you to get to know me a little better first."

"Told me what?"

"I was never erased. I just lied about that. It's all there on the shelf, everything that happened, the betrayals, the dirt, the failures. And there were lots of those. I just never had the guts to go through with it. Same with the dentist. That's why I've got such lousy teeth. I *meant* to. I had the money—at least for a while, after the divorce, but I thought. . . ." She shrugged, took a swallow from the cup, grimaced, and smiled, this time almost friendly.

"What did your husband do?"

"Why do you ask that?"

"Well, you seem to want to tell the whole story. I guess I wanted to sound interested."

She shook her head. "You still don't have a glimmering, do you?"

"Of what?" He did have a glimmering, but he refused to believe it.

"Well then, since you just insist, I'll have to tell you, won't I? *You* were the husband you're asking about. And you haven't changed one damned bit. You're the same stupid schmuck you were then."

"I don't believe you."

"That's natural. After spending so much to become innocent, who would want to see their investment wiped out like . . ." She tried to snap her fingers. ". . . that."

"There's no way you could have found me here. The Institute never releases that information. Not even to their employees."

"Oh, computers are clever these days (*you* know that), and for a couple thousand dollars it's not hard to persuade a salaried employee to tickle some data out of a locked file. When I found out where you'd gone, I packed my bags and followed you. I *told* you before you were erased that I'd track you down, and what you said was, 'Try, just try.' So that's what I did."

"You can be sent to prison for what you've done. Do you know that?"

"You'd like that, wouldn't you? If you could have had me locked up before, you wouldn't have had to get erased. You wouldn't have damned near killed me."

She said it with such conviction, with such a weariness modifying the anger, that it was hard to hold on to his reasonable doubt. He remembered how he'd identified with Judd Gray, the murderer of Albert Snyder.

"Don't you want to know *why* you tried to kill me?" she insisted.

"Whatever you used to be, Ms. Astor, you're not my wife now. You're a washed-up, forty-year-old drunk teaching an adult education course in the middle of nowhere."

"Yeah. Well, I could tell you how I got that way. Schmuck."

He stood up. "I'm leaving."

"Yes, you've said that before."

Two blocks from her house he remembered his overshoes. To hell with his overshoes! To hell with people who don't shovel their sidewalks! Most of all to hell with her!

That woman, his wife! What sort of life could they have lived together? All the questions about his past that he'd subdued so successfully up till now came bubbling to the surface: who he'd been, what he'd done, how it had all gone wrong. And she had the answers. The temptation to go back was strong, but before he could yield to it, the bus came in the homeward direction and he got on, his mind unchanged, his anger burning brightly.

5

Even so it was a week before he'd mustered the righteous indignation to call the Delphi Institute and register a formal complaint. They took down the information and said they'd investigate, which he assumed was a euphemism for their ignoring it. But in fact a week later he got a registered letter from them stating that Ms. Lady Astor of 1972 Follet Avenue in Boulder, Colorado, had never been his wife, nor had there ever been any other connection between them. Further, three other clients of the Institute had registered similar complaints about the same Ms. Astor. Unfortunately there was no law against providing erasees with misinformation about their past lives, and it was to be regretted that there were individuals who took pleasure in disturbing the equanimity of the Institute's clients. The letter pointed out that he'd been warned of such possibilities while he was at the halfway house.

Now in addition to feeling angry and off-balance he felt like an asshole as well. To have been so easily diddled! To have believed the whole unlikely tale without even the evidence of a snapshot!

Three days before Christmas she called him at work. "I didn't want to bother you," she said in a meek little whisper that seemed, even now, knowing everything, utterly sincere, "but I had to apologize. You did pick a hell of a time to come calling. If I hadn't been drunk I would never have spilled the beans."

"Uh-huh," was all he could think to say.

"I know it was wrong of me to track you down and all, but I

couldn't help myself." A pause, and then her most amazing lie of all: "I just love you too much to let you go."

"Uh-huh."

"I don't suppose we could get together? For coffee, after work?"

When they got together for coffee, after work, he led her on from lie to lie until she'd fabricated a complete life for him, a romance as preposterous as any soap on TV, beginning with a tyrannical father, a doting mother, a twin brother killed in a car crash, and progressing through his years of struggle to become a painter. (Here she produced a brittle polaroid of one of his putative canvases, a muddy jumble of ochres and umbers. She assured him that the polaroid didn't do it justice.) The tale went on to tell how they'd met, and fallen in love, how he'd sacrificed his career as an artist to become an animation programmer. They'd been happy, and then—due to his monstrous jealousy—unhappy. There was more, but she didn't want to go into it, it was too painful. Their son. . . .

Through it all he sat there nodding his head, seeming to believe each further fraud, asking appropriate questions, and (another First) enjoying it hugely—enjoying *his* fraudulence and her greater gullibility. Enjoying, too, the story she told him about his imaginary life. He'd never imagined a past for himself, but if he had he doubted if he'd have come up with anything so large, so resonant.

"So tell me," he asked, when her invention finally failed her, "why did I decide to be erased?"

"John," she said shaking flakes of dandruff from her long black hair, "I wish I could answer that question. Partly it must have been the pain of little Jimmy's death. Beyond that, I don't know."

"And now? . . ."

She looked up, glittery. "Yes?"

"What is it you want?"

She gave a sigh as real as life. "I hoped . . . oh, you know."

"You want to get married again?"

"Well, no. Not till you've got to know me better anyhow. I mean I realize that from *your* point of view I'm still pretty much a stranger. And you've changed too, in some ways. You're like you were when I first met you. You're—" Her voice choked up, and tears came to her eyes.

He touched the clasp of his briefcase, but he didn't have the heart to take out the xerox of the letter from the Delphi Institute that he'd been intending to spring on her. Instead he took the bill from under the saucer and excused himself.

"You'll call me, won't you?" she asked woefully.

"Sure, sure. Let me think about it a while first. Okay?"

She mustered a brave, quavering smile. "Okay."

In April to mark the conclusion of the first year of his new life and just to glory in the weather that made such undertakings possible again, he took the lift up Mount Lifton, then hiked through Corporation Canyon past New Focus and the site of the pyramid—only eight feet at its highest edge so far, scarcely a tourist attraction—and on up the Five Waterfall Trail. Except for a few boot-challenging stretches of vernal bogginess the path was stony and steep. The sun shone, winds blew, and the last sheltered ribs of snow turned to water and sought, trickle by trickle, the paths of least resistance. By one o'clock he'd reached his goal, Lake Silence, a perfect little mortuary chapel of a tarn colonnaded all round with spruces. He found an unshadowed, accommodating rock to bask on, took off his wet boots and damp socks, and listened as the wind did imitations of cars on a highway. Then, chagrined, he realized it wasn't the wind but the shuddering roar of an approaching helicopter.

The helicopter emerged like a demiurge from behind the writhing tops of the spruces, hovered a moment above the tarn, then veered in the direction of his chosen rock. As it passed directly overhead a stream of water spiraled out of the briefly opened hatch, dissolving almost at once in the machine's rotary winds into a mist of rainbow speckles. His first thought was that he was being bombed, his next that the helicopter was using Lake Silence as a toilet. Only when the first tiny trout landed, splat, on the rock beside him did he realize that the helicopter must have been from the Forest Service and was seeding the lake with fish. Alas, it had missed its mark, and the baby trout had fallen on the rocks of the shore and into the branches of the surrounding trees. The waters of Lake Silence remained unrippled and inviolate.

He searched among those fallen along the shore—there were dozens—for survivors, but all that he could find proved inert and lifeless when he put them in the water. Barefoot, panicky, totally devoted to the trout of Lake Silence, he continued the search. At last among the matted damp needles beneath the spruces he found three fish still alive and wiggling. As he lowered them, lovingly, into the lake he realized in a single lucid flash what it was he had to do with his life.

He would marry Lady Astor.

He would join new Focus and help them build a pyramid.

And he would buy a car.

(Also, in the event that she became orphaned, he would adopt little Rochelle Rockefeller. But that was counting chickens.)

He went to the other side of Lake Silence, to the head of the trail, where the Forest Service had provided an emergency telephone link disguised as a commemorative plaque to Governor Dent. He inserted his credit card into the slot, the plaque opened, and he punched Lady Astor's number. She answered at the third ring.

"Hi," he said. "This is Richard Roe. Would you like to marry me?"

"Well, yes, I guess so. But I ought to tell you—I was never really your wife. That was a story I made up."

"I knew that. But it was a nice story. And I didn't have one that I could tell you. One more thing, though. We'll have to join New Focus and help them build their pyramid."

"Why?"

"You can't ask why. That's one of their rules. Didn't you know that?"

"Would we have to live up there?"

"Not year-round. It'd be more like having a summer place, or going to church on Sunday. Plus some work on the pyramid."

"Well, I suppose I could use the exercise. Why do you want to get married? Or is that another question I shouldn't ask?"

"Oh, probably. One more thing: what's your favorite color?"

"For what?"

"A car."

"A car! Oh, I'd *love* a car! Be a show-off—get a red one. When do you want to do it?"

"I'll have to get a loan from the bank first. Maybe next week?"

"No, I meant getting married."

"We could do that over the phone. Or up here, if you want to take the lift to New Focus. Do you want to meet me there in a couple hours?"

"Make it three. I need a shampoo, and the bus isn't really reliable."

And so they were married, at sunset, on the stump of the unfinished pyramid, and the next week he bought a brand new Alizarin Crimson Ford Fundamental. As they drove out of the dealer's lot, he felt, for the first time in his life, that this was what it must be like to be completely human.

A Rarebit
of Magic

✳   ✳   ✳

John Morressy

F&SF has published many series stories; one of the most popular in recent years has been John Morressy's delightful run of stories about Kedrigern the wizard, master of the counterspell. In this tale, Kedrigern's lovely princess, whose voice has long flown, regains her sweet speech through a toenail ingrown . . .

✳   ✳   ✳

THE sun was warm, but not too warm for comfort; bright, but not dazzling to Kedrigern's overworked and slightly nearsighted eyes. Birds sang, but not too loudly, and every note rang clear. The mild breeze was freighted with rich fragrance. It was a perfect spring day.

Kedrigern made his unhurried way along the forest path, humming a little wordless tune which he made up as he walked to where his horse awaited. He was in excellent spirits, and at peace with the world. In plain fact, this spring day had filled him with the ebullient, unfocused glee of a small boy on holiday, and he was in a mood to do handsprings and cut capers right here on this green-roofed pathway. Only the pouch at his side, filled with freshly gathered herbs of great virtue, prevented him. The herbs were much too delicate to withstand gymnastics.

On an impulse, he laid the pouch gently at the base of a tree. He sprang into the air, tapping his heels together. Selecting a level open patch of green beside the path, he did a headstand. At last, laughing for pure joy, he tumbled onto his back and lay looking up at the sunny sky through the tapestry of new leaves.

And then, faint in the distance, he heard a moan.

At once he was on his feet, busily brushing himself off. His expression became somber. It would not do for ordinary citizens to see a respected senior wizard bounding about the woods like a silly lamb. Taking up his pouch of herbs and simples, he proceeded in the direction of the mournful sound, guided by frequent repetitions which became louder and more distinct as he drew near. His pace was stately, but rapid, and before long he came upon a huddled figure by the wayside.

It was a young man, dressed in once-gaudy finery which was now stained and worn from travel. He sat with his back to a flat rock, his bare feet stuck straight out before him. His hands were limp and forlorn in his lap, his head slumped forward in a posture of utter desolation. Looking about, Kedrigern saw a single boot lying a good way down the road, as if it had been flung there. Something unusual was going on here, he thought, and resolved to find out what it might be.

He cleared his throat, and in his most disarming voice said, "Good morrow, traveler. Is all well with you?"

At the first sound, the young man jerked up his head. He brushed back his tangled black hair and gazed up at Kedrigern with large, sad brown eyes. "Look you, sir, how I am crippled entirely with the curse of ingrown toenails, and it not ten days since Black Ivor Gruffydd placed it on me," said he in a deep voice speaking in a lilting manner that fell halfway between oratory and incantation.

"Ingrown toenails can be very painful. Particularly if one is required to do much walking," Kedrigern said sympathetically.

"True enough, that is. And a *cerddor* must do much walking, and that is to say nothing of taking care of his harp, and the keeping his head filled with sweet sound, or he will be forced to sleep in the woods and feed on nuts and berries," the young man lamented.

"Ah . . . you're a minstrel, then."

"I am a minstrel now. But despite my youth, I was near to being *bardd teulu*, household bard to a great lord, and would now hold such a position of dignity, mind you, except for the dirty underhanded scheming of the Gruffydds to snatch away what was justly mine and give it to whining whey-faced Red Gruffydd."

"I've heard that it's a highly competitive business," said Kedrigern, "but didn't you say your enemy was Black Ivor? How does Red Gruffydd fit into this?"

"There is sharp you are, mister," said the young minstrel appreciatively. "It was Black Ivor Gruffydd put the curse on me, indeed, and him known as Black Ivor not for the color of hair or eyes or skin but for the black of his nature. I have not seen him, nor he me, since I left my home these two years gone. But I saw him at the fair ten days ago, where he was peddling his lechery and bawdry, and I said for all to hear what kind of nastiness is in him. And it is then he put the curse of ingrown toenails on me."

"What do you plan to do?"

The young man's eyes flashed, black as buttons. "I will soak my feet in a pail of the Gruffydd's blood, that is what I will do, as soon as I can walk without the pains of hell to cripple me."

"That's a bit drastic, isn't it? Surely it won't do anything for your toenails."

"There is peace of mind it will give me, mister," the minstrel said grimly.

Kedrigern nodded, acknowledging the desirability of peace of mind. He settled down at the minstrel's side. For a time, neither of them spoke, then Kedrigern, looking off into the trees, said casually, "The local lord is a man we all call Breborn the Just. He got his name from his practice of tracking down and executing everyone suspected of crime in his domain. As a rule he hangs murderers, but every now and then he impales one. Just for a change."

"I would be away from here like smoke, look you. No man would find me."

"When you can hardly walk? Give it up, my boy. Revenge is silly. Very entertaining on the stage, but totally unworkable in day-to-day affairs," Kedrigern said with a wise, avuncular smile.

"There is a great fool I am, and have always been," said the minstrel with a deep sigh. "When we were lads, studying at the feet of the great *pen ceirdd* Twm ap Tudur, the Gruffydds learned all the spells for rapid advancement and discomfort to enemies, and far it is that their wicked knowledge has brought them."

"What did you learn?"

"Every spell for eloquence and sweetness of speech in the Green Book of Maelgwyn I have by heart. I can make the stones of the ground to sing, look you, and the croaking toad to converse with the voice of an angel. And I would trade it all for a charm to cure my ingrown toenails."

Kedrigern turned a broad, beaming smile on the woebegone minstrel and clapped him solidly on the shoulder. "It's a deal, my boy," he said.

"There is cruel you are to mock me, mister," said the youth.

"I'm not mocking you. I can get you back on your feet in no time. In exchange, I want you to use your spells for eloquence. I'm a wizard. Semi-retired at the moment, but I do private work in counterspells. The name's Kedrigern," said the wizard, extending a hand.

"And I am Rhys ap Gwallter," said the minstrel, accepting the offered welcome. "Though it is small need you have of my spells, mister, to hear the talking of you."

"It's more for a friend. You'll understand when we get to my house. We should arrive just in time for lunch," Kedrigern said, rising and brushing the leaves from his seat.

"I will be slow in the walking, look you. More like it will be breakfast time two days hence," Rhys warned.

"No need to walk at all. I'll summon my horse."

Rhys looked up, wide-eyed. "A great excitement it will be to me to see how a true wizard summons his horse."

Kedrigern frowned, puzzled. "Why? All I do is whistle."

"Oh," said the minstrel, crestfallen.

Kedrigern thrust two fingers in his mouth and gave a sharp, long whistle. In a very short time, the sound of measured hoofbeats echoed up the forest path, and soon a shaggy black horse came into sight.

"That is a horse I would expect to see a great barbarian warrior riding, and not a kindly wizard," said Rhys, hauling himself to his feet.

"It belonged to a barbarian warrior once," Kedrigern said, recalling his encounter with Buroc the Depraved. "He got all stiffened up. Doesn't ride any more."

With a bit of assistance from Kedrigern, Rhys ap Gwallter mounted the black horse. Kedrigern handed up the minstrel's harp and skimpy pack, and his own pouch of herbs, and they started off for the wizard's home, where Princess awaited.

As they emerged from the forest, and Silent Thunder Mountain loomed before them, far across the rolling grasslands, Rhys uncovered his small harp and began to play a sweet, sad melody. It was a very fine performance, but not at all suited to Kedrigern's mood, which was improving with every homeward step. He requested something merry, and the minstrel obliged.

Kedrigern was certain that he had at last found the solution to Princess' problem. The power of the charms over speech and eloquence known to the Cymric bards was the envy of wizard's everywhere. More than once, Kedrigern had given serious consideration to obtaining bardic help for his wife, but every time he had been discouraged by the bards' notorious reluctance to share their magic with outsiders. And now the magic of the Cymri was his for the asking, in exchange for a small, simple healing spell. It seemed to Kedrigern to be a sign that the universe was in good hands after all. He smiled placidly and began to hum along with the harp.

They arrived at the cottage just at midday. As Kedrigern was helping Rhys down from the horse, he felt the minstrel stiffen.

"What is that, now?" Rhys cried, alarmed.

A grotesque little creature, about knee-high, consisting almost entirely of a large ugly head, big hands and feet, and ears like wide-flung shutters, was bouncing up and down on the flagstones of the dooryard, salivating liberally. It cried "Yah! Yah!" joyously, in a piercing voice.

"Tell Princess I'm back, Spot," Kedrigern called, waving a greeting. As the little apparition bounded into the house, he said to the minstrel, "That's our house-troll. A good hard worker, and absolutely devoted to us."

"That is a thing I have never seen before," Rhys said guardedly.

"No, I suppose not. Well, you have to get them young, or it's no use at all, and it's not easy to find a troll with any kind of decent family background." At this point Spot reappeared, and Kedrigern ordered the troll to bring a basin of warm salt water. "You can sit here in the sun and give your feet a nice restful soak until lunch is ready. After lunch we'll get down to business," he explained.

Princess appeared in the doorway. She wore a pale green robe, trimmed with white. Her ebony hair hung loose to her waist. A slim golden circlet bound her brows. Rhys ap Gwallter looked on, bedazzled by her beauty, as Kedrigern kissed her warmly, then took her hand and conducted her to their guest. She curtseyed deeply to his bow, then she smiled a smile that made the spring morning seem dull and cheerless by comparison. Without having spoken, she withdrew.

"There is a fine-looking woman your wife is, Master Kedrigern," said Rhys reverently. "I have seen queens and princesses and fine ladies, but next to her, look you, they are all as ugly as toads."

"Funny you should put it that way," Kedrigern said. "Would you believe, Rhys, that only—"

The arrival of Spot, bearing a great wooden tub of steaming water, interrupted Kedrigern's response. The troll set it down in front of a chair, and Rhys, at Kedrigern's bidding, immersed his pained feet in the tub with a great sigh of relief.

"Nothing like a good long soak when your feet hurt," Kedrigern said. "Make yourself comfortable. Lunch will be ready shortly. As I started to say," he went on, pulling up a chair for himself, "you'd hardly believe that only a few years ago, that beautiful woman was hopping about in a bog."

"In a bog, now? There is strange in that."

"Not so strange, actually. She was a toad at the time."

"A toad?"

"Yes. A fine-looking toad she was, too. I knew there was something special about that toad the minute I laid eyes on it."

"Why would such a woman want to be a toad, indeed?" Rhys asked.

"Oh, it wasn't her idea. Her parents had neglected to invite the local bog-fairy to her christening—the invitation went to some silly nixie by mistake—so the bog-fairy put a curse on the child. Princess turned into a toad on her eighteenth birthday. Didn't even get to open her presents. Bog-fairies can be very mean-minded when they think they've been insulted. Touchy lot."

"And you it was who changed her back into the lovely lady, then, with the magic of you?"

"Yes. As I mentioned earlier, I specialize in remedial magic. Counterspells and such, Undoing other people's nasty magic. Been remarkably successful at it, too, as you can see. There's only one small—"

Princess emerged from the doorway bearing a silver tray on which rested a chunk of deep golden cheese, a round of dark bread, and a square of pale yellow butter. Behind her bounded Spot, with a frost-coated pitcher in one hand and three stone mugs clutched in the other.

Kedrigern, rising and bidding Rhys remain seated, pulled up a chair for Princess, kissed her cheek, and took the tray.

"Brereep," she said, smiling gloriously.

Rhys gave a little start. Water sloshed from the tub, darkening the flagstones.

"I was just telling Rhys about our first meeting, my dear, and how I used my arts to restore you to your proper—and most exquisite— form. Rhys is having a bit of a problem himself, with a curse some- one has placed on him," Kedrigern said as he helped Princess to her seat.

"Brereep?" she asked.

"Exactly, my dear. And in return, Rhys will place at our service his knowledge of the Cymric spells for eloquence and sweetness of speech, which he has learned from the Green Book of Maelgwyn. I believe we've found the solution to your troubles at last, my dear," Kedrigern said, patting her hand tenderly.

"Brereep? Brereep!" she exclaimed happily.

"Look you now, this is a bit more complicated than I thought it might be," Rhys said apprehensively.

"Surely the power of the Green Book of Maelgwyn can deal with a little croak," Kedrigern said, pouring foaming ale into the first mug.

"A great difference there is, Master Kedrigern, between taking a tongue-tied *creddor* and instilling in him sweetness of discourse, and taking a lady who croaks like a toad—a very fine and melodious croak it is, lady, I do assure you—" he quickly added, "and putting words to her tongue. Oh, a very great difference, indeed."

"We have every confidence in you, Rhys, and in the Green Book of Maelgwyn," Kedrigern said, pouring into the second mug. "And if our confidence is misplaced, you will find your toenails growing out of the top of your head."

"Brereep," Princess said softly. She shook her head and placed her hand on Kedrigern's forearm.

Kedrigern's sighed, nodded, and said contritely, "Yes, of course, my dear. You're absolutely right. That was in bad form." Handing Rhys ap Gwallter the foam-capped mug, he said, "There will be no reprisals, my boy. You must do your best for Princess, and in return, I will free you of Black Ivor's curse. Agreed?"

"Agreed," the minstrel said eagerly, looking much relieved.

They partook of a leisurely and satisfying lunch. When they had finished, and Spot had removed the dishes and empty mugs, and Rhys had dried his feet and donned a pair of soft slippers provided by his host, Rhys readied himself for the curing of Princess. He took up his small harp, struck a few notes, tightened two of the strings, played the notes once more, and then cleared his throat.

"For my first charm, I will attempt Ceiriog's spell of unlocking," he announced with a pleasant smile. "It is much favored for stirring speech in those who appear reluctant or incapable."

"That sounds as though it might fit," said Kedrigern.

"Brereep," Princess agreed.

"Do you want me to leave? I'd really like to stay and watch, but if I'm going to make you nervous, . . ." Kedrigern said, half-rising.

"I am accustomed to an audience, Master Kedrigern. Stay," said the minstrel.

The wizard smiled gratefully and resumed his seat. Rhys struck a chord, then began to play a simple melody, like a child's song, to which he sang lyrics of great subtlety and very sophisticated poetic technique. When he was done, he put down his harp and he and Kedrigern turned to Princess.

"How is it with you, lady?" Rhys asked cautiously.

Princess took a deep breath, swallowed, let out the breath, blinked twice, drew a more normal breath, and slowly said, "I can talk."

"That's marvelous, my dear! Well done, Rhys!" Kedrigern cried.

"Oh! Oh! I can talk!" Princess repeated, rising from her chair.

"On the first try! Oh, this is wonderful, my dear!"

"Do you hear me talk?"

"Yes. It's lovely," Kedrigern said warmly.

"Look! Look!" she shouted, and the two men twisted their necks in sudden alarm. But they saw only the little troll, who reappeared and was now running about, picking up scraps and tidying the front yard.

"See Spot run!" she cried. "Run, Spot, run!"

"Yes, my dear," said Kedrigern, dubiously.

She turned to him, and the look in her eyes was enough to wring his heart. "I can talk. Do you hear me talk? I talk *dumb!*"

"Considering that it's only a starting point, . . ." Kedrigern began, looking to Rhys for encouragement.

"Look you, Ceiriog's spell is a great thing for the children, but I am thinking that maybe it is not such a good thing for a grownup," Rhys said, with an uneasy glance at Princess.

"I talk like a baby. I am a lady. I want to talk like a lady. I do not want to sound like a baby all my life," said Princess. Kedrigern noticed that she was getting a bit red in the face.

"I will try something else," said Rhys.

"Oh! Oh! I hope it works. If it doesn't—"

"Now, my dear," Kedrigern said, reaching out to pat her hand. "We mustn't upset the young man. He's doing his best."

She seated herself demurely, folding her hands in her lap. "I will be good," she said.

Rhys took up his harp once again. This time, the melody he played was so intricate, and so lively, that it filled Kedrigern and Princess with wonder to see it played by only two hands and ten fingers. The chant that he sang to this whirlwind of music was dark and harsh, and impossible to follow. Kedrigern recognized all the signs of a powerful charm, and kept a close eye on Princess. She seemed fascinated by the web of words and sounds, but quite alert.

At last Rhys laid his harp down, and wiped his brow, damp from the strain of concentration. In the silence, Princess spoke. Her words came slowly, as if she were choosing each syllable and placing it as carefully as an artisan might place the stones of a mosaic.

Mute, tame, Oh! long my tongue lay;
Maelgwyn's words made go away
Toad's gruff croak. T'was good coming
Brought Rhys, best bard, to sing.

Rhys ap Gwallter looked at Princess with awe, and joy, and an expression that rapidly came to resemble that of a man who has scuffed his foot in the pebbles of a pathway and come upon a tub of precious gems. He turned expectantly to Kedrigern, who was gazing vacantly at his wife.

"Look you now, there is poetry for you!" Rhys cried proudly. "That is the true *cywydd*, embellished with the beauties of *cynghanedd*. Oh, that is fine, indeed."

"Is she always going to talk that way?" Kedrigern asked without taking his eyes off Princess.

"She will improve with practice. There was a bit of weakness in the second line, where the rhyme should properly have come on an unstressed syllable, and I did not count more than three consonants recurring in any line. But it is very tidy for a first effort. In a few years the lady will be a great bard," Rhys said confidently.

"A few years? . . . Will I ever know what she's talking about?" Kedrigern murmured, dazed.

Great bard? I grant better days
May follow—but must always
I be rhyming? Right cramping
T'would be; word bound. Better sing
Small songs, some lesser in grace,
Quite modest, neat, commonplace;
Speak as plain lass, prosily—
So my dear deciphers me, said the Princess.

Kedrigern scratched his head, working on her utterance. The last line had sounded very good, but he was not sure about what went before. Poetry was not his forte.

"That was a proper first line," Rhys said respectfully. "Five consonants I counted, repeated in order. You do not often find that in a beginner, lady. Are you certain you do not wish to speak forever in *cywydd*, adorning your verses with *cynghanedd*?"

Princess smiled to acknowledge the compliment, but she shook her head decisively. After a pause, she said,

Plain discourse will please me best;
Simple speech is the sweetest.

Kedrigern sighed with relief. Rhys ap Gwallter shook his head slowly, sadly, as if at a great act of ingratitude, but took up his harp once more.

"For my third charm, I will recite something that has long been a favorite of mine. It is a simple rhyming spell that is attributed to Hywel Morgan," said the minstrel.

"Don't you know anything that doesn't involve rhyming?" Kedrigern asked plaintively.

"I have tried a spell without rhyme to it, and it was a disaster, with this lovely lady speaking like a three-year-old, and not a very clever one, look you."

"Just asking. Go right ahead with Hywel Morgan's spell."

Rhys began again, and this time his music was merry and bright, a tune to dance to. His small audience could not refrain from tapping their feet in time with the harp. The words were quick and clever, and several times Princess and Kedrigern glanced at one another and shared a smile. Rhys ended on an abrupt chord and looked at Princess with an expectant grin.

"Speak to us now, lady!" he cried.

"Your magic has worked like a charm! It has done me all good, and no harm."

"I have done it this time," Rhys said proudly.

"But she still speaks in rhyme," Kedrigern pointed out.

"Stop complaining, and give me your arm!" Princess said.

Kedrigern did as she bade him. Princess pulled him to his feet, and with her arm in his, they danced around the beaming young minstrel. At last, flushed and breathless, they fell into their chairs, laughing for sheer joy. Princess leaned forward and laid her hand on Rhys's. Giggling a bit, brushing back a long strand of hair, she said, "Young man, you're an absolute winner! I insist on your staying to dinner. I'll give orders to Spot, to get everything hot—"

"You speak well, my dear, for a beginner," Kedrigern observed.

"Look you now," Rhys asked, "Could you fix my feet? There is pain."

"Do it promptly, my sweet," Princess said. "I'm sure you know how."

Kedrigern rose, saying, "I'll see to it now."

"There is plenty of time till we eat," Princess assured them.

She left them, and Kedrigern set about his part of the bargain. Black Ivor Gruffydd's spell turned out to be a simple one, and he removed it easily. As he pronounced the last word of the counterspell, Rhys's face lit up with relief, and he heaved a great sigh.

"There is good you are with your magic, Master Kedrigern," he said. "I did not feel a thing."

Kedrigern gave a self-deprecating smile and waved off the compliment. "No reason you should. It was a small spell."

"It did not feel so small when it was in my feet."

"They never do. Rhys . . . I'm curious about something. . . ."

"I will answer you gladly," said the minstrel, rising.

"It seems to me . . . now, maybe I've just got rhyming on my mind . . . but it seems to me that when we were talking with Princess just now, we were all falling into rhyme. Is that right?"

Rhys ap Gwallter took a few gingerly steps. He grinned at Kedrigern, walked firmly around his chair, then did a vigorous little dance. "Better than ever I am, look you, Master Kedrigern. I could walk from here to the ocean without stopping, thanks to you. Yes, it may be that we were all rhyming. The charm is fresh and new, you see, and it spreads out around the lady, touching others."

"Will it always be like that?"

"The rhyming is a fragile gift. Indeed, if the lady does not remain in constant practice, she will be speaking in prose before you know it," Rhys said.

Kedrigern smiled. "All things considered, that might be for the best."

That night, the three of them dined lavishly and drank deeply of Kedrigern's most treasured stock, the very best from the vineyards of Vosconu the Openhanded. It was well into morning when the last song was sung, and the last health was drunk. With muffled yawns and weary "good-nights," Kedrigern and Princess left Rhys to curl up on a soft mat before the fire while they made their way to their bedchamber.

Kedrigern awoke to a bright morning, refreshed by a night's unbroken rest. He yawned and stretched, and turned to Princess. She was already awake, and was staring up with a preoccupied air.

"My dear, did you have a good sleep?" he asked.

She replied thoughtfully, "For a time, it was restful and deep. But I woke with a cry—"

"Did you really? But why?"

"I dreamed I'd relapsed to 'Brereep.' "

He took her hand and pressed it for reassurance. She snuggled closer, and they lay warm and quiet for a little while. Then Princess said, "Did you notice, my dear, that we rhyme?"

"It will go away in a short time," Kedrigern replied, automatically. Then, thinking on her words, he realized that he really was falling into the patterns of his wife's speech. It was all harmless, he knew; but something in him made him chary of all spells. "Let us rise," he said tersely.

"Yes," said Princess. "It's best we consider our guest."

Kedrigern nodded, but remained warily silent. As they entered the dining hall, Princess in the lead, Rhys sat up, scratching himself and looking about confusedly. Kedrigern signaled to him to remain silent. The minstrel, seeing his gestures, looked even more confused, and asked, "Look you now, what is this pantomime?"

So Kedrigern gave up the struggle. All that day and the next, any conversation that took place in the presence of Princess was in limerick form, and there were no deviations from the rule. If Kedrigern deliberately tried to jumble the rhythm, the outcry from Spot supplied the missing beats. But when, on the morning of the third day after his arrival, Rhys ap Gwallter left them, the rhyming charm seemed to depart with him. Princess spoke in a voice as sweet and musical as an angel, but she spoke in prose.

As they sat over lunch, Kedrigern said, "It took a long time, my dear, but you have your voice back at last."

"Thanks to you, Keddie. I knew you'd do it."

"I've disappointed you a number of times, I'm afraid. I needed Rhys's charms to bring it about."

"If it weren't for your powers, Rhys would never have helped you. I've heard you say hundreds of times that the bards of Cymri are very close with their magic. More ale?"

"Just a drop, thank you." Kedrigern reflected for a time, and said, "Yes, I suppose you're right. It's all professional courtesy, but nothing would have been done if I weren't a wizard of some standing."

"Exactly. So the credit is yours."

"It was a privilege, my dear. And now that you're speaking again, what shall we do to celebrate? Shall we invite a few friends, and have a party?"

"All my friends are toads," Princess pointed out. "Not much point inviting *them*. And your friends are scattered all over the place."

"True," Kedrigern said, nodding. "Perhaps we could take a little trip. There's a convention coming up. I hadn't planned on going— you know how I am about travel—but if you'd like to—"

"It's hard to think. Actually, all I want to do for a time is talk. I want to talk about the meaning of life, and gossip about people I hardly know, and I want to discuss great art and literature and music, and tell silly jokes, and sing songs, and recite poetry, and complain about the way you leave indescribable things lying about the house when you're in the middle of an enchantment—"

"I'm sorry, my dear. I didn't realize—"

"And congratulate you when you work a difficult magic just right. And talk with another woman about all the things that interest me but don't interest you."

"We could invite the wood-witch for a weekend. Bess is a good sort."

"That's a start. I want to talk and talk and talk, Keddie. I want to say everything."

"I'm sure there's one thing you won't be saying."

"What's that, my love?"

"Brereep," he said.

In Midst
of Life

✳   ✳   ✳

James Tiptree, Jr.

Alice Sheldon, who wrote SF for twenty years under the pseudonym "James Tiptree, Jr.," shot and killed her ailing husband and then herself in May 1987, at their home in McLean, Virginia. "Bullets End 2 Fragile Lives" said the headline on page one of the Washington Post, *and they also brought an end to one of the most powerful voices in science fiction. Mrs. Sheldon, who served in the Army Air Corps in World War II and later taught experimental psychology, started writing SF in the late 1960s. Her best known stories include: "Love Is the Plan, the Plan is Death," "Houston, Houston, Do You Read," and "The Women Men Don't See" (F&SF, December 1973). The story you are about to read was the last work her agent received before Alice Sheldon's death.*

✳   ✳   ✳

THE first sign of Amory Guilford's mortal sickness showed up in the spring when he was forty-five.

His wife heard him stirring. When she looked up, he was sitting on the edge of his bed, his head in his hands.

"Is anything wrong, dear?"

"No . . . I don't want to get dressed."

She sat up. "Do you feel all right? We shouldn't have stayed at the Blairs' so late."

"It isn't that. I tell you, I just don't want to get dressed."

"But—"

"I'm sick and tired of getting dressed. My pants—left foot in, right foot up and in. I've done some figuring. Call it four hundred times a year, counting dressing for dinner. That's four thousand times a decade—sixteen thousand times now. Add in changing into exercise clothes, breeches—call it twenty thousand times I've put my pants on so far. I'm *tired* of it. Bored! And I forgot the pajamas—that's another sixteen thousand."

"I'll ask Manuel to help you get dressed, dear."

"No—I don't *want* Manuel to help me get dressed. I don't want to get dressed, I'm bored with getting dressed, that's all. . . . Do you know what would happen if I went down to the office this way?"

"Oh dear—"

"I'll tell you. They'd all say, 'Good morning, Mr. Guilford,' as if nothing were different. And if I went over to the computer and pulled up our position on a couple of random stocks and then sat down looking thoughtful, Tony would have George on the modem before I said a word. And that would be all that would happen, except that sometime in the afternoon, those stocks would go up a tick because of that leak I still haven't spiked. . . . I have a good notion to do it. Except that Mrs. Hewlett would phone Peters to bring down a suit of clothes, and I'd still have to get dressed. Like she did when they found me still in my dinner jacket that time. . . . God, I'm *bored!*"

"With getting dressed, dear? Perhaps you want a vacation."

"No, I don't need a vacation. Besides, I'd still have to get dressed."

But he was grinning now, and going into his dressing room, where Manuel waited with his business clothes, and it all passed over.

The next time came a couple of months later and was more serious.

"Amory dear! What are you doing home? Did you forget something?"

"No . . . I just couldn't face it."

"Face the office? But you love the office, your work. And isn't this the morning when the firm you're taking over was supposed to make you some kind of offer? You told me about that."

"Yes, yes . . . Pickering Drill. They'll pay up; I've got them over a log. . . . But I don't know: at the tunnel I just suddenly didn't give one damn about the whole thing. I told Peters to make a U-turn at Palisades Avenue and bring me home."

"You *do* need a vacation. And I think you should see Dr. Ellsworth; some little thing may be bothering you. I'll make an appointment. This isn't like you, Amory dear."

"I know."

He sat down heavily, dropping the morning paper. "Suddenly I don't *care* what Pickering offers. Another $30, $40 million; God knows we don't need it. I just don't care about Pickering Drill, or Yamahito, or Aleman, or Four-L Bits—my empire building!" He gave a derisive snort. "I've worked so hard putting it all together—and now I don't care."

"Tony won't understand," Margo said thoughtfully.

"No. None of them will. All they see is my go-go-go."

"And you'll be go-go-go again, dear. This is just a mood. But I'm sure Dr. Ellsworth—"

"No. I don't want Dr. Ellsworth . . . I want—I don't know *what* I want . . . just to *stop*, maybe."

"Oh Amory!"

"No, I don't mean that. . . ."

"Well, I better call Mrs. Hewlett and tell her something has come up," she said after a pause.

"Yes—No, wait. I don't know." He got up and paced around the room. Was his mood lifting?

Yes. Sure enough, a little later he called Peters and went on his way into town, right in the old groove. And Pickering Drill came up with an offer that netted him $35 million, which he accepted, and turned to other targets. And the days passed as usual.

But the next week the "mood" came back and settled in heavily, so that he twice went into the library and opened the drawer where lay his old .45 Colt, and looked at it. The second time, he reached in and touched the cool checkered grip. But he closed the drawer decisively and let Margo talk him out of canceling the dinner they were giving that night.

At dinner he behaved normally, except that he disturbed a few guests by giving them long, probing looks in silence, so that conversation died. And next day he agreed to go away for three weeks on a newly opened Caribbean beach that Margo had got wind of.

Those weeks, and the four months beyond them, were the most appalling time of Amory Guilford's experience. The engines of his life seemed to have stopped, and nothing he could do would start them. He could find no motivation, no zest or joy or the mildest interest in anything at all, though he stoically went through the motions. He felt literally bored unto death.

He and Margo had long lived, like most of their friends, in friendship without passion. Their children were both in colleges and effectively out of their lives. It had been tacitly understood that his passion was invested in his work, and incidentally in his stream of more or less mechanical erotic investigations of the new faces in his company. It says much for Amory's desperation now that he twice attempted to revive with Margo the activities of former days.

But he could in no way keep this up, and presently turned to the girl they had brought down with them in case his interest in work resurfaced. This ended as abruptly as it had begun.

By the end of their stay at St. Antrim, he could barely make the effort to get into his swim trunks, and looked with blank eyes at the scuba gear he had used to enjoy. He took to slopping about permanently in an old terry beach robe, until Margo brought him home.

Of the next four months, nothing more need be said. The end of them came one afternoon when he walked into the library, took out his gun, and without ceremony thrust it into his mouth and pulled the trigger.

There was a blinding, soundless crash.

Then, to his amazement, he found himself rising to his feet. He was facing the door, through which people were now rushing. He looked behind him and perceived—something—on the floor behind him. He looked away. People closed around.

Avoiding the people, he made his way from the room. Movement was light and easy, without pain. He was, he thought, walking—with an utter lack of effort that he had never known before.

"But, but—" he murmured silently.

Leaving the uproar behind him, he came out into the entry foyer.

Here he hesitated a moment. The feeling of finality was strong; he sensed that what he left now he could never return to. So be it.

After a minute he went on through the foyer and out the front door, and began walking down the curving drive. Peters was there, standing beside the town car and looking up at the house.

"Hello," Amory said.

Peters did not seem to hear or see him. Amory went on, and came to the wrought-iron gates. Here he stopped and looked back one last time.

A milky sort of mist or film already lay between him and the house.

He knew now, absolutely and finally, that he was dead.

And, apparently, in the land of death.

It did not appear much different. Outside the gates lay the familiar two-lane blacktop road, set about with big trees. The day was overcast, the light vaguely greenish.

He went through the gates—he was not quite sure how—and began walking along the road.

He had no goal, and for a time needed none. He was content to pace along through an increasingly ambiguous landscape. All was silent; he saw no people, nor did cars pass him. Presently the road changed, imperceptibly, to the streets of a small town. But it was a silent town, without traffic or people. After a time the street changed again; it became, block by block, a street in a silent city.

He walked and walked, and still the pale light held steady, though he knew it was time for darkness. His watch, he found, had stopped at 3:48.

But now and then a car silently crossed the street ahead of him, and disappeared in the side streets. Once one came so close that he shouted and ran after it, but when he came to the corner, still shocked by the sound of his own voice, it had vanished.

He strolled on, bemused by a growing feeling of familiarity. This corner, that building—he had seen them before, he knew; perhaps many times. But here they seemed oddly jumbled together, misjuxtaposed.

He passed a block of luxury condominiums. Among them was the well-known building where friends lived on the penthouse level. Should he go in and see what he could rouse up? He peered into the lighted lobby. It was empty. There seemed to be a dark, moveless shadow behind the front desk. Was this someone who could tell him where he was? He doubted it, and found himself walking on.

Still, everything was overlaid with the feeling of déjà vu. Never did he see anything unexpected or strange, except for the emptiness. He couldn't be sure what city he was in. But were these not the streets that he passed on his daily commutings? Or were they from an earlier time? He couldn't tell.

Ahead of him lay a smoggy, mistlike curtain through which he could not see very far ahead. When he turned around, he found the same curtain hiding the blocks he had already passed.

He found himself wishing to be out of the city. On this street he passed route signs, though he was not familiar with the number. But they must mean that this street turned to a highway at the city's outskirts. Good. It would be a long hike, but this gait was untiring, and there was no alternative. He hastened his step, moved more purposefully.

He was beginning to be puzzled—more than puzzled, resentful —at the lack of any reception. Surely he had passed a significant boundary, from life into death. Was he not due some kind of recognition or explanation? A sign, anyhow, to tell him where he was or what was going on?

This strange existence was nothing from any religion he had ever heard about. He himself was a quiet unbeliever, but he had read a bit, and Margo occasionally took him to church for weddings or memorials. He knew he wasn't in Hell or Heaven; if he had been judged, he'd had no notification of it. Could it be that he was in some Eastern scenario, waiting to be born again? As, he hoped, a human being rather than some animal. He wasn't aware that he had done anything so wrong as to deserve being, say, a cockroach. Indeed, he wasn't aware of any particular wrongdoing, outside of being born rich and making himself more so. He had always given freely to charities, if that counted as virtue, and he had helped several people along the way—Margo had seen to that. What was he being held here for?

And where was here?

It came to him that in some doctrine there was a place called Limbo, which was neither Heaven nor Hell. He seemed to recall that certain doubtful cases ended there—unbaptized infants, for example. He hoped this wasn't Limbo; it sounded unbearably tedious, and the sentences as he remembered them were indefinite. No, please, not Limbo, he murmured to himself.

There occurred to him then the explanation for all this world. It was all a patchwork of his memories, old and new, conscious and forgotten. Everything here was from his own mind—he was in effect living in his mind, wandering through what was nothing but that which he had seen or heard of or experienced. Wandering in my wits, he mumbled and made a bark of laughter that echoed crazily in the bare street.

The thought displeased him, yet he couldn't get rid of it. It threatened an eternity of boredom, if this was to be eternity. Or perhaps, like a story he had read, all his walking had taken place in an instant of real time, the instant between the bullet's entry and the stoppage of his brain—and he would presently "awaken" to die for real. Certainly he had expected that death would be nothingness, a total erasure of Amory Guilford. That had been what he longed for, not this vapid excursion through random memory.

And why were there no people? Of course he remembered people, too. And traffic. Was this some kind of a morality message that he hadn't paid enough attention to people? Some corny hint for him to repent? Well, what of? He'd paid as much attention to people as most men of his class and type, he thought defensively. He didn't deserve this—this isolation ward. . . . And if he did repent, what good would it do? This was a nasty retribution, and useless, with no people here for him to notice.

Or was this a hint that he really *was* going to be reborn, to have another chance? He scuffed his feet, resentful again. The idea of becoming a helpless, squalling infant did not appeal to him.

And now he noticed something else, which shocked him.

The misty curtain in which the street ahead ended seemed to be *drawing closer*. He wheeled about, and saw the same effect behind. So few blocks were visible now! He counted ahead—five, six, and he could make out no more. Surely there had been eight or nine only a short time ago? The clear space that traveled with him was *shrinking*!

Oh no! He became frightened; his pulse raced. Yet he could do nothing but walk a bit faster, dreading what would happen if his space shrank to nothing. The thought terrified him—to be swaddled into the mist, alone with his own mind.

Could this be some kind of substitute for the night that should have fallen?

He couldn't know, but merely hiked on, almost at a run now. He was so eager to be out of the city, into free air, where, he thought confusedly, the mist couldn't close him in as easily.

And suddenly he saw that he *was* getting out of the city. On both sides now were big gas stations, and then a shopping mall—signs of suburbia. He hurried on.

And now another thought came to him. He had heard of men who got shot in the head and yet did not die, but survived as horrible vegetables, living on tubes and machines. Maybe that had happened to him! Maybe his body was even now in a hospital, invaded by heart-lung machines and metabolic supports, while his mind walked free. Maybe the apparent closing-in of the world signified his return to his body, to take up the "life" of an idiot!

"Oh God!" He invoked a purely verbal deity, then flinched, wondering if he had offended some Unknown.

Well, if he had missed killing himself, the obvious thing to do was to complete the job now. To kill himself dead, right here. But how? There were no weapons to be had here.

He surveyed the line of shops in the nearest mall. No gun shop, of course. No hardware store, even. And no one manned those stores. Well, if he could spot a hardware, he could just walk in and pick up a knife. That would be messy, and painful as well. But he thought he could do it.

He passed another mall on his right. Still no hardware store. But there was bound to be one soon; he remembered them so clearly.

He strode on, watching alertly, until a sound behind him made him turn.

On what was now clearly an interstate highway, a big truck was overtaking him at speed.

He could throw himself in front of that! Surely it would finish him.

People managed to kill themselves that way, he knew. And his body was agile and well coordinated. He could try. Yes.

He scrambled off the shoulder of the road and crouched behind some bushes.

The huge twelve-wheeler bore down frighteningly fast. It was blue and white, with a great glittering grillwork nose. He caught a flash of "LEROY'S TRANSPORT" over the windshield. Quickly—*now*—
He leaped out, directly in its path.
But even as he jumped, he knew he had done it too soon. There was a blare of brakes, and the monster swerved by him, bowling him over in its air blast.
As he picked himself up, he saw the truck stopping. For some reason he tottered futilely toward it.
"What do you want to do, get killed?"
The driver was climbing down from the cab, a shiny wrench in his hand. To Amory's relief, he was a short man, though brawny, with thinning red hair. As they neared each other, he repeated his query, "You trying to get dead?"
"Yes," said Amory humbly. "I missed."
"Oh, a jumper, huh? Well, you didn't miss; I missed you. You ought to be grateful. You jumpers never think what you could do to the rig. The driver. Never think a-tall!"
"I'm sorry," said Amory distractedly. He was noticing something. All around the truck and driver, the world seemed different. The landscape was brighter, more detailed, and the mist had receded to be barely visible. And there were ordinary noises again. A man shouted at the filling station ahead, and Amory could see live people there—not dark ghosts like in the lobby, but real men, moving. And there was sunlight. Wonderful!
"Are you Leroy?" he asked the driver slowly.
"Yeah. That's my rig; you could have trashed it."
"I really am sorry. I didn't think a human body could damage anything that big and hard."
"Ah, you never think. I ought to turn you in."
Amory was thinking fast. He had never known a truck driver. Leroy must be real, not another dead man like himself. If this was Leroy's world, it was very different from his. Preferable. Not to lose touch with him, that was it.
"Please don't. My name is Amory. I'd like to ride with you a ways. To someplace, someplace cheerful. Could you take me?"
" 'Gainst regulations. No riders."

Amory found his wallet was still in his pocket and took it out. Inside were a couple of hundreds and his gold credit card. He fingered out the bills.

"Would this help, Mr. Leroy? I could give you more if you'd stop by a bank. And you could always say you picked me up wandering crazy and are taking me to a hospital. . . . The first part is true, but I don't want the hospital. What do you say?"

Leroy didn't look at Amory's hand, but somehow his hand took the bills neatly.

"I guess I could do that," he said slowly.

"Great!" For a moment, Amory felt an actual surge of cheer. "So let's get going—if your, ah, rig is all right."

"Oh, she's O.K., no thanks to you. Go on, get in."

Amory went around the big nose, reached up, and climbed in. All he knew about trucks was that they had many gears and, he had heard, a bunk up back of the seat where the driver could nap. Sure enough, there was one here. It was empty.

Seeing the fresh paint, the newness, he said, "This is a beautiful truck. You said 'she.' Does she have a name?"

Leroy was stowing the wrench in a built-in tool box. "Daisy," he said with a trace of shyness. "I call her Daisy because she's a daisy."

"Beautiful. . . . Where are you headed?"

Leroy set the gears and put the giant motor into action. They rolled ponderously off the shoulder and picked up speed.

"I have a load for Chicago," he said.

"Do you plan to drive straight through? I'm afraid I'm not a qualified driver so I could spell you."

"Oh, hell no. On this run I usually stop at Overlook. That's a big trucker's rest. Deluxe. They have everything there, at Overlook—stores, theater, yeah, a bank. You could spend a week there."

"Oh good. I meant it about the bank; I need some money, too. I can get it with this type of card." In Leroy's world, it was clear, the usual rules held. You paid for what you got. Good enough; he could use some reality. But Amory was becoming more and more cheered. Certainly a trucker's rest was well out of his own experience! He wondered: Was it normal here for the dead to meet? Perhaps the recently dead? Mysterious. . . .

"How long have you been here?" he asked.

Leroy's head snapped around at him, wearing a strange, hostile look. Amory regretted his question; things were tenuous enough.

"What do you mean, 'here'?"

"Oh, I misspoke myself. I mean here in this cab. Driving." The little man relaxed again. "Thirty years come March. This rig, one year—it's the first one I've ever owned free and clear."

"I can see why you were so mad at me for nearly damaging it. Truly I didn't think it was possible."

"They never do," Leroy said glumly. His eyes sought Amory's face again. "Say, are you after—are you an investigator, about that hassle back at the Pennsy docks?"

"What hassle? I never heard of the Pennsy docks, Leroy. And I for sure am no investigator—I'm just what I look like."

Leroy slowly seemed to believe him. "H'mm. I guess no 'spector would jump like that. O.K."

But Amory had the idea now. There must have been some accident at those docks. And Leroy was killed. But he wasn't admitting it; he was simply denying that anything had happened to him, living in his ghost world. How could he be driving his truck? Well, his truck was as much a part of his persona, his self-image, as Amory's clothes were of his. And he had walked away from, from that library in his suit. These must be ghost clothes, though—he fingered his vest—they felt perfectly solid and had his wallet in the pocket. Just so, whenever whatever had happened at the Pennsy docks killed Leroy, he must have driven off in his ghost truck as easily as Amory had walked away in his suit.

He must be careful not to disturb the little man's belief in the reality of all this, or he might collapse the world Amory found so reassuring. But there seemed no danger of that—he was sure that if he told Leroy he was dead, he would get only laughter. "What do you mean, I'm dead?" And indeed, Amory thought, what do I mean?

They were barreling on through the endless sunset, the big truck eating up the road. The road wasn't empty now, Amory saw. Occasional traffic met them or passed them, the drivers seeming notably well behaved, perhaps a happy memory of Leroy's.

Desultorily, they conversed, discussing makes of cars and the ways of drivers. Amory was charmed, learning about trucks and trucking. If he ever got back to a computer, he thought, he had a couple of names of firms to look up. Nothing like first hand reports from the consumer! It seemed incredible. He reminded him that he was *dead*, and most unlikely to have a use for the information.

The only hint of his state was that the gold sky did not fade. It was the beautiful time of the evening, when neon and arc lights bloomed against the colored sky. And it remained that way. Leroy did not comment on the unnatural length of the day. As they neared a big triple overpass, the little man pointed ahead.

"There's Overlook!" he said with satisfaction.

On the upper level was a substantial group of buildings topped by a big sign: OVERLOOK—TRUCKERS BAR AND GRILL. Below, it said: BEDS AND BREAKFAST—ALL SERVICES—24 Hours—No private cars.

It looked like a medieval castle on a hill, Amory thought.

They pulled off the overpass into an enclave ending in a parking lot full of big trucks and trailers. On their left was a Kmart store, on the right the two-story bar and grill. All the roadways and turns were truck-sized. Leroy trundled Daisy into the parking lot and took a ticket from a cute girl in a uniform.

"Full tonight, Patty."

"Yes sir, Mr. Leroy." Professional smile from Patty.

"They all know me," he confided to Amory with a grin, skillfully backing into a slot between two behemoths. As they walked out, Amory felt impressed and exhilarated by the sheer size of the great trucks lined up here. This really was something new to him!

"The bank's in here." Leroy was leading him into the Kmart.

"At this time of night?"

"Twenty-four hours. You'll see. Nothing closes at Overlook."

Beyond the aisles of clothing and appliances, in a back corner, Amory saw the grilles and counters of a small bank branch. Not one Amory had an account with. He made another futile mental note; an enterprising outfit.

After a brief, completely normal hassle with another cute girl, he got five thousand on his gold bank card. While she was making her phone check, Amory wondered who or what was on the other end. Limbo Central? Impossible to believe that all this, and the five bills she presently handed him, were substanceless, figments of his memory.

He pulled off a thousand and pushed it at Leroy.

"Just so you won't forget and pull out without me," he smiled.

The little man protested, but finally allowed himself to be persuaded to put it in his dog-eared wallet.

"I tell you where I'm not going tonight," he told Amory. "Not with this."

"Where?"

"To the blackjack table."

"Oh, so there's a casino, too."

"I told you. *Everything.*" Looking up at Amory with a shy smile, he added primly, "Girls, too. *Hostesses.*"

"Oh yes?"

"Oh yes. Man!" Leroy slapped his cap on his leg.

They came out into the golden light and crossed the roadway into the bar and grill. Convivial sounds rose; two or three voices called out to Leroy. He waved. The bar was a cheerful, heavily wood-trimmed big room, with an oak bar and booths, just beginning to be full. All the guests were clearly truckers, mostly huge mountains of men like their vehicles.

Amory felt like an interloper in his dark three-piece suit, among Leroy's friends. Among Leroy's *imaginary* friends, he corrected himself. For God's sake, not to forget that he was a ghost, living in another ghost's memories!

But it was all so real, so persuasive . . . the solidity, the detail of Leroy's mental world!

The big TV was showing what was evidently a sports cable. Music was also coming from a side room, where dancing seemed to be going on.

Leroy made straight for the bar; Amory followed.

"Yo, Leroy," said the bartender, a husky individual with curly black hair.

"Two light," said Leroy, smacking his cap on the bar.

Amory had felt no thirst or hunger, indeed, no physical needs. But the beers looked tempting. He tasted his—and found it flavorful. Some of Leroy's zest must be spilling onto him. He drank more.

A woman came from the dance room and circulated professionally through the bar. Finding no takers, she went away.

"Dot here tonight?" Leroy inquired of the barkeep.

"Oh yeah, sure."

"Wait till you see her," Leroy told Amory. "Oh hey—there she is now!"

A tall, well-built young brunette was coming in.

"Hey Dot! Dottie! Over here."

"Hey, my man!" Dot undulated toward them, looking curiously at Amory.

"Friend of yours, hon?"

"Yeah, he's with me. He's no trucker, though."

"So I see." She smiled at Amory, her eyes nearly level with his. "Find him a nice girl, will you?"

"Oh no, no," protested Amory. "Thanks, but no thanks—I'm still a little shook up." Have sex with a ghost or whatever—no way, he thought.

"O.K.," said Leroy. To Dot, he explained, "He had a near miss out on 91."

"Oh well, mister, a nice girl would just fix you up."

Amory's protests finally ended the matter. Dot had a beer, and Leroy downed another, showing signs of impatience. Amory noticed that there was a staircase up off beyond the bar.

"Rooms up there," said Leroy. "Real nice. . . . Hey Georgio, give us a key, will you?"

He pulled out a hundred, and got back twenty-five in change. Amory saw Dot and the barkeep exchange nods.

"C'mon, hon." He boosted Dot away from the bar.

"What I like," Dot laughed at Amory, "is these long engagements."

"See you."

With that, Leroy hustled Dottie to the staircase, seeming undisturbed by the slightly ludicrous figure he cut with the woman; she was a good head taller than he. Like his big truck, Amory thought.

As they left him, he felt a pang of loss. The lights seemed to dim down a bit as the couple ascended into the shadows above. And a kind of slowness came over the scene, though the noise of the room stayed the same.

It was as if Leroy's world was weakening behind him as he left the scene. Would it vanish, if he removed himself too far? Panicked, Amory saw that the bartender had turned static, pouring a shot. Yet the liquid didn't overflow.

In a surge of fear, Amory ran to the staircase and called up.
"Hey! Hey Leroy!"
They didn't hear him. He was about to call again, louder, when
a voice spoke almost in his ear.
"Are you out of your senses, man? Let the poor ghost have his
privacy."
Amory whirled. The man who had spoken to him was sitting at
the bar alone. Amory had noticed his sharp black eyes.
"But—but—," Amory said, utterly confused by his need. "Who
are you?"
"Don't you recognize me?" the man asked. "You called me in
yourself."
"Called you in?"
The man gestured to Amory to take the seat beside him. Amory
saw he had a very white face, in which his eyes burned like black embers
and felt a thrill of fear. When he was seated, the man said neutrally,
"I am Death. To be more accurate, his delegate."
In spite of Amory's fascinated horror, he felt a prick of satisfaction.
At last some explanations were about to begin. The man who called
himself Death's delegate was unremarkable, save for his eyes, and clad
in a suit no darker than Amory's own. This was no ghost, no figment. . . . What was he? Before Amory could speak, he went on, "Now
you can do something for me."
Another woman was turning through the room, a cute little blonde,
moving as slowly as a zombie. Hers was the only movement in the
room now, but still the noise of an active bar went on, rising up the
stairs. The blonde bent toward Amory, her open mouth making a kind
of low moaning, like a slowed-down tape.
"What?" said Amory distractedly. "Look, without him everything
goes wrong. It's—it's grotesque, horrible."
"That bothers you? Of course." The man raised his hand and
snapped his fingers. At once the lights came back bright, and everything
speeded up to normal tempo. The blonde whirled away, laughing.
"Better?"
"Oh yes. Uh, thank you."
The man looked him over. There was something clinical in his
gaze.
"Do you understand all this?" Amory asked.

"Yes."

"Then where are we?"

"In the country of the dead. One of them."

"And all this is just memory, right? Someone's memories?"

"Right."

"Then why were my memories so weak? And foggy?"

"Because death touched you while you were still alive."

Amory thought this over. It sounded like what he had felt, back then. The touch of death. Yes.

"Why?" The man didn't answer him directly. Instead, he said, "We are of a kind. I smelled it as soon as you came near. You will, too."

Amory thought some more. "But this *is* death?"

"Yes."

"It isn't like what I believed. I believed I'd simply stop. Nothingness. Zero."

"That's the one belief that's not fulfilled."

"Why not? I mean, it's logical. Where does a candle flame go when you blow the candle out?"

"Perhaps the spark of consciousness, once ignited, is not so easy to put out."

"No, it should be easy." Amory summoned a lifetime of quiet but impassioned argument. "Look, consciousness is one of the last developments. The last. So it should be fragile. It is, to—look at the effect of a few drinks, a tap on the head. Gone. Poof!"

"Perhaps," the pale man said noncommittally.

"You say it's the one belief that's not fulfilled," Amory said thoughtfully. "You mean, you fulfill all the others? If I'd believed in the usual stuff—pearly gates, Saint Peter, judgment, Heaven and Hell—I'd have found that?"

"Yes. Or any other faith."

"What if I'd believed I was going straight to Hell?"

"You'd have got that. If you really believed it."

"But that's terrible! Hell . . . for how long? Forever? And when does *this* end? What happens?"

Death's delegate looked down at his hands. "I said this was just one of Death's kingdoms. For a special type. The unbelievers, do you see?"

"That's me."

"Exactly. But as I also said, you're special, too." Abruptly his tone changed. "Would you come outside with me for a moment? There's something I want to show you."

Casting a perfunctory look upstairs, where there was no sign of Leroy, Amory followed the pale man out.

Outside, the golden daylight still held. Two big semis were rolling in. His new acquaintance halted near the entrance.

"Look at the sky over there where it's dark. Can you see a kind of light on the clouds?"

Amory squinted, and made out a patch of pale luminescence, like a reflection of a light below. As he gazed, it seemed to shift a little, as if whatever was reflected was moving internally.

"Do you think you could drive over there, to the light?"

"Sure, if the road leads there. What is it, a town?"

"All roads lead there. . . . No, it's the main arrival point for this area. I should be there now, but I'm making a swing around to catch the incomers I missed." He made a gesture to Amory to follow him around the corner of the building. "The numbers keep increasing, you see. The old policy was to meet everyone individually, but—" He opened his hands in a helpless gesture. "Now we can cope only with the active questioners. You'll soon get to sense them; they stand out. People like your friend don't call for attention. They're satisfied. Maybe after a while he'll start to need help, but not soon. Anyway, there's where I need your help."

"*My* help? What do you mean?"

"Oh, just to drive around until you sense somebody who needs attention. Then you stop and talk with him. The ones who seem satisfied, you don't need to bother with."

"You mean you're trying to delegate your job to *me?*" Amory demanded incredulously.

"Oh, only a portion of it, I assure you. There's plenty for me, too. Ah, here's my car."

They had come to a small parking line for ordinary autos; he was pointing at a dark maroon BMW much like Amory's own, and getting out his keys.

"As I said, we're alike. Here—" Before Amory could resist, he found the keys thrust into his hand. "I'm giving it to you."

"Why? What's all this about? I don't want it."

"Yes, you do. You'll feel more comfortable, at first anyway. And it's nothing—here one gets such things by simply wishing—in the right way."

"Huh? You mean . . . I'll get anything I wish for?"

"Yes. Virtually anything. Except living people. Try."

"Try wishing for something?"

"Yes."

As Amory stood nonplussed, to his surprise he found he had a wish. For a dog he'd owned in his youth, a black Labrador. He wished for it, finding it awkward to phrase. At the last moment he remembered to ask for Dory as he'd been early on, not the old dog he had become.

Nothing happened.

And then, suddenly, a black shadow that was a dog came bursting around the corner—stopping to pee as Dory always had, then galloping toward Amory. Despite his conviction that the thing was a phantasm, a figment, as the dog approached, so real, so living, Amory couldn't help holding out his hand to him—and then going down on one knee to receive the Labrador's familiar, enthusiastic greeting. Strangely, he felt a sense of comfort.

The man beside him smiled. "Nice dog."

"Yeah. . . ." Amory got up and dusted off his knee. "Sit, Dory."

Dory did.

"You see?" Death's delegate was taking off his dark jacket. He looked away, oddly, for a moment as if concentrating. A moment later, long, dark wings extended themselves from his shoulders and spread wide. "Well, you'll be all right now," he said to Amory.

"Wait!" Amory cried. "What do I *tell* them? You haven't told me a thing!"

The wings seemed to enlarge. "I've told you all I know," the man said. "That's all the one who recruited me told me."

He gave an experimental wing flap. "I specified that these should be easy to work," he confided to Amory.

"But—but—"

Beside him the Labrador gave a low growl in his throat and raised his hackles at the winged man.

"Leroy," Amory said helplessly. "My friend—"

"He'll be all right." Death's delegate flapped again and rose a little in the air. "Oh, I almost forgot," he said. "Remember this: *Death is not mocked.*"

With a great sweep of his new black wings, the man lofted over the near roof—and went soaring out of sight in the sunset.

Amory stood looking after him dumbfounded, the car keys in his hand. Dory was looking up at him expectantly. But he couldn't go back in the bar with his dog, and he didn't want to wish him out of existence. What to do? Should he start out on this crazy business he'd been dragooned into? That seemed to be what the man expected. And he acted as if he had some kind of authority here. Or did he? "The one who recruited me," he'd said. Did that mean he was just another ghost who'd been hustled into being a reception committee? And what did that make Amory? Death's delegate's delegate? Or were there more behind that? This could be a whole chain of delegations, with nobody knowing anything. . . . And what did that mean, *Death is not mocked?* It sounded ominous. Maybe some kind of warning to take this seriously.

Dory gave a little whine. Amory remembered that the dog loved riding in cars. Amory looked up at the dark sky again; the light patch was still visible. And the road seemed to run straight toward it. He might as well try; he'd nothing to lose.

He opened the door. "Up and in, old boy."

Dory jumped in eagerly and settled himself in the passenger seat. The car smelled new. And he liked BMWs. The motor started, purring out its happy song of good engineering.

The man had said he'd spot people in need of help. How? Maybe he should lower the window, to let vibrations or whatever in. And what *would* he tell them? Anything he liked, it seemed. But that caution against mockery might refer to this—not to tell too fantastic a tale.

At least I'm not bored, he thought. As he thought it, a dire premonition hit him. Even this job could get boring, with time and repetition. He checked himself hurriedly. Not to think that way! Not to believe it. What you believe is what you get, here.

Determinedly, he pushed the thought away and eased the car into gear.

Rolling out to the highway, an old quotation came to him. He twisted it around: *In midst of Death I am alive.* He gave a snort of laughter. Dory barked, startling him. He had forgotten that habit the dog had of barking when anyone laughed. Did that mean that Dory was at least a little real? That he, too, was a "spark of consciousness"? He hoped so. And what would happen if he wished for Dory to be real? A big sign in the sky, saying *TILT*? Better not try.

He headed down the highway, to encounter the existential Unknown.

Surviving

*   *   *

Judith Moffett

Judith Moffett is a professor of English at the University of Pennsylvania. She had written several books of poetry and criticism, but "Surviving" (which evokes memories of Tarzan but turns into something quite different) was her first published SF story. It received several award nominations and was followed by a well-received novel, Pennterra.

*   *   *

FOR nearly eighteen years I've been keeping a secret to honor the memory of someone, now pretty certainly dead, who didn't want it told. Yet over those years I've come gradually to feel uncomfortable with the idea of dying without recording what I know—to believe that science would be pointlessly cheated thereby, and Sally, too; and just lately, but with a growing urgency, I've also felt the need to write an account of my own actions into the record.

Yet it's difficult to begin. The events I intend to set down have never, since they happened, been out of my mind for a day; nevertheless the prospect of reexperiencing them is painful and my silence the harder to break on that account.

I'll start, I guess, with the afternoon an exuberant colleague I scarcely knew at the time spotted me through the glass door and barged

139

into the psychology department office calling, "Hey, Jan, you're the expert on the Chimp Child—wait'll you hear this, you're not gonna believe it!"

People were always dashing to inform me of some item, mostly inconsequential, relating to this subject. I glanced across at John from the wall of mailboxes, hands full of memos and late papers, one eyebrow probably raised. "What now?"

"We've *hired* her!" And when I continued to look blank: "No kidding, I was just at a curriculum committee meeting in the dean's office, and Raymond Lickorish in Biology was there, and he told me: they've definitely given Sally Barnes a tenure-track appointment, to replace that old guy who's retiring this year, what's his name, Ferrin. The virus man. Raymond says Barnes's Ph.D. research was something on viruses and the origin of life on earth and her published work is all first-rate and she did well in the interview—he wasn't there so he didn't meet her, but they were all talking about it afterward—and she seems eager to leave England. So the department made her an offer and she accepted! She'll be here in September, I swear to God!"

By this point I'm sure I was showing all the incredulous excitement and delight a bearer of happy tidings could possibly have wished. And no wonder: I wrote my *dissertation* on Sally Barnes; I went into psychology chiefly because of the intense interest her story held for me. In fact the Chimp Child had been a kind of obsession of mine—part hobby, part mania—for a long time. I was a college freshman, my years of Tarzan games in the woods less far behind me than you might suppose, in 1990, when poachers hauled the screeching, scratching, biting, terrified white girl into a Tanzanian village and told its head man they would be back to collect the reward. Electrified, I followed the breaking story from day to day.

The girl was quickly and positively identified as Sally, the younger daughter of Martin and Hilary Barnes, Anglican missionary teachers at a secondary school in the small central African republic of Malawi, who had been killed when the light plane in which they and she were traveling from Kigoma had crashed in the jungle. A helicopter rescue crew found only the pilot's body in the burned-out fuselage. Scavengers may have dragged the others away and scattered the bones; improbable survivors of the crash may have tried to walk out—the plane had come down in the mountains, something less than 150 kilometers east of

Lake Tanganyika—and starved, or been killed by anything from leopards to thieves to fever. However it was, nothing had been heard or seen of the Barnes family after that day in 1981; it was assumed that one way or another all three had died in the bush.

No close living relatives remained in England. An older daughter, left at home that weekend with an attack of malaria, had been sent to an Anglican school for the children of missionaries, somewhere in the Midlands. There was no one but the church to assume responsibility for her sister the wild girl, either.

The bureaucracies of two African nations and the Church of England hummed, and after a day or two Sally was removed to the Malosa School in Southern Malawi, where the whole of her life before the accident had been lived. She could neither speak nor understand English, seemed stunned, and masturbated constantly. She showed no recognition of the school, its grounds or buildings, or the people there who had been friendly with her as a small child. But when they had cleaned her up, and cropped her matted hair, *they* recognized that child in *her*; pictures of Sally at her fourth birthday party, printed side by side in the papers with new ones of the undersized thirteen-year-old she had become, were conclusive. Hers was one of those faces that looks essentially the same at six and sixty.

But if the two faces obviously belonged to the same person, there was a harrowing difference.

A long time later Sally told me, gazing sadly at this likeness of herself: "Shock. It was nothing but shock, nothing more beastly. On top of everything else, getting captured must have uncovered my memories of the plane crash—violence; noise; confusion; my parents screaming, then not answering me—I mean, when the poachers started shooting and panicked everybody, and then killed the Old Man and flung that net over me, I fought and struggled, of course, but in the end I sort of went blank. Like the accident, but in reverse."

"Birth Trauma Number Three?" We were sitting cross-legged on the floor before the fireplace in my living room, naked under blankets, like Mohicans. I could imagine the scene vividly, had in fact imagined it over and over: the brown child blindly running, running, in the green world, the net spreading, dropping in slow motion, the child pitching with a crash into wet vegetation. Helplessness. Claustrophia. Uttermost bowel-emptying terror. The hysterical shrieks, the rough handling . . .

Sally patted my thigh, flushed from the fire's heat, then let her hand stay where it was.

"No point looking like that. What if they *hadn't* found me then? At University College, you know, they all think it was only just in time."

"And having read my book, you know I think so, too." We smiled; I must have pressed my palm flat to her hot, taut belly, or slipped my hand behind her knee or cupped her breast—some such automatic response. "The wonder is that after that double trauma they were able to get you back at all. You had to have been an awfully resilient, tough kid, as well as awfully bright. A survivor in every sense. Or you'd have died of shock and grief after the plane crashed, or of shock and grief when the poachers picked you up, or of grief and despair in England from all that testing and training, like spending your adolescence in a pressure cooker." I can remember nuzzling her shoulder, how my ear grazed the rough blanket. "You're a survivor, Sal."

In the firelight Sally smiled wanly. "Mm. Up to a point."

Any standard psych text published after 2003 will describe Sally Barnes as the only feral child in history to whom, before her final disappearance, full functional humanity had been restored. From the age of four and a half until just past her thirteenth birthday, Sally acted as a member of a troop of chimpanzees in the Tanzanian rain forest; from sixteen or seventeen onward, she was a young Englishwoman, a person. What sort of person? The books are vague on this point. Psychologists, naturally enough, were wild to know; Sally herself, who rather thought she did know, was wild to prevent them from turning her inside out all her life in the interest of *science*. I was (and am) a psychologist and a partisan, but professional integrity is one thing and obsession is quite another, and if I choose finally to set the record straight it's not because I respect Sally's own choice any less.

From the very first, of course, I'd been madly infatuated with the *idea* of Sally, in whose imagined consciousness—that of a human girl accepted by wild creatures as one of themselves—I saw, I badly wished to see, myself. The extreme harshness of such a life as hers had been —with its parasites, cold rains, bullying of the weak by the strong, and so forth—got neatly edited out of this hyperromantic conception; yet the myth had amazing force. I don't know how many times I read the *Jungle Books* and the best of the Tarzan novels between the ages of eight and fifteen, while my mother hovered uneasily in the background, dropping hints about eye makeup and stylish clothes. Pah.

So that later, when a real apechild emerged from a real jungle and the Sunday supplements and popular scientific magazines were full of her story, for me it was an enthralling and fabulous thing, one that made it possible to finish growing up, at graduate school, *inside* the myth: a myth not dispelled but amplified, enhanced, by scientific scrutiny. The more one looked at what had happened to Sally, the more wonderful it seemed.

Her remarkable progress had been minutely documented, and I had read every document and published half a dozen of my own, including my dissertation. It was established that she had talked early and could even read fairly well before the accident, and that her early family history had been a happy, stable one; all we experts were agreed that these crucial factors explained how Sally, alone among feral children, had been able to develop, or reacquire, normal language skills in later life. She was therefore fortunate in her precocity; fortunate, too, in her foster society of fellow primates. Almost certainly she could not have recovered, or recovered so completely, from eight years of life as a wolf or a gazelle. Unlike Helen Keller, she had never been sensually deprived; unlike Kaspar Hauser, also sensually deprived, she had not been isolated from social relations—wild chimpanzees provide one another with plenty of those; unlike the wolf girls of India, she had learned language before her period of abstention from the use of it. And like Helen Keller, Sally had a very considerable native intelligence to assist her.

It may seem odd that despite frequent trips to England, I had never tried to arrange a meeting with the subject of all this fascinated inquiry, but in some way my fixation made me shy, and I would end each visit by deciding that another year would do as well or better. That Sally might come to America, and to my own university, and to stay, was a wholly unlooked-for development. Now that chance had arranged it, however, shyness seemed absurd. Not only would we meet, we would become friends. Everyone would expect us to, and nothing seemed more natural.

My grandfather used to claim, with a forgiving chuckle, that his wedding night had been the biggest disappointment of his life. I thought bleakly of him the September evening of the annual cocktail party given by the dean of arts and sciences so that the standing faculty could make the acquaintance of their newly hired colleagues. A lot of people knew about Sally Barnes, of course, and among psychologists she was really famous, a prodigy; everybody wanted to meet her, and more than a few wanted to be there when I met her, to witness the encounter. I was exasperated with myself for being so nervous, as well as annoyed that the meeting would occur under circumstances so public, but when the moment arrived and I was actually being introduced to Sally—the dean had stationed himself beside her to handle the crush, and did the honors himself—these feelings all proved maddeningly beside the point.

There she stood, the Chimp Child of all my theories and fantasies: a small, utterly ordinary-seeming and -sounding young woman who touched my hand with purely mechanical courtesy. The plain black dress did less than nothing for her plain pale face and reddish hair; history's only rehabilitated feral child was a person you wouldn't look at twice in the street, or even once. That in itself meant nothing; but her expression, too, was indifferent and blank, and she spoke without any warmth at all, in an "educated" English voice pitched rather high: "How d'you do, a pleasure to meet you . . ." There she actually stood, saying her canned phrase to me, sipping from her clear plastic container of white wine, giving away nothing at all.

I stared at the pale, round, unfamiliar face whose shape and features I knew so well, unable to believe in it or let go of the hand that felt so hard in mine. The room had gradually grown deafening. Bright, curious eyes had gathered round us. The moment felt utterly weird and wrong. Dean Eccles, perhaps supposing his difficult charge had failed to catch my name, chirped helpfully, "Of course Janet is the author of that fascinating book about *you*," and beamed at Sally as if to say, "*There* now, you lucky girl!"

Only a flicker of eyelids betrayed her. "Oh, I see," she said, but her hand pulled out of mine with a little yank as she spoke, and she looked pointedly past me toward the next person in the receiving line —a snub so obvious that even the poor dean couldn't help but notice. Flustered, he started to introduce the elderly English professor Sally's attention had been transferred to.

We had hardly exchanged a dozen words. Suddenly I simply had to salvage something from the wreck of the occasion. "Look—could I call you in a week or two? Maybe we could get together for lunch or a drink or something after you're settled in?"

"Ah, I'm afraid I'll be rather busy for quite some time," said the cool voice, not exactly to me. "Possibly I might ring you if I happen to be free for an hour one afternoon." Then she was speaking to the old gentleman and I had been eased out of the circle of shoulders and that was that.

I went home thoroughly despondent and threw myself on the sofa. An hour or so later, the phone rang: John, who had witnessed the whole humiliating thing. "Listen, she acted that way with *everybody*, I watched her for an hour. Then I went through the line and she acted like that with *me*. She was probably jet-lagged or hates being on display—she was just pretending to drink that wine, by the way, sip, sip, sip, but the level never went down the whole time I was watching. You shouldn't take it personally, Jan. I doubt she had any idea who you were in that mob of freak-show tourists."

"Oh, she knew who I was, all right, but that doesn't make you wrong. O.K., thanks. I just wish the entire department hadn't been standing around with their tongues hanging out, waiting to see us fall weeping on each other's necks." Realizing I wasn't sure which I minded more, the rejection or its having been witnessed in that way, made me feel less tragic. I said good night to John, then went and pulled down the foldable attic stairs, put on the light, and scrounged among cartons till I found the scrapbook; this I brought downstairs and brooded over, soothed by a glass of rosé.

The scrapbook was fat. The Chimp Child had been an international sensation when first reclaimed from the wild, and for years thereafter picture essays and articles had regularly appeared where I could clip or copy them. I had collected dozens of photographs of Sally: arriving at Heathrow, a small, oddly garbed figure, face averted, clinging to a uniformed attendant; dressed like an English schoolgirl at fifteen, in blazer and tie, working at a table with the team of psychologists at University College, London; on holiday with the superb teacher Carol Cheswick, who had earned a place for herself in the educators' pantheon beside Jean-Marc Itard and Annie Sullivan by virtue of her brilliant achievements with Sally; greeting Jane Goodall, very old and frail, on one of Goodall's last visits to England; in her rooms at Newnham College, Cambridge, an average-looking undergraduate.

The Newnham pictures were not very good, or so I had always thought. Only now that I'd seen her in person . . . I turned back to the yellow newspaper clipping, nearly twenty years old, of a wild thing with matted, sawed-off hair; and now for the first time the blank face beneath struck me as queerly like this undergraduate's, and like the face I had just been trying to talk to at the party. The expressive adolescent's face brought into being sometime during the nineties—what had become of it? Who was Sally Barnes, after all? That precocious, verbally gifted little girl . . . I closed the cover, baffled. Whoever she was, she had long since passed the stage of being studied without her consent.

Yet I wanted so badly to know her. As fall wore on to winter, I would often see her on campus, walking briskly, buttoned up in her silver coat with a long black scarf wrapped round her, appearing to take no notice of whatever leaves or slush or plain brickwork happened to be underfoot, or of the milling, noisy students. She always carried reading equipment and a black shoulder bag. Invariably she would be alone. I doubt that I can convey more than a dim impression of the bewilderment and frustration with which the sight of her affected me thoughout those slow, cold months. I knew every detail of the special education of Sally Barnes, the dedication of her teachers, her own eagerness to learn; and there had been *nothing*, nothing at all, to suggest that once "restored to human status," she would become ordinary—nothing to foreshadow this standoffish dullness. Of course it was understandable that she would not wish to be quizzed constantly about her life in the wild; rumor got round of several instances when somebody unintimidated by her manner had put some question to her and been served with a snappish "Sorry, I don't talk about that." But was it credible that the child whom this unique experience had befallen had been, as her every word and action now implied, a particularly unfriendly, unoriginal, bad-tempered child who thereafter had scuttled straight back to sour conventionality as fast as ever she could?

I simply did not believe it. She had to be deceiving us deliberately. But I couldn't imagine why, nor entirely trust my own intuition: I wanted far too badly to believe that *no* human being who had been a wild animal for a time, and then become human again, could possibly really be the sort of human Sally seemed to be.

And yet why not (I would argue with myself)? Why doubt that a person who had fought so hard for her humanity might desire, above all else, the life of an ordinary human?

But is it ordinary to be so antisocial (I would argue back)? Of course she never got in touch with me. A couple of weeks after the party, I nerved myself up enough to call her office and suggest meeting for lunch. The brusqueness of that refusal took some getting over; I let a month go by before trying again. "I'm sorry," she said. "But what was it you wanted to discuss? Perhaps we could take care of it over the phone."

"The idea wasn't to discuss anything, particularly. I only thought—new people sometimes find it hard to make their way here at first, it's not a very friendly university. And then, naturally I'd like to—well, just talk. Get acquainted. Get to know you a bit."

"Thanks, but I'm tremendously busy, and in any event there's very little I could say." And then, after a pause: "Someone's come to the door. Thanks for ringing."

It was no good, she would have nothing to do with me, beyond speaking when we met on campus—I could, and did, force her to take that much notice of me. Where was she living? I looked it up, an address in the suburbs, not awfully far from mine. Once I pedaled past the building, a shabby older high-rise, but there was no way of telling which of the hundreds of windows might be hers. I put John up to questioning his committee acquaintance in Biology, learning in this way: that Sally had coolly repulsed every social overture from people in her department, without exception; that student gossip styled her a Britishly reserved but better-than-competent lecturer; that she was hard at work in the lab on some project she never discussed with anybody. Not surprisingly, her fellow biologists had soon lost interest. She had speedily trained us all to leave her alone.

The psych department lost interest also, not without a certain tiresome belaboring of me, jokes about making silk purses out of chimps' ears and Ugly Chimplings and the like. John overheard a sample of this feeble mailbox badinage one day and retorted with some heat, "Hey, Janet only said she's *human* in that book. If education made you nice and personable, I know lots of people around here besides Sally Barnes who could stand to go back to school." But John, embroiled in a romance with a first-year graduate student, now found Sally a dull subject himself; besides, what he had said was true. My thesis had not been invalidated, nor Carol Cheswick and the team at University College overrated. It was simply the case, in fact, that within six months of her arrival, Sally—billed in advance as an exotic ornament to the university—had compelled us all to take her for neither more nor less than the first-rate young microbiologist she had come among us to be.

My personal disappointment grew by degrees less bitter. But still I would see the silver coat and subduedly fashionable boots, all points and plastic, moving away across the quad and think: Lady, had it been given unto me to be the Chimp Child, by God I'd have made a better job of it than you do!

Spring came. Between the faculty club and the library, the campus forsythia erupted along its straggling branches, the azaleas flowered as usual a week earlier in the city than in my garden fifteen miles away. Ridley Creek, in the nearby state park, roared with rains and snowmelt and swarmed with stocked trout and bulky anglers; and cardinals and titmice, visible all winter at the feeders, abruptly began to sing. Every winter I used to lose interest in the park between the first of February and the middle of March; every spring rekindled my sense of the luck and privilege of having it so near. During the first weeks of trout season, the trails, never heavily used, were virtually deserted, and any sunny day my presence was not required in town I would stuff a sandwich, a pocket reader, and a blanket into a daypack and pedal to the park. Generally I stayed close to the trails, but would sometimes tough my way through some brambly thicket of blackberry or raspberry canes, bright with small new chartreuse-colored leaves, to find a private spot where I could take off my shirt in safety.

Searching for this sort of retreat in a tract of large beech trees one afternoon in April, I came carefully and painfully through a tangle of briars to be thunderstruck by the sight of young Professor Barnes where she seemed at once least and most likely to be: ten meters up in one of the old beeches. She was perfectly naked. She sat poised on a little branch, one shoulder sat against the smooth gray bole of the bare tree, one foot dangling, the opposite knee cocked on the branch, the whole posture graced by a naturalness that smote me with envy in the surreal second or two before she caught sight of me. She was rubbing herself, and seemed to be crying.

One after another, like blows, these impressions whammed home in the instant of my emerging. The next instant Sally's face contorted with rage, she screamed, snapped off and threw a piece of dead branch at me (and hit me, too, in the breastbone), and was down the tree and running almost faster than I could take in what had happened, what was still happening. While part of my brain noted with satisfaction, *She didn't hear me coming!* a different part galvanized my frenzied shouting: "No! Sally, for God's sake, stop! Stop! Come back here, I won't tell anybody, I won't, I swear! *Sally!*" Unable to move, to chase her, I could only go on yelling in this semihysterical vein; I felt that if she got away now, I would not be able to bear it. I'd have been heard all over that side of the park if there had been anybody to hear, outside the zone of noise created by the creek. It was the racket I was making, in fact, that made her come pelting back—that, and the afterthought that all her clothes were back there under the tree, and realizing I had recognized her.

"All right, I'm not going anywhere, now *shut up!*" she called in a low, furious voice, crashing through undergrowth. She stomped right up to me barefoot and looked me in the eye. "God damn it to hell. What will you take to keep your mouth shut?" Did she mean right now? But I *had* stopped shouting. My heart went right on lurching about like a tethered frog, though, and the next moment the view got brighter and began to drift off to the right. I sat down abruptly on something damp.

"I was scared witless you wouldn't come back. Wait a second, let me catch my breath."

"You're the one who wrote that book. Morgan," she said between her teeth, "God damn it to *hell.*" In a minute she sat down, too, first pushing aside the prickly stems unthinking. The neutral face that gave away nothing had vanished. Sally Barnes, angry and frightened, looked exactly as I had wished to see her look; incredibly, after so much fruitless fantasy, here we were in the woods together. Here she sat, scratching a bare breast with no more special regard than if it had been a nose or a shoulder. It was pretty overwhelming. I couldn't seem to pull myself together.

Sally's skin had turned much darker than mine already, all over —plainly this was not her first visit to the bare-branched woods. Her breasts were smallish, her three tufts of body hair reddish, and all her muscles large and smooth and well-molded as a gymnast's. I said what came into my head: "I was a fairly good tree-climber as a kid, but I could never have gotten up one with a trunk as thick as that, and those high, skinny branches. Do you think if I built my arms and shoulders up, lifted weights or something—I mean, would you teach me? Or maybe I'm too old," I said. "My legs aren't in such bad shape, I run a few kilometers three times a week, but the top half of my body is a flabby mess—"

"Don't play stupid games," Sally burst out furiously. "You had to come blundering in here today, you're the worst luck I ever had. I'm asking again: will you take money not to tell anyone you saw me? Or is there something else you want? If I can get it, you can have it, only you've *got* to keep quiet about seeing me out here like this."

"That's a rotten way to talk to people!" I said, furious myself. "I was blundering around in these woods for years before you ever set foot in them. And I'm sorry if you don't like my book, or is it just me you don't like? Or just psychologists? If it weren't for you, I probably wouldn't even *be* one." My voice wobbled up and down, I'd been angry with Sally for seven months. "Don't worry, I won't say anything. You don't need to bribe me."

"Yes, but you will, you see. Sooner or later you'll be at some dinner party, and someone will ask what the Chimp Child is like *really*"—I looked slantwise at her; this had already happened a couple of times—"and you won't be able to resist. 'There I was, walking along minding my own business, and whoever do you think I saw—stark naked and gone right up a tree like a monkey!' Christ," Sally said through her teeth, "I could *throttle* you. Everything's spoilt." She got up hastily; I could feel how badly she wanted to clobber me again.

But I was finally beginning to be able to think, and to call upon my expertise. "Well, then, make me *want* not to tell. Make it a question of self-interest. I don't want money, but I wasn't kidding: I'd absolutely love to be able to get around in a forest like a chimp does. Teach me to climb like one—like you do. If the story gets out, the deal's off. Couldn't you agree to that?"

Sally's look meant, "What kind of idiot do you take me for?" Quickly I said, "I know it sounds crazy, but all through my childhood—and most of my adolescence, too—for whatever wacky reason, I wanted in the *worst* way to be Tarzan! And for the past twenty years, I've gone on wanting even more to be *you*! I don't know why—it's irrational, one of those passions people develop for doing various weird things, being fans or collecting stamps or—I used to know a former world champion fly caster who'd actually gone fishing only a couple of times in his life!" I drew a deep breath, held it, let it out in a burst of words: "Look—even if I don't understand it, I *know* that directly behind *The Chimp Child and the Human Family*—and the whole rest of my career, for that matter—is this ten-year-old kid who'd give anything to be Tarzan swinging through the trees with the Great Apes. I can promise that so long as you were coaching me, you'd be safe. I'll never get a better chance to act out part of that fantasy, and it would be worth—just everything! One *hell* of a lot more than keeping people entertained at some dinner party, I'll tell you that!"

"You don't want to be me," said Sally in a flat voice. "I was right the first time; it's a stupid game you're playing at." She looked at me distastefully, but I could see that at any rate she believed me now.

The ground was awfully damp. I got up, starting to feel vastly better. Beech limbs webbed the sky; strong sunshine and birdsong poured through the web; it was all I could do, suddenly, not to howl and dance among the trees. I could see she was going to say yes.

Sally set conditions, all of which I accepted promptly. I was not to ask snoopy professional questions, or do any nonessential talking. At school we were to go on as before, never revealing by so much as a look or gesture that an association existed between us. I was not to tell *anybody*. Sally could not, in fact, prevent my telling people, but I discovered that I hadn't any desire to tell. My close friends, none of whom lived within 150 kilometers of the city, could guess I was concealing a relationship but figured I would talk about it when I got ready; they tended to suppose a married man, reason enough for secrecy. Sally and I both taught our classes, and Sally had her work in the lab, and I my private patients.

Once in midweek and once each weekend, we met in the beech grove; and so the "lessons" got under way.

I acquired some light weights and began a program of exercise to strengthen my arms, shoulders, chest, and back, but the best way to build up the essential muscles was to climb a lot of trees. Before long the calluses at the base of each finger, which I had carried throughout my childhood, had been re-created (and I remembered then the hardness of Sally's palm when I'd shaken hands with her at the cocktail party in September). Seeing how steadily my agility and toughness increased, Sally was impressed and, in spite of herself, gratified. She was also nervous; she'd had no intention of letting herself enjoy this companionship that had been forced upon her.

It was a queer sort of blackmail. I went along patiently, working hard and trying to make my company too enjoyable to resist; and in this way the spring semester ended.

Sally was to teach summer school, I to prepare some articles for publication and continue to see my patients through the summer. By June all the trout had been hooked and the beech woods had grown risky; we found more inaccessible places on the riding-trail side of the park where I could be put through my training-exercise routines. By the Fourth of July my right biceps measured thirty-seven centimeters and Sally had finally begun to relax in my presence, even to trust me.

That we shortly became lovers should probably surprise nobody. All the reports describe the pre-accident Sally as an affectionate child, and her family as a loving one. From my reading I knew that in moments of anxiety or fear, chimps reassure one another by touching, and that in placid ones they reaffirm the social bond by reciprocal grooming. Yet for a decade, ever since Carol Cheswick died and she'd gone up to Cambridge, Sally had protected herself strictly against personal involvements, at the cost of denying herself all emotional and physical closeness. Cheswick, a plump, middle-aged, motherly person, had hugged and cuddled Sally throughout their years together, but after Cheswick's death—sick of the pokings and peerings of psychologists and of the curious public, resentful and guilty about the secret life she had felt compelled to create for herself—Sally had simply done without. Now she had me.

Except for the very beginning, in London, there had always been a secret life.

She abruptly started to talk about it late one horribly hot afternoon, at the end of a workout. We had dropped out of the best new training tree, a century-old white oak, then shaken out a ragged army blanket, sat on it cross-legged, and passed a plastic canteen and a bunch of seedless grapes between us. I felt sticky and spent, but elated. Sally looked me over critically. "You're filling out quite well, it's hard to believe these are the same scrawny shoulders." She kneaded the nearer shoulder with her hard hand, while I carefully concealed my intense awareness that except to correct an error, she had never touched me anywhere before. The hand slipped down, gripped my upper arm. When I "made a muscle" the backs of her brown fingers brushed my pale-tan breast; our eyes met, and I said lightly, "I owe it all to you, coach," but went warmer still with pleasure and the rightness of these gestures, which had the feeling of a course correction.

Sally plucked several grapes and popped them in her mouth, looking out over the creek valley while she chewed. After a bit she said, "They let me go all to pot in London. All anybody cared about was guiding me out of the wilderness of ignorance, grafting my life at thirteen back onto the stump of my life at four and then making up for the lost years how they could. The lost years . . . mind you, they had their hands full, they all worked like navvies and so did I. But I'd got absolutely consumptive with longing for the bush before they brought Carol in, and she noticed and made them let me out for a fortnight's holiday in the countryside. I'd lost a lot of strength by then, but it was only just a year so it came back quick enough."

She stopped there, and I didn't dare say anything; we ate grapes and slapped mosquitoes. It was incredibly hot. After a bit, desperate to hear more, I was weighing the risks of a response when she went on without prodding:

"At University College, though, they didn't much care to have me swinging about in trees. I think they felt, you know, 'Here *we* are, slaving away trying to drag the ape kid into the modern world, and what does she do the minute our backs are turned but go dashing madly back to her savage ways.' Sort of, 'Ungrateful little beast.' They *never* imagined I might miss that benighted life, or anything about it, but when I read *Tarzan of the Apes* myself a few years later, the part toward the end where Tarzan strips off his suit and tie and shoes and leaps into the branches swearing he'll never, never go back—I cried like anything."

I said, "What could you do about it, though?" breaking Sally's no-questions rule without either of us noticing.

"Oh, on my own, not much. But Carol had a lot to say about what I should and shouldn't do. They respected her tremendously. And she was marvelous. After I'd got so I could talk and read pretty well, she'd take me to the South Downs on weekends and turn me loose. We had a tacit agreement that if she didn't ask, I needn't tell. We were so close, she certainly knew I was getting stronger and my hands were toughening up, but *she* never took the view that those years in the wild were best forgotten. She arranged for me to meet Jane Goodall once . . . I couldn't have borne it without her. I never should have left England while she lived. If it weren't for Carol—" For several minutes Sally's hand had been moving of its own accord, short rhythmic strokes that ceased abruptly when, becoming aware of this movement, she broke off her sentence and glanced—sharply, in alarm—at me.

I made a terrific effort to control my face and voice, a fisherman angling for the biggest trout in the pool. "She must have been remarkable."

For a wonder Sally didn't get up without a word and stalk away. Instead she said awkwardly, "I—do you mind very much my doing this? I've always done it—for comfort, I suppose—ever since I was small, and it's a bit difficult to talk about all these things . . . without . . ."

From the first day of training, I had determined never to let Sally force a contrast between us; I would adapt to her own sense of fitness out here. If she climbed naked, so would I, tender skin or not. If she urinated openly, and standing, so would I—and without a doubt there was something agreeable about spraddling beside Sally while our waters flowed. A civilized woman can still pass the whole length of her life without ever seeing another woman's urine, or genitalia, or having extended, repeated, and matter-of-fact exposure to another woman's naked body—and yet how many *men*, I had asked myself, ever gave these homely matters a second thought?

Then why on earth should we?

Certainly no woman had ever before done in my presence what Sally had been doing. Mentally, I squared my shoulders. "Why should I mind? Look, I'll keep you company"—suiting action to words with a sense of leaping in desperation into unknown waters, graceless but absolutely determined—"O.K.?"

It was the very last thing Sally had looked for. For a second I was afraid she thought I was ridiculing her in some incomprehensible way; but she only watched, briefly, before saying, "O.K. For a psychologist you're not a bad sort. The first bloody thing they did at that mission school was make me stop doing this in front of people.

"So anyway. Carol knew I was longing for the wild life, and knew it was important, not trivial or wrong, so she gave it back to me as well as she could. But she couldn't give me back"—her voice cracked as she said this—"the chimpanzees. The people I knew. And I did miss them dreadfully—certain ones, and living in the troop—the thing is, I was a child among them, and in a lot of ways it was a lovely life for a child, out there. The wild chimps are so direct and excitable, their feelings change like lightning, they're perfectly uninhibited—they squabble like schoolkids with no master about. And the babies are so sweet! But it's all very—very, you know, physical; and I missed it. I thought I should die with missing it, before Carol came." The grapes were all gone. Sally chucked the stem into the brambles and lay back on the blanket, left arm bent across her eyes, right hand rocking softly.

"Part of my training in London was manners and morals: to control myself, play fair, treat people politely whether I liked them or not. I'd *enjoyed* throwing tantrums and swatting the little ones when they got in my road, and screaming when I was furious and throwing my arms around everybody in reach when I was excited or happy, and being hugged and patted—like this," patting her genitals to demonstrate the chimpanzees' way of reassuring one another, "when I was upset. Chimps have no superego. It's hard to have to form one at thirteen. By then, pure selfishness without guilt is hard to conquer. Oh, I had a lot of selfishness to put up with from the others—I was very low-ranking, of course, being small and female—but I never got seriously hurt. And a knockabout life makes you tough, and then I had the Old Man for a protector as well." Sally lifted her arm and looked beneath it, up at me. "For a kid, most of the time, it was a pretty exhilarating life, and I missed it. And I missed," she said, "getting fucked. They were not providing any of that at University College, London."

"What?" My thumb stopped moving. "Ah—were you old enough? I mean, were the males interested, even though you didn't go pink?" I began to rub again, perhaps faster.

"For the last year or thereabouts—I'm not quite sure how long. It must have been, I don't know, pheromones in the mucus, or something in my urine, but I know it was quite soon after my periods started that they'd get interested in me *between* periods, when I would have been fertile, even without the swelling. I knew all about it, naturally; I'd seen plenty of copulating right along, as far back as I could remember. A pink female is a very agitating social element, so I'd needed to watch closely, because one's got to get out of the way, except while they're actually going at it. That's when all the little ones try to make them stop—don't ask me why," she added quickly, then grinned. "Sorry. That's one thing every primatologist has wanted to know." Sally's movements were freer now; watching, I was abruptly pierced by a pang of oddity, which I clamped down on as best I could. This was definitely not the moment for turning squeamish.

"It frightened me badly that first time; adult male chimps who want something don't muck about. When they work themselves up, you know, they're quite dangerous. I usually avoided them, except for the Old Man, who'd sort of adopted me not long after the troop took me in . . . any road the first time hurt, and then of course everybody always wants a piece of the action, and it went on for *days*. By the time it was over, I'd got terribly sore. But later . . . well, after I'd recovered from that first bout, I found it didn't really hurt anymore. In fact, I liked it. Quite a lot, actually, once I saw I needn't be frightened. The big males are frightfully strong, the only time I could ever dare be so close to so many of them was then, when I came in season, and one or another of them would sort of summon me over to him, and then they'd all queue up and press up behind me, one after another . . ."

More relieved than she realized at having broken the long silence at last, Sally went on telling her story; and of course, the more vividly she pictured for me her role in this scene of plausible bizarreness, elaborating, adding details, the more inevitable was the outcome of our own unusual scene. All the same, when the crisis struck us, more or less simultaneously, it left me for the moment speechless and utterly nonplussed, and Sally seemed hardly less flustered than I.

But after that momentary shock, we each glanced sidelong at each other's flushed, flummoxed face and burst into snorts of laughter; and we laughed together—breathlessly, raggedly, probably a little hysterically—for quite a while. And pretty soon it was all right. Everything was fine.

It was all right, but common sense cautioned that if Sally's defenses were too quickly breached, she would take fright. So many barriers had collapsed at once as to make me grateful for the several days that must elapse before the next coaching session. Still, when I passed her figure in its floppy navy smockdress and dark glasses on campus the following morning, I was struck as never before by the contrast between the public Sally and the powerful glowing creature nobody here had seen but me. A different person in her situation, I thought, would surely have exploited the public's natural curiosity: made movies, written books, gone on the lecture circuit, endorsed products and causes. Instead, to please her teachers, everything that had stubbornly remained Chimp Child in Sally as she learned and grew had had to be concealed, denied.

But because the required denial was a concealment and a lie, she had paid an exorbitant price for it; too much of what was vital in her had living roots in those eight years of wildness. Sally was genuinely fond of and grateful to the zealous psychologists who had given back her humanity. At the same time she resented them quite as bitterly as she resented a public interested only in the racier parts of her life in the wild and in her humanity not at all. One group starved her, the other shamed her. Resentments and gratitudes had split her life between them. She would never consent to display herself *as* the Chimp Child on any sort of platform, yet without the secret life she would have shriveled to a husk. When I surprised her in the park, she had naturally feared and hated me. Not any more.

Success despite such odds made me ambitious. I conceived a plan. Somehow I would find a way—become a way!—to integrate the halves of Sally's divided self; one day she would walk across this quad, no longer alone, wearing her aspect of the woods (though clothed and cleaner). I'd worked clinically with self-despising homosexuals, and with the children of divorced and poisonously hostile parents; Sally's case, though unique in one way, was common enough in others. Charged with purpose, I watched as the brisk, dark shape entered a distant building and swore a sacred oath to the Principle of Human Potential: I would finish the job, I would dedicate myself to the saving of Sally Barnes. Who but I could save her now? At that fierce moment I knew exactly how Itard had felt when finally, for the first time, he had succeeded in reducing Victor to the fundamental humanity of tears.

Saturday looked threatening, but I set off anyway for the park. The mid-afternoon heat was oppressive; I cut my muscle-loosening jog to a kilometer or two, then quartered through the woods to the training oak. Early as I was, Sally had come before me. I couldn't see her, high in the now dense foliage, but her clothing was piled in the usual place and I guessed she had made a day-nest at the top of that tree or one nearby, or was traveling about up there somewhere. After a long drink from the canteen I peeled off my own sweaty shorts, toweling shirt, shoes, and the running bra of heavy spandex, smeared myself with insect repellent, and dried my hands on my shirt. Then I crouched slightly, caught a heavy limb well over two meters above the ground and pulled myself into the tree.

For ten minutes I ran through a set of upper-body warmups with care and concentration; I'd pulled one muscle in my shoulder four times and once another in my back, before finding an old book on gymnastics explaining how to prevent (and treat) such injuries. The first few weeks I had worn lightweight Keds, and been otherwise generally scraped and skinned. But now my skin had toughened—I hadn't known it would do that—and greater strength made it easier to forgo the clambering friction of calves and forearms; now, for the most part, my hands and feet were all that came in contact with the bark. A haircut had nicely solved the problems of snarling twigs and obscured vision.

Warm and loose, I quickly climbed ten meters higher and began another series of strengthening and balancing exercises, swinging back and forth, hand over hand, along several slender horizontal limbs, standing and walking over a heavier one, keeping myself relaxed.

After half an hour of this, I descended to the massive lowest limb and practiced dropping to the ground, absorbing the shock elastically with both hands and both feet, chimp-style. Again and again I sprang into the tree, poised, and landed on the ground. I was doing quite well, but on about the fifteenth drop I bruised my hand on a rock beneath the leaf mold and decided to call it an afternoon; my hair was plastered flat with sweat, and I was as drenched as if I'd just stepped out of a shower. I had a long, tepid drink and was swabbing myself down with my shirt when Sally left the tree by the same limb, landed with a negligent, perfect pounce, came forward and—without meeting my eye—relieved me of the canteen, at the same time laying her free arm briefly across my shoulders. "That one's looking pretty good," she said, nodding at the branch to indicate my dropping-to-the-ground exercise. The arm slid off, she picked up the squirter of Tropikbug—"but did you ever see such monstrous mosquitoes in your life?"

"It's the humidity, I was afraid the storm would break before I could get through the drill. Maybe we better skip the rest and try to beat it home."

Sally squirted some repellent into her palm and wiped it up and down her limbs and over her brown abdomen. She squirted out some more. "Yours is all sweated off," she said, still not meeting my eye; and instantly Hugo Van Lawick's photographs of chimps soliciting grooming flashed into my mind, and I turned my shoulder toward Sally, who rubbed the bug stuff into it, then anointed the other shoulder, and my back and breasts and stomach for good measure, and then handed the flask dreamily to me, presenting her own back to be smeared with smelly goop. At that instant the first dramatic thunderclap banged above the park, making us both jump; and for a heart-stopping second Sally's outstretched arm clutched round me.

We bundled the blanket back into its plastic pouch and cached it, and pulled on clothes, while rain began to fall in torrents. My jogging shoes were clearly goners. I didn't bother to put on the bra, rolling it up on the run and sticking it inside my waistband. We floundered out of the trees in a furious commotion of wind and *crackle*-WHAM of lightning, and dashed in opposite directions for our parked cars. It took me fully fifteen minutes to reach mine, and twenty more to pedal home by roads several centimeters deep in rain, with the heater going full blast, and another half hour to take a hot shower and brew some tea. Then, wrapped in a bathrobe, I carried the tea tray and Jane Goodall's classic study *In the Shadow of Man* into the living room, and reread for the dozenth time the passages on the social importance of physical contact among wild chimpanzees.

Over and over, as I sat there, I relived the instant of Sally's instinctive quasi-embrace in the storm, and each time it stopped my breath. What must Sally herself be feeling then? What terrifying conflict of needs? She must realize, just as I did, that a torrent had begun to build that would sweep her carefully constructed defenses away, that she could not stop it now, that she must flee or be changed by what would follow.

When I thought of *change*, it was as something about to happen to Sally, though change was moving just as inexorably down upon me. Three or four times in my life, I've experienced that sense of *courting* change, of choosing my life from moment to moment, the awareness of process and passage that exalted me that evening but never before or since with such intensity. I alone had brought us to this, slowly, over months of time, as the delicate canoe is portaged and paddled to where the white water begins. Day by day we had picked up speed; now the stream was hurtling us forward together; now, with all our skill and nerve and strength, we would ride the current—we would shoot through. There is a word for this vivid awareness: existential.

If I feared anything then, it was that Sally might hurl herself out of the canoe.

The next day was not a regular coaching day, but the pitch of nervous excitement made desk work impossible. I drove to the park in mid-afternoon to jog, and afterward decided, in preference to more disciplined routines, to practice my traveling-from-tree-to-tree. My speed and style at this—that of a very elderly, very arthritic ape—was still not half bad (I thought) for a human female pushing forty, though proper brachiation still lay well beyond my powers. The run, as usual, had settled me down. The creek, still aboil with muddy runoff from the storm, was racketing along through a breezy, beautiful day. I chose an ash with a low fork, stuffed my clothes into my fanny pack, buckled it on, and started to climb.

I hadn't expected to find Sally at the training tree, but saw her without surprise—seated below me, cross-legged on the grubby blanket—when, an hour later, I had made my way that far. She stood up slowly while I descended the familiar pattern of limbs and dropped from the bottommost one. Again without surprise I saw that she looked awful, shaky and sick, that assurance had deserted her—and understood then that *whatever* happened now would not surprise me, that I was ready and would be equal to it. While I stood before Sally, breathing hard, unfastening the buckle, the world arranged itself into a patterned whole.

Then, as I let the pack fall, Sally crouched low on the blanket, whimpering and twisting with distress. I knelt at once and gathered her into my arms, holding her firmly, all of her skin close against all of mine. She clutched at me, pressed her face into my neck. Baffled moaning sounds and sobs came out of her. She moved inside this embrace; still moaning, eyes squeezed shut, her blind face searched until she had taken the nipple and end of my left breast into her mouth. As she sucked and mouthed at this, with her whole face pushed into the breast, her body gradually unknotted, relaxed, curled about mine, so I could loosen my hold to stroke her with the hand not suporting her head. Soon, to relieve the strain of the position, I pressed the fanny pack—I could just reach it—into service as a pillow and lay down on my side, still cradling Sally's head.

Time passed, or stopped. The nipple began to be sore.

At last, seemingly drained, she rolled away onto her back. Her face was smeared with mucus and tears; I worked my shirt out of the pack one-handed and dried it. At once she rolled back again, pushing herself against me with a long, groaning sigh. "The past couple of nights, God, I've had all sorts of dreams. Not bad dreams, not exactly, but—there was this old female in the troop, maybe her baby died, it must have done . . . I'd completely forgotten this. This must have been when they first found me. *She* found me, I think . . . I think I'd been alone in the forest without food long enough to be utterly petrified and apathetic with terror. But when she found me . . . I remember she held me against her chest and shoved the nipple in—maybe just to relieve her discomfort, or to replace her own child with a substitute, who knows. I think I would certainly have died except for that milk, there was such all-encompassing fear and misery. I don't know how many weeks or months she let me nurse. She couldn't have lived very long, though."

Sally weighed my breast in her hand. "Last night I dreamed I was in some terrible place, so frightened I couldn't move or open my eyes, and somebody . . . picked me up and held me, and then I was suckling milk from a sort of teat, and felt, oh, ever so much better, a great flood of relief. Then I opened my eyes and saw we were in the bush—I recognized the actual place—but it was *you*, the person holding me was you! You had a flat chest with big rubbery chimpanzee nipples" —lifting the tender breast on her palm—"and a sort of chimp face, but you were only skin all over, and I realized it was you."

I put my hand firmly over hers, moved it down along her forearm. "How did you feel when you knew it was me?"

"Uncomfortable. Confused. Angry." Then reluctantly: "Happy, too. I woke up, though, and then mostly felt just astonished to remember that that old wet nurse had saved my life and I'd not given her a single thought for twenty-five years." She lay quiet under my caressing: neck, breasts, stomach, flank; her eyes closed again. "What's queer is that I should remember *now*, but not when Carol first took charge of me, and not when I first read *Tarzan*, even though the Tarzan story's nearly the same as mine. I don't understand why now and not then."

"Do you feel you need to? I mean, does it seem important to understand?"

"I don't know." She sounded exhausted. "I certainly don't feel like even trying to sort it all out now."

"Well. It'll probably sort itself out soon enough, provided you don't start avoiding whatever makes these disturbing memories come back."

Sally opened her eyes and smiled thinly. "Start avoiding you, you mean. No. I shan't, never fear." She snuggled closer, widening and tilting herself; in my "therapist" frame of mind I tried to resist this, but my hand—stroking on automatic for so long—slid downward at once of its own volition, and I ceased at the same instant to ignore a response I'd been blocking without realizing it for a good long while. I was still lying on my side, facing Sally; my top knee shifted without permission, and seconds later another afternoon had culminated in a POW that made my ears ring.

I was destined to know very well indeed the complicated space between Sally's muscular thighs, far better than I would ever know the complicated space inside her head, but that first swift unforeseen climax had a power I still recall with astonishment. My sex life, though quite varied, had all been passed in the company of men. I'd never objected to homosexuality in any of its forms, on principle and by professional conviction, but before that day no occasion of proving this personally had happened to occur. As for Sally, her isolation had allowed for no sex life at all with humans male *or* female; and though the things we did together meant, if possible, even more to her than they did to me, she didn't really view them in a sexual light. To Sally's way of thinking, *sex* was a thing that happened more or less constantly during several days each month, and had to do with dark, shaggy, undeniable maleness forcing itself upon you—with brief, rough gusto—from behind. She continued to miss this fear-laced excitement just as before. Our physical involvement, which was regularly reinforced, and which often ended as it had that afternoon, was a source of immeasurable pleasure and solace to her, but she viewed it as the natural end of a process that had more to do with social grooming than with sex.

But for me it was a revelation, and late in August, when the coarse, caterpillar-chewed foliage hung dispiritedly day after day in the torpid air, I went away for a week to remind myself of what ordinary sex was like with an ordinary man. Afterwards I returned to Sally having arrived at a more accurate view of the contrast: not as pudendum versus penis, but as the mythic versus the mundane. Sleeping with my comfy old flame had been enjoyable as ever, but he was no wild thing living a split life and sharing the secret half with me alone.

"Are you in love with somebody?" Bill asked me on our last evening together. "Is that what's up with you? It's got to have something to do with your being in this incredible physical shape—wait! don't tell me! you've conceived a fatal passion for a jock!" I laughed and promised to let him in on the secret when I could; and though his eyes were sharp with curiosity, he didn't press the point. And for that, when the time came, Bill was one of half a dozen friends I finally did tell about Sally.

But even then, after it could no longer matter materially, I was unable to answer his question. Was I in love with Sally, or she with me? No. Or yes. For more than a year I worked hard to link her with the human community, she to school me for a role in a childhood fantasy of irresistible (and doubtless neurotic) appeal. Each of us was surely fated to love what the other symbolized; how could we help it? But I've wondered since whether I was ever able to see Sally as anything but the Chimp Child, first and last. For each of us, you see, there was only *one*. In such a case, how can individual be told from type, how can the love be personal? And when not personal, what does "love" mean, anyway?

Whatever it was or meant, it absorbed us, and I was as happy that summer as ever in my life. As the season waned and the fall semester began, my skills and plans both moved forward obedient to my will. After workouts we would spread the blanket on its plastic ground sheet and ourselves across the blanket, giving our senses up to luxuriant pleasure, while the yellow leaves tapped down about us, all but inaudibly.

And afterward we'd talk. It was at this stage that bit by bit I was able to breach Sally's quarantine by turning the talk to our work: her research, my theoretical interests, gifted or maddening students, departmental politics, university policy. Even then, when I encountered Sally on campus, her indifference toward me as toward everyone appeared unchanged; and at first these topics annoyed and bored her. But bit by bit I could see her begin to take an interest in the personalities we worked among, form judgments about them, distinguish among her students. To my intense delight, colorful chimp personalities began to swim up from her memory, with anecdotes to illustrate them, and she spoke often of Carol Cheswick, and—less frequently—of the team of psychologists at University College.

Cambridge provided no material of this sort, for by the time the church fellowship had sent her up, Cheswick was dead and Sally left to devise ways of coping on her own with the nosy public while protecting her privacy and the purposes it served. Antisocial behavior had proved an effective means to that end at Cambridge, as it was to do subsequently at our own university. She had concentrated fiercely on her studies. In subjects that required an intuitive understanding of people—literature, history, the social sciences—her schoolwork had always been lackluster; in mathematics and hard science, she had excelled from the first. At Cambridge she read biology. Microbiology genuinely fascinated her; now, thus late in her career, Sally was discovering the pleasures of explaining an ongoing experiment to a listener only just able to follow. In fact, she was discovering gossip and shop talk.

By the time cold temperatures and bare trees had forced me to join a fitness center and Sally to work out alone in a thermal skinsuit and thin pigskin gloves and moccasins, she was able to say: "I remember that old mother chimpanzee because she saved me out of a killing despair, and so did you. So did you, Jan. That day you discovered me crying in the beech, remember? I actually believed I was coping rather well then, but the truth is I was dying. I might really have died, I think—like a houseplant, slowly, of heat and dryness and depleted soil." And to me as well, this seemed no more than the simple truth.

That winter, one measure of our progress was that I could sometimes coax Sally to my house. Had close friends of mine been living nearby, or friendly neighbors or relatives, this could not have been possible; as it was she would leave her pedalcar several blocks away and walk to the house by varying routes, and nearly always after dark. But once inside, with doors locked and curtains drawn, we could be easy, eat and read, light a fire to sit before, snuggle in bed together. In winter, outdoor sex was impractical and we could never feel entirely safe from observation in the denuded woods, whose riding trails wound through and through it. And Sally's obsessive concealment of the fact that she had made a friend, and that her privacy could therefore be trespassed upon, seemed to weaken very little despite the radical changes she had passed through.

Truly, I found myself in no hurry to weaken it. I could not expect, nor did I wish, to have Sally to myself forever. Indeed my success would be measured by how much more fully she could learn to function in society—develop other friendships and activities and so on—eventually. It is true that I could not quite picture this, though I went on working toward it in perfect confidence that the day would come. Yet for the time being, like a mother who watches her child grow tall with mingled pride and sorrow, I kept our secret willingly and thought *eventually* would be here soon enough.

As spring drew closer, Sally began sleeping badly and to be troubled again by dreams. She grew oddly moody also. All through the winter she had dressed and slipped out to her car in the dark; now I would sometimes wake in the morning to find her still beside me. Several times her mutterings and thrashings disturbed me in the night, and then I would soothe and hold her till we both dozed off again. That a crisis was brewing looked certain, but though the dreams continued for weeks, she soon stopped telling me anything about them and said little else to reveal the nature of her distress. In fact, I believed I knew what the trouble was. The first dreams, those she had described, were all about Africa and England and seemed drenched in yearning for things unutterably dear, lost beyond recall. They seemed dreams of mourning—for her parents, her lost wild life in Tanzania, her teacher. Events of the past year, I thought, had rendered the old defenses useless. She could not escape this confrontation any longer.

I was very glad. Beyond the ordeal of grief lay every possibility for synthesizing the halves of her life into one coherent human whole. I believed that Cheswick's death in Sally's twenty-third year had threatened to touch off a mourning for all these losses at once, and that to avoid this she had metamorphosed into the Cambridge undergraduate of my scrapbook: intellectual, unsociable, dull. "You're a survivor," I had told her one night that winter, and she had replied, "Up to a point." Now it seemed she felt strong enough at last to do the grieving and survive *that*, and break through to a more complete sort of health and strength.

Either that, or the year's developments had weakened her ability to compensate, and she would now be swiftly destroyed by the forces held so long in check; but I thought not.

Weeks passed while Sally brooded and sulked; our partnership, so long a source of happy relief, had acquired ambiguities she found barely tolerable. Once she did avoid me for nine days despite her promise—only to turn up, in a state of feverish lust, for a session as unlike our lazy summertime trysts as possible. Afterward she was heavy and silent, then abruptly tearful. I bore with all this patiently enough, chiefly by trying to foresee what might happen next and what it might mean, and so was not much surprised when she said finally, "I've decided not to teach this summer after all. I want to go to England for a month or so, after I've got the experiment written up."

I nodded, thinking, *Here it is.* Huge green skunk cabbages were thick now in the low places on the floor of the April woods, and fly fisherfolk thick along and in the creek; once again we had the mild, bare, windy, hairy-looking forest to ourselves, and were perched together high in a white-topped sycamore hung with balls. "Sounds like a good plan, though I'll miss you. Where to, exactly, or have you decided yet?"

"Well—London for a start, and Cambridge, and here and there. I might just pop in on my sister, not that there's much point to *that.*" Sally's sister Helen had married the vicar of a large church in Liverpool and produced four children. "But about missing me. You like England, you're always telling me. Why not come along?"

"Really?" I hadn't foreseen everything, it seemed. "Of course I'll come, I'd love to. Or no, wait a minute"—squirming round on the smooth limb to watch her face—"have you thought this through? I mean, suppose the papers get wind of it? 'Chimp Child Returns to Foster Country.' Or even: 'Chimp Child, Friend, Visit England.' If we're traveling together, people are bound to *see* us together—sure you want to risk it?"

"Oh well, so what," said the Chimp Child, for all the world as if she hadn't been creeping up to my house under cover of night all winter long. "I want to talk to the blokes at the university, Snyder and Brill and a couple of others—get them to show me the files on *me.*" She swung free of the branch and dangled by one hand to hug me with the opposite arm. "Sorry I've been such a bore lately. There's something I'm suddenly madly curious about, I've had the most appalling dreams, night after night, for weeks." She swung higher in the tree, climbing swiftly by her powerful arms alone, flashing across gaps as she worked her way to the high outermost branches and leapt outward and downward into another tree with the action I loved to see. "Right," she called back across the gulf between us, "get to work then, you lazy swine. We'll put on a show for Helen's kids that'll stop traffic all over the ruddy parish."

And so we flew to England; and now my part of the story is nearly finished.

Sally did not quite feel ready to come out, as it were, to the extent of going anywhere in my company at school, though she'd smile now with some naturalness when our paths would cross there, and even exchange a few words in passing. We arrived separately at the airport. But from that point on, we were indeed "traveling together," and she never tried to make it seem otherwise.

She had wanted a couple of days in Cambridge before tackling the records of her unique education, as if to work backward in time by bearable degrees, and so it was together that we climbed the wide stairs on a Tuesday afternoon early in June to look into her first-year room in Newnham College. Unfortunately the present occupant knew the Chimp Child had once been quartered in her room and recognized Sally immediately; she must have felt perplexed and dismayed at the grimness of the famous pilgrim, who glared round without comment, refused a cup of tea, and stalked away leaving me to render thanks/ apologies on behalf of us both. I caught Sally on the stairs. Nothing was said till we had proceeded the length of two green courts bordered with flower beds and come out into the road. Then: "God, I was wretched here!" she burst out. "I went through the whole three years in a—in a chromatic daze, half unconscious except in the lab, and going through that door again—it was as if all the color and warmth began to drain out of a hole in the floor of the day, and I could only stand helplessly watching. The very *smell* of the place means nothing but death to me. What bloody, bloody waste."

And "What a waste," more thoughtfully the next morning, as we walked back to the station from our bed-and-breakfast across the river and the common with its grazing Friesians and through the Botanical Gardens. "One sees why other people could manage to be so jolly and smug here, while I'd go skulking down to Grantchester at five in the morning to work out in the only wood for miles, terrified every day I should be caught out, and skulking back to breakfast every day relieved, like an exhibitionist who thinks, 'Well, there's one more time I got away with it.' " A few minutes later she added, "Of course it got much better when I was working on my thesis . . . only those years don't seem real at *all* when I try to remember them. All I can remember is the lab, I expect that's why."

"Why it got better, or why it's unreal?"

"Both, very likely."

She was pensive on the train. I fell asleep and woke as we were pulling into Liverpool Street, feeling tired and headachy, the beginnings of the flu that put me to bed for a crucial week when I might otherwise have done something, just by staying well, to affect the course of events. By late afternoon of that Wednesday, I felt too miserable to be embarrassed at imposing myself on Dr. Snyder's wife and filling their tiny guest room with my awkward germiness. For four or five days, I had a dry, wheezy cough and a fever so high that Mrs. Snyder was beginning to talk rather worriedly of doctors; then the fever broke and my head, though the size of a basketball, no longer burned, and I rallied enough to take in that Sally was gone.

She had spent the early days of my illness at University College, reading, asking occasional questions, searching—as it seemed—for something she couldn't describe but expected to recognize when she found it. Late on the fourth day, the day my temperature was highest, she came in and sat on the bed. "Listen, Jan. I'm off to Africa tomorrow."

I swam wearily to the surface. "Africa? But . . . don't you have to get, uh, inoculations or something? Visas?" I didn't wonder, within the remoteness of my fever, why she was going. Nor did I much care that evidently she would be going without me.

"Only cholera and yellow fever, and I've had them. Before we left, just in case; and yesterday afternoon I bagged the last seat on a tourist charter to Dar es Salaam. The flight returns in a fortnight, by which time you should be fit again, and we can go on up north then or wherever you like." When I didn't reply, she added, unnecessarily, "I've got to visit the school, Malosa School, and sort of stare the forest in the face again. It's terribly important, though I can't say just why. Maybe when I've got back, when you're better. Only, I've made my mind up to take this chance while it's going, because I do feel I've absolutely got to go through with it, as quick as I can."

My eyes ached. I closed them, shutting out the floating silhouette of Sally's head and shoulders. "I know. I wish . . ."

"Never mind. It'll be all right. Sorry I didn't tell you before, but first I wanted to make sure." I felt her hand beneath my pajama jacket. "God, you're *hot*," she said, surprised. "Perhaps I ought to leave it till you're a bit better."

Distantly amused at this display of superego, I said, "You know a fever's always highest at night, old virologist. Anyway, you can't do any good here. We'll have a doctor in soon if it doesn't go down." I made a truly tremendous effort. "It's probably a good idea, Sally, the trip. I hope you can find whatever it is you're looking for." Clumsily I patted the hand inside my pajamas. "But don't miss the plane coming back, I'll be dying to hear what happened."

"I shan't, I promise you," she said with relief; and when I woke the next morning, she had gone.

We know that Sally reached Dar es Salaam after an uneventful flight, spent the night in an airport hotel, flew Air Malawi to the Chileka airfield the next morning, and hired a driver to take her the 125 kilo-meters overland to Machinga and the Malosa Secondary School, where she was greeted with pleased astonishment by those of the staff who remembered her—everyone, of course, knew of her connection with the school. She stayed there nearly a week, questioning people about the details of her early childhood and of exactly what had happened when the church officials brought her in, in the weeks before she had been whisked to London. She spent hours prowling about the grounds and buildings, essentially the same as thirty years before despite some modest construction and borrowed the school's Land Rover several times to drive alone into the countryside of the Shire Highlands and the valley beyond. Her manner had been alternately brusque and preoccupied, and she had impressed them all as being under considerable strain.

The school staff confirmed that Sally had been driven back to Chileka by a couple, old friends of her parents, who at her request had dropped her at the terminal without coming in to see her off. She had told them she intended to fly back to Dar that evening in order to catch her charter for London the next day, and that she hated a dragged-out good-bye; the couple had no way of knowing that her ticket had specified a two-week stay abroad. Inside the terminal she bought a round-trip ticket for Ujiji, in Tanzania.

From Ujiji a helicopter shuttle took her to Kogoma on Lake Tanganyika. Once there, Sally had made inquiries, then gone straight to the town's tiny branch of Bookers Ltd., a safari agency operating out of a closet-sized cubbyhole in the VW dealership. She told the Bookers agent—a grizzled old Indian—that she wanted to hire two men to help her locate the place where a plane had crashed in the mountains east of the lake, some thirty years before. She produced detailed directions and maps; and the agent, though openly doubtful whether the wreckage would not have rusted into the ground after so long, agreed for a stiff price to outfit and provision the trip. He assigned his cousin to guide her, and a native porter. Forty-eight hours later this small expedition set off into the mountains in the agency's battered four-wheel-drive safari van.

The cousin had parked the van beside the road of ruts that had brought them as far as roads could bring them toward the area marked on Sally's maps, much nearer than any road had approached it on the day of the crash, but still not near. They had then followed a footpath into the forest for several kilometers before beginning to slash a trail away from it westward, toward the site where the plane had gone down. Something like fifty kilometers of rain-forested mountainous terrain had to be negotiated on foot, a difficult, unpleasant, suffocating sort of passage. Sally must have been assailed by frustration at the clumsiness of their progress; the guide called her a bad-tempered bitch, probably for good reason. On the third morning her patience had evidently snapped. When the men woke up, Sally was not in camp. They waited, then shouted, then searched, but she never replied or reappeared. And I knew what they could not: that she must have slipped away and taken to the trees, flying toward a goal now less than fifteen kilometers distant.

I had gone out to meet Sally's plane, due into Gatwick on the same day the reporters got hold of the story of her disappearance. When she proved not to be aboard, and to have sent no word, all my uneasiness broke out like sweat, and back in the city I must have hurried past any number of news agents before the *Guardian* headline snatched at my attention: WILD WOMAN MISSING IN JUNGLE, SEARCH CONTINUES. I bought a paper and stood shaking on the pavement to read: "Dodoma (Tanzania), Tuesday. Sally Barnes, the wild girl brought up by chimpanzees, has been missing in the mountains of Tanzania since Friday . . . two companions state . . . no trace of the Chimp Child . . . police notified and a search party . . ." and finally: "Searchers report sighting several groups of wild chimpanzees in the bush near the point of her disappearance."

All the rest is a matter of record. Day by day the newspapers repeated it: No trace, No trace, and at last, Presumed dead. The guide and porter were questioned but never tried for murder. In print and on the video news, it was noted that Dr. Barnes had vanished into the jungle only a few kilometers east of the spot where she had emerged from it twenty years earlier. Investigators quickly discovered that Sally and I had been together in Cambridge and London, and I, too, was forced to submit to questioning; I told them we had met on the plane and spent a few days as casual traveling companions, and that when I fell ill, her friends had kindly taken me in. I denied any closer connection between us, despite my having studied her case professionally —mentioning that she was well known at the university for her solitary ways. Sally herself had said nothing in particular to the Snyders about us, and I had been too sick. No one was alive in all the world to contradict the essential elements of this story, and, as it appeared to lead nowhere, they soon let me alone. (Some years later, however, I told Dr. Snyder the whole truth.)

It developed that no one had any idea why Sally had gone to Tanzania, why she was looking for the site of the plane crash.

For me that fall was hellish. By the time I returned to the States, only a few days before the new semester was to get under way, Sally's apartment—the apartment I had never seen, though she had called me from it two or three times during the final weeks of spring—had been stripped of its contents by strangers and her effects shipped to the Liverpool sister. At school, people were overheard to suggest, only half jokingly, that Sally had rejoined the chimps and was living now in the jungle, wild again. Such things were freely voiced in my presence; indeed, the loss of Sally, so shocking, so complete, was the more difficult to accept because not a single person on my side of the Atlantic could have the least suspicion that I had lost her.

My acting, I believe, was flawless. Though I went dazedly about my work, nobody seemed to see anything amiss. But might-have-beens tormented me. Save for my interference, Sally would almost certainly still have been alive. Or (more excruciating by far), had she not met defeat in the jungle, her search would almost certainly have left her healed of trauma, able to fit the halves of her life together. I had nearly freed her; now she was dead, the labor come to nothing, the child stillborn. I did believe she was dead. Yet I felt as angry with her, at times, as if she had purposely abandoned and betrayed me, disdained the miracle of healing I had nearly brought off—as if she had really chosen to return to the wild. For now neither of us could ever, ever complete the crossing into those worlds each had been training the other to enter for the preceding year.

I did not see how I was going to survive the disappointment, nor could I imagine what could possibly occupy, or justify, the rest of my life. The interlude with Sally had spoiled me thoroughly for journeyman work. It would not be enough, any longer, to divide my time between educating healthy minds and counseling disturbed ones. Long before that bleak winter was out, I had begun to cast about fretfully for something else to do.

This document has been prepared in snatches, over many evenings, by kerosene lanternlight in my tent in the Matangawe River Nature Reserve overlooking Lake Malawi, 750 kilometers northwest across the immense lake from Sally's birthplace. The tent is set up inside a chimp-proof cage made of Cyclone fencing and corrugated iron. Outside, eleven chimpanzees of assorted ages and stages of reacclimatization to independent survival in the wild are sleeping (all but the newest arrival, who is crying to get in). A few of these chimps were captured as infants in the wild; the rest are former subjects of language and other learning experiments, ex-laboratory animals or animals who were reared in homes until they began to grow unmanageable.

This may seem an unlikely place in which to attempt the establishment of a free-living population of rehabilitant chimpanzees, for the ape has been extinct in Malawi for a couple of centuries at least, and the human population pressure is terrific, the highest in Africa. In fact, to "stare the forest in the face," Sally was forced to go on back to Tanzania, where there was (and still is) some riverine forest left standing. Yet private funding materialized, and I've been here since the reserve was created, nearly fifteen years. Despite some setbacks and failures— well, there were bound to be some!—the project is doing very well indeed. At this writing, thirty-four chimps have mastered the course of essential survival skills and moved off to establish breeding, thriving communities on their own in the reserve. For obvious reasons these societies fascinate the primatologists, who often come to study them. We've lost a few to disease and accidents, and two to poachers, but our success, considering the problems inherent to the enterprise, might even be called spectacular. We've been written up in *National Geographic* and the *Smithsonian*, which in primate studies is how you know when you've arrived, and similar projects in several more suitable West African countries have been modeled on ours.

I started alone, with three adolescent chimpanzee "graduates in psychology" from my university who, having outgrown their usefulness along with their tractable childhoods, faced long, dull lives in zoos or immediate euthanasia. Now a staff of eight works with me: my husband, John (yes, the same John), and seven graduate students from my old department and from the Department of Biology, which used to be Sally's. She would be pleased with my progress in brachiation, though arthritis in my hands and shoulders has begun to moderate my treetop traveling with my charges. (That skill, incidentally, has given me a tactical edge over every other pioneer in the field of primate rehabilitation.)

To all the foregoing I will add only that I have found this work more satisfying than I can say. And that very often as I'm swinging along through lush forest in the company of four or five young chimps, "feeding" with them on new leaves and baobab flowers, showing them how to build a sturdy nest in the branches, I know a deep satisfaction that now, at last, there's no difference that matters between Sally and me.

Cage 37

*   *   *

Wayne Wightman

Wayne Wightman has contributed a dozen stories to F&SF over the last six years. He is one of our most reliable writers, in the sense that he is always entertaining without repeating himself. A Wightman story can be relentlessly grim or totally lighthearted. Here is an example of the latter, a fast and funny tale about a high school science project that begins in a haunted house and ends up in some very odd places indeed.

*   *   *

I TRIED to ignore the screaming while Ray, the class skinhead, sliced open another rat and snipped out its cherry-sized heart before it stopped beating. This was his end-of-the-year science project to demonstrate how the Aztecs did surgery, and Mr. Boren Zick, our fundamentalist sub-head teacher, stood beside him and nodded his approval. Zick was about thirty-five, but he looked like a worn-out fifty—mealy-skinned, soft-bodied, and he smelled like a Salvation Army store.

"Quickly, Ray, quickly now. Hmm," as he studied Ray's mutilation and pushed his wire-rimmed glasses up his oily nose. Zick wore string ties and white shirts and usually had a fat red pimple somewhere on his face. Today it was on the side of his nose, and his glasses were always sliding over it. I imagined swarms of meat-eating bacteria churning around inside his pustule, eating him alive. Today he also had rat-blood splatters across his pen-filled pocket protector and the right side of his shirt.

Skinhead Ray held up the rat's heart, and all over the room, girls were shrieking and grabbing at their faces. All except for Andrea, Ray's frilly girlfriend—she sat next to me and leaned over and displayed her six amazing inches of tight-boobed cleavage and the tops of her tan nipples. Tits and blood and screaming. It was a complicated scene. I had heard that being a teenager was difficult, but it didn't seem to me that adults ever talked about going through stuff like this.

"There it is," Ray said, holding the little heart up in front of his face. Ray was a sect leader of the Rude Shitz, so he was probably used to doing this kind of thing. Rat blood streamed down through his fingerless gloves and under his inch-thick wristwatch cassette-player bracelet. "I think it's still beating." He frowned and focused his narrow eyes on it. "Well. . . ." He shook it twice. "It *was* beating. It quit," he said accusatorily and threw it hard into the porcelain sink, where it hit with a wet thunk.

"Must have been a bunch of sick rats," Zick said, snuffling and pushing his glasses up his nose and over his pimple. He grimaced a little.

"Can I have another one, please?" Ray asked. He looked at me and grinned. "Maybe if I *dinked* it around a little, I could get a new *slant* on it."

"I don't know," Zick said thoughtfully, scratching the oily cleft in his chin and then straightening the two strings of his tie. Blood smeared from the pen protector across to his buttons. "We have only two rats left."

"Maybe I could use a different *slope* with the razor blade," he said, looking at me.

Andrea was still leaning over, fiddling around with the pink shoe box she had under her desk and threatening to spill her boobs in my direction. Ray didn't notice—and he had become well known over the years for bopping anyone who even thought nude thoughts about his girlfriends. And Andrea inspired nude thoughts. Andrea inspired problems standing up at the end of class. I had known her and Ray since fifth grade, and they had always been the same—except Ray's fists and Andrea's boobs were all bigger now.

"I think this is cruel," a girl whined from one of the front rows. "Ray's already got to kill three today, and I need one for my project."

"This is *science*," Zick said stiffly, pushing up his wire-rimmed glasses and smearing rat blood on the side of his nose. "We were made the lords of our world. We can do anything we want with nature. Eighth Psalm. 'Thou makest man master over all thy creatures; thou hast put everything under his feet . . . all the wild beasts, the birds in the air and the fish in the sea.' Read it and weep, my tenderhearted friends."

"Could I please use another rat?" Ray said politely.

"Certainly," Zick said. Then he glanced at his wristwatch and shook his head. "Well, I don't know if we have time to kill another one today, Ray. And we need to save one for Cindy."

"I bet I could do better on a cat," Ray said. "I need something bigger. Maybe it wouldn't get so *gooked* up when I slice it open." He glanced at me again while Andrea swung her chest and made a soft kissing noise at me.

"A cat, hm?" Zick turned to the class and pushed his glasses up his nose. "Anyone have a cat they want to donate?"

"I bet Dell does," Ray said. "He's got a whole houseful of the things."

Zick looked at me. "Dell, do you have a cat you don't need?"

"No," I said, "I don't." I knew I was going to get in trouble, and I wanted to go to college in the fall with a nice-looking transcript, but the idea of Ray killing more animals was something I figured even a teenager shouldn't have to put up with. "I don't have any cats I don't need," I said, "and if Ray kills another animal, I'm going to report what's been going on in this class to the SPCA." My throat tightened up, and I barely squeaked out the last word.

Ray feigned shock, and Mr. Zick smiled. "Ah," he said. "So we have here an animal rights fanatic. I see. A defender of dumb animals. Do you think animals have souls, Dell? Don't you believe what it says in Psalms? Are you an atheist?"

Behind his back, Ray made his eyebrows dance as he jammed an index finger in and out of his other fist.

"Do you think the lives of dumb animals are more important than human knowledge, Dell? Do you think pussycats have human emotions, Mr. Honor List Student?"

"I don't think animals should be killed for fun."

Andrea whispered to me, "You can kill mine for fun anytime." She had her big purse and her pink shoe box up on her desk now.

"If I promise not to enjoy it," Ray said, "can I open up a couple of cats tomorrow, Mr. Zick? If the Aztecs did it, I know I can." Zick wasn't looking at him, and, like a lizard, Ray flicked out his tongue a couple of times and grinned.

Andrea whispered, "You can open mine up anytime, Dell."

Zick ignored Ray and focused on me. "It is in the nature of animals to kill each other. Our Lord gave us the same right. The greater eat the lesser, and in the world, we are the greater."

"*I* ain't going to eat these rats!" Ray yukked.

The class laughed with him, but Zick kept staring at me. "You objected to my presentation on the creation of the universe, Mr. Honor Student, and you insisted on believing in evolution, despite the overwhelming evidence I presented to the contrary. I think we have a failure in communication here."

"I just did book reports on some books I'd read, sir." Calling him "sir" made me want to gag, but if I got anything less than a "C" in the class, I'd have to retake it in college.

Zick pushed his glasses up on his oily nose and grimaced as they bumped over his pimple. I felt a little weird being on the side of the bacteria, but today it seemed natural. He planted his hands on the worktable and leaned forward. Light gleamed on his slick face, and the mutilated body lay soaked in blood in front of his belt buckle. "You wrote those things to antagonize me, didn't you? You read those books just because they contradicted me."

"Maybe he just wanted to get another *slant* on it," Ray said.

"You could get me slanted anytime," Andrea whispered. "Or standing up, if you want."

I was having a tough time concentrating on anything, and I had the feeling that Zick was about to unload on me. I felt like an adult who needed a drink.

"Class," he said, "you all have the final projects schedule I gave you last week, and Dell is scheduled for a week from Friday—is that not so, Dell?"

I nodded. Out of the corner of my eye, I could see that Andrea had propped up her purse on her shoe box so Ray and Zick couldn't see, and had then slipped one of her hands under the breast nearest me. She was fondling herself. Why was she doing this to me? Ray would kill me if he saw her.

"You could do this," she breathed.

"Well, class," Zick said, "the schedule has been changed. Dell, you're on *this* Friday." He smiled. "Forty-eight hours. Tell me, have you decided what you're going to do yet? I think you were a little unsure the last time I asked you."

"Actually, sir, I was still planning to do what I told you before."

He smiled. "Remind me."

"Well, sir, ever since I was in grammar school, I've heard this rumor about a house on Oak Street that's haunted. I thought I'd set up some equipment and do some observation and interview some people."

"A haunted house," Zick said, and nodded deeply. Disks of reflected light moved up and down his nose.

Behind him, Ray was making more finger-in-the-fist gestures at me.

"It fits," Zick said. "It all fits. You think animals have souls, you're an evolutionist, and now you're into Satanism. It all fits. I'm not really surprised." He gazed out the window toward the evergreens that lined the edge of the tennis courts. "A lot of you so-called *smart* people," he said philosophically, "idolize your intelligence. This leads you into paths of lies and untruths and those things that have no validity."

"I'm not a Satanist, sir." I could still peripherally see Andrea pinching the end of her boob, but I was losing interest. Zick was getting serious with me. He'd never climbed on me before with such delight, and I could end up taking extra units in college.

He pushed up his glasses again and tilted his head back and looked down his nose at me. "Hm," he grunted.

"You're—," I said and then shut my mouth. I tried to be sensible: the semester was only two weeks from ending, and with a few decent grades, I could get into college without having to take a lot of low-level courses, and Zick was a sub-head, which was a lot more of a problem for him than it was for me. So, I thought, I should pay more attention to Andrea's tender teenage tits than to Zick's paranoid accusations and just hope the bacteria won.

"I'm *what?*" Zick asked.

"Nothing, sir. I apol—"

"I'm a *nothing?* Is that what you think of me, Mr. Honor Student? Your teacher is a *nothing?*"

"No, sir," I said, figuring I could eat a little shit to avoid an extra couple hundred hours of college work. I just wanted to get through and be left alone. "I was going to say that you're assuming I'm a Satanist just because I'm curious about a haunted house. I'm not a Satanist."

Ray was standing up there grinning and smearing blood from his mesh gloves onto his cheeks, and Zick was patiently shaking his head side to side like he was feeling sorry for me, and I heard myself saying, "You think *I'm* a Satanist? I'm not the one slicing open animals and pulling their hearts out. You showed us how to do that." Why was I saying this? I had to be crazy, but my mouth kept talking. "I wasn't the one to put mice in a decompression jar and make people watch their eyes pop out."

"Are you suggesting, Mr. Honor Student, that I, your instructor, Mr. Boren Zick, am in league with the Evil One?" He was grinning as he pushed up his glasses. His zit had turned a fiery red.

"All I want to do is my project and not have to watch any more public mutilations of animals."

"You have until Friday," Zick said. "And this project had better not have any Satanist overtones."

Behind him, Ray was silently laughing and pointing at me and then wildly poking his finger into his fist.

"Andrea," Zick said, "when will your project be ready?"

"I can give my report tomorrow, Mr. Zick." Her shoulders went up and down when she spoke, and the front of her blouse strained tight. She glanced at me and smiled.

The bell rang, and everyone leapt to their feet except me and Andrea. She leaned toward me and said in a whisper just loud enough for me to hear over the commotion of books and backpacks and clumping feet, "That Ray is such an animal. You can do it to me anytime. I can do it better than your little Oriental friend." She squeezed her purse and shoe box up under her boobs.

Hormones made my ears ring. My nostrils probably flared.

"Well," she said, moving her shoulders and making everything above her waist wobble, "if you've got the want, I've got the. . . ." She winked and flounced away. I hobbled out the door.

After I bought a sandwich at the lunch counter, I met Pham out under one of the plum trees by the track. The sun was warm, and on the football field, a dozen people were playing fris-ball. Yellow butterflies flittered across the grass. This seemed like real life. I knew that big things ate small things and that sooner or later everything gets eaten, but Zick's idea that we were entitled to snuff life at will seemed like low-grade arrogance. And I was afraid of what he would let Ray do in class the next day.

Pham sat down next to me and opened up a plastic box with her lunch in it—rice balls wrapped in black seaweed. She was small and slim, and her skin was as smooth as warm butter. Her black hair was clipped back behind her ears with yellow clips and hung to the middle of her back. When she talked, she spoke almost in a whisper. Her voice was mostly breath.

She had been in the U.S. two years. During her escape on a boat with forty other people, she had seen pirates shoot her brother in the back of the head and throw her mother overboard for screaming about it. She watched her mother slowly drown. Now she lived with her aunt.

She offered me part of her lunch.

"Thanks," I said. "I need to ask you a favor. Zick moved up the date of my project, and I have to have it done by Friday. Would your uncle mind if I came over this evening and set up some equipment?"

"I think that be fine," she said. "He never go in that room anyway. How come you have to do project Friday?"

"I told Zick I didn't like seeing animals killed in class. Ray was killing rats today. He was cutting out their hearts."

"Cutting out their hearts? Why he does this?"

"He wanted to see if he could cut out a heart fast enough that it would keep beating."

"How come?"

"Ray likes to do demonstrations that bother people."

"Oh." She seemed to understand now. She bit a rice ball in half. "He would like my country."

"One time in fifth grade, he showed a friend how to hit somebody so it would hurt a lot. He used me as a part of the demonstration and then asked me which way hurt the most."

"Ah."

"He's a jerk." I wanted to change the subject. "Do you think there are ghosts in your uncle's house?"

She shrugged her thin shoulders. "He thinks so. Last night he call to say there was a mir-oh . . . a mir-ror—did I say that right?—a mirror in the closet."

"My mom has a mirror in her closet."

"But he d'not put it there. And he says it was a bad mirror. It d'not show his face in it. He says it—"

"Well, hi guys." It was Ray, with Andrea clinging to his side. She was all grins and squeezes, and she chewed her gum without closing her mouth. "Hey Dell, wanna be a member of the Rude Shitz? We're doing a membership drive. Wanna be a member and get some respect? All you gotta do is kill a dog with your bare hands." The blood on his cheek had dried to a flaky brown.

Andrea giggled and wiggled and popped her gum.

"The dog's gotta be over ten years and weigh less than fifteen pounds," he said. "And you're allowed to use a tire iron."

"Oh *Ray*," Andrea said.

"And it has to be a gook dog. Wanna be a member? We'll get you a white girlfriend, too."

"He is a rectum," Pham said to me in her soft, airy voice. "Is that what I mean?"

"Yes. That's what you mean."

Andrea stopped chewing her gum.

"Watch your mouth, slope," Ray said.

I started to stand up, but Pham grabbed my arm and pulled me down. I was thinking about crushing his fucking skull.

"Stay," she said to me. "There are too many rectums in world to clean all of them. I know. I've seen many *big* ones." She grinned and made a loop with her arm.

Andrea started chewing her gum again. "C'mon, Ray."

"I seen you looking at Andrea in class," Ray said to me. "You remember what I done last year to that fat plughole that grabbed her tits?"

"You grabbed his tits back, didn't you?"

"C'mon, Ray."

He looked at me, and I ate a rice ball.

"C'mon, Ray."

He started grinning, as though he had just thought of something clever. "Yeah, babe." He reached behind her and squeezed one of her buns. "Yeah, let's go. I'll be seeing you later, slope-sucker."

Andrea was all grins and squeezes, and she chewed her gum without closing her mouth. Without Ray's seeing, she raised her eyebrows twice at me. "See you later," she said, and they walked away clinging to each other.

"I wish there were justice," I said.

"Can't have justice," Pham said. "Spend time wishing for nice weather. I heard American saying: 'Best revenge is living well.' Spend time living well. Can't be justice when rectums have legs. Old Vietnamese saying." With a smile, she offered me a second rice ball.

I liked her. She had gone through a hundred times what I ever would, and she was smiling. If there wasn't justice, maybe there was something else. Endurance, maybe. Or laughing.

"When could we go over to your uncle's?"

"Anytime. You want to go there in afternoon or evening?"

"About five? Can I meet you there?"

She started rolling her shoulders around like Andrea and said, "You can meet me anywhere, white boy."

I liked her.

When I got home, my dad was sitting on the piano bench staring at the keyboard. My dad is an interesting person. He is an enigma, but he is an interesting enigma. He has a business card that reads "VLADO VERMICELLI: troubleshooter." That isn't his real name, but since he was in the army as a teenager, he doesn't know exactly who he is or what he is. In fact, it's very hard to know what he does know.

He thinks the army used him in some experiment that wiped out the boundary between his conscious and unconscious minds. So he says one name is as good as another. On some weekends, he goes over to San Francisco and does stand-up comedy in nightclubs under the name of Walter Roscoe. The rest of the time, he solves problems for people.

Last week, Mr. Sammartini, owner of a local TV station asked him if he could write a theme song for some program, and Dad had been working on that for several days now. When I came in the back door, it sounded like he was playing chopsticks very slowly backwards.

"Hi, Dad. How's it going?"

He was sitting there in a denim jacket and white boxer shorts with his hair sticking out in twenty directions. He looked like a madman, but when your conscious and unconscious minds are right in there together, in the same place at the same time, I guess once in a while you forget about combing your hair or putting your pants on. "Anything turning out?"

"I don't know," he said. He looked confused. "All I can figure out is that if you hit two keys that are next to each other, it sounds bad."

"When does Mr. Sammartini want this theme song?"

"Tomorrow. Boy, I don't know." He looked worried. He scratched under one of his arms. "A lot of keys here. Do you know why they made the black ones so small and put them up here where they're hard to reach?"

"Beats me. I think they're called sharps and flats."

"Strange," he said, staring at them.

"Dad, my science teacher moved up the due date of my project. Have you been able to get that stuff you were telling me about?"

"Stuff?"

"The camera, recording thermometer and barometer, that stuff?"

"Oh yeah." He hit a couple of keys down at the lower end. "I wonder who thought this thing up," he mumbled. "I called Mr. Sammartini, and he was very helpful. I got you a biostatic charge detector and a Kirlian photographic panel big enough to ride a bike through," he said. "And don't put your face in front of the open end of that tube gizmo—it's a net gun a guy at the zoo loaned him and that he loaned me."

"A net gun?"

"They use it on the baboons when they start to party."

"Thanks, Dad." I thought of Ray. "I might be able to find a use for it."

"Anytime." He plunked a few times on the keyboard and shook his head. "Why did they put so many keys on this thing?"

"What happens if you don't get the music done in time?"

"Mr. Sammartini said I'd work better if I didn't know. I told him no sweat. I was sure I'd studied music." He shrugged and sighed. "This is really complicated," he mumbled. "Did I study music?"

"If you did, it was before my time. Good luck, Dad. Is Mom home yet?"

"She's in the bedroom."

I went down the hall and looked in. She was sleeping on top of the bed in her clothes. They were trying something new at the hospital where she worked—rotating the shifts in ways no one could understand under the pretext of trying to see if they could get more work out of people. Mom had worked eighteen hours straight. She was an emergency room nurse, and with the new scheduling, she was irritable, crabby, and withdrawn, and that wasn't like her. Mom was usually really nice. I liked her.

I went back down to where my dad was. He was slowly experimenting with hitting three keys at a time. It sounded bad.

"Mom doesn't look so good, does she?"

"Nope." He made his hands like claws and dramatically hit a random bunch of keys. "That doesn't work either," he mumbled. "You may have noticed that she didn't take her uniform off before going to sleep."

"Yeah."

"She has to go back to work in an hour."

"Why doesn't she quit?"

"She's trying to wait them out." He looked up from the keyboard. "Son, what are you going to do with all that stuff?"

"Pham's uncle thinks his closet is haunted."

"You're looking for ghosts?"

"Who knows? Maybe just rats."

He seemed to be thinking very hard. "Well, either way, if you see Richard Nixon, ask him how much he got paid for arranging Pearl Harbor." Then he started playing chopsticks backwards again, but I could see a little of his Walter Roscoe grin showing.

My dad.

I got all the stuff wedged into the trunk and backseat and was on my way over to Pham's Uncle Heng, when I noticed there was a car following me. It wasn't being subtle either—whoever it was, was right on my tail, but I couldn't see much because the Kirlian panel and the biostatic charge detector blocked most of my view.

At a stop sign, I felt a jolt as the other car's bumper hit mine. I stuck my head out the window and looked back—and there she was: Andrea, her head out the car window, waving and yelling at me, "Pull over—I have to tell you something! Pull over!"

So I did.

When she got in the front seat with me, hugging her purse and ever-present shoe box to her body, I said, "Look, I have only a minute. I have to set up all this stuff right away, or Zick's going to ream my transcript."

"Oh, that nasty man." Andrea had on white shorts that looked like they had been glued to her, and her tank top was so stretched out at her armpits that I could see that she had a pencil-eraser-sized mole on the side of her left breast.

I started to get that graspy feeling in my chest.

She put her big purse in the seat between us and held her shoe box on her beautiful knees. "I know you're kind of stuck on that Pham refugee person, but Dell. . . ." She rolled her shoulders, and her mole moved in little jiggling circles. "Dell, I can offer you things she can't. Big things. You don't know what you're missing."

"True, I don't," I said. My heart felt like it was sucking air. I had some pictures under my mattress of women who looked like Andrea, but I'd also seen Ray bang on guys who had done less than I already had. "Ray wouldn't like this," I said, but I was already asking myself just how much getting hit a few times would hurt. . . .

"Ray's a pinhead," she cooed, leaning toward me. Her tank top opened up, and so did my mouth. I could feel my heartbeat in my eyeballs. "I like guys who can think with something besides their privates. Just answer me one question."

She leaned forward even more. I could see nipple. It was pale brown. I could see nipple. Oh God.

"Just tell me this," she said. She took my left hand and turned it palm up and pressed it against her hanging boob. "Just tell me what that feels like."

"Uh. . . ."

"In your own words, just tell me what it's like."

"Soft. It feels soft."

"Tell me more," she purred.

"Warm," I said, choking up. Did adults do things like this? Did they risk death out of lust?

She put the shoe box on the dashboard and hooked her fingers over the upper edge of her tank top and pulled it all the way down and then let it snap back up under her breasts. She rolled her shoulders, and everything moved. Even in me, everything moved.

"Now," she said softly, "tell me what they look like."

All I could think was, "Thank you, God; thank you, God; thank you." I was an animal.

"You look funny," Pham said.

It was 5:20, and she met me in Heng's dirt and cement-chunk driveway. When I got out of the car, my legs were still rubbery.

"You O.K.?"

"Somebody ran into my back bumper at a stop sign," I said. "It rattled me a little." I was looking at Pham, but all I could see was Andrea's chest . . . Andrea's and those swooping curves . . . and that white skin and those brown circles and—

"You look real nervous."

"It was pretty scary." I went around to the trunk and put the key in the lock. I wasn't much for symbolic things, but when that key slid in, my knees buckled and banged into the bumper. I was still a virgin, but I was a virgin with a dream.

"What is all that stuff in backseat?"

"The two silver panels can tell if there's an electrical field between them that's caused by a living organism, and the square thing that looks like a door will take a picture of it. Here." I handed her the recording barometer and thermometer out of the trunk.

She took them and said with a nod toward me, "Pants unzipped."

I probably jumped like I had been stabbed. I turned my back and pulled the zipper up. It had been only halfway down.

"You *very* nervous," Pham said as she went toward the front door.

The zipper wasn't Andrea's fault. Not directly anyway. Mere man-made materials were not meant to take such stress.

Heng's place was basically a dump that he had scraped and shoveled out and then moved into. The neighborhood was a mixture of white trash, brown trash, black trash, blighted trees, yellow lawns, dusty streets, and Heng. In Vietnam he had been the manager of a bicycle factory.

He didn't look like he had moved since I had been to his house the one time before. He sat rocking in a scabbed-up old rocking chair in the corner of the living room. He looked seventy or eighty, but Pham said he was sixty-one. He was always smiling very hard, with his narrow eyes squinched up into thin slits and his face furrowed with dark wrinkles.

"Hello, Mr. Heng," I said, smiling and bowing a little. I didn't know exactly what to do, but it seemed to be the right thing.

"Yes," Heng said, nodding and rocking at the same time. "Thank you."

"I wanted to thank you for letting me come in your house and set up this equipment." I gestured a little with the barometer I was holding.

"Thank you," Heng said, still nodding. "Hello."

"He likes you," she said, leading me into the back room where the allegedly haunted closet was.

I nodded again at Heng and followed her. "He likes me? Why?"

"You treat him like he not crazy."

"In truth, it crossed my mind."

"Oh, Uncle Heng very crazy. He very bad zerked-out. But you treat him O.K."

The back room was about twelve by twelve feet, and empty except for the closet that had been built into the corner and stuck out into the room. The closet was about three feet square, hardly big enough to have the reputation it had.

The walls of the room had been painted brown and green and black at different times, wallpapered with a yellow vine pattern, and then apparently scraped down with a steel garden rake. The window had been broken out and then boarded up with a sheet of plywood, and the only light was a clear bulb in the overhead socket. The air smelled like old, damp wallpaper glue. It was the kind of room where Andrea could strip naked, and all I'd want to do would be leave.

Well, maybe not, but it would be a tough decision.

I turned the cracked glass doorknob on the closet and pulled it open. Empty. Just more dead air and a few lint balls in the corners. It didn't look haunted. On one of the inside walls, someone had written in orange crayon, "José loves Lauralee Poontang."

Maybe this was all a big mistake. Zick was going to enjoy hosing me over on this one.

We hauled in all the stuff, and every time I passed through the living room, Heng would be rocking and smiling and I would smile back and he would say, "Yes, thank you very much. O.K."

By the time I'd hooked up everything like the directions said, it was a little after eight, and the room was cluttered with power lines layered across the floor, chairs that Heng had dragged in to put some of the stuff on, and the Kirlian screen looked really impressive. I set it up right in front of the closet. It was an aluminum-framed rectangle, shaped like a door, and on its inside edges were what looked like steel comb-teeth. A coil-table connected it to a little printer that simultaneously charted out horizontal and vertical fluctuations in the patterns it picked up.

Pham had gone out and got a pizza, and when we finished, we sat against one of the few vacant spots against a wall and ate and admired the setup. It was very serious-looking, even if we ended up recording only a few rats.

Heng even got up and shuffled over and looked at it. He said something to Pham in Vietnamese and went back to his rocking chair.

"He say bad mirror show up at nine o'clock," she said between bites. "And he say he d'not want any pizza. He call it 'blood pie' because it have meat on it."

"Nine o'clock? How does he know?"

Pham shrugged. "Maybe every night the same."

"You said Uncle Heng was crazy."

"Oh yes. Very bats."

"Has he always been like that?"

"Oh no. Communists bury him alive and then dig him up fi' times. It make him zerked-out."

I had stopped chewing. "Five times they buried him alive?"

"Better than bury him dead." She bit into her third piece.

"Well," I said, "at least he smiles a lot."

"Oh, he not smiling," she said to me. "That like a . . . like this—" She clenched her teeth and drew back her lips. "What you call that?"

"A grimace."

"That what he do. At first I call him 'Happy Uncle Heng,' but I found out the sadder he got, the more he look like he smile. He not very happy since last time they bury him."

"Jesus."

We heard the front screen door slam and heavy footsteps clumping across the empty living room.

Ray stuck his head through the door. "Hi, guys," he said with a grin. Ray sauntered in, holding a pillowcase in one hand. Inside it, an animal thrashed around. "Cat," Ray said. "Probably a gook cat. Pretty frisky. Bet he's got a good heart." He looked around the room and pursed his lips. "Oooo. Lookit all the high-puke equipment you got in here. Looks like there's some torrid upchuck about to squirt down." He ran his fingers along the toothed inner edge of the Kirlian detector. "Hey phlegm-boy, your wacko old man steal this stuff for you?"

Ray stepped back and swung the cat at the frame. It hit it with a thump, and the cat yowled and the frame crashed into the recording barometer.

"God damn it, Ray!" I yelled, grabbing for the frame and missing it.

"Oh darn," Ray said. "This stupid cat busted something." He held up the pillowcase with one hand and drew back his other fist. On the pillowcase there was a small spot of blood. "Kitty needs to be punished."

"I give you fi' dollar for the cat," Pham said calmly.

Ray looked at her in mock surprise. He nodded his head at the pizza box. "Didn't you get enough to eat?"

"Fi' dollar," Pham said. She reached in her pocket and pulled out a metal clip with some ones in it. "Here. Fi' dollar for the cat."

"Whillikers," Ray said, lifting his eyebrows and bugging his eyes. "The football team must be payin' in quarters these days."

I swung at him, and he swung the cat at me, and we both missed each other, but the cat hit one of the biostatic charge detector panels, and the panel clanged and broke against the wall. When I looked back at Ray, he had his knife in one hand and the pillowcase in the other. The knife was spade-shaped, not more than six inches long, but it was an inch wide and it gleamed under the clear light bulb.

"Now," he said to Pham, "I'll give you the cat for five bucks and a piece of ass right now. Dell, you have to watch, and if I don't see some dink tit before I count to five, I do some Aztec surgery in the here and now." He teased the knife point around the lumps in the pillowcase. The cat moved feebly now. It made a small squeak when Ray poked it with the knife. "One-two," he said quickly.

Pham looked at me, and I looked at her, and then her eyes went very large and very round and she pointed at the closet. Ray saw it, too, and he turned to face it, but he still held the knife up to the cat.

Inside the closet, filling it up completely, was a thing that looked like a silver bubble—like a mirror—only it was curved, and inside it, behind the distorted reflection of the room, we could see vague dark shapes moving slowly back and forth.

The bubble bulged out and contracted and then bulged out again, as though it were breathing.

"What is this?" Ray demanded. His voice was a little unsteady. "Is this some scabass trick your wacko old man came up with? What is this? What the vuk is this?"

He backed up, and when the thing bulged out into the room again, he gave the cat a short swing and threw it at the bubble. It vanished inside the bubble's surface without a sound. And just like an autoteller giving a receipt, the instant the last corner of the pillowcase disappeared, a small slip of paper popped out of the bubble and fluttered down to the cruddy floor.

Ray looked at us, and we looked at each other. And on the piece of paper, we could all read the neat block letters printed on the front side:

CAT

"Neat trick," Ray said with a grin. "I bet if I shove the gook in, I'll get a piece of paper back that says TWAT."

He grabbed her, and I grabbed the net gun. It was a tube about the size of my forearm and looked scary. I was thinking of netting them both and then kicking Ray in the head five or six times. I was starting to feel the need to get some relief.

"What's that?" Ray barked suspiciously, holding Pham with her back to him, one hand on her neck and the other clamped on her wrist.

"It's a net gun, Ray. They use it on baboons. It won't hurt either of you, but I will."

The mirror-bubble bloated a foot out of the closet door. Ray eyed it carefully and then gave Pham a shove away from him.

"Here," he said, "you can have back your slope." He was moving sideways toward the door, not taking his eyes off me, and I seriously considered wrapping him up right there and seeing what happened when he was shoved through the bubble.

Just before he got to the door, he said, "Oh yeah. One other thing, zit-dick." He reached over and knocked the recording thermometer off a chair, and it crashed on the floor. "This is a guarantee. Before graduation, the Rude Shitz are going to put a hog clamp on your nuts and then take your picture for your mom and dad. No way you can stop it. So poke your slope while you still can. Ta-ta."

I stood there even after the screen door had slammed, wishing I had webbed him. Now I had something else to look forward to.

Pham's hand touched my shoulder. "He very small rectum," she said. "Let's try something, to see what that thing is."

I put down the net gun and picked up the broken thermometer. "Let's put this into it," I said.

She nodded, and I stepped over to the thing. It had retracted till it was about even with the doorsill. Our reflections in it showed us with big noses.

Slowly I touched the edge of the bubble with the corner of the thermometer. I expected some resistance, but there wasn't any. Behind the swollen reflection of my hand, I could see those dark shapes, like blurry fish, moving slowly back and forth.

All at once the thermometer was snatched out of my hand and a slip of paper popped back out and slid between my fingers. On it was printed the word JUNK.

"Comedians," Pham said.

"What do you think's in there?"

"CIA," she said.

"I don't know . . . ," I said. This looked a little beyond any technology I'd heard about. "Maybe they're aliens. Or maniacs from the tenth dimension. Or the Welfare Department checking to see if Uncle Heng is having too much fun. D'you have some paper?"

From her purse, over by the grease-stained pizza box, she took out a little pink tablet and a ballpoint and gave them to me.

On one paper I printed, "Who are you?" and ripped it off and pushed it into the bubble. Again, instantaneously, another slip of paper was returned into my fingers, and on it was printed in neat block letters, WE ARE CURIOUS.

"CIA," Pham said, nodding.

I wrote another note: "We are also curious. What are you curious about?"

The answer was: WE WANT TO KNOW HOW YOU LIKE IT THERE.

Pham was reading the note, when Heng appeared in the doorway wearing his grimace-smile. He said some stuff to Pham and waved at the bubble.

"He wants to know if the mirror talks," she said. She looked again at the note and translated it for him.

Heng threw back his head and barked a mirthless "*Ha!*" and quickly jabbered something else.

"He say to tell them he d'not like it here and that politicians are shit-worms."

"O.K." I wrote it down.

"For me, tell them, 'Too much mean stuff.' " As I wrote that down, she said, "Ray a bad guy. Bad guys all over."

I wondered if I should add something of my own. How did I like it here? Here, in this room? In this town? How did I like being seventeen in this world? I thought of my mom and dad and Zick and Ray and of Heng being buried five times . . . and of Andrea. And I thought of what Ray might do with his knife if he knew I had given Andrea a breast exam.

For my message, I wrote, "At best, it's very risky." Then I thought a second and added, "How do you like it where you are? And where are you?"

I slipped it through the membrane, and the instantaneous answer was: WE'RE SOMEWHERE ELSE AND WE LIKE IT FINE.

I wrote, "If you're somewhere else, where are we?"

"CIA tell you nothing," Pham muttered.

I put the note through, and the return message said simply: CAGE 37.

"What that mean?" Pham asked.

I shrugged. "It doesn't mean anything to me." I started to write a note asking about "Cage 37," but at that moment the mirrored bubble stopped being there. It didn't pop or melt away—it just wasn't anymore. All it left behind was a little noise like a coin hitting the floor in the closet.

Cautiously, I stuck my head in, and in the corner on the floor, under the "José loves Lauralee Poontang" sign, was a metal disk. It was shiny and a little larger than a dime, but when I picked it up, it weighed nothing, and on one side were three little depressions, two above the other one, in the shape of a triangle. I hadn't ever seen anything like it, and neither had Pham, but it didn't look like anything special. It could have fallen off the wall when the bubble disappeared. Or the bubble could have left it. I shrugged again. Since puberty, nothing ever seemed to make a whole lot of sense.

"What we do now?" Pham asked.

"Go home, I guess." I looked around at the wrecked equipment. All of it, except the net gun, was trash. Mr. Sammartini would probably have my dad kneecapped. I had twenty-two hundred dollars saved for college, and that would probably about cover the cost of the printer. Well, if I couldn't go to college, I could go to work, I suppose.

"I wonder what happen to the cat," Pham said.

I thought a second. "Ask Heng if this thing comes back every night."

We both went into the living room. Heng sat there rocking and grimacing, and when Pham finished talking, he said very distinctly, "Yes." Then he pointed at me and said something else to her in Vietnamese.

Pham nodded at the coin-thing I was holding. "Uncle Heng ask if you want more of those."

"O.K.," I said. "Sure."

Heng got up out of his chair and did his bowlegged shuffle into the kitchen. I wondered what he had been like before he was buried five times. He opened the oven and took out a cigar box filled with the things and shoved them at me.

"Goo'ni'," he barked, and flailed his hand at the door.

We left.

When I got home, Mom was at work again and Dad was asleep. I had just enough energy to count the number of disks in the box Heng had given us—there were sixty-two—and pull off my clothes and get in bed. It had been a long day . . .

. . . humiliation in class; titillation in Andrea's car; strange weirdness in Heng's closet; realizing that I really liked Pham, but that Andrea, whom I didn't like very much at all, made my hormones scream for mercy. . . . Did adults have to put up with stuff like this? Greeps. And

I got to see my college career get trashed . . . maybe I could sell mobile homes for a while and try again next year . . . and in return I got a box full of funny buttons, probably left there by José when he was snaking Lauralee Poontang. . . . Was this those "great teenage years" I had heard so much about? Was this what I was supposed to enjoy so much because adulthood was such a pain in the ass?

I had the distinct feeling that some crucial information had been left out somewhere, like the directions for my life had been written in Hong Kong and badly translated. "Be sure assemble emotion limiter before extending thorough pubberty, and handle limiter and external breasticals with foresight." Sure. And avoid maniacs regardless of what dimension they come from.

I rolled over and went to sleep. I dreamed of Pham. She had silver boobs that expanded and contracted and spoke to me in a foreign tongue, which I understood. I woke up out of the dream and wondered, What else can happen? How much worse can it get?

"This is my science project," Andrea said, putting her huge purse and her pink shoe box on the lab table in front of her. She clicked on the slide projector. Behind her, the screen lit up with the words MY SCIENCE PROJECT.

Today Andrea was wearing a blue and white checked sundress with spaghetti straps. I noticed I wasn't the only male paying close attention. Ray, however, was drawing pictures of exploding spaceships on his desk.

"As you all know," Andrea went on primly, "Ray is my boyfriend."

"Yo!" Ray said as he waved one hand over his head.

"Thank you," Mr. Zick said sourly. He sat off to the side of the room with his gradebook open and his pencil poised. With the eraser end he pushed his wire-rims up his nose. He really grimaced this time as the nosepads slid over his pimple. It was coming to a head. "Continue, Andrea."

"Well," she said, "I got Ray for my boyfriend because I wanted to do this project on—" she studied at her notes—"on 'The Effect of Lust on One's Sense of Self-Preservation.' "

Ray was looking up from his airplane now. "She got me for the lust part," he said proudly.

"Actually," she said, "Ray was for the threatening part. Here are the two subjects of my experiment." She clicked to the next slide. It was of me and Ray. This didn't look promising.

"What is this?" I heard Ray mutter.

"What I wanted to do my project on," Andrea said, "was if lust could make a person disregard his own safety."

I felt my gonads begin to shrivel up. There were ugly ingredients here.

"Here," she said, "we can see the early stages." She ran through a succession of five or six slides of me looking down her dress. "I made these pictures using a camera concealed in this ordinary-looking shoe box."

That goddamned pink shoe box.

"Wait a minute," Ray was saying. "Wait a minute. You mean he was—"

"Quiet, Ray," Zick said tiredly, "or you won't get to use the spare rat after Andrea's finished. You take care of your personal business outside class."

"Right. I will, too."

There were a few *Oooo's* from around the room, and Ray's little pig eyes had images of the slaughterhouse in them.

"The most fascinating element of my experiment is that I'm going to do the last part of it right here in class, right after I show you the later stages of my subject's development." She was looking at me. I was her subject. Apparently I had developed. At the moment I was rapidly developing a lot of sweat.

She took a small tape recorder from her purse and turned it on loud. In the background was the sound of passing traffic. "In the later stages," she said, "the subject disregarded all personal safety." She clicked the slide projector.

There I was in her car, facing her and looking down her dress. "I shouldn't be here," my voice said. "If Ray found out, he'd murder me." Click of the projector, and there I was with my hands glued to her tank top, and like a moron I was saying, "Warm . . . they're very warm."

I glimpsed Zick studying the screen very carefully, and Ray was getting up from his desk.

The projector clicked, and there I was, the grinning fishhead, with my hands on her naked boobs, and the tape recorder was playing, "Oh God, if Ray finds out, oh God, oooh God. . . ."

Ray was already coming at me, but he had three rows of desks to get through and the door was on my side of the room, so I had a chance.

"Thus we see the conclusion of my experiment," Andrea said, making a wide gesture at me and Ray and the developing chaos.

"Hold it!" Zick was yelping. "What's going on?"

As I was on my way out the door, I heard Andrea saying, "And today, as a result of my project, I was accepted at U.C. Berkeley." Behind me there was lot of crashing and yelling, and I made myself gone.

I crept into my room, but no one seemed to be home anyway. My gray cat, Kubo, was lying asleep on a piece of paper on the middle of my bed. He stretched and opened his eyes and rolled over on his back.

I really didn't want to explain the ugly mess to my folks, even though they would try to understand. Except for all the wrecked equipment. Well, they might understand, but they certainly wouldn't like it. I had heard a rumor that Mr. Sammartini had killed his own parents to get control of his family's trucking business—but who knows? Maybe he was just lucky. Imagining my dad trying to explain in his wacked-out way to Sammartini that a hundred thousand dollars of his frontline equipment had been trashed in a West Side slumhouse. . . . It made me feel wormy inside.

Yesterday I was a happy guy. In twenty-four hours I had developed at least two life-threatening problems. But I got in a few incredible feels.

Kubo rolled over and said, "*Meah*," and when I looked over at him, I saw that the piece of paper was a note. It said, "Call Pham," and it gave a number I didn't recognize. So I called it.

It didn't get to finish one ring before she said, "Hello?" There was a lot of noise in the background.

"Where are you?" I asked.

"School. I heard abou' Andrea's project. Ray said he going to cut your dick off."

"Somehow I'm not surprised."

"I d'not think you should stay home. It would really hurt, you know? Go to my house, O.K.? He'd not know where I live. My aunt fix you dinner with us. O.K.?"

"Yeah, I appreciate it, Pham. I mean, if you heard what I did with Andrea and you're still willing to talk to me, I really appreciate it."

"It is O.K. I also never see real big ones like that till I come to California either. Bring those things Uncle Heng give you, you know? O.K.?"

"O.K."

"Go to my house now. Ray left school soon as principal told him he couldn't leave. So go now."

"Thanks. I will." We said good-bye and hung up. While we had been talking, Kubo had left the room and had come back in dragging the white sock he played with. He put it at my feet and looked up. The sock was his imitation mouse. If only people could be that civilized . . . at least Ray and Mr. Sammartini.

I gave him a few quick strokes. "Maybe later," I said. "I have to save my ass now."

I had the cigar box of metal things under my arm, and I was about to let the back screen slam, when I saw my mom and dad. They were out in the backyard, standing under the mulberry tree with their arms around each other. Mom still had her hospital whites on, and she was standing with her cheek pressed against Dad's chest.

I didn't want to intrude, but I was a little curious about what they were saying, and since I could just barely hear them, I slowed down a moment and listened.

". . . and so I quit," Mom was saying. "I fooled myself into thinking that I had to play by their rules. I didn't." She moved her cheek against him. "I forgot what was important."

Dad said something I couldn't make out.

"No," Mom said, "I won't regret it. As long as I have you, I can deal with whatever I need to deal with."

My mom.

Pham's aunt fixed us a dinner of fried chicken, corn on the cob, and mashed potatoes. She was very proud of her "ethnic American cuisine." She used to teach history at the University of Saigon, but now she spends her days clipping coupons and cleaning other people's houses.

A couple of times she admiringly referred to "the great American experiment," but given her circumstances, I didn't see how she could be so cheerful about it.

After dinner, which looked normal but which tasted strangely spicy, tangy, and generally great, Pham and I cleared off the table for her and spread out the box of buttons Uncle Heng had given us.

"All alike," Pham said.

They were about the size of big dimes, about the same color, with the three indentations on the lower half of one side, one below the other two.

"These belong to some American machine?" Pham asked.

"Not that I know of, but I suppose they could. From the sharpness of the edges and the way these dents are so precise, they look to me like they were pretty carefully made."

"No scratches either," Pham said, holding one at an angle to the light.

Now that was unusual, considering they had all been thrown together in a box.

We tapped on them against each other, rolled them around, stacked and restacked them, and I felt like a rat failing an intelligence test. I arranged several of them under the chair leg and tried to bend or break one, but nothing happened.

"Well," I said, "now what?"

Pham was looking very closely at the dents on one of the coins. "You know what," she said slowly, "in the middle of each of these little pits, there a dull spot, like something been rubbed on it. Like you stick something into pit."

I already had my Swiss pocketknife out. I pulled the toothpick out of it, picked up a coin, and poked into one of the top dents.

A strange thing happened.

The upper half of the coin face looked like it kind of went soft—moltenlike—and the number *1* formed and turned black. I ran my finger over its raised shape.

"I never see this kind of thing before," Pham said.

"Me either." I poked the toothpick into the dent again. The *1* turned into a *2*. And each time I touched the bottom of the indentation, the number ratcheted up.

Pham leaned close to me with her arm across the back of my

shoulder and her fingertips touching my neck at the edge of my collar. I liked it.

I poked the other top indentation, and a second digit formed in the metal. I had a *41.* I also had the bottom indentation gleaming a bright red at me.

"Uh-oh," I said.

"What does this mean?" she asked under her breath. "Is it a bomb?"

I picked up one of the other disks and held it up to the light. In the bottom of that third indentation, there was the same shiny spot, probably meaning that somebody—using the term loosely—somebody else had poked something into it any number of times and it hadn't blown up.

I poised the toothpick over it. "Shall I?" I asked.

"Sure."

And while I was thinking twice, I remembered that on one of the messages from the thing in the closet, when I'd asked where we were, it said, "Cage 37."

"Let's try thirty-seven," I said, and poked the dents till that number came up. The red dot gleamed as bright as ever.

"O.K.," I said, and stuck the toothpick into it.

Nothing happened. I was glad.

"It d'not blow us up," Pham said.

"Well, let's try thirty-eight." I poked at the dents till I got thirty-eight. I stuck the toothpick into the gleaming red dot.

Weird stuff happened.

The first thing was more of a pukey feeling than anything else. Then I noticed that it hurt where I was leaning my elbows on the table—and the reason was that the table was no longer a slick Formica—it was rough, splintery planks. I looked up at Pham, and she was staring back at me in horror.

God knows what I looked like, but she was buck-toothed; had oily, stringy hair; dirty pockmarks across her cheeks; and crusted snot around the insides of her nostrils.

I fumbled with the disk I was holding, punched the upper right dent a bunch of times till I got a thirty-seven, and then I poked the red dot. It was like the film jerked, I had a wave of pukiness, and there we were again, sitting at a neat and clean Formica table, and Pham looked even better than ever.

"That wa' *ho*rrible," she said. "Worse than movies."

"Wanta do it again?" I asked.

"This time," she said, "do a thirty-six, you know, so it only take one push on that thing to get back here."

"You think well," I said.

"I practice."

So I did a thirty-six. My guts churned again, but the rest of it wasn't nearly so bad. First thing, we checked out each other, and we looked the same. Several of the kitchen appliances were a different color, and the TV in the living room was on, and some guy was using a language we could only half-understand.

"Something smell bad," Pham said.

Something smelled like oily plastic. Out the window, through the twilight, I saw rows of towering chimneys, all pouring billows of gloom into the evening sky.

"Dirty place," Pham said. "Let's go home."

I got us back to thirty-seven.

"Say, what time is it?"

She looked over her shoulder at the clock on the wall. "Seven-thirty."

"I'd be interested in being at your Uncle Heng's at nine o'clock. We could ask the thing in the closet some interesting questions about this." I looked at the disk in my hand. "O.K.," I said, "let's try a high number."

"I d'know," Pham said slowly. "If thirty-eight was that bad . . ."

"O.K.," I said, "how about we try a ninety-seven, and that way it'll take only four pokes at the first digit to get it back here."

"I d'know. That could be sixty times worse than this."

"Or it could just be sixty times more different." A part of me kind of hoped she'd talk me out of it.

"O.K. How fast can you poke into that four time?"

"Like lightning. Like the wind."

I set it for ninety-seven, looked at Pham, she took a deep breath, and said, "Let's go," and we did.

First I felt pukey, and then I saw the goddamned weasels—or *something* with a lot of teeth and claws—rushing me through some underground tunnel. They were as big as dogs, and they were really mad about something. I looked around for Pham, and if that was Pham, then I probably had a weevil head, too, and a mouth that looked like a slab of black meat in a bunch of briars. Somebody—or some*thing* —started screaming, and like a maniac I started raking at the disk I held in my claws, got some other number to come up, and got us out of there like quick.

Pham looked like a dog, sort of, except what should have been hair looked like moss, and we were standing up to each of our four knees in some kind of thick mud. First, I noticed there were bugs crawling all over us; second, that it was raining; and third, that the disk that was lying in front of me was going to be a little difficult to manipulate with paws and teeth. Bugs crawled around my snout, and I heard Pham whimper.

Pham . . . what I assumed was Pham . . . shifted her feet as she watched for predators and water dripped off her black nose. Heavy, dead-looking trees rose up out of the swamp, and in their upper branches, hook-necked birds carefully watched us.

I was glad there were no weasels to deal with this time, because it took about five minutes and a dozen mouthfuls of mud to get my incisors to press into the disk to make us gone.

We ended up in sixteen. Sixteen was not a bad place. Pham and I looked like ourselves again, and there were a lot of slow things grazing around us that looked like something between cows and hippopotamuses. We were on a grassy plain, and some miles away, even though it was late evening, we could see the silver spires of a city.

"We could come back here," Pham said. "But I want to go home now."

I set the disk to thirty-seven and touched the red dot. Again we were sitting in her kitchen, leaning forward on her bright Formica table. I asked her what time it was, and she looked at the kitchen clock.

"Seven thirty-five. That d'not take any time at all."

We were both amazed. And we had sixty-two of the things.

We tried out a few more tricks with them and found they had a range of about two and a half feet, and it took about three seconds for the transfer to take place. In those three nauseous seconds, you could back off from the disk and stay here. If I went to nineteen while Pham stood away from me and watched, she just saw me standing there looking glazed for a second or two, even though it seemed to me I was walking around for five minutes in this gloomy warehouse before I pressed in thirty-seven and came back. But she didn't see me move at all. Nineteen was a grim place. All in all, by 8:30 we'd checked out a dozen or so places, and only sixteen wasn't bleak or creepy or like ninety-seven, which was just a screaming psycho's nightmare. We stayed out of the nineties altogether.

"Let's go to your uncle's now," I said. "D'you have a tablet and pen we could take? We have some better questions to ask tonight."

Outside, the air was warm and sweet with the smell of jasmin from the trellis on her aunt's patio. In the southern sky, Mars stood close to Antares, the red star in the heart of Scorpio. Together, they were like eyes.

Pham knocked on the screen door and called, "Uncle Heng?"

"O.K., be inside," he called back. "Open door."

He was sitting in his rocking chair in the corner of the room, rocking and grinning.

"We wanted to look in the closet again," I said, nodding once deeply. "May we, please?"

"Yes, thank you, O.K.," he said, waving his hand in front of his face as though shooing away gnats. "Yes, yes."

We moved some of the trash aside—everything looked hopelessly wrecked—and I started worrying again about my dad and Mr. Sammartini. Maybe I could sell some of the disks to keep my dad out of the hot water I was going to put him in. I didn't get to worry anymore, because right then, right on the dot of nine o'clock, the closet filled up with the slow-pulsing mirrored bubble.

I turned off the overhead light, and Pham and I eased up to it and tried to see through the surface into the inside. It was just like in the movies. Without even realizing it, we were nearly cheek to cheek, holding hands, and inside the thing was a faint yellow glow that lit up our faces. We couldn't see anything clearly, but there were vague angular outlines of things that didn't move and taller thin things—the "people," I guess—that seemed to drift back and forth, like they lived inside of Jell-O or something.

I wrote the first note: "We know how to use the metal disks."

Just like before, there was no time lag—I pushed the front edge of the slip of paper into the surface, and one of their notes popped out of it and fluttered to the floor.

In block letters the response was: GOOD FOR YOU.

Pham wrote, "What are those places?" and as the answer popped out, she said, "I meant *where*," and she shook her head and looked disgusted with herself.

The card read: THOSE ARE OTHER CAGES.

I looked at Pham, and Pham looked at me, and we both reread the card. Other cages?

"Other cages?" Pham said to me. "Like rats?"

I wrote the next question: "What are the cages for?"

The answer was: INTERACTIVE BIOLOGICAL SYSTEMS ANALYSIS.

"What that mean?" Pham asked.

"I think it means they like to watch how we animals get along with each other."

"Like rats," Pham said.

On the notepad I wrote, "Are we your science project?"

The block letters on the card read, ONE OF MANY. NOTHING PERSONAL.

"Like rats," Pham said.

There was some clomping around in the living room, the screen door banged, and I heard Heng jabbering something angry-sounding.

Pham and I both got over to the door to see Ray holding off Heng with one arm—he turned his head and gave us a quick tongue-flicking grin. In his free hand he held a drawstring bag with a cat in it—he had the string pulled tight around the cat's neck so only its head stuck out. Its eyes bulged from choking.

"Hi, guys," he said as he swung the bag in a high overhead loop and brought it down on Heng's back. The cat screamed as it whumped on the old man's bent shoulders. Heng staggered off backward and sat down again in his rocker.

Ray looked pleased with himself. "See," he said, pointing at Heng, who was grinning-grimacing fiercely. "Gooks like to be knocked around."

"Whi' shi'," Heng said through his teeth. Ray didn't understand him.

"Lookit here," Ray said, holding up the bag by the drawstring. "This one's bigger. It'll be easier to get to his parts, Aztec style."

It was Kubo. His eyes were going wide and glassy, and then the lids would close halfway.

"This one's for tomorrow," Ray said with a smile. "Whatsa matter?"

"That's my cat," I said. One of us wasn't going to walk away from this one.

"It's mine now, unless you want to try to take him away from me." He had his bright spade-shaped knife out before I knew what he was doing, and held the tip at Kubo's throat. "Wanta try to take him away from me, pinprick?"

"I'll buy him from you," I said. "How much?"

"I give you twenty minutes with me," Pham interrupted.

"Half hour," Ray said, poking Kubo's neck with the knifepoint. Kubo made a slow *eeeea* squeak.

"Twenty minutes," Pham said. "If you need more, you a whi' weenie."

"O.K., let's do it. In there," he said, nodding at the room with the weird closet. "Come on, zit-brain. You need to see my technique."

I backed through the door, thinking about where I'd last seen the net gun—and then I saw it, in the far corner, under a tipped-over chair. Ray saw it, too.

He hooked the drawstring of the bag over a nail in the wall, and Kubo hung there looking dazed, but he recognized me and opened his mouth but couldn't make any noise. He probably thought I had some part in doing this to him since I wasn't helping him.

"Hand me that," Ray said to Pham, pointing at the net gun. "Pick it up by the open end, slot."

He didn't take his eyes off me when he reached for it, but I didn't care anymore—he was ruining my life for the fun of it. I grabbed the nearest thing—the broken Kirlian frame—and swung it over my head at him, but the net gun made a *poopf* sound, and I was tangled in cords and thrown backward. The edges of the net had weights in them, and they whipped around me, wrapped me tight, and I fell on my back and cracked my head on something very hard. For a second I couldn't see anything. Pham watched it all without expression.

"O.K., white boy," she said to Ray, "show it to me."

As he reached for his zipper, he turned and winked at me and Pham buried the toe of her sneaker square between his legs, right behind his nuts. It sounded like she had kicked a block of cement. Ray took a sudden deep breath and looked surprised, frozen there, still holding his zipper between his fingers. Pham popped him in the same place again, and this time her foot crushed his knuckles, and I could hear fingers breaking.

Ray just stood there looking paralyzed. Pham looked around, picked up the empty net gun and, holding it in both hands, swung it back over her head and then brought it forward hard enough that when it slammed down on Ray's head, her toes came off the floor.

He rocked around with his mouth hanging open and his arms doing limp-wristed slow-motion flailing. Pham's lower jaw jutted out, and she put her hands on her hipbones and stepped toward him as though she had a few things she wanted to get off her mind. Ray backed up two steps, and his left heel touched the silver bubble in the closet.

Whatever was in there liked him. He was pulled slowly through, and when half his leg had disappeared into the thing, he saw what was happening and started to make, "Aah, aah, ahh!" noises. Up on the wall, Kubo stared with blurry interest.

When his other leg slipped through and he was up to his waist, he recovered enough from his beating to focus on Pham and wave his arms at her. "*Please,*" he begged, "save me! Pull me out! Please!"

"We d'not need more rectums," Pham said.

Ray was up to his waist now, and inside the silver bubble where his body was being slowly pulled through, several dark shapes hovered and bobbled. "I can be good," he whimpered, glancing toward the door.

Through the slack in the net, I could barely see Uncle Heng standing there, grinning or grimacing as broadly as ever. "Whi' shi'," he mumbled.

Ray was up to his chest and trying to reach the closet doorframe with his hands, when Pham came over to me with the knife Ray had dropped, and began cutting me out.

"I'll be good!" Ray said, up to his neck. "It was just a joke!" And then his face went through, and the last we saw was the greasy top of his head—and as soon as that vanished, a cat popped out, just like one of the messages, and landed on its feet.

It was the one Ray had banged around and cut up the night before—but now the cat looked fine. Healthy and well fed, even, like it had had a lot of time to recuperate. It took one look at the three of us and trotted out the door between Heng's feet, tail high in the air.

"My ca' come back," Heng said, and turned and went back to his chair.

As I went over to unhook Kubo from the wall, a card with a message popped out of the bubble, and then the bubble blinked out of existence, leaving the closet empty.

Pham picked up the card, read it, and showed it to me. It said: THANKS. THIS ONE IS BIGGER.

I woke up the next morning to a lot of screaming and thumping. For a few seconds I thought I was in Cage 97 again and the weasels were after me. But when I was completely awake, I realized the yelling had an Italian accent.

Sammartini had returned. He'd probably seen his expensive equipment piled in the backseat of the car. It took up a lot less room than it used to.

I climbed out of bed and prepared to go take the heat, give Sammartini my college money, and offer myself into slavery to pay off the rest of it. On my dresser was the box of disks, and I blearily thought how neat it would be to just check out—go to Cage 17 and watch the hippo-cows until Sammartini forgot about me . . . or . . .

Inspiration is a wonderful thing.

I got a robe on and got out there fast. My dad was sitting on the piano bench looking very confused.

Most of Sammartini's head was bloodshot—his eyes looked like they'd been washed out with martinis, and cobwebs of broken veins colored his cheeks and nose a blotchy red. But his suit looked very good—very expensive and custom-tailored to fit his overhung belly and square-cheeked bubble-buns. He was a rich man who couldn't believe that anyone who had less money than he had would dare offend him. He just couldn't believe it. It was beyond him.

"Your father owes me fifteen thousand dollars for the equipment I loaned him—*and* another ten thousand for breach of contract. You can't even read music!" he bellowed, and stomped his foot. His veins glowed. "Go ahead, play that," he said, pointing to the sheet of Chopin on the music rack. "Play it, you cockroach. Jesus Christ. Jesus Christ."

My dad shrugged.

"*I* wrecked your stuff, Mr. Sammartini."

"I can't believe this. Jesus H. Christ. A whole family of them. Jesus Christ. Where do you kind of people come from anyway? You guys niggers or something? You lie, you bust up my stuff—you guys don't belong in the real world, you know that? The next time I hear the university needs some test animals, I'll recommend you people. Jesus. Wrecking my stuff, you know, could result in you having some serious medical problems. Jesus H. Christ."

"Actually, sir," I said, "I'll pay for the stuff if you want me to."

My dad looked amused.

"*Want* you to?" Mr. Sammartini looked amazed. He threw his manicured hands over his head.

"And," I said, "as a token of my appreciation for the loan of the equipment, I wanted to give this to you as a kind of prepayment."

He looked at the disk carefully. "What kind of shit is this?"

"Well, sir—" (I handed him the toothpick out of my Swiss knife and stood back.) "—if you just press the little red light with this—"

"What is this 'ninety-seven' shit on here? I don't need this. I need my theme song and fifteen thousand dollars, snotbrain." But he took the toothpick and he pressed the red light on the disk, and then he just stood there looking like somebody had hit him with a Cadillac.

Originally, I'd set it on thirty-eight, just to get him worried and settle him down a little. But he was a ninety-seven-type scuzz.

After twenty seconds or so, my dad said, "Mr. Sammartini? Are you all right?" He looked at me. "Is he all right?"

I shrugged. "Looks to me like he's having some kind of seizure." Out the front window I could see his Continental with his driver leaning on the roof smoking a cigarette. "Why don't you go call that guy to come in and get him?"

While my dad was out of the room, I got the yardstick out of the hall closet and knocked the disk out of Sammartini's hands. I would deal with turning it off later.

When my dad got back into the room with the driver, Sammartini was sitting on the floor in the doorway, saying, "Face . . . face. . . ." Having dealt once with those weasels, I guessed they'd probably been throwing him around like a piece of meat and nibbling on his eyelids.

"Gosh," Dad said, "he looks like a little boy who does . . . does . . ." A strange look came over his face. He looked at the piano and murmured, ". . . who does fine . . . ," and then he looked back at Sammartini, who was mumbling, "Face . . . face . . . ," and then back at the piano again, and shouted, *"That's it!"*

"It is?" the driver said. He was a big horse-faced guy in a cheap suit, and he looked confused. A thoroughbred bent-nose.

Dad sat down at the piano bench, glanced at the sheet of Chopin, and started ripping it off across the keyboard at incredible speed. When he finished, he turned around, beaming, and pointed to the sheet music and said, "F-A-C-E and Every-Good-Boy-Does-Fine. *Ha!* I couldn't remember what notes went on the lines and spaces, but that's it!" He turned around and played a few measures of something big and dramatic and then looked back over his shoulder and said expansively, "How about a margarita, everybody?"

"Well," I said, "it's only 7:30, and I have to go to school."

"I'll have one," the driver said nervously. "I get, y'know, nervous, if I have to, y'know, touch him like physically."

The fat man sat there on the floor mumbling like an idiot, and I kind of felt sorry for him, but jeez. When you threaten somebody's family, I guess you can't kick too much if somebody throws a bunch of weasels at you and you get a bit chewed up.

"Dad?"

"Yes, Son?"

"You still have that button-maker thing, you know, that makes buttons that pin on your shirt?"

"It's in the top of my closet."

"Thanks. I might need it for my science project today."

The bent-nose had a margarita with my dad, and while I was getting ready for school, I heard him say he always suspected this would happen, since Mr. S. had such a temper. He was very apologetic, and after a nice little chat about his wife and kids, he and my dad dragged Sammartini out and dumped him in the backseat of the Continental. Sammartini drooled and babbled the whole way. Now he had a cage all to himself.

When I finally left, with my books under my arm, my dad was at the piano with a smile on his face and he was playing beautiful stuff, right straight out of his head.

My dad.

* * *

Pham had wished me well when she met me in the corridor outside my science class, and while we were talking, Andrea went in, smiled, and stuck her chest out a bit more.

"You got speech memorized?" Pham asked at the last minute.

"Well . . . sort of."

"You do O.K.," she said, and gave my arm a squeeze. "School be all over next week."

"I'm just a little worried Zick's going to be all over me in the meantime."

The bell rang, but I was in my seat before it stopped, and Zick was waiting for me, grinning and leaning forward on the demonstration table.

"Good morning, Dell. Spend last night with your demon friends?" Today the top of his pimple was white.

"My report's ready, sir."

"Report? Just a report? Where are your visual aids?"

"Um, there were some diagrams I was going to put on the board."

"Sure," I heard Andrea whisper.

"No demonstrations and no visual aids? Chalk diagrams alone aren't good enough, Dell. Don't you have any other visual aids? If you don't have any visual aids to go with your project, it just isn't going to be acceptable."

"I have lots of information to present—"

He was looking at the ceiling and shaking his head. "You have no charts, no demonstrations, and you expect me to let you try to brainwash these students into believing some Satanic litany you've got cooked up? You expect me to do that?"

"I just expected to be able to present my project, sir."

He was looking at me now. Behind her hand, Andrea whispered, "Bye-bye, loverboy."

"You expected to use my class as a forum for your deviant ideas, and that isn't going to happen. I've looked at your high school records, Dell, and I think a little extra college science would do you some good. Next project."

Before anyone could answer, I raised my hand and said, "Mr. Zick, I accept your decision. And to show you there are no hard feelings on my part, I wanted to give you this." I took the button out of my pocket. I hadn't had time to do a great job on it that morning, but a little glue and some low-grade artwork was all it took.

I got out of my desk and held the button in front of me so he could read it before he could tell me to sit down . . . and a big smile broke across his face.

"Ha-ha-haa!" he sort of laughed. " 'Darwin Was a Red'—maybe there's hope for you yet, Dell."

I moved fast, hit the red dot of the disk I'd glued into the back of the button, and tried to get away from him in three seconds, before the field took hold. I dropped it on his desk in front of him and caught just a glimpse of buzzard-sized bats coming out of the air at us and hoped my momentum would carry me past him and out of range of the thing before it could get a hold on me.

And I made it.

So there was Zick, standing immobilized in front of the class, his glasses sliding slowly over his pimple and down his nose as his head filled with visions of Cage 58. Fifty-eight wasn't so bad if you didn't mind rather large bats.

The class watched him for half a minute, and during that time, all he did was make a kind of "Buhh" sound and start to sweat pretty heavily. I sat back down, and then, like everyone else, I took out some homework and started doing that. The class was calm. After dealing with puberty for a few years, not much strikes us as too weird. Zick buhhed a few more times, and then the bell rang and we all left.

It was a beautiful day. Pham offered me part of her lunch, and we sat and ate and watched some people out on the field play fris-ball.

"What you want to do with all those little metal things?" Pham asked.

"Well, I'd kind of like to check out some of the other cages, but on the other hand, I'm using those things like a big animal who wants to beat up on the littler ones." I looked out across the football field and watched the white Frisbee sail in a long slow-motion arc. "I don't know. It seems like everybody is doing something mean to someone else—all for the best of reasons, of course."

A yellow butterfly landed on the plastic box her lunch had been in. It dipped its wings twice and flew toward the field. "Maybe Cage 37 made to be that way," she said.

"A depressing thought."

"Yes," she said, spreading out her hands and grinning, "but here we are."

She had a point. She had *the* point. It's a mean miracle, but here we are.

Across from us, the white Frisbee sailed through the summer air, and yellow butterflies flickered in the sun like scraps of notepaper dropped from the sky.

While You're Up

✳   ✳   ✳

Avram Davidson

Avram Davidson is a former editor of F&SF, *one of only five in forty years, and the only one to have edited the magazine from Central America. His wonderful and distinctive short stories have been appearing in* F&SF *since 1954 ("My Boy Friend's Name Is Jello") and 1955 ("The Golem"). His most recent story is "While You're Up," a very short tale about an* almost *perfect moment.*

✳   ✳   ✳

THE scene might have been painted by Maxfield Parrish, perhaps the best of painters during that rich, lost era that also gave the world Leonardo and Rembrandt. While the latter two have their spokesmen, nay, their devotees, even they would have to concede that neither ever painted so blue a sky, and that there are those who deny that such blue skies ever indeed existed is (as Sexton often explained) beside the point. "They ought to have existed," Tony said now to the few friends, to Mother Ruth—his wife of many years—all sitting in the large front room to which his preeminence and seniority entitled him. "They *ought* to have existed, for, as we see now, sometimes they almost do—and—look! a cloud!"

Mother Ruth, who had certainly seen clouds from this room before, merely smiled and murmured something soft and inaudible; the others craned and clearly spoke of their delight and good fortune. All, except of course, for Samjo, who continued sitting with his mouth open. Tony Sexton more than once had said, though—they could all well remember—"Don't ever underestimate Samjo. He sees more than you think, and he adds things up, too."

"The wine should be warm enough to drink in a few minutes," Sexton said now. "We brought it up from the cellar several hours ago."

Barnes, from his chair with the wooden arms, declared, hands sweeping the air, "Good friends, a good view, good thoughts, and— good wine, too." Overfamiliarity may have perhaps tarnished the quotation, but Barnes's enthusiasm was always contagious.

Maria said, "This moment, with the view and the blue and the cloud and, shortly, the wine—will be a moment that I shall always remember." She peered forward, probably seeking to look into Mother Ruth's eyes, for such was Maria's habit; when she said something worthy, she felt, of notice, she sought someone's eyes and, as it were, sought to bring forth an evident approval: a smile, a nod, an expression of the face, a gesture. But this time it was not forthcoming. Perhaps Maria, for all she knew, was just a bit annoyed.

Perhaps Tony understood all this, for he smiled his famous Sexton smile, and said, "Mother Ruth often looks into her apron as the ancient sibyls did into their crystal bowls." For it was true, Mother Ruth dared to wear the antique apron, so long outlawed; and almost it did seem to make her look like something from antique eras.

Barnes picked up the metaphor and asked—Barnes often asked very odd questions—"Father, were those crystal bowls empty when the sibyls looked into them, or did they contain something, a . . . a liquid, perhaps?"

Tony Sexton very slightly pursed his lips. "Wine, I suppose, would have been too precious for such a use; water would always be in short supply. What, then? A thick soup would surely have interfered with the visioning, so—broth perhaps?"

Barnes in a moment went bright: A new concept! Then the brightness went. "One never knows when you are making a joke," he muttered.

"I wanted to have a few friends over," Sexton said, lightly leaving the subject. "Wine and five glasses waiting, a day with a lot of blue, and, if we were lucky . . . and I felt we would be lucky . . . even a cloud. A day to be remembered."

Murmurs from all assured him that the day would surely be remembered. With an effect most odd, Sexton's face turned gray, and his body seemed to fall in upon itself. For a second only, his face—like a dim, thin, crusted mask—rested on what seemed a pile of ashes; then it, too, dissolved.

The reaction of the others was varied. Maria started to rise, fell back, composed herself, looked about with a rueful air. Mother Ruth sagged. "Oh, Tony, Tony," she said, her voice very small. Barnes exclaimed loudly, beat his hands upon the costly arms of his chair. "He didn't *renew!*" cried Barnes. "Time and time again, I asked, I begged—much good that will do now," he said, deeply annoyed. He bent over, removed from the still settling pile the small tag of malleable substance, read aloud, "Your warranty expires on or about the hour of noon on the 23rd of April, 2323." Several voices declared that Tony Sexton had timed it just about right—leave it to Sexton! they said.

Maria now rose all the way. "I think," she said, "that now is *just* the time to drink that container of wine Sexton was saving; he'd want that, wouldn't he?"

"Bound to!" exclaimed Barnes. "Absolutely!"

Mother Ruth looked up from her lap. "Maria, dear. While you're up. *Would* you mind also bringing back with you the dustpan *and* the broom? Thank you, dear."

Samjo had as usual seemed to have been thinking of nothing at all; as often, this semblance was deceptive. He had been wiping, first his eyes, then his nose, with an article of cloth quite as archaic as Mother Ruth's apron. Then he spoke. "Only four glasses now, Maria," said he.

Who could help chuckling?

Eidolons

✳   ✳   ✳

Harlan Ellison

Most F&SF readers know Harlan Ellison through his passionate and uncompromising films column, "Harlan Ellison's Watching," which has been appearing since 1984. Ellison has also written book reviews for F&SF and, who knows, one day he may even contribute a science column. We've also been fortunate to publish a fair sampling of his short fiction, including such classics as "The Deathbird," "Jeffty Is Five," and "All the Lies that Are My Life." His most recent story is this strange and unsettling tale, which offers the parting gift of the man known as Vizinczey.

✳   ✳   ✳

EIDOLON: a phantom, an apparition, an image.

A NCIENT geographers gave a mystic significance to that extremity of land, the borderland of the watery unknown at the southwestern tip of Europe. Marinus and Ptolemy knew it as *Promentorium Sacrum*, the sacred promontory. Beyond that beyondmost edge, lay nothing. Or rather, lay a place that was fearful and unknowable, a place in which it was always the twenty-fifth hour of the day, the thirtieth or thirty-first of February; a turbid ocean of lost islands where golden mushroom trees reached always toward the whispering face of the moon; where tricksy life had spawned beasts and beings more of satin and ash than of man and woman; dominion of dreams, to which the unwary might journey, but whence they could never return.

My name is Vizinczey, and my background is too remarkable to be detailed here. Suffice to note that before Mr. Brown died in my arms, I had distinguished myself principally with occupations and behavior most cultures reward by the attentions of the headsman and the *strappado*. Suffice to note that before Mr. Brown died in my arms, the most laudable engagement in my *vita* was as the manager and sole roustabout of an abattoir and ossuary in Li Shih-min. Suffice to note that there were entire continents I was forbidden to visit, and that even my closest acquaintances, the family of Sawney Beane, chose to avoid social intercourse with me.

I was a pariah. Whatever land in which I chose to abide, became a land of darkness. Until Mr. Brown died in my arms, I was a thing without passion, without kindness.

While in Sydney—Australia being one of the three remaining continents where hunting dogs would not be turned out to track me down—I inquired if there might be a shop where authentic military minatures, toy soldiers of the sort H. G. Wells treasured, could be purchased. A clerk in a bookstore recalled "a customer of mine in Special Orders mentioned something like that . . . a curious little man . . . a Mr. Brown."

I got onto him, through the clerk, and was sent round to see him at his home. The moment he opened the door and our eyes met, he was frightened of me. For the brief time we spent in each other's company, he never ceased, for a moment, to fear me. Ironically, he was one of the few ambulatory creatures on this planet that I meant no harm. Toy soldiers were my hobby, and I held in high esteem those who crafted, painted, amassed, or sold them. In truth, it might be said of the Vizinczey that was I in those times before Mr. Brown died in my arms, that my approbation for toy soldiers and their aficionados was the sole salutary aspect of my nature. So, you see, he had no reason to fear me. Quite the contrary. I mention this to establish, in spite of the police records and the warrants still in existence, seeking my apprehension, I had nothing whatever to do with the death of Mr. Brown.

He did not invite me in, though he stepped aside with a tremor and permitted entrance. Cognizant of his terror at my presence, I was surprised that he locked the door behind me. Then, looking back over his shoulder at me with mounting fear, he led me into an enormous central drawing room of his home, a room expanded to inordinate size by the leveling of walls that had formed adjoining areas. In that room, on every horizontal surface, Mr. Brown had positioned rank after rank of the most astonishing military miniatures I had ever seen.

Perfect in the most minute detail, painted so artfully that I could discern no brushstroke, in colors and tones and hues so accurate and lifelike that they seemed rather to have been created with pigmentations inherent; the battalions, cohorts, regiments, legions, phalanxes, brigades and squads of metal figurines blanketed in array without a single empty space; every inch of floor, tables, cabinets, shelves, window ledges, risers, showcases, and countless numbers of stacked display boxes.

Enthralled, I bent to study more closely the infinite range of fighting men. There were Norman knights and German Landsknecht, Japanese Samurai and Prussian dragoons, foot grenadiers of the French Imperial Guard and Spanish Conquistadors; U.S. 7th Cavalry troopers from the Indian Wars; Dutch musketeers and pikemen who marched with the army of Maurice of Nassau during the long war of independence fought by the Netherlands against the Spanish Habsburgs; Greek hoplites in bronze helmets and stiff cuirasses, cocked-hat riflemen of Morgan's Virginia Rifles who repulsed Burgoyne's troops with their deadly accurate Pennsylvania long-barrels; Eygptian chariot-spearmen and French Foreign Legionnaires; Zulu warriors from Shaka's legions and English longbowmen from Agincourt; Anzacs and Persian Immortals and Assyrian slingers; Cossacks and Saracen warriors in chainmail and padded silk; 82nd Airbone paratroopers and Israeli jet pilots and Wehrmacht Panzer commanders and Russian infantrymen and Black Hussars of the 5th Regiment.

And as I drifted through a mist of wonder and pleasure, from array to array, one overriding observation dominated even my awe in the face of such artistic grandeur.

Each and every figure—to the last turbaned Cissian, trousered Scythian, wooden-helmeted Colchian or Pisidian with an oxhide shield—every one of them bore the most exquisite expression of terror and hopelessness. Faces twisted in anguish at the precise moment of death—or more terribly, the moment of *realization* of personal death

—each soldier looked up at me with eyes just fogging with tears, with mouth half-open to emit a scream, with fingers reaching toward me in splay-fingered hope of last-minute reprieve.

These were not merely painted representations.

The faces were individual. I could see every follicle of beard, every drop of sweat, every frozen tic of agony. They seemed able to complete the shriek of denial. They looked as if, should I blink, they would spring back to life and then fall dead as they were intended.

Mr. Brown had left narrow aisles of carpet among the vast armadas, and I had wandered deep into the shoe-top grassland of the drawing room, with the little man behind me, still locked up with fear but attendant at my back. Now I rose from examining a raiding party of Vietcong frozen in attitudes of agony as the breath of life stilled in them, and I turned to Mr. Brown with apparently such a look on my face that he blurted it out. I could not have stopped the confession had I so desired.

They were not metal figurines. They were flesh turned to pewter. Mr. Brown had no artistic skill save the one ability to snatch soldiers off the battlefields of time, to freeze them in metal, to miniaturize them, and to sell them. Each commando and halberdier captured in the field and reduced, at the moment of his death . . . realizing in that moment that Heaven or whatever Valhalla in which he believed, was to be denied him. An eternity of death in miniature.

"You are a greater ghoul than ever I could have aspired to become," I said.

His fright overcame him at that moment. Why, I do not know. I meant him no harm. Perhaps it was the summation of his existence, the knowledge of the monstrous hobby that had brought him an unspeakable pleasure through his long life, finally caught up with him. I do not know.

He spasmed suddenly as though struck at the base of his spine by a maul, and his eyes widened, and he collapsed toward me. To prevent the destruction of the exquisite figurines, I let him fall into my arms; and I carefully lowered him into the narrow aisle. Even so, his lifeless left leg decimated the ranks of the thirteenth-century Mongol warriors who had served Genghis Khan from the China Sea in the east to the gates of Austria in the west.

He lay face down, and I saw a drop of blood at the base of his neck. I bent closer as he struggled to turn his head to the side to speak, and saw the tiniest crossbow quarrel protruding from his rapidly discoloring flesh, just below the hairline.

He was trying to say something to me, and I knelt close to his mouth, my ear close to the exhalations of dying breath. And he lamented his life, for though he might well have been judged a monster by those who exist in conformity and abide within the mundane strictures of accepted ethical behavior, he was not a bad man. An obsessed man, certainly; but not a bad man. And to prove it, he told me haltingly of the *Promentorium Sacrum*, and of how he had found his way there, how he had struggled back. He told me of the lives and the wisdom and the wonders to be found there.

And he made one last feeble gesture to show me where the scroll was hidden. The scroll he had brought back, which had contained such knowledge as had permitted him to indulge his hobby. He made that last feeble gesture, urging me to find the scroll and to remove it from its hidden niche, and to use it for ends that would palliate his life's doings.

I tried to turn him over, to learn more, but he died in my arms. And I left him there in the narrow aisle among the Nazi Werewolves and Royal Welsh Fusiliers; and I threaded my way through the drawing room large enough to stage a cotillion; and I found the secret panel behind which he had secreted the scroll; and I removed it and saw the photograph he had taken in that beyond that lay beyond the beyondmost edge; the only image of that land that has ever existed. The whispering moon. The golden mushroom trees. The satin sea. The creatures that sit and ruminate there.

I took the scroll and went far away. Into the Outback, above Arkaroo Rock where the Dreamtime reigns. And I spent many years learning the wisdom contained in the scroll of Mr. Brown.

It would not be hyperbole to call it an epiphany.

For when I came back down, and re-entered the human stream, I was a different Vizinczey. I was recast in a different nature. All that I had been, all that I had done, all the blight I had left in my track . . . all of it was as if from someone else's debased life. I was now equipped and anxious to honor Mr. Brown's dying wish.

And that is how I have spent my time for the past several lifetimes. The scroll, in a minor footnote, affords the careful reader the key to immortality. Or as much immortality as one desires. So with this added benison of longevity, I have expended entire decades improving the condition of life for the creatures of this world that formerly I savaged and destroyed.

Now, due to circumstances I will not detail (there is no need to distress you with the specifics of vegetables and rust), the time of my passing is at hand. Vizinczey will be no more in a very short while. And all the good I have done will be the last good I can do. I will cease to be, and I will take the scroll with me. Please trust my judgment in this.

But for a very long time I have been your guardian angel. I have done you innumerable good turns. Yes, even you reading these words: I did you a good turn just last week. Think back and you will remember a random small miracle that made your existence prettier. That was I.

And as parting gift, I have extracted a brief number of the most important thoughts and skills from the scroll of the *Promentorium Sacrum*. They are the most potent runes from that astonishing document. So they will not burn, but rather will serve to warm, if properly adduced, if slowly deciphered and assimilated and understood. I have couched them in more contemporary, universal terms. I do this for your own good. They are not quite epigraphs, nor are they riddles; though set down in simple language, if pierced to the nidus, they will enrich and reify; they are potentially analeptic.

I present them to you now, because you will have to work your lives without me from this time forward. You are, as you were for millennia, alone once again. But you can do it. I present them to you because, from the moment Mr. Brown died in my arms, I have been unable to forget the look of human misery, endless despair, and hopelessness on the face of a Spartan soldier who lay on a carpet in a house in Sydney, Australia. This is for him, for all of them, and for you.

--- **1** ---

It's the dark of the sun. It's the hour in which worms sing madrigals, tea leaves tell their tales in languages we once used to converse with the trees, and all the winds of the world have returned to the great throat that gave them life. Messages come to us from the core of quiet. A friend now gone tries desperately to pass a message from the beyond, but the strength of ghosts is slight: all he can do is move dustmotes with great difficulty, arranging them with excruciating slowness to form words. The message comes together on the glossy jacket of a book casually dropped on a table more than a year ago. Laboriously laid, mote by mote, the message tells the friend still living that friendship must involve risk, that it is merely a word if it is never tested, that anyone can claim *friend* if there is no chance of cost. It is phrased simply. On the other side, the shade of the friend now departed waits and hopes. He fears the inevitable: his living friend despises disorder and dirt: what if he chances on the misplaced book while wearing his white gloves?

2

Do they chill, the breezes that whisper of yesterday, the winds that come from a hidden valley near the top of the world? Do they bite, the shadowy thoughts that lie at the bottom of your heart during daylight hours, that swirl up like wood smoke in the night? Can you hear the memories of those who have gone before, calling to you when the weariness takes you, close on midnight? They are the winds, the thoughts, the voices of memory that prevail in the hour that lies between awareness and reverie. And on the other side of the world, hearing the same song, is your one true love, understanding no better than you, that those who cared and went away are trying to bring you together. Can you breach the world that keeps you apart?

3

This is an emergency bulletin. We've made a few necessary alterations in the status quo. For the next few weeks, there will be no madness; no imbecile beliefs; no paralogical, prelogical, or paleological thinking. No random cruelty. For the next few weeks, all the impaired mentalities will be frozen in stasis. No attempts to get you to believe that vast and cool intelligences come from space regularly in circular vehicles. No runaway tales of yetis, sasquatches, hairy shamblers of a lost species. No warnings that the cards, the stones, the running water, or the stars are against your best efforts. This is the time known in Indonesia as *djam karet*—the hour that stretches. For the next few weeks you can breathe freely and operate off these words by one who learned too late, by one who has gone away, who was called Camus: "It is not man who must be protected, but the possibilities within him." You have a few weeks without hindrance. Move quickly.

4

The casement window blows open. The nightmare has eluded the guards. It's over the spiked wall and it's in here with you. The lights go out. The temperature drops sharply. The bones in your body sigh. You're all alone with it. Circling with your back to the wall. Hey, don't be a nasty little coward; face it and disembowel it. You've got time. You have *always* had time, but the fear slowed you, and you were overcome. But this is the hour that stretches . . . and you've got a chance. After all, it's only your conscience come to kill you. Stop shivering and put up your dukes. You might beat it this time, now that you know you have some breathing space. For in this special hour, anything that has ever happened will happen again. Except, this time, it's *your* turn to risk it all.

5

In the cathedral at the bottom of the Maracot Deep, the carillon chimes for all the splendid thinkers you never got to be. The memories of great thoughts left unspoken rise from their watery tomb and ascend to the surface. The sea boils at their approach, and a siege of sea eagles gathers in the sky above the disturbance. Fishermen in small boats listen as they have never listened before, and all seems clear for the first time. These are warnings of storms made only by men. Tempests and sea-spouts, tsunamis and bleeding oceans the color of tragedy. For men's tongues have been stilled, and more great thoughts will die never having been uttered. Memories from the pit of the Deep rise to lament their brethren. Even now, even in the hour that stretches, the past silently cries out not to be forgotten. Are you listening, or must you be lost at sea forever?

6

Did you have one of those days today, like a nail in the foot? Did the pterodactyl corpse dropped by the ghost of your mother from the spectral *Hindenburg* forever circling the Earth come smashing through the lid of your glass coffin? Did the New York strip steak you attacked at dinner suddenly show a mouth filled with needle-sharp teeth, and did it snap off the end of your fork, the last solid-gold fork from the set Anastasia pressed into your hands as they took her away to be shot? Is the slab under your apartment building moaning that it cannot stand the weight on its back a moment longer, and is the building stretching and creaking? Did a good friend betray you today, or did that good friend merely keep silent and fail to come to your aid? Are you holding the razor at your throat this very instant? Take heart, comfort is at hand. This is the hour that stretches. *Djam karet.* We are the cavalry. We're here. Put away the pills. We'll get you through this bloody night. Next time, it'll be your turn to help us.

------------------------------ 7 ------------------------------

You woke in the night, last night, and the fiery, bony hand was enscribing mystic passes in the darkness of your bedroom. It carved out words in the air, flaming words, messages that required answers. One picture is worth a thousand words, the hand wrote. "Not in *this* life," you said to the dark and the fire. "Give me one picture that shows how I felt when they gassed my dog. I'll take less than a thousand words and make you weep for the last Neanderthal crouched at the cliff's edge at the moment he realized his kind were gone . . . show me your one picture. Commend to me the one picture that captures what it was like for me in the moment she said it was all over between us. Not in *this* life, Bonehand" So here we are, once again in the dark, with nothing between us in this hour that stretches but the words. Sweet words and harsh words and words that tumble over themselves to get born. We leave the pictures for the canvas of your mind. Seems only fair.

------------------------------ 8 ------------------------------

Rain fell in a special pattern. I couldn't believe it was doing that. I ran to the other side of the house and looked out the window. The sun was shining there. I saw a hummingbird bury his stiletto beak in a peach on one of the trees, like a junkie who had turned himself into the needle. He sucked deeply and shadows flowed out of the unripe peach: a dreamy vapor that enveloped the bird, changing its features to something jubilantly malevolent. With juice glowing in one perfect drop at the end of its beak, it turned a yellow eye toward me as I pressed against the window. Go away, it said. I fell back and rushed to the other side of the house where rain fell in one place on the sunny street. In my soul I knew that not all inclement weather meant sorrow, that even the brightest day held dismay. I knew this all had meaning, but there was no one else in the world to whom I could go for interpretation. There were only dubious sources, and none knew more than I, not really. Isn't that the damnedest thing: there's never a good reference when you need one.

9

Through the jaws of night we stormed, banners cracking against the icy wind, the vapor our beasts panted preceding us like smoke signals, warning the enemy that we looked forward to writing our names in the blood of the end of their lives. We rode for Art! For the singing soul of Creativity! Our cause was just, because it was the only cause worth dying for. All others were worth living for. They stood there on the black line of the horizon, their pikes angrily tilted toward us. *For Commerce*, they shouted with one voice. *For Commerce!* And we fell upon them, and the battle was high-wave traffic, with the sound of metal on metal, the sound of hooves on stone, the sound of bodies exploding. We battled all through the endless midnight till at last we could see nothing but hills and valleys of dead. And in the end, we lost. We always lost. And I, alone, am left to tell of that time. Only I, alone of all who went to war to measure the height of the dream, only I remain to speak to you here in the settling silence. Why do *you* feel diminished . . . you weren't there . . . it wasn't your war. Hell hath no fury like that of the uninvolved.

10

Hear the music. Listen with all your might, and you needn't clap to keep Tinker Bell from going into a coma. The music will restore her rosy cheeks. Then seek out the source of the melody. Look long and look deep, and somewhere in the murmuring world you will find the storyteller, there under the cabbage leaves, singing to herself. Or is that a she? Perhaps it's a he. But whichever, or whatever, the poor thing is crippled. Can you see that now? The twisting, the bending, the awkward shape, the milky eye, the humped back, do you now make it out? But if you try to join in, to work a duet with wonder, the song ceases. When you startle the cricket, its symphony ceases. Art is not by committee, nor is it by wish fulfillment. It is that which is produced in the hour that stretches, the timeless time wherein *all* songs are sung. In a place devoid of electrical outlets. And if you try to grasp either the singer or the song, all you will hold is sparkling dust as fine as the butter the moth leaves on glass. How the bee flies, how the lights go on, how the enigma enriches and the explanation chills . . . how the music is made . . . are not things we were given to know. And only the fools who cannot hear the song ask that the rules be posted. Hear the music. And enjoy. But do not cry. Not everyone was intended to reach A above high C.

11

Ah, there were giants in the land in those days. There was a sweet-faced, honey-voiced girl named Barbara Wire, whom we called Nancy because no one had the heart to call her Barb Wire. She tossed a salamander into a window fan to see what would happen. There was Sofie, who had been bitten by *The Sun Also Rises* at a tender age, and who took it as her mission in life to permit crippled virginal boys the enjoyment of carnal knowledge of her every body part: harelips, lepers, paraplegics, albinos with pink eyes, aphasiacs, she welcomed them all to her bed. There was Marissa, who could put an entire unsegmented fried chicken in her mouth all at once, chew without opening her lips or dribbling, and who would then delicately spit out an intact skeleton, as dry and clean as the Gobi Desert. Perdita drew portraits. She would sit you down, and with her pad and charcoal, quickly capture the depth and specificity of your most serious flaws of honor, ethic, and conscience, so accurately that you would rip the drawing to pieces before anyone else could see the nature of your corruption. Jolanda: who stole cars and then reduced them to metal sculpture in demolition derbies, whose residence was in an abandoned car-crusher. Peggy: who never slept but told endlessly of her waking dreams of the things the birds told her they saw from on high. Naomi: who was white, passing for black, because she felt the need to shoulder some of the guilt of the world. Ah, there were giants in the land in those days. But I left the room, and closed the door behind me so that the hour that stretches would not leak out. And though I've tried portal after portal, I've never been able to find that room again. Perhaps I'm in the wrong house.

12

I woke at three in the morning, bored out of sleep by dreams of such paralyzing mediocrity that I could not lie there and suffer my own breathing. Naked, I padded through the silent house: I knew that terrain as my tongue knows my palate. There were rolls of ancient papyrus lying on the counter. I will replace them, high in a dark closet, I thought. Then I said it aloud . . . the house was silent, I could speak to the air. I took a tall stool and went to the closet, and climbed up and replaced the papyrus. Then I saw it. A web. Dark and billowing in the corner of the ceiling, not silvery but ashy. Something I could not bear to see in my home. It threatened me. I climbed down, moved through the utter darkness, and struggled with the implements in the broom closet, found the feather duster, and hurried back. Then I killed the foaming web and left the closet. Clean the feather duster, I thought. In the backyard I moved to the wall, and shook it out. Then, as I returned, incredible pain assaulted me. The cactus pup with its cool, long spikes had embedded itself in the ball of my naked right foot. My testicles shrank and my eyes watered. I took an involuntary step, and the spines drove deeper. I reached down to remove the agony, and a spike embedded itself in my thumb. I shouted. I hurt. Limping, I got to the kitchen. In the light of the kitchen, I tried to pinch out the spines. They were barbed. They came away with bits of flesh attached. The poison was already spreading. I hurt very much. I hobbled to the bathroom to put antiseptic or the Waters of Lethe on the wounds. They bled freely. I salved myself, and returned to the bed, hating my wife who slept unknowing; I hated my friend who lay dreaming in another part of the house. I hated the world for placing random pain in my innocent path. I lay down and hated all natural order for a brief time.

Then I fell asleep. Relieved. Boredom had been killed with the billowing web. Somehow, the universe always provides.

13

Like all men, my father was a contradiction in terms. Not more than two or three years after the Great Depression, when my family was still returning pop bottles for the few cents deposit, and saving those pennies in a quart milk bottle, my father did one of the kindest things I've ever known: he hired a man as an assistant in his little store; an assistant he didn't really need and couldn't afford. He hired the man because he had three children and couldn't find a job. Yet not more than a week later, as we locked up the stationary shop late on a Saturday night, and began to walk down the street to the diner where we would have our hot roast beef sandwiches and french fries, with extra country gravy for dipping the fries, another man approached us on the street and asked for twenty-five cents to buy a bowl of soup. And my father snarled, "No! Get away from us!" I was more startled at that moment than I had ever been—or ever *would* be, as it turned out, for my father died not much later that year—more startled than by anything my father had ever said or done. If I had known the word at that age—I was only twelve—I would have realized that I was *dumbfounded*. My gentle father, who never raised his voice to me or to anyone else, who was unfailingly kind and polite even to the rudest customer, who has forever been a model of compassion for me, *my father* had grown icy and stony in that exchange with an innocent stranger. "Dad," I asked him, as we walked away from the lonely man, "how come you didn't give that fella a quarter for some soup?" He looked down at me, as if through a crack in the door of a room always kept locked, and he said, "He won't buy a bowl of soup. He'll only buy more liquor." Because my father never lied to me, and because I knew it was important for him always to tell me the truth, I didn't ask anything more about it. But I never forgot that evening; and it is an incident I can never fit into the film strip of loving memories I run and rerun starring my father. Somehow I feel, without understanding, that it was the most important moment of human frailty and compassion in the twelve years through which I was permitted to adore my father. And I wonder when I will grow wise enough to understand the wisdom of my father.

*   *   *

Thus, my gift. There were six more selections from the scroll of the *Promentorium Sacrum*, but once having entered them here, I realized they would cause more harm than good. Tell me truly: Would you really want the power to bend others to your will, or the ability to travel at will in an instant to anyplace in the world, or the facility for reading the future in mirrors? No, I thought not. It is gratifying to see that just the wisdom imparted here has sobered you to that extent.

And what would you do with the knowledge of shaping, the talent for sending, the capturing of rainbows? You already possess such powers and abilities as the world has never known. Now that I've left you the time to master what you already know, you should have no sorrow at being denied these others. Be content.

Now I take my leave. Passage of an instant sort has been arranged. Vizinczey, the I that I became, goes finally on the journey previously denied. Until I had fulfilled the dying request of Mr. Brown, I felt it was unfair of me to indulge myself. But now I go to the sacred promontory; to return the scroll; to sit at the base of the golden mushroom trees and confabulate with astonishing creatures. Perhaps I will take a camera, and perhaps I will endeavor to send back a snap or two, but that is unlikely.

I go contentedly, for all my youthful crimes, having left this a prettier venue than I found it.

And finally, for those of you who always wash behind your ears because, as children, you heeded the admonition "go wash behind your ears," seeing motion pictures of children being examined by their parents before being permitted to go to the dinner table, remembering the panels in comic strips in which children were being told, "Go back and wash behind your ears," who always wondered why that was important—after all, your ears fit fairly close to your head—who used to wonder what one could possibly have behind one's ears—great masses of mud, dangerous colonies of germs, could vegetation actually take root there, what are we talking about and why such obsessive attention to something so silly?—for those of you who were trusting enough to wash behind your ears, and still do . . . for those of you who know the urgency of tying your shoelaces tightly . . . who have no fear of vegetables or rust . . . I answer the question you raise about the fate of those tiny metal figurines left in eternal anguish on the floor of Mr. Brown's drawing room. I answer the question in this way:

There was a man standing behind you yesterday in the checkout line at the grocery store. You casually noticed that he was buying the most unusual combinations of exotic foods. When you dropped the package of frozen peas, and he stooped to retrieve it for you, you noticed that he had a regal, almost one might say *militaristic*, bearing. He clicked his heels as he proffered the peas, and when you thanked him, he spoke with a peculiar accent.

Trust me in this: not even if you were Professor Henry Higgins could you place the point of origin of that accent.

Dedicated to the memory of Mike Hodel

Face Value

*   *   *

Karen Joy Fowler

Karen Joy Fowler is another of the fine new voices in science fiction. A collection of her short fiction, Artificial Things, *was published in 1987. This story—about a husband/wife team and their study of an alien race that has lost the ability to fly—is SF at its best, in which we read about something truly alien and discover something about humans.*

*   *   *

I T was almost like being alone. Taki, who had been alone one way or another most of his life, recognized this and thought he could deal with it. What choice did he have? It was only that he had allowed himself to hope for something different. A second star, small and dim, joined the sun in the sky, making its appearance over the rope bridge that spanned the empty river. Taki crossed the bridge in a hurry to get inside before the hottest part of the day began.

Something flashed briefly in the dust at his feet, and he stooped to pick it up. It was one of Hesper's poems, half finished, left out all night. Taki had stopped reading Hesper's poetry. It reflected nothing, not a whisper of her life here with him, but was filled with longing for things and people behind her. Taki pocketed the poem on his way to the house, stood outside the door, and removed what dust he could

230

with the stiff brush that hung at the entrance. He keyed his admittance; the door made a slight sucking sound as it resealed behind him.

Hesper had set out an iced glass of ade for him. Taki drank it at a gulp, superimposing his own dusty fingerprints over hers sketched lightly in the condensation on the glass. The drink was heavily sugared and only made him thirstier.

A cloth curtain separated one room from another, a blue sheet, Hesper's innovation since the dwelling was designed as a single, multifunctional space. Through the curtain, Taki heard a voice and knew Hesper was listening again to her mother's letter—Earth weather, the romances of her younger cousins. The letter had arrived weeks ago, but Taki was careful not to remind Hesper how old its news really was. If she chose to imagine the lives of her family moving along the same timeline as her own, then this must be a fantasy she needed. She knew the truth. In the time it had taken her to travel here with Taki, her mother had grown old and died. Her cousins had settled into marriages happy or unhappy or had faced life alone. The letters that continued to arrive with some regularity were an illusion. A lifetime later, Hesper would answer them.

Taki ducked through the curtain to join her. "Hot," he told her as if this were news. She lay on their mat stomach down, legs bent at the knees, feet crossed in the air. Her hair, the color of dried grasses, hung over her face. Taki stared for a moment at the back of her head. "Here," he said. He pulled out her poem from his pocket and laid it by her hand. "I found this out front."

Hesper switched off the letter and rolled onto her back away from the poem. She was careful not to look at Taki. Her cheeks were stained with irregular red patches, so that Taki knew she had been crying again. The observation caused him a familiar mixture of sympathy and impatience. His feelings for Hesper always came in these uncomfortable combinations; it tired him.

" 'Out front,' " Hesper repeated, and her voice held a practiced tone of uninterested nastiness. "And how did you determine that one part of this featureless landscape was the 'front'?"

"Because of the door. We have only the one door, so it's the front door."

"No," said Hesper. "If we had two doors, then one might arguably be the front door and the other the back door, but with only one it's just the door." Her gaze went straight upward. "You use words so carelessly. Words from another world. They mean nothing here." Her eyelids fluttered briefly, the lashes darkened with tears. "It's not just an annoyance to me, you know," she said. "It can't help but damage your work."

"My work is the study of the mene," Taki answered. "Not the creation of a new language." And Hesper's eyes closed.

"I really don't see the difference," she told him. She lay a moment longer without moving, then opened her eyes and looked at Taki directly. "I don't want to have this conversation. I don't know why I started it. Let's rewind, run it again. I'll be the wife this time. You come in and say, 'Honey, I'm home!' and I'll ask you how your morning was."

Taki began to suggest that this was a scene from another world and would mean nothing here. He had not yet framed the sentence, when he heard the door seal release and saw Hesper's face go hard and white. She reached for her poem and slid it under the scarf at her waist. Before she could get to her feet, the first of the mene had joined them in the bedroom.

Taki ducked through the curtain to fasten the door before the temperature inside the house rose. The outer room was filled with dust, and the hands that reached out to him as he went past left dusty streaks on his clothes and his skin. He counted eight of the mene, fluttering about him like large moths, moths the size of human children, but with furry vestigial wings, hourglass abdomens, sticklike limbs. They danced about him in the open spaces, looked through the cupboards, and pulled the tapes from his desk. When they had their backs to him, he could see the symmetrical arrangement of dark spots that marked their wings in a pattern resembling a human face. A very sad face, very distinct. Masculine, Taki had always thought, but Hesper disagreed.

The party that had made initial contact under the leadership of Hans Mene so many years ago had wisely found the faces too whimsical for mention in their report. Instead they had included pictures and allowed them to speak for themselves. Perhaps the original explorers had been asking the same question Hesper posed the first time Taki showed her the pictures. Was the face really there? Or was this only evidence of the ability of humans to see their own faces in everything? Hesper had a poem titled "The Kitchen God," which recounted the true story of a woman about a century ago who had found the image of Christ in the burn marks on a tortilla. "Do *they* see it, too?" she had asked Taki, but there was as yet no way to ask this of the mene, no way to know if they had reacted with shock and recognition to the faces of the first humans they had seen, though studies of the mene eye suggested a finer depth perception, which might significantly distort the flat image.

Taki thought that Hesper's own face had changed since the day, only six months ago calculated as Travel-time, when she had said she would come here with him and he thought it was because she loved him. They had sorted through all the information that had been collected to date on the mene, and her face had been all sympathy then. "What would it be like," she asked him, "to be able to fly and then to lose this ability? To outgrow it? What would a loss like that do to the racial consciousness of a species?"

"It happened so long ago, I doubt it's even noticed as a loss," Taki had answered. "Legends, myths not really believed, perhaps. Probably not even that. In the racial memory not even a whisper."

Hesper had ignored him. "What a shame they don't write poetry," she had said. She was finding them less romantic now as she joined Taki in the outer room, her face stoic. The mene surrounded her, ran their string-fingered hands all over her body, inside her clothing. One mene attempted to insert a finger into her mouth, but Hesper tightened her lips together resolutely, dust on her chin. Her eyes were fastened on Taki. Accusingly? Beseechingly? Taki was no good at reading people's eyes. He looked away.

Eventually the mene grew bored. They left in groups, a few lingering behind to poke among the boxes in the bedroom, then following the others until Hesper and Taki were left alone. Hesper went to wash herself as thoroughly as their limited water supply allowed; Taki swept up the loose dust. Before he finished, Hesper returned, showing him her empty jewelry box without a word. The jewelry had all belonged to her mother.

"I'll get them when it cools," Taki told her.

"Thank you."

It was always Hesper's things that the mene took. The more they disgusted her—pawing over her, rummaging through her things, no way to key the door against clever mene fingers even if Taki had agreed to lock them out, which he had not—the more fascinating they seemed to find her. They touched her twice as often as they touched Taki, and much more insistently. They took her jewelry, her poems, her letters, all the things she treasured most; and Taki believed, although it was far too early in his studies really to speculate with any assurance, that the mene read something off the objects. The initial explorers had concluded that mene communication was entirely telepathic, and if this were accurate, then Taki's speculation was not such a leap. Certainly the mene didn't value the objects for themselves. Taki always found them discarded in the dust on this side of the rope bridge.

The fact that everything would be easily recovered did nothing to soften Hesper's sense of invasion. She mixed herself a drink, stirring it with the metal straw that poked through the dustproof lid. "You shouldn't allow it," she said at last, and Taki knew from the time that had elapsed that she had tried not to begin this familiar conversation. He appreciated her effort as much as he was annoyed by her failure.

"It's part of my job," he reminded her. "We have to be accessible to them. I study them. They study us. There's no way to differentiate the two activities, and certainly no way to establish communication except simultaneously."

"You're letting them study us, but you're giving them a false picture. You're allowing them to believe that humans intrude on each other in this way. Does it occur to you that they may be involved in similar charades? If so, what can either of us learn?"

Taki took a deep breath. "The need for privacy may not be as intrinsically human as you imagine. I could point to many societies, prior to the plagues, that afforded very little of this. As for any deliberate misrepresentations on their part—well, isn't that the whole rationale for not sending a study team? Wouldn't I be further along if I were working with environmentalists, physiologists, linguists? But the risk of contamination increases exponentially with each additional human. We would be too much of a presence. Of course, I will be very careful. I am far from the stage in my study where I can begin to draw conclusions. When I visit them. . . ."

"Reinforcing the notion that such visits are ordinary human behavior. . . ." Hesper was looking at Taki with great coolness.

"When I visit them I am much more circumspect," Taki finished. "I conduct my study as unobtrusively as possible."

"And what do you imagine you are studying?" Hesper asked. She closed her lips tightly over the straw and drank. Taki regarded her steadily and with exasperation.

"Is this a trick question?" he asked. "I imagine I am studying the mene. What do you imagine I am studying?"

"What humans always study," said Hesper. "Humans."

You never saw one of the mene alone. Not ever. One never wandered off to watch the sun set or took its food to a solitary hole to eat without sharing. They did everything in groups, and although Taki had been observing them for weeks now and was able to identify individuals and had compiled charts of the groupings he had seen, trying to isolate families or friendships or work-castes, still the results were inconclusive.

His attempts at communication were similarly discouraging: He had tried verbalizations, but had not expected a response to them; he had no idea how they processed audio information, although they could hear. He had tried clapping and gestures, simple hand signals for the names of common objects. He had no sense that these efforts were noticed. They were so unfocused when he dealt with them, fluttering here, fluttering there. Taki's esp-quotient had never been measurable, yet he tried that route, too. He tried to send a simple command. He would trap a mene hand and hold it against his own cheek, trying to form in his mind the picture that corresponded to the action. When he released the hand, sticky mene fingers might linger for a moment or they might slip away immediately, tangle in his hair instead, or tap his teeth. Mene teeth were tiny and pointed like wires. Taki saw them only when the mene ate. At other times they were hidden inside the folds of skin that almost hid their eyes as well. Taki speculated that the skin flaps protected their mouths and eyes from the dust. Taki found mene faces less expressive than their backs. Head-on they appeared petaled and blind as flowers. When he wanted to differentiate one mene from another, Taki looked at their wings.

Hesper had warned him there would be no art, and he had asked her how she could be so sure. "Because their communication system is perfect," she said. "Out of one brain and into the next with no loss of meaning, no need for abstraction. Art arises from the inability to communicate. Art is the imperfect symbol. Isn't it?" But Taki, watching the mene carry water up from their underground deposits, asked himself where the line between tools and art objects should be drawn. For no functional reason that he could see, the water containers curved in the centers like the shapes of the mene's own abdomens.

Taki followed the mene below-ground, down some shallow, rough-cut stairs into the darkness. The mene themselves were slightly luminescent when there was no other light; at times and seasons some were spectacularly so, and Taki's best guess was that this was sexual. Even with the dimmer members, Taki could see well enough. He moved through a long tunnel with a low ceiling that made him stoop. He could hear water at the other end of it, not the water itself, but a special quality to the silence that told him water was near. The lake was clearly artificial, collected during the rainy season, which no human had seen yet. The tunnel narrowed sharply. Taki could have gone forward, but felt suddenly claustrophobic and backed out instead. What did the mene think, he wondered, of the fact that he came here without Hesper?

Did they notice this at all? Did it teach them anything about humans that they were capable of understanding?

"Their lives together are perfect," Hesper said. "Except for those useless wings. If they are ever able to talk with us at all, it will be because of those wings."

Of course Hesper was a poet. The world was all language as far as she was concerned.

When Taki first met Hesper, at a party given by a colleague of his, he had asked her what she did. "I name things," she had said. "I try to find the right names for things." In retrospect, Taki thought it was bullshit. He couldn't remember why he had been so impressed with it at the time, a deliberate miscommunication when a simple answer, "I write poetry," would have been so clear and easy to understand. He felt the same way about her poetry itself, needlessly obscure, slightly evocative, but it left the reader feeling that he had fallen short somehow, that it had been a test and he had flunked it. It was unkind poetry, and Taki had worked so hard to read it then.

"Am I right?" he would ask her anxiously when he finished. "Is that what you're saying?" But she would answer that the poem spoke for itself.

"Once it's on the page, I've lost control over it. Then the reader determines what it says or how it works." Hesper's eyes were gray, the irises so large and intense within their dark rings that they made Taki dizzy. "So you're always right. By definition. Even if it's not remotely close to what I intended."

What Taki really wanted was to find himself in Hesper's poems. He would read them anxiously for some symbol that could be construed as him, some clue as to his impact on her life. But he was never there.

It was against policy to send anyone into the field alone. There were pros and cons, of course, but ultimately the isolation of a single professional was seen as too cruel. For shorter projects there were advantages in sending a threesome, but during a longer study the group dynamics in a trio often became difficult. Two was considered ideal, and Taki knew that Rawji and Heyen had applied for this post, a husband-and-wife team in which both members were trained for this type of study. He had never stopped being surprised that the post had been offered to him instead. He could not even have been considered if Hesper had not convinced the committee of her willingness to accompany him, but she must have done much more. She must have impressed someone very much for them to decide that one trained xenologist and one poet might be more valuable than two trained xenologists. The committee had made some noises about possible "contamination" occurring between the two trained professionals, but Taki found this argument specious. "What did you say to them?" he asked her after her interview, and she shrugged.

"You know," she said. "Words."

Taki had hidden things from the committee during his own interview. Things about Hesper. Her moods, her deep attachment to her mother, her unreliable attachment to him. He must have known it would never work out, but he walked about in those days with the stunned expression of a man who had been given everything. Could he be blamed for accepting it? Could he be blamed for believing in Hesper's unexpected willingness to accompany him? It made a sort of equation for Taki. *If* Hesper were willing to give up everything and come with Taki, *then* Hesper loved Taki. An ordinary marriage commitment was reviewable every five years; this was something much greater. No other explanation made any sense.

The equation still held a sort of inevitability for Taki. *Then* Hesper loved Taki, *if* Hesper were willing to come with him. So somehow, sometime, Taki had done something that lost him Hesper's love. If he could figure out what, perhaps he could make her love him again. "Do you love me?" he had asked Hesper, only once; he had too much pride for these thinly disguised pleadings. "Love is such a difficult word," she had answered, but her voice had been filled with a rare softness and had not hurt Taki as much as it might.

The daystar was appearing again when Taki returned home. Hesper had made a meal, which suggested she was coping well today. It included a sort of pudding made of a local fruit they had found themselves able to tolerate. Hesper called the pudding "boxty." It was apparently a private joke. Taki was grateful for the food and the joke, even if he didn't understand it. He tried to keep the conversation lighthearted, talking to Hesper about the mene water jars. Taki's position was that when the form of a practical object was less utilitarian than it might be, then it was art. Hesper laughed. She ran through a list of human artifacts and made him classify them.

"A paper clip," she said.

"The shape hasn't changed in centuries," he told her. "Not art."

"A safety pin."

Taki hesitated. How essential was the coil at the bottom of the pin? Very. "Not art," he decided.

"A hairbrush."

"Boar bristle?"

"Wood handle."

"Art. Definitely."

She smiled at him. "You're confusing ornamentation with art. But why not? It's as good a definition as any," she told him. "Eat your boxty."

They spent the whole afternoon alone, uninterrupted. Taki transcribed the morning's notes into his files and reviewed his tapes. Hesper recorded a letter whose recipient would never hear it and sang softly to herself.

That night he reached for her, his hand along the curve at her waist. She stiffened slightly, but responded by putting her hand on his face. He kissed her, and her mouth did not move. His movements became less gentle. It might have been passion; it might have been anger. She told him to stop, but he didn't. Couldn't. Wouldn't. "Stop," she said again, and he heard she was crying. "They're here. Please stop. They're watching us."

"Studying us," Taki said. "Let them." But he rolled away and released her. They were alone in the room. He would have seen the mene easily in the dark. "Hesper," he said. "There's no one here."

She lay rigid on her side of their bed. He saw the stitching of her backbone disappearing into her neck, and had a sudden feeling that he could see everything about her, how she was made, how she was held together. It made him no less angry.

"I'm sorry," Hesper told him, but he didn't believe her. Even so, he was asleep before she was. He made his own breakfast the next morning without leaving anything out for her. He was gone before she had gotten out of bed.

The mene were gathering food, dried husks thick enough to protect the liquid fruit during the two-star dry season. They punctured the husks with their needle-thin teeth. Several crowded about him, greeting him with their fingers, checking his pockets, removing his recorder and passing it about until one of them dropped it in the dust. When they returned to work, Taki retrieved it, wiped it as clean as he could. He sat down to watch them, logged everything he observed. He noted in particular how often they touched each other, and wondered what each touch meant. Affection? Communication? Some sort of chain of command?

Later he went underground again, choosing another tunnel, looking for one that wouldn't narrow so as to exclude him, but finding himself beside the same lake with the same narrow access ahead. He went deeper this time until it gradually became too close for his shoulders. Before him he could see a luminescence; he smelled the dusty odor of the mene and could just make out a sound, too, a sort of movement, a grass-rubbing-together sound. He stooped and strained his eyes to see something in the faint light. It was like looking into the small end of a pair of binoculars. The tunnel narrowed and narrowed. Beyond it must be the mene homes, and he could never get into them. He contrasted this with the easy access they had to his home. At the end of his vision, he thought he could just see something move, but he wasn't sure. A light touch on the back of his neck and another behind his knee startled him. He twisted around to see a group of the mene crowded into the tunnel behind him. It gave him the feeling of being trapped, and he had to force himself to be very gentle as he pushed his way back and let the mene go through. The dark pattern of their wings stood in high relief against the luminescent bodies. The human faces grew smaller and smaller until they disappeared.

"Leave me alone," Hesper told him. It took Taki completely by surprise. He had done nothing but enter the bedroom; he had not even spoken yet. "Just leave me alone."

Taki saw no signs that Hesper had ever gotten up. She lay against the pillow, and her cheek was still creased from the wrinkles in the sheets. She had not been crying. There was something worse in her face, something that alarmed Taki.

"Hesper?" he asked. "Hesper? Did you eat anything? Let me get you something to eat."

It took Hesper a moment to answer. When she did, she looked ordinary again. "Thank you," she said. "I am hungry." She joined him in the outer room, wrapped in their blanket, her hair tangled around her face. She got a drink for herself, dropping the empty glass once, stooping to retrieve it. Taki had the strange impression that the glass fell slowly. When they had first arrived, the gravitational pull had been light, just perceptibly lighter then Earth's. Without quite noticing, this had registered on him in a sort of lightheartedness. But Hesper had complained of feelings of dislocation, disconnection. Taki put together a cold breakfast that Hesper ate slowly, watching her own hands as if they fascinated her. Taki looked away. "Fork," she said. He looked back. She was smiling at him.

"What?"

"Fork."

He understood. "Not art."

"Four tines?"

He didn't answer.

"Roses carved on the handle."

"Well then, art. Because of the handle. Not because of the tines." He was greatly reassured.

The mene came while he was telling her about the tunnel. They put their dusty fingers in her food, pulled it apart. Hesper set her fork down and pushed the plate away. When they reached for her, she pushed them away, too. They came back. Hesper shoved harder.

"Hesper," said Taki.

"I just want to be left alone. They never leave me alone." Hesper stood up, towering above the mene. The blanket fell to the floor. "We flew here," Hesper said to the mene. "Did you see the ship? Didn't you see the pod? Doesn't that interest you? Flying?" She laughed and flapped her arms until they froze, horizontal at her sides. The mene reached for her again, and she brought her arms in to protect her breasts, pushing the mene away repeatedly, harder and harder, until they tired of approaching her and went into the bedroom, reappearing with her poems in their hands. The door sealed behind them.

"I'll get them back for you," Taki promised, but Hesper told him not to bother.

"I haven't written in weeks," she said. "In case you hadn't noticed. I haven't finished a poem since I came here. I've lost that. Along with everything else." She brushed at her hair rather frantically with one hand. "It doesn't matter," she added. "My poems? Not art."

"Are you the best person to judge that?" Taki asked.

"Don't patronize me." Hesper returned to the table, looked again at the plate that held her unfinished breakfast, dusty from handling. "My critical faculties are still intact. It's just the poetry that's gone." She took the dish to clean it, scraped the food away. "I was never any good," she said. "Why do you think I came here? I had no poetry of my own, so I thought I'd write the mene's. I came to a world without words. I hoped it would be clarifying. I knew there was a risk." Her hands moved very fast. "I want you to know I don't blame you."

"Come and sit down a moment, Hesper," Taki said, but she shook her head. She looked down at her body and moved her hands over it.

"They feel sorry for us. Did you know that? They feel sorry about our bodies."

"How do *you* know that?" Taki asked.

"Logic. We have these completely functional bodies. No useless wings. Not art." Hesper picked up the blanket and headed for the bedroom. At the cloth curtain she paused a moment. "They love our loneliness, though. They've taken all mine. They never leave me alone now." She thrust her right arm suddenly out into the air. It made the curtain ripple. "Go away," she said, ducking behind the sheet.

Taki followed her. He was very frightened. "No one is here but us, Hesper," he told her. He tried to put his arms around her, but she pushed him back and began to dress.

"Don't touch me all the time," she said. He sank onto the bed and watched her. She sat on the floor to fasten her boots.

"Are you going out, Hesper?" he asked, and she laughed.

"Hesper is out," she said. "Hesper is out of place, out of time, out of luck, and out of her mind. Hesper has vanished completely. Hesper was broken into and taken."

Taki fastened his hands tightly together. "Please don't do this to me, Hesper," he pleaded. "It's really so unfair. When did I ask so much of you? I took what you offered me; I never took anything else. Please don't do this."

Hesper had found the brush and was pulling it roughly through her hair. He rose and went to her, grabbing her by the arms, trying to turn her to face him. "Please, Hesper!"

She shook loose from him without really appearing to notice his hands, and continued to work through the worst of her tangles. When she did turn around, her face was familiar, but somehow not Hesper's face. It was a face that startled him.

"Hesper is gone," it said. "We have her. You've lost her. We are ready to talk to you. Even though you will never, never, never understand." She reached out to touch him, laying her open palm against his cheek and leaving it there.

Buffalo Gals, Won't You Come Out Tonight

✳ ✳ ✳

Ursula K. Le Guin

*One of science fiction's most distinguished novelists, Ursula Le Guin
has been honored with both the Hugo and Nebula awards, as well as a
National Book Award. Her books include* The Left Hand of Darkness,
The Dispossessed, *and* Always Coming Home. *"Buffalo Gals . . . ,"
a wonderfully different "animal" story, won a Hugo award and a World
Fantasy Award in 1988.*

✳ ✳ ✳

1

"YOU fell out of the sky," the coyote said.

Still curled up tight, lying on her side, her back pressed
against the overhanging rock, the child watched the coyote
with one eye. Over the other eye she kept her hand cupped, its back
on the dirt.

"There was a burned place in the sky, up there alongside the
rimrock, and then you fell out of it," the coyote repeated, patiently, as
if the news was getting a bit stale. "Are you hurt?"

She was all right. She was in the plane with Mr. Michaels, and
the motor was so loud she couldn't understand what he said even when

he shouted, and the way the wind rocked the wings was making her feel sick, but it was all right. They were flying to Canyonville. In the plane.

She looked. The coyote was still sitting there. It yawned. It was a big one, in good condition, its coat silvery and thick. The dark tear line back from its long yellow eye was as clearly marked as a tabby cat's.

She sat up slowly, still holding her right hand pressed to her right eye.

"Did you lose an eye?" the coyote asked, interested.

"I don't know," the child said. She caught her breath and shivered. "I'm cold."

"I'll help you look for it," the coyote said. "Come on! If you move around, you won't have to shiver. The sun's up."

Cold, lonely brightness lay across the falling land, a hundred miles of sagebrush. The coyote was trotting busily around, nosing under clumps of rabbitbrush and cheatgrass, pawing at a rock. "Aren't you going to look?" it said, suddenly sitting down on its haunches and abandoning the search. "I knew a trick once where I could throw my eyes way up into a tree and see everything from up there, and then whistle, and they'd come back into my head. But that goddamn bluejay stole them, and when I whistled, nothing came. I had to stick lumps of pine pitch into my head so I could see anything. You could try that. But you've got one eye that's O.K.; what do you need two for? Are you coming, or are you dying there?"

The child crouched, shivering.

"Well, come if you want to," said the coyote, yawned again, snapped at a flea, stood up, turned, and trotted away among the sparse clumps of rabbitbrush and sage, along the long slope that stretched on down and down into the plain streaked across by long shadows of sagebrush. The slender gray-yellow animal was hard to keep in sight, vanishing as the child watched.

She struggled to her feet and—without a word, though she kept saying in her mind, "Wait, please wait"—she hobbled after the coyote. She could not see it. She kept her hand pressed over the right eye socket. Seeing with one eye, there was no depth; it was like a huge, flat picture. The coyote suddenly sat in the middle of the picture, looking back at her, its mouth open, its eyes narrowed, grinning. Her legs began to steady, and her head did not pound so hard, though the deep black ache was always there. She had nearly caught up to the coyote, when it trotted off again. This time she spoke. "Please wait!" she said.

"O.K.," said the coyote, but it trotted right on. She followed, walking downhill into the flat picture that at each step was deep.

Each step was different underfoot; each sage bush was different, and all the same. Following the coyote, she came out from the shadow of the rimrock cliffs, and the sun at eye level dazzled her left eye. Its bright warmth soaked into her muscles and bones at once. The air, which all night had been so hard to breathe, came sweet and easy.

The sage bushes were pulling in their shadows, and the sun was hot on the child's back when she followed the coyote along the rim of a gully. After a while the coyote slanted down the undercut slope, and the child scrambled after, through scrub willows to the thin creek in its wide sand bed. Both drank.

The coyote crossed the creek, not with a careless charge and splashing like a dog, but single foot and quiet like a cat; always it carried its tail low. The child hesitated, knowing that wet shoes make blistered feet, and then waded across in as few steps as possible. Her right arm ached with the effort of holding her hand up over her eye. "I need a bandage," she said to the coyote. It cocked its head and said nothing. It stretched out its forelegs and lay watching the water, resting but alert. The child sat down nearby on the hot sand and tried to move her right hand. It was glued to the skin around her eye by dried blood. At the little tearing-away pain, she whimpered; though it was a small pain, it frightened her. The coyote came over close and poked its long snout into her face. Its strong, sharp smell was in her nostrils. It began to lick the awful, aching blindness, cleaning and cleaning with its curled, precise, strong, wet tongue, until the child was able to cry a little with relief, being comforted. Her head was bent close to the gray-yellow ribs, and she saw the hard nipples, the whitish belly fur. She put her arm around the she-coyote, stroking the harsh coat over back and ribs.

"O.K.," the coyote said, "let's go!" And set off without a backward glance. The child scrambled to her feet and followed. "Where are we going?" she said, and the coyote, trotting on down along the creek, answered, "On down along the creek. . . ."

There must have been a time while she was asleep that she walked because she felt like she was waking up, but she was walking along only in a different place. They were still following the creek, though the gully had flattened out to nothing much, and there was still sagebrush range as far as the eye could see. The eye—the good one—felt rested. The other one still ached, but not so sharply, and there was no use thinking about it. But where was the coyote?

She stopped. The pit of cold into which the plane had fallen reopened, and she fell. She stood falling, a thin whimper making itself in her throat.

"Over here!"

The child turned.

She saw a coyote gnawing at the half-dried-up carcass of a crow, black feathers sticking to the black lips and narrow jaw.

She saw a tawny-skinned woman kneeling by a campfire, sprinkling something into a conical pot. She heard the water boiling in the pot, though it was propped between rocks, off the fire. The woman's hair was yellow and gray, bound back with a string. Her feet were bare. The upturned soles looked as dark and hard as shoe soles, but the arch of the foot was high, and the toes made two neat curving rows. She wore blue jeans and an old white shirt. She looked over at the girl. "Come on, eat crow!" she said.

The child slowly came toward the woman and the fire, and squatted down. She had stopped falling and felt very light and empty; and her tongue was like a piece of wood stuck in her mouth.

Coyote was now blowing into the pot or basket or whatever it was. She reached into it with two fingers, and pulled her hand away, shaking it and shouting, "Ow! Shit! Why don't I ever have any spoons?" She broke off a dead twig of sagebrush, dipped it into the pot, and licked it. "Oh boy," she said. "Come on!"

The child moved a little closer, broke off a twig, dipped. Lumpy pinkish mush clung to the twig. She licked. The taste was rich and delicate.

"What is it?" she asked after a long time of dipping and licking.

"Food. Dried salmon mush," Coyote said. "It's cooling down." She stuck two fingers into the mush again, this time getting a good load, which she ate very neatly. The child, when she tried, got mush all over her chin. It was like chopsticks: it took practice. She practiced. They ate turn and turn until nothing was left in the pot but three rocks.

The child did not ask why there were rocks in the mush pot. They licked the rocks clean. Coyote licked out the inside of the pot-basket, rinsed it once in the creek, and put it onto her head. It fit nicely, making a conical hat. She pulled off her blue jeans. "Piss on the fire!" she cried, and did so, standing straddling it. "Ah, steam between the legs!" she said. The child, embarrassed, thought she was supposed to do the same thing, but did not want to, and did not. Bare-assed, Coyote danced around the dampened fire, kicking her long, thin legs out and singing:

> *Buffalo gals, won't you come out tonight*
> *Come out tonight, come out tonight,*
> *Buffalo gals, won't you come out tonight,*
> *And dance by the light of the moon?*

She pulled her jeans back on. The child was burying the remains of the fire in creek sand, heaping it over, seriously, wanting to do right. Coyote watched her.

"Is that you?" she said. "A Buffalo Gal? What happened to the rest of you?"

"The rest of me?" The child looked at herself, alarmed.

"All your people."

"Oh. Well, Mom took Bobbie—he's my little brother—away with Uncle Norm. He isn't really my uncle or anything. So Mr. Michaels was going there anyway, so he was going to fly me over to my real father, in Canyonville. Linda—my stepmother, you know—she said it was O.K. for the summer anyhow if I was there, and then we could see. But the plane."

In the silence the girl's face became dark red, then grayish white. Coyote watched, fascinated. "Oh," the girl said, "oh—oh—Mr. Michaels—he must be—Did the—"

"Come on!" said Coyote, and set off walking.

The child cried, "I ought to go back—"

"What for?" said Coyote. She stopped to look round at the child, then went on faster. "Come on, Gal!" She said it as a name; maybe it was the child's name, Myra, as spoken by Coyote. The child, confused and despairing, protested again, but followed her. "Where are we going? Where *are* we?"

"This is my country," Coyote answered with dignity, making a long, slow gesture all round the vast horizon. "I made it. Every goddamn sage brush."

And they went on. Coyote's gait was easy, even a little shambling, but she covered the ground; the child struggled not to drop behind. Shadows were beginning to pull themselves out again from under the rocks and shrubs. Leaving the creek, Coyote and the child went up a long, low, uneven slope that ended away off against the sky in rimrock. Dark trees stood one here, another way other there; what people called a juniper forest, a desert forest, one with a lot more between the trees than trees. Each juniper they passed smelled sharply—cat-pee smell the kids at school called it—but the child liked it; it seemed to go into her mind and wake her up. She picked off a juniper berry and held it in her mouth, but after a while spat it out again. The aching was coming back in huge black waves, and she kept stumbling. She found that she was sitting down on the ground. When she tried to get up, her legs shook and would not go under her. She felt foolish and frightened, and began to cry.

"We're home!" Coyote called from way on up the hill.

The child looked with her one weeping eye, and saw sagebrush, juniper, cheatgrass, rimrock. She heard a coyote yip far off in the dry twilight.

She saw a little town up under the rimrock: board houses, shacks, all unpainted. She heard Coyote call again, "Come on, pup! Come on, Gal, we're home!"

She could not get up, so she tried to go on all fours, the long way up the slope to the houses under the rimrock. Long before she got there, several people came to meet her. They were all children, she thought at first, and then began to understand that most of them were grown people, but all were very short; they were broad-bodied, fat, with fine, delicate hands and feet. Their eyes were bright. Some of the women helped her stand up and walk, coaxing her, "It isn't much farther, you're doing fine." In the late dusk, lights shone yellow-bright through doorways and through unchinked cracks between boards. Woodsmoke hung sweet in the quiet air. The short people talked and laughed all the time, softly. "Where's she going to stay?"—"Put her in with Robin, they're all asleep already!"—"Oh, she can stay with us."

The child asked hoarsely, "Where's Coyote?"

"Out hunting," the short people said.

A deeper voice spoke: "Somebody new has come into town?"

"Yes, a new person," one of the short men answered.

Among these people the deep-voiced man bulked impressive; he was broad and tall, with powerful hands, a big head, a short neck. They made way for him respectfully. He moved very quietly, respectful of them also. His eyes when he stared down at the child were amazing. When he blinked, it was like the passing of a hand before a candle flame.

"It's only an owlet," he said. "What have you let happen to your eye, new person?"

"I was—We were flying—"

"You're too young to fly," the big man said in his deep, soft voice. "Who brought you here?"

"Coyote."

And one of the short people confirmed: "She came here with Coyote, Young Owl."

"Then maybe she should stay in Coyote's house tonight," the big man said.

"It's all bones and lonely in there," said a short woman with fat cheeks and a striped shirt. "She can come with us."

That seemed to decide it. The fat-cheeked woman patted the child's arm and took her past several shacks and shanties to a low, windowless house. The doorway was so low even the child had to duck down to enter. There were a lot of people inside, some already there and some crowding in after the fat-cheeked woman. Several babies were fast asleep in cradle-boxes in the corner. There was a good fire, and a good smell, like toasted sesame seeds. The child was given food and ate a little, but her head swam, and the blackness in her right eye kept coming across her left eye, so she could not see at all for a while. Nobody asked her name or told her what to call them. She heard the children call the fat-cheeked woman Chipmunk. She got up courage finally to say, "Is there somewhere I can go to sleep, Mrs. Chipmunk?"

"Sure, come on," one of the daughters said, "in here," and took the child into a back room, not completely partitioned off from the crowded front room, but dark and uncrowded. Big shelves with mattresses and blankets lined the walls. "Crawl in!" said Chipmunk's daughter, patting the child's arm in the comforting way they had. The child climbed onto a shelf, under a blanket. She laid down her head. She thought, "I didn't brush my teeth."

—————————————— **2** ——————————————

She woke; she slept again. In Chipmunk's sleeping room it was always stuffy, warm, and half dark, day and night. People came in and slept and got up and left, night and day. She dozed and slept, got down to drink from the bucket and dipper in the front room, and went back to sleep and doze.

She was sitting up on the shelf, her feet dangling, not feeling bad anymore, but dreamy, weak. She felt in her jeans pocket. In the left front one was a pocket comb and a bubble gum wrapper; in the right front, two dollar bills and a quarter and a dime.

Chipmunk and another woman—a very pretty, dark-eyed, plump one—came in. "So you woke up for your dance!" Chipmunk greeted her, laughing, and sat down by her with an arm around her.

"Jay's giving you a dance," the dark woman said. "He's going to make you all right. Let's get you all ready!"

There was a spring up under the rimrock, which flattened out into a pool with slimy, reedy shores. A flock of noisy children splashing in it ran off and left the child and the two women to bathe. The water was warm on the surface, cold down on the feet and legs. All naked, the two soft-voiced, laughing women, their round bellies and breasts, broad hips and buttocks gleaming warm in the late-afternoon light, sluiced the child down, washed and stroked her limbs and hands and hair, cleaned around the cheekbone and eyebrow of her right eye with infinite softness, admired her, sudsed her, rinsed her, splashed her out of the water, dried her off, dried each other off, got dressed, dressed her, braided her hair, braided each other's hair, tied feathers on the braid-ends, admired her and each other again, and brought her back down into the little straggling town and to a kind of playing field or dirt parking lot in among the houses. There were no streets, just paths and dirt; no lawns and gardens, just sagebrush and dirt. Quite a few people were gathering or wandering around the open place, looking dressed up, wearing colorful shirts, bright dresses, strings of beads, earrings. "Hey there, Chipmunk, Whitefoot!" they greeted the women.

A man in new jeans, with a bright blue velveteen vest over a clean, faded blue work shirt, came forward to meet them, very handsome, tense, and important. "All right, Gal!" he said in a harsh, loud voice, which startled among all these soft-speaking people. "We're going to get that eye fixed right up tonight! You just sit down here and don't worry about a thing." He took her wrist, gently despite his bossy, brassy manner, and led her to a woven mat that lay on the dirt near the middle of the open place. There, feeling very foolish, she had to sit down, and was told to stay still. She soon got over feeling that everybody was looking at her, since nobody paid her more attention than a checking glance or, from Chipmunk or Whitefoot and their families, a reassuring wink. Every now and then, Jay rushed over to her and said something like, "Going to be as good as new!" and went off again to organize people, waving his long blue arms and shouting.

Coming up the hill to the open place, a lean, loose, tawny figure—and the child started to jump up, remembered she was to sit still, and sat still, calling out softly, "Coyote! Coyote!"

Coyote came lounging by. She grinned. She stood looking down at the child. "Don't let that Bluejay fuck you up, Gal," she said, and lounged on.

The child's gaze followed her, yearning.

People were sitting down now over on one side of the open place, making an uneven half circle that kept getting added to at the ends until there was nearly a circle of people sitting on the dirt around the child, ten or fifteen paces from her. All the people wore the kind of clothes the child was used to—jeans and jeans jackets, shirts, vests, cotton dresses—but they were all barefoot; and she thought they were more beautiful than the people she knew, each in a different way, as if each one had invented beauty. Yet some of them were also very strange: thin black shining people with whispery voices, a long-legged woman with eyes like jewels. The big man called Young Owl was there, sleepy-looking and dignified, like Judge McCown who owned a sixty-thousand acre ranch. And beside him was a woman the child thought might be his sister, for like him she had a hook nose and big, strong hands; but she was lean and dark, and there was a crazy look in her fierce eyes. Yellow eyes, but round, not long and slanted like Coyote's. There was Coyote sitting yawning, scratching her armpit, bored. Now somebody was entering the circle: a man, wearing only a kind of kilt and a cloak painted or beaded with diamond shapes, dancing to the rhythm of the rattle he carried and shook with a buzzing fast beat. His limbs and body were thick yet supple, his movements smooth and pouring. The child kept her gaze on him as he danced past her, around her, past again. The rattle in his hand shook almost too fast to see; in the other hand was something thin and sharp. People were singing around the circle now, a few notes repeated in time to the rattle, soft and tuneless. It was exciting and boring, strange and familiar. The Rattler wove his dancing closer and closer to her, darting at her. The first time, she flinched away, frightened by the lunging movement and by his flat, cold face with narrow eyes, but after that she sat still, knowing her part. The dancing went on, the singing went on, till they carried her past boredom into a floating that could go on forever.

Jay had come strutting into the circle and was standing beside her. He couldn't sing, but he called out, "Hey! Hey! Hey! Hey!" in his big, harsh voice, and everybody answered from all round, and the echo came down from the rimrock on the second beat. Jay was holding up a stick with a ball on it in one hand, and something like a marble in the other. The stick was a pipe: he got smoke into his mouth from it and blew it in four directions and up and down and then over the marble, a puff each time. Then the rattle stopped suddenly, and everything was silent for several breaths. Jay squatted down and looked intently into the child's face, his head cocked to one side. He reached forward, muttering something in time to the rattle and the singing that had started up again louder than before; he touched the child's right eye in the black center of the pain. She flinched and endured. His touch was not gentle. She saw the marble, a dull yellow ball like beeswax, in his hand; then she shut her seeing eye and set her teeth.

"There!" Jay shouted. "Open up. Come on! Let's see!"

Her jaw clenched like a vise, she opened both eyes. The lid of the right one stuck and dragged with such a searing white pain that she nearly threw up as she sat there in the middle of everybody watching.

"Hey, can you see? How's it work? It looks great!" Jay was shaking her arm, railing at her. "How's it feel? Is it working?"

What she saw was confused, hazy, yellowish. She began to discover, as everybody came crowding around peering at her—smiling, stroking and patting her arms and shoulders—that if she shut the hurting eye and looked with the other, everything was clear and flat; if she used them both, things were blurry and yellowish, but deep.

There, right close, was Coyote's long nose and narrow eyes and grin. "What is it, Jay?" she was asking, peering at the new eye. "One of mine you stole that time?"

"It's pine pitch," Jay shouted furiously. "You think I'd use some stupid secondhand coyote eye? I'm a doctor!"

"Ooooh, ooooh, a doctor," Coyote said. "Boy, that is one ugly eye. Why didn't you ask Rabbit for a rabbit dropping? That eye looks like shit." She put her lean face yet closer, till the child thought she was going to kiss her; instead, the thin, firm tongue once more licked accurately across the pain, cooling, clearing. When the child opened both eyes again, the world looked pretty good.

"It works fine," she said.

"Hey!" Jay yelled. "She says it works fine! It works fine; she says so! I told you! What'd I tell you?" He went off waving his arms and yelling. Coyote had disappeared. Everybody was wandering off.

The child stood up, stiff from long sitting. It was nearly dark; only the long west held a great depth of pale radiance. Eastward, the plains ran down into night.

Lights were on in some of the shanties. Off at the edge of town, somebody was playing a creaky fiddle, a lonesome chirping tune.

A person came beside her and spoke quietly: "Where will you stay?"

"I don't know," the child said. She was feeling extremely hungry. "Can I stay with Coyote?"

"She isn't home much," the soft-voiced woman said. "You were staying with Chipmunk, weren't you? Or there's Rabbit, or Jackrabbit; they have families. . . ."

"Do you have a family?" the girl asked, looking at the delicate, soft-eyed woman.

"Two fawns," the woman answered, smiling. "But I just came into town for the dance."

"I'd really like to stay with Coyote," the child said after a pause, timid but obstinate.

"O.K., that's fine. Her house is over here." Doe walked along beside the child to a ramshackle cabin on the high edge of town. No light shone from inside. A lot of junk was scattered around the front. There was no step up to the half-open door. Over a battered pine board, nailed up crooked, said: "Bide-A-Wee."

"Hey, Coyote? Visitors," Doe said. Nothing happened.

Doe pushed the door farther open and peered in. "She's out hunting, I guess. I better be getting back to the fawns. You going to be O.K.? Anybody else here will give you something to eat—you know. . . . O.K.?"

"Yeah. I'm fine. Thank you," the child said.

She watched Doe walk away through the clear twilight, a severely elegant walk, small steps, like a woman in high heels, quick, precise, very light.

Inside Bide-A-Wee it was too dark to see anything, and so cluttered that she fell over something at every step. She could not figure out where or how to light a fire. There was something that felt like a bed, but when she lay down on it, it felt more like a dirty-clothes pile, and smelled like one. Things bit her legs, arms, neck, and back. She was terribly hungry. By smell, she found her way to what had to be a dead fish hanging from the ceiling in one corner. By feel, she broke off a greasy flake and tasted it. It was smoked, dried salmon. She ate one succulent piece after another until she was satisfied, and licked her fingers clean. Near the open door, starlight shone on water in a pot of some kind; the child smelled it cautiously, tasted it cautiously, and drank just enough to quench her thirst, for it tasted of mud and was warm and stale. Then she went back to the bed of dirty clothes and fleas, and lay down. She could have gone to Chipmunk's house, or other friendly households; she thought of that as she lay forlorn in Coyote's dirty bed. But she did not go. She slapped at fleas until she fell asleep.

Along in the deep night, somebody said, "Move over, pup," and was warm beside her.

Breakfast, eaten sitting in the sun in the doorway, was dried-salmon-powder mush. Coyote hunted, mornings and evenings, but what they ate was not fresh game but salmon, and dried stuff, and any berries in season. The child did not ask about this. It made sense to her. She was going to ask Coyote why she slept at night and waked in the day like humans, instead of the other way round like coyotes, but when she framed the question in her mind, she saw at once that night is when you sleep and day when you're awake; that made sense, too. But one question she did ask, one hot day when they were lying around slapping fleas.

"I don't understand why you all look like people," she said.

"We are people."

"I mean, people like me, humans."

"Resemblance is in the eye," Coyote said. "How is that lousy eye, by the way?"

"It's fine. But—like you wear clothes—and live in houses—with fires and stuff—"

"That's what *you* think. . . . If that loudmouth Jay hadn't horned in, I could have done a really good job."

The child was quite used to Coyote's disinclination to stick to any one subject, and to her boasting. Coyote was like a lot of kids she knew, in some respects. Not in others.

"You mean what I'm seeing isn't true? Isn't real—like TV or something?"

"No," Coyote said. "Hey, that's a tick on your collar." She reached over, flicked the tick off, picked it up on one finger, bit it, and spat out the bits.

"Yecch!" the child said. "So?"

"So, to me, you're basically grayish yellow and run on four legs. To that lot"—she waved disdainfully at the warren of little houses next down the hill—"you hop around twitching your nose all the time. To Hawk, you're an egg, or maybe getting pinfeathers. See? It just depends on how you look at things. There are only two kinds of people."

"Humans and animals?"

"No. The kind of people who say, 'There are two kinds of people,' and the kind of people who don't." Coyote cracked up, pounding her thighs and yelling with delight at her joke. The child didn't get it, and waited.

"O.K.," Coyote said. "There're the first people, and then the others. Those're the two kinds."

"The first people are—?"

"Us, the animals . . . and things. All the old ones. You know. And you pups, kids, fledglings. All first people."

"And the—others?"

"Them," Coyote said. "You know. The others. The new people.

The ones who came." Her fine, hard face had gone serious, rather formidable. She glanced directly, as she seldom did, at the child, a brief gold sharpness. "We are here," she said. "We are always here. We are always here. Where we are is here. But it's their country now. They're running it. . . . Shit, even I did better!"

The child pondered and offered a word she had used to hear a good deal: "They're illegal immigrants."

"Illegal!" Coyote said, mocking, sneering. "Illegal is a sick bird. What the fuck's illegal mean? You want a code of justice from a coyote? Grow up kid!"

"I don't want to."

"You don't want to grow up?"

"I'll be the other kind if I do."

"Yeah. So," Coyote said, and shrugged. "That's life." She got up and went around the house, and the child heard her pissing in the backyard.

A lot of things were hard to take about Coyote as a mother. When her boyfriends came to visit, the child learned to go stay with Chipmunk or the Rabbits for the night, because Coyote and her friend wouldn't even wait to get on the bed, but would start doing that right on the floor or even out in the yard. A couple of times, Coyote came back late from hunting with a friend, and the child had to lie up against the wall in the same bed and hear and feel them doing that right next to her. It was something like fighting and something like dancing, with a beat to it, and she didn't mind too much except that it made it hard to stay asleep. Once she woke up and one of Coyote's friends was stroking her stomach in a creepy way. She didn't know what to do, but Coyote woke up and realized what he was doing, bit him hard, and kicked him out of bed. He spent the night on the floor, and apologized next morning—"Aw, hell, Ki, I forgot the kid was there; I thought it was you—"

Coyote, unappeased, yelled, "You think I don't got any standards? You think I'd let some coyote rape a kid in my *bed*?" She kicked him out of the house, and grumbled about him all day. But a while later he spent the night again, and he and Coyote did that three or four times.

Another thing that was embarrassing was the way Coyote peed anywhere, taking her pants down in public. But most people here didn't seem to care. The thing that worried the child most, maybe, was when Coyote did number two anywhere and then turned around and talked to it. That seemed so awful. As if Coyote were—the way she often seemed, but really wasn't—crazy.

The child gathered up all the old dry turds from around the house one day while Coyote was having a nap, and buried them in a sandy place near where she and Bobcat and some of the other people generally went and did and buried their number twos.

Coyote woke up, came lounging out of Bide-A-Wee, rubbing her hands through her thick, fair, grayish hair and yawning, looked all round once with those narrow eyes, and said, "Hey! Where are they?" Then she shouted, "Where are you? Where are you?"

And a faint chorus came from over in the draw: "Mommy! We're here!"

Coyote trotted over, squatted down, raked out every turd, and talked with them for a long time. When she came back, she said nothing, but the child, red-faced and heart pounding, said, "I'm sorry I did that."

"It's just easier when they're all around close by," Coyote said, washing her hands (despite the filth of her house, she kept herself quite clean, in her own fashion).

"I kept stepping on them," the child said, trying to justify her deed.

"Poor little shits," said Coyote, practicing dance steps.

"Coyote," the child said timidly. "Did you ever have any children? I mean real pups?"

"Did I? Did I have children? Litters! That one that tried feeling you up, you know? That was my son. Pick of the litter. . . . Listen, Gal. Have daughters. When you have anything, have daughters. At least they clear out."

3

The child thought of herself as Gal, but also sometimes as Myra. So far as she knew, she was the only person in town who had two names. She had to think about that, and about what Coyote had said about the two kinds of people; she had to think about where she belonged. Some persons in town made it clear that as far as they were concerned, she didn't and never would belong there. Hawk's furious stare burned through her; the Skunk children made audible remarks about what she smelled like. And though Whitefoot and Chipmunk and their families were kind, it was the generosity of big families, where one more or less simply doesn't count. If one of them, or Cottontail, or Jackrabbit, had come upon her in the desert lying lost and half blind, would they have stayed with her, like Coyote? That was Coyote's craziness, what they called her craziness. She wasn't afraid. She went between the two kinds of people; she crossed over. Buck and Doe and their beautiful children were really afraid, because they lived so constantly in danger. The Rattler wasn't afraid, because he was so dangerous. And yet maybe he was afraid of her, for he never spoke, and never came close to her. None of them treated her the way Coyote did. Even among the children, her only constant playmate was one younger than herself, a preposterous and fearless little boy called Horned Toad Child. They dug and built together, out among the sagebrush, and played at hunting and gathering and keeping house and holding dances, all the great games. A pale, squatty child with fringed eyebrows, he was a self-contained but loyal friend; and he knew a good deal for his age.

"There isn't anybody else like me here," she said as they sat by the pool in the morning sunlight.

"There isn't anybody much like me anywhere," said Horned Toad Child.

"Well, you know what I mean."

"Yeah. . . . There used to be people like you around, I guess."

"What were they called?"

"Oh—people. Like everybody. . . ."

"But where do *my* people live? They have towns. I used to live in one. I don't know where they are, is all. I ought to find out. I don't know where my mother is now, but daddy's in Canyonville. I was going there when. . . ."

"Ask Horse," said Horned Toad Child sagaciously. He had moved away from the water, which he did not like and never drank, and was plaiting rushes.

"I don't know Horse."

"He hangs around the butte down there a lot of the time. He's waiting till his uncle gets old and he can kick him out and be the big honcho. The old man and the women don't want him around till then. Horses are weird. Anyway, he's the one to ask. He gets around a lot.

And his people came here with the new people; that's what they say, anyhow."

Illegal immigrants, the girl thought. She took Horned.Toad's advice, and one long day when Coyote was gone on one of her unannounced and unexplained trips, she took a pouchful of dried salmon and salmonberries and went off alone to the flat-topped butte miles away in the southwest.

There was a beautiful spring at the foot of the butte, and a trail to it with a lot of footprints on it. She waited there under willows by the clear pool, and after a while Horse came running, splendid, with copper-red skin and long, strong legs, deep chest, dark eyes, his black hair whipping his back as he ran. He stopped, not at all winded, and gave a snort as he looked at her. "Who are you?"

Nobody in town asked that—ever. She saw it was true: Horse had come here with her people, people who had to ask each other who they were.

"I live with Coyote," she said cautiously.

"Oh sure, I heard about you," Horse said. He knelt to drink from the pool. Long, deep drafts, his hands plunged in the cool water. When he had drunk, he wiped his mouth, sat back on his heels, and announced, "I'm going to be king."

"King of the horses?"

"Right! Pretty soon now. I could lick the old man already, but I can wait. Let him have his day," said Horse, vainglorious, magnanimous. The child gazed at him, in love already, forever.

"I can comb your hair, if you like," she said.

"Great!" said Horse, and sat still while she stood behind him, tugging her pocket comb through his coarse, black, shining, yard-long hair. It took a long time to get it smooth. She tied it in a massive ponytail with willow bark when she was done. Horse bent over the pool to admire himself. "That's great," he said. "That's really beautiful!"

"Do you ever go . . . where the other people are?" she asked in a low voice.

He did not reply for long enough that she thought he wasn't going to; then he said, "You mean the metal places, the glass places? The holes? I go around them. There are all the walls now. There didn't used to be so many. Grandmother said there didn't use to be any walls.

Do you know Grandmother?" he asked naively, looking at her with his great, dark eyes.

"Your grandmother?"

"Well, yes—Grandmother—you know. Who makes the web. Well, anyhow. I know there're some of my people, horses, there. I've seen them across the walls. They act really crazy. You know, we brought the new people here. They couldn't have got here without us: they have only two legs, and they have those metal shells. I can tell you that whole story. The king has to know the stories."

"I like stories a lot."

"It takes three nights to tell it. What do you want to know about them?"

"I was thinking that maybe I ought to go there. Where they are."

"It's dangerous. Really dangerous. You can't go through—they'd catch you."

"I'd just like to know the way."

"I know the way," Horse said, sounding for the first time entirely adult and reliable; she knew he did know the way. "It's a long run for a colt." He looked at her again. "I've got a cousin with different-color eyes," he said, looking from her right to her left eye. "One brown and one blue. But she's an Appaloosa."

"Bluejay made the yellow one," the child explained. "I lost my own one. In the . . . when. . . . You don't think I could get to those places?"

"Why do you want to?"

"I sort of feel like I have to."

Horse nodded. He got up. She stood still.

"I could take you, I guess," he said.

"Would you? When?"

"Oh, now, I guess. Once I'm king I won't be able to leave, you know. Have to protect the women. And I sure wouldn't let my people get anywhere near those places!" A shudder ran right down his magnificent body, yet he said, with a toss of his head, "They couldn't catch *me*, of course, but the others can't run like I do. . . ."

"How long would it take us?"

Horse thought for a while. "Well, the nearest place like that is over the red rocks. If we left now, we'd be back here around tomorrow noon. It's just a little hole."

She did not know what he meant by "a hole," but did not ask.
"You want to go?" Horse said, flipping back his ponytail.
"O.K.," the girl said, feeling the ground go out from under her.
"Can you run?"
She shook her head. "I walked here, though."
Horse laughed, a large, cheerful laugh. "Come on," he said, and
knelt and held his hands back-turned like stirrups for her to mount to
his shoulders. "What do they call you?" he teased, rising easily, setting
right off at a jog trot. "Gnat? Fly? Flea?"
"Tick, because I stick!" the child cried, gripping the willow bark
tie of the black mane, laughing with delight at being suddenly eight
feet tall and traveling across the desert without even trying, like the
tumbleweed, as fast as the wind.

Moon, a night past full, rose to light the plains for them. Horse jogged
easily on and on. Somewhere deep in the night, they stopped at a
Pygmy Owl camp, ate a little, and rested. Most of the owls were out
hunting, but an old lady entertained them at her campfire, telling them
tales about the ghost of a cricket, about the great invisible people, tales
that the child heard interwoven with her own dreams as she dozed and
half woke and dozed again. Then Horse put her up on his shoulders,
and on they went at a tireless, slow lope. Moon went down behind
them, and before them the sky paled into rose and gold. The soft night
wind was gone; the air was sharp, cold, still. On it, in it, there was a
faint, sour smell of burning. The child felt Horse's gait change, grow
tighter, uneasy.
"Hey, Prince!"
A small, slightly scolding voice: the child knew it, and placed it
as soon as she saw the person sitting by a juniper tree, neatly dressed,
wearing an old black cap.
"Hey, Chickadee!" Horse said, coming round and stopping. The
child had observed, back in Coyote's town, that everybody treated Chickadee with respect. She didn't see why. Chickadee seemed an ordinary
person, busy and talkative like most of the small birds, nothing so
endearing as Quail or so impressive as Hawk or Great Owl.
"You're going on that way?" Chickadee asked Horse.
"The little one wants to see if her people are living there," Horse
said, surprising the child. Was that what she wanted?

Chickadee looked disapproving, as she often did. She whistled a few notes thoughtfully, another of her habits, and then got up. "I'll come along."

"That's great," Horse said thankfully.

"I'll scout," Chickadee said, and off she went, surprisingly fast, ahead of them, while Horse took up his steady, long lope.

The sour smell was stronger in the air.

Chickadee halted, way ahead of them on a slight rise, and stood still. Horse dropped to a walk, and then stopped. "There," she said in a low voice.

The child stared. In the strange light and slight mist before sunrise, she could not see clearly, and when she strained and peered, she felt as if her left eye were not seeing at all. "What is it?" she whispered.

"One of the holes. Across the wall—see?"

It did seem there was a line, a straight, jerky line drawn across the sagebrush plain, and on the far side of it—nothing? Was it mist? Something moved there. . . .

"It's cattle!" she said.

Horse stood silent, uneasy. Chickadee was coming back toward them.

"It's a ranch," the child said. "That's a fence. There're a lot of Herefords." The words tasted like iron, like salt in her mouth. The things she named wavered in her sight and faded, leaving nothing—a hole in the world, a burned place like a cigarette burn. "Go closer!" she urged Horse. "I want to see."

And as if he owed her obedience, he went forward, tense but unquestioning.

Chickadee came up to them. "Nobody around," she said in her small, dry voice, "but there's one of those fast turtle things coming."

Horse nodded but kept going forward.

Gripping his broad shoulders, the child stared into the blank, and as if Chickadee's words had focused her eyes, she saw again: the scattered whitefaces, a few of them looking up with bluish, rolling eyes—the fences—over the rise a chimneyed house roof and a high barn—and then in the distance, something moving fast, too fast, burning across the ground straight at them at terrible speed. "Run!" she yelled to Horse. "Run away! Run!" As if released from bonds, he wheeled and ran, flat out, in great reaching strides, away from sunrise, the fiery burning chariot, the smell of acid, iron, death. And Chickadee flew before them like a cinder on the air of dawn.

──────────── **4** ────────────

"Horse?" Coyote said. "That prick? Cat food!"

Coyote had been there when the child got home to Bide-A-Wee, but she clearly hadn't been worrying about where Gal was, and maybe hadn't even noticed she was gone. She was in a vile mood, and took it all wrong when the child tried to tell her about where she had been.

"If you're going to do damn fool things, next time do 'em with me; at least I'm an expert," she said, morose, and slouched out the door. The child saw her squatting down, poking an old white turd with a stick, trying to get it to answer some question she kept asking it. The turd lay obstinately silent. Later in the day the child saw two coyote men, a young one and a mangy-looking older one, loitering around near the spring, looking over at Bide-A-Wee. She decided it would be a good night to spend somewhere else.

The thought of the crowded rooms of Chipmunk's house was not attractive. It was going to be a warm night again tonight, and moonlit. Maybe she would sleep outside. If she could feel sure some people wouldn't come around, like the Rattler. . . . She was standing indecisively halfway through town when a dry voice said, "Hey, Gal."

"Hey, Chickadee."

The trim, black-capped woman was standing on her doorstep shaking out a rug. She kept her house neat, trim like herself. Having come back across the desert with her, the child now knew, though she still could not have said, why Chickadee was a respected person.

"I thought maybe I'd sleep out tonight," the child said, tentative.

"Unhealthy," said Chickadee. "What are nests for?"

"Mom's kind of busy," the child said.

"Tsk!" went Chickadee, and snapped the rug with disapproving vigor. "What about her little friend? At least they're decent people."

"Horny-toad? His parents are so shy. . . ."

"Well. Come in and have something to eat, anyhow," said Chickadee.

The child helped her cook dinner. She knew now why there were rocks in the mush pot.

"Chickadee," she said, "I still don't understand; can I ask you? Mom said it depends who's seeing it, but still; I mean, if I see you wearing clothes and everything like humans, then how come you cook this way, in baskets, you know, and there aren't any—any of the things like they have—there where we were with Horse this morning?"

"I don't know," Chickadee said. Her voice indoors was quite soft and pleasant. "I guess we do things the way they always were done, when your people and my people lived together, you know. And together with everything else here. The rocks, you know. The plants and everything." She looked at the basket of willow bark, fern root, and pitch, at the blackened rocks that were heating in the fire. "You see how it all goes together. . . ."

"But you have fire—That's different—"

"Ah!" said Chickadee, impatient, "you people! Do you think you invented the sun?"

She took up the wooden tongs, plopped the heated rocks into the water-filled basket with a terrific hiss and steam and loud bubblings. The child sprinkled in the pounded seeds and stirred.

Chickadee brought out a basket of fine blackberries. They sat on the newly shaken-out rug and ate. The child's two-finger scoop technique with mush was now highly refined.

"Maybe I didn't cause the world," Chickadee said, "but I'm a better cook than Coyote."

The child nodded, stuffing.

"I don't know why I made Horse go there," she said after she had stuffed. "I got just as scared as he did when I saw it. But now I feel again like I have to go back there. But I want to stay here. With my friends, with Coyote. I don't understand."

"When we lived together, it was all one place," Chickadee said in her slow, soft home-voice. "But now the others, the new people, they live apart. And their places are so heavy. They weigh down on our place, they press on it, draw it, suck it, eat it, eat holes in it, crowd it out. . . . Maybe after a while longer, there'll be only one place again, their place. And none of us here. I knew Bison, out over the mountains. I knew Antelope right here. I knew Grizzly and Graywolf, up west there. Gone. All gone. And the salmon you eat at Coyote's house, those are the dream salmon, those are the true food; but in the rivers, how many salmon now? The rivers that were red with them in spring?

Who dances, now, when the First Salmon offers himself? Who dances by the river? Oh, you should ask Coyote about all this. She knows more than I do! But she forgets. . . . She's hopeless, worse than Raven; she has to piss on every post; she's a terrible housekeeper. . . ." Chickadee's voice had sharpened. She whistled a note or two, and said no more.

After a while the child asked very softly, "Who is Grandmother?"

"Grandmother," Chickadee said. She looked at the child and ate several blackberries thoughtfully. She stroked the rug they sat on. "If I built the fire on the rug, it would burn a hole in it," she said. "Right? So we build the fire on sand, on dirt. . . . Things are woven together. So we call the weaver the Grandmother." She whistled four notes, looking up the smoke hole. "After all," she added, "maybe all this place—the other places, too—maybe they're all only one side of the weaving. I don't know. I can look with one one eye at a time; how can I tell how deep it goes?"

Lying that night rolled up in a blanket in Chickadee's backyard, the child heard the wind soughing and storming in the cottonwoods down in the draw, and then slept deeply, weary from the long night before. Just at sunrise she woke. The eastern mountains were a cloudy dark red as if the level light shone through them as through a hand held before the fire. In the tobacco patch—the only farming anybody in this town did was to raise a little wild tobacco—Lizard and Beetle were singing some kind of growing song or blessing song, soft and desultory, *huh*-huh-huh-huh, *huh*-huh-huh-huh, and as she lay warm-curled on the ground, the song made her feel rooted in the ground, cradled on it and in it, so where her fingers ended and the dirt began, she did not know, as if she were dead—but she was wholly alive; she was the earth's life. She got up dancing, left the blanket folded neatly on Chickadee's nest and already empty bed, and danced up the hill to Bide-A-Wee. At the half-open door, she sang:

Danced with a gal with a hole in her stocking
And her knees kept a knocking and her toes kept a rocking,
Danced with a gal with a hole in her stocking,
Danced by the light of the moon!

Coyote emerged, tousled and lurching, and eyed her narrowly. "Sheeeoot," she said. She sucked her teeth and then went to splash water all over her head from the gourd by the door. She shook her head, and the water drops flew. "Let's get out of here," she said. "I have had it. I don't know what got into me. If I'm pregnant again, at my age, oh shit. Let's get out of town. I need a change of air."

In the fuggy dark of the house, the child could see at least two coyote men sprawled snoring away on the bed and floor.

Coyote walked over to the old white turd and kicked it. "Why didn't you stop me?" she shouted.

"I *told* you," the turd muttered sulkily.

"Dumb shit," Coyote said. "Come on, Gal. Let's go. Where to?" She didn't wait for an answer. "I know. Come on!"

And she set off through town at that lazy-looking, rangy walk that was so hard to keep up with. But the child was full of pep, and came dancing, so that Coyote began dancing, too, skipping and pirouetting and fooling around all the way down the long slope to the level plains. There she slanted their way off northeastward. Horse Butte was at their backs, getting smaller in the distance.

Along near noon the child said, "I didn't bring anything to eat."

"Something will turn up," Coyote said. "Sure to." And pretty soon she turned aside, going straight to a tiny gray shack hidden by a couple of half-dead junipers and a stand of rabbitbrush. The place smelled terrible. A sign on the door said: Fox. Private. No Trespassing!—but Coyote pushed it open, and trotted right back out with half a small smoked salmon. "Nobody home but us chickens," she said, grinning sweetly.

"Isn't that stealing?" the child asked, worried.

"Yes," Coyote answered, trotting on.

They ate the fox-scented salmon by a dried-up creek, slept a while, and went on.

Before long the child smelled the sour burning smell, and stopped. It was as if a huge, heavy hand had begun pushing her chest, pushing her away, and yet at the same time as if she had stepped into a strong current that drew her forward, helpless.

"Hey, getting close!" Coyote said, and stopped to piss by a juniper stump.

"Close to what?"

"Their town. See?" She pointed to a pair of sage-spotted hills. Between them was an area of grayish blank.

"I don't want to go there."

"We won't go all the way in. No way! We'll just get a little closer and look. It's fun," Coyote said, putting her head on one side, coaxing. "They do all these weird things in the air."

The child hung back.

Coyote became businesslike, responsible. "We're going to be very careful," she announced. "And look out for big dogs, O.K.? Little dogs I can handle. Make a good lunch. Big dogs, it goes the other way. Right? Let's go, then."

Seemingly as casual and lounging as ever, but with a tense alertness in the carriage of her head and the yellow glance of her eyes, Coyote led off again, not looking back; and the child followed.

All around them the pressures increased. It was as if the air itself were pressing on them, as if time were going too fast, too hard, not flowing but pounding, pounding, pounding, faster and harder till it buzzed like Rattler's rattle. "Hurry, you have to hurry!" everything said. "There isn't time!" everything said. Things rushed past screaming and shuddering. Things turned, flashed, roared, stank, vanished. There was a boy—he came into focus all at once, but not on the ground: he was going along a couple of inches above the ground, moving very fast, bending his legs from side to side in a kind of frenzied, swaying dance, and was gone. Twenty children sat in rows in the air, all singing shrilly, and then the walls closed over them. A basket, no, a pot, no, a can, a garbage can, full of salmon smelling wonderful, no, full of stinking deer hides and rotten cabbage stalks—keep out of it. Coyote! Where was she?

"Mom!" the child called. "Mother!"—standing a moment at the end of an ordinary small-town street near the gas station, and the next moment in a terror of blanknesses, invisible walls, terrible smells and pressures and the overwhelming rush of Time straightforward rolling her helpless as a twig in the race above a waterfall. She clung, held on trying not to fall—"Mother!"

Coyote was over by the big basket of salmon, approaching it, wary but out in the open, in the full sunlight, in the full current. And a boy and a man borne by the same current were coming down the long, sage-spotted hill behind the gas station, each with a gun, red hats—hunters; it was killing season. "Hey, will you look at that damn coyote in broad daylight big as my wife's ass," the man said, and cocked, aimed, shot—all as Myra screamed and ran against the enormous drowning torrent. Coyote fled past her yelling, "Get out of here!" She turned and was borne away.

Far out of sight of that place, in a little draw among low hills, they sat and breathed air in searing gasps until, after a long time, it came easy again.

"Mom, that was *stupid*," the child said furiously.

"Sure was," Coyote said. "But did you see all that food!"

"I'm not hungry," the child said sullenly. "Not till we get all the way away from here."

"But they're your folks," Coyote said. "All yours. Your kith and kin and cousins and kind. Bang! Pow! There's Coyote! Bang! There's my wife's ass! Pow! There's anything—BOOOOM! Blow it away, man! BOOOOOOM!"

"I want to go home," the child said.

"Not yet," said Coyote. "I got to take a shit." She did so, then turned to the fresh turd, leaning over it. "It says I have to stay," she reported, smiling.

"It didn't say anything! I was listening!"

"You know who to understand? You hear everything, Miss Big Ears? Hears all—See all with her crummy, gummy eye—"

"You have pine-pitch eyes, too! You told me so!"

"That's a story," Coyote snarled. "You don't even know a story when you hear one! Look, do what you like; it's a free country. I'm hanging around here tonight. I like the action." She sat down and began patting her hands on the dirt in a soft four-four rhythm and singing under her breath, one of the endless, tuneless songs that kept time from running too fast, that wove the roots of trees and bushes and ferns and grass in the web that held the stream in the streambed and the rock in the rock's place and the earth together. And the child lay listening.

"I love you," she said.

Coyote went on singing.

Sun went down the last slope of the west and left a pale green clarity over the desert hills.

Coyote had stopped singing. She sniffed. "Hey," she said. "Dinner." She got up and moseyed along the little draw. "Yeah," she called back softly. "Come on!"

Stiffly, for the fear-crystals had not yet melted out of her joints, the child got up and went to Coyote. Off to one side along the hill was one of the lines, a fence. She didn't look at it. It was O.K. They were outside it.

"Look at that!"

A smoked salmon, a whole chinook, lay on a little cedar-bark mat.

"An offering! Well, I'll be darned!" Coyote was so impressed she didn't even swear. "I haven't seen one of these for years! I thought they'd forgotten!"

"Offering to whom?"

"Me! Who else? Boy, *look* at that!"

The child looked dubiously at the salmon.

"It smells funny."

"How funny?"

"Like burned."

"It's smoked, stupid! Come on."

"I'm not hungry."

"O.K. It's not your salmon anyhow. It's mine. My offering, for me. Hey, you people! You people over there! Coyote thanks you! Keep it up like this, and maybe I'll do some good things for you, too!"

"Don't, don't yell, Mom! They're not that far away—"

"They're all my people," said Coyote with a great gesture, and then sat down cross-legged, broke off a big piece of salmon, and ate.

Evening Star burned like a deep, bright pool of water in the clear sky. Down over the twin hills was a dim suffusion of light, like a fog. The child looked away from it, back at the star.

"Oh," Coyote said. "Oh shit."

"What's wrong?"

"That wasn't so smart, eating that," Coyote said, and then held herself and began to shiver, to scream, to choke—her eyes rolled up; her long arms and legs flew out jerking and dancing; foam spurted out between her teeth. Her body arched tremendously backward, and the child, trying to hold her, was thrown violently off by the spasms of her limbs. The child scrambled back and held the body as it spasmed again, twitched, quivered, went still.

By moonrise, Coyote was cold. Till then there had been so much warmth under the tawny coat that the child kept thinking maybe she was alive, maybe if she just kept holding her, keeping her warm, Coyote would recover, she would be all right. The child held her close, not looking at the black lips drawn back from the teeth, the white balls of the eyes. But when the cold came through the fur as the presence of death, the child let the slight, stiff corpse lie down on the dirt.

She went nearby and dug a hole in the stony sand of the draw, a shallow pit. Coyote's people did not bury their dead; she knew that. But her people did. She carried the small corpse to the pit, laid it down, and covered it with her blue and white bandanna. It was not large enough; the four stiff paws stuck out. The child heaped the body over with sand and rocks and a scurf of sagebrush and tumbleweed held down with more rocks. She also heaped dirt and rocks over the poisoned salmon carcass. Then she stood up and walked away without looking back.

At the top of the hill, she stood and looked across the draw toward the misty glow of the lights of the town lying in the pass between the twin hills.

"I hope you all die in pain," she said aloud. She turned away and walked down into the desert.

5

It was Chickadee who met her, on the second evening, north of Horse Butte.

"I didn't cry," the child said.

"None of us do," said Chickadee. "Come with me this way now. Come into Grandmother's house."

It was underground, but very large, dark and large, and the Grandmother was there at the center, at her loom. She was making a rug or blanket of the hills and the black rain and the white rain, weaving in the lightning. As they spoke, she wove.

"Hello, Chickadee. Hello, New Person."

"Grandmother," Chickadee greeted her.

The child said, "I'm not one of them."

Grandmother's eyes were small and dim. She smiled and wove. The shuttle thrummed through the warp.

"Old Person, then," said Grandmother. "You'd better go back there now, Granddaughter. That's where you live."

"I lived with Coyote. She's dead. They killed her."

"Oh, don't worry about Coyote!" Grandmother said with a little huff of laughter. "She gets killed all the time."

The child stood still. She saw the endless weaving.

"Then I—Could I go back home—to her house—?"

"I don't think it would work," Grandmother said. "Do you, Chickadee?"

Chickadee shook her head once, silent.

"It would be dark there now, and empty, and fleas. . . . You got outside your people's time, into our place; but I think that Coyote was taking you back, see. Her way. If you go back now, you can still live with them. Isn't your father there?"

The child nodded.

"They've been looking for you."

"They have?"

"Oh yes. Ever since you fell out of the sky. The man was dead, but you weren't there—they kept looking."

"Serves him right. Served them all right," the child said. She put her hands up over her face and began to cry terribly, without tears.

"Go on, little one, Granddaughter," Spider said. "Don't be afraid. You can live well there. I'll be there, too, you know. In your dreams, in your ideas, in dark corners in the basement. Don't kill me, or I'll make it rain. . . ."

"I'll come around," Chickadee said. "Make gardens for me."

The child held her breath and clenched her hands until her sobs stopped and let her speak.

"Will I ever see Coyote?"

"I don't know," the Grandmother replied.

The child accepted this. She said, after another silence, "Can I keep my eye?"

"Yes. You can keep your eye."

"Thank you, Grandmother," the child said. She turned away then and started up the night slope toward the next day. Ahead of her in the air of dawn for a long way, a little bird flew, black-capped, light-winged.

The Boy
Who Plaited
Manes

✫　　　✫　　　✫

Nancy Springer

"The Boy Who Plaited Manes" appeared in our 37th anniversary issue along with stories from some of the best-known writers in SF, yet this was the story that received the most attention and went on to win several awards. Nancy Springer's recent novels include The Hex Witch of Seldom *and* Apocalypse.

✫　　　✫　　　✫

THE boy who plaited the manes of horses came, fittingly enough, on the day of the Midsummer Hunt: when he was needed worst, though Wald the head groom did not yet know it. The stable was in a muted frenzy of work, as it had been since long before dawn, every groom and apprentice vehemently polishing. The lord's behest was that all the horses in his stable should be brushed for two hours every morning to keep the fine shine and bloom on their flanks, and this morning could be no different. Then there was also all the gear to be tended to. Though old Lord Robley of Auberon was a petty manor lord, with only some hundred of horses and less than half the number of grooms to show for a lifetime's striving, his lowly status made him all the more keen to present himself and his retinue grandly before the more powerful lords who would assemble for the Hunt. Himself and his retinue and his lovely young wife.

Therefore it was an eerie thing when the boy walked up the long stable aisle past men possessed with work, men so frantic they took no notice at all of the stranger, up the aisle brick-paved in chevron style until he came to the stall where the lady's milk-white palfrey stood covered withers to croup with a fitted sheet tied on to keep the beast clean, and the boy swung open the heavy stall door and walked in without fear, as if he belonged there, and went up to the palfrey to plait its mane.

He was an eerie boy, so thin that he seemed deformed, and of an age difficult to guess because of his thinness. He might have been ten, or he might have been seventeen with something wrong about him that made him beardless and narrow-shouldered and thin. His eyes seemed too gathered for a ten-year-old, gray-green and calm yet feral, like woodland. His hair, dark and shaggy, seemed to bulk large above his thin, thin face.

The palfrey's hair was far better cared for than his. Its silky mane, coddled for length, hung down below its curved neck, and its tail was bundled into a wrapping, to be let down at the last moment before the lady rose, when it would trail on the ground and float like a white bridal train. The boy did not yet touch the tail, but his thin fingers flew to work on the palfrey's mane.

Wald the head groom, passing nearly at a run to see to the saddling of the lord's hotblooded hunter, stopped in his tracks and stared. And to be sure it was not that he had never seen plaiting before. He himself had probably braided a thousand horses' manes, and he knew what a time it took to put even a row of small looped braids along a horse's crest, and how hard it was to get them even, and how horsehair seems like a demon with a mind of its own. He frankly gawked, and other grooms stood beside him and did likewise, until more onlookers stood gathered outside the palfrey's stall than could rightly see, and those in the back demanded to know what was happening, and those in the front seemed not to hear them, but stood as if in a trance, watching the boy's thin, swift hands.

For the boy's fingers moved more quickly and deftly than seemed human, than seemed possible, each hand by itself combing and plaiting a long, slender braid in one smooth movement, as if he no more than stroked the braid out of the mane. That itself would have been wonder enough, as when a groom is so apt that he can curry with one hand and follow after with the brush in the other, and have a horse done in half the time. A shining braid forming out of each hand every minute, wonder enough—but that was the least of it. The boy interwove them as he worked, so that they flowed into each other in a network, making of the mane a delicate shawl, a veil, that draped the palfrey's fine neck. The ends of the braids formed a silky hem curving down to a point at the shoulder, and at the point the boy spiraled the remaining mane into an uncanny horsehair flower. And all the time, though it was not tied and was by no means a cold-blooded beast, the palfrey had not moved, standing still as stone.

Then Wald the head groom felt fear prickling at the back of his astonishment. The boy had carried each plait down to the last three hairs. Yet he had fastened nothing with thread or ribbon, but merely pressed the ends between two fingers, and the braids stayed as he had placed them. Nor did the braids ever seem to fall loose as he was working, or hairs fly out at random, but all lay smooth as white silk, shimmering. The boy, or whatever he was, stood still with his hands at his sides, admiring his work.

Uncanny. Still, the lord and lady would be well pleased. . . . Wald jerked himself out of amazement and moved quickly. "Get back to your work, you fellows!" he roared at the grooms, and then he strode into the stall.

"Who are you?" he demanded. "What do you mean coming in here like this?" It was best, in a lord's household, never to let anyone know you were obliged to them.

The boy looked at him silently, turning his head in the alert yet indifferent way of a cat.

"I have asked you a question! What is your name?"

The boy did not speak, or even move his lips. Then or thereafter, as long as he worked in that stable, he never made any sound.

His stolid manner annoyed Wald. But though the master groom could not yet know that the boy was a mute, he saw something odd in his face. A halfwit, perhaps. He wanted to strike the boy, but even worse he wanted the praise of the lord and lady, so he turned abruptly and snatched the wrapping off the palfrey's tail, letting the cloud of white hair float down to the clean straw of the stall. "Do something with that," he snapped.

A sweet, intense glow came into the boy's eyes as he regarded his task. With his fingers he combed the hair smooth, and then he started a row of small braids above the bone.

Most of the tail he left loose and flowing, with just a cluster of braids at the top, a few of them swinging halfway to the ground. And young Lady Aelynn gasped with pleasure when she saw them, and with wonder at the mane, even though she was a lord's daughter born and not unaccustomed to finery.

It did not matter, that day, that Lord Robley's saddle had not been polished to a sufficient shine. He was well pleased with his grooms. Nor did it matter that his hawks flew poorly, his hounds were unruly and his clumsy hunter stumbled and cut its knees. Lords and ladies looked again and again at his young wife on her white palfrey, its tail trailing and shimmering like her blue silk gown, the delicate openwork of its mane as dainty as the lace kerchief tucked between her breasts or her slender gloved hand that held the caparisoned reins. Every hair of her mount was as artfully placed as her own honey-gold hair looped in gold-beaded curls atop her fair young head. Lord Robley knew himself to be the envy of everyone who saw him for the sake of his lovely wife and the showing she made on her white mount with the plaited mane.

And when the boy who plaited manes took his place among the lord's other servants in the kitchen line for the evening meal, no one gainsaid him.

Lord Robley was a hard old man, his old body hard and hale, his spirit hard. It took him less than a day to pass from being well pleased to being greedy for more: no longer was it enough that the lady's palfrey should go forth in unadorned braids. He sent a servant to Wald with silk ribbons in the Auberon colors, dark blue and crimson, and commanded that they should be plaited into the palfrey's mane and tail. This the stranger boy did with ease when Wald ordered him to, and he used the ribbon ends to tie tiny bows and love knots and leave a few shimmering tendrils bobbing in the forelock. Lady Aelynn was enchanted.

Within a few days Lord Robley had sent to the stable thread of silver and of gold, strings of small pearls, tassels, pendant jewels, and fresh-cut flowers of every sort. All of these things the boy who plaited manes used with ease to dress the lady's palfrey when he was bid. Lady Aelynn went forth to the next hunt with tiny bells of silver and gold chiming at the tip of each of her mount's dainty ribbon-decked braids, and eyes turned her way wherever she rode. Nor did the boy ever seem to arrange the mane and tail and forelock twice in the same way, but whatever way he chose to plait and weave and dress it seemed the most perfect and poignant and heartachingly beautiful way a horse had ever been arrayed. Once he did the palfrey's entire mane in one great, thick braid along the crest, gathering in the hairs as he went, so that the neck seemed to arch as mightily as a destrier's, and he made the braid drip thick with flowers, roses and great lilies and spires of larkspur trailing down, so that the horse seemed to go with a mane of flowers. But another time he would leave the mane loose and floating, with just a few braids shimmering down behind the ears or in the forelock, perhaps, and this also seemed perfect and poignant and the only way a horse should be adorned.

Nor was it sufficient, any longer, that merely the lady's milk-white palfrey should go forth in braids. Lord Robley commanded that his hot-blooded hunter also should have his mane done up in stubby ribboned braids and rosettes in the Auberon colors, and the horses of his retinue likewise, though with lesser rosettes. And should his wife choose to go out riding with her noble guests, all their mounts were to be prepared like hers, though in lesser degree.

All these orders Wald passed on to the boy who plaited manes, and the youngster readily did as he was bid, working sometimes from before dawn until long after dark, and never seeming to want more than what food he could eat while standing in the kitchen. He slept in the hay and straw of the loft and did not use even a horseblanket for covering until one of the grooms threw one on him. Nor did he ask for clothing, but Wald, ashamed of the boy's shabbiness, provided him with the clothing due to a servant. The master groom said nothing to him of a servant's pay. The boy seemed content without it. Probably he would have been content without the clothing as well. Though in fact it was hard to tell what he was thinking or feeling, for he never spoke and his thin face seldom moved.

No one knew his name, the boy who plaited manes. Though many of the grooms were curious and made inquiries, no one could tell who he was or where he had come from. Or even what he was, Wald thought sourly. No way to tell if the young snip was a halfwit or a bastard or what, if he would not talk. No way to tell what sort of a young warlock he might be, that the horses never moved under his hands, even the hotblooded hunter standing like a stump for him. Scrawny brat. He could hear well enough; why would he not talk?

It did not make Wald like the strange boy, that he did at once whatever he was told and worked so hard and so silently. In particular he did not like the boy for doing the work for which Wald reaped the lord's praise; Wald disliked anyone to whom he was obliged. Nor did he like the way the boy had arrived, as if blown in on a gust of wind, and so thin that it nearly seemed possible. Nor did he like the thought that any day the boy might leave in like wise. And even disliking that thought, Wald could not bring himself to give the boy the few coppers a week which were his due, for he disliked the boy more. Wald believed there was something wrongheaded, nearly evil, about the boy. His face seemed wrong, so very thin, with the set mouth and the eyes both wild and quiet, burning like a steady candle flame.

Summer turned into autumn, and many gusts of wind blew, but the boy who plaited manes seemed content to stay, and if he knew of Wald's dislike he did not show it. In fact he showed nothing. He braided the palfrey's mane with autumn starflowers and smiled ever so slightly as he worked. Autumn turned to the first dripping and dismal, chill days of winter. The boy used bunches of bright feathers instead of flowers when he dressed the palfrey's mane, and he did not ask for a winter jerkin, so Wald did not give him any. It was seldom enough, anyway, that the horses were used for pleasure at this season. The thin boy could spend his days huddled under a horseblanket in the loft.

Hard winter came, and the smallpox season.

Lady Aelynn was bored in the wintertime, even more so than during the rest of the year. At least in the fine weather there were walks outside, there were riding and hunting and people to impress. It would not be reasonable for a lord's wife, nobly born (though a younger child, and female), to wish for more than that. Lady Aelynn knew full well that her brief days of friendships and courtships were over. She had wed tolerably well, and Lord Robley counted her among his possessions, a beautiful thing to be prized like his gold and his best horses. He was a manor lord, and she was his belonging, his lady, and not for others to touch even with their regard. She was entirely his. So there were walks for her in walled gardens, and pleasure riding and hunting by her lord's side, and people to impress.

But in the wintertime there were not even the walks. There was nothing for the Lady Aelynn to do but tend to her needlework and her own beauty, endlessly concerned with her clothes, her hair, her skin, even though she was so young, no more than seventeen—for she knew in her heart that it was for her beauty that Lord Robley smiled on her, and for no other reason. And though she did not think of it, she knew that her life lay in his grasping hands.

Therefore she was ardently uneasy, and distressed only for herself, when the woman who arranged her hair each morning was laid abed with smallpox. Though as befits a lady of rank, Aelynn hid her dismay in vexation. And it did not take her long to discover that none of her other tiring-women could serve her nearly as well.

"Mother of God!" she raged, surveying her hair in the mirror for perhaps the tenth time. "The groom who plaits the horses' manes in the stable could do better!" Then the truth of her own words struck her, and desperation made her willing to be daring. She smiled. "Bring him hither!"

Her women stammered and curtseyed and fled to consult among themselves and exclaim with the help in the kitchen. After some few minutes of this, a bold kitchen maid was dispatched to the stable and returned with a shivering waif: the boy who plaited manes.

It was not to be considered that such a beggar should go in to the lady. Her tiring-women squeaked in horror and made him bathe first, in a washbasin before the kitchen hearth, for there was a strong smell of horse and stable about him. They ordered him to scrub his own hair with strong soap and scent himself with lavender, and while some of them giggled and fled, others giggled and stayed, to pour water for him and see that he made a proper job of his ablutions. All that was demanded of him the boy who plaited manes did without any change in his thin face, any movement of his closed mouth, any flash of his feral eyes. At last they brought him clean clothing, jerkin and woolen hose only a little too large, and pulled the things as straight as they could on him, and took him to the tower where the lady waited.

He did not bow to the Lady Aelynn or look into her eyes for his instructions, but his still mouth softened a little and his glance, calm and alert, like that of a woodland thing, darted to her hair. And at once, as if he could scarcely wait, he took his place behind her and lifted her tresses in his hands. Such a soft, fine, honey-colored mane of hair as he had never seen, and combs of gold and ivory lying at hand on a rosewood table, and ribbons of silk and gold, everything he could have wanted, his for the sake of his skill.

He started at the forehead, and the lady sat as if in a trance beneath the deft touch of his hands.

Gentle, he was so gentle, she had never felt such a soft and gentle touch from any man, least of all from her lord. When Lord Robley wanted to use one of his possessions he seized it, not so hard as to hurt, but still firmly enough to take control. But this boy touched her as gently as a woman, no, a mother, for no tiring-woman or maid had ever gentled her so. . . . Yet unmistakably his was the touch of a man, though she could scarcely have told how she knew. Part of it was power, she could feel the gentle power in his touch, she could feel—uncanny, altogether eerie and uncanny, what she was feeling. It was as if his quick fingers called to her hair in soft command and her hair obeyed just for the sake of one quick touch, all the while longing to embrace. . . . She stayed breathlessly still for him, like the horses.

He plaited her hair in braids thin as bluebell stems, only a wisp of hairs to each braid, one after another with both his deft hands as if each was as easy as a caress, making them stay with merely a touch of two fingers at the end, until all her hair lay in a silky cascade of them, catching the light and glimmering and swaying like a rich drapery when he made her move her head. Some of them he gathered and looped and tied up with the ribbons which matched her dress, blue edged with gold. But most of them he left hanging to her bare back and shoulders. He surveyed his work with just a whisper of a smile when he was done, then turned and left without waiting for the lady's nod, and she sat as if under a spell and watched his thin back as he walked away. Then she tossed her head at his lack of courtesy. But the swinging of her hair pleased her.

She had him back to dress her hair the next day, and the next, and many days thereafter. And so that they would not have to be always bathing him, her tiring-women found him a room within the manorhouse doors, and a pallet and clean blankets, and a change of clothing, plain coarse clothing, such as servants wore. They trimmed the heavy hair that shadowed his eyes, also, but he looked no less the oddling with his thin, thin face and his calm burning glance and his mouth that seemed scarcely ever to move. He did as he was bid, whether by Wald or the lady or some kitchen maid, and every day he plaited Lady Aelynn's hair differently. One day he shaped it all into a bright crown of braids atop her head. On other days he would plait it close to her head so that the tendrils caressed her neck, or in a haughty crest studded with jewels, or in a single soft feathered braid at one side. He always left her tower chamber at once, never looking at the lady to see if he had pleased her, as if he knew that she would always be pleased.

Always, she was.

Things happened. The tiring-woman who had taken smallpox died of it, and Lady Aelynn did not care, not for the sake of her cherished hair and most certainly not for the sake of the woman herself. Lord Robley went away on a journey to discipline a debtor vassal, and Lady Aelynn did not care except to be glad, for there was a sure sense growing in her of what she would do.

When even her very tresses were enthralled by the touch of this oddling boy, longing to embrace him, could she be otherwise?

When next he had plaited her mane of honey-colored hair and turned to leave her without a glance, she caught him by one thin arm. His eyes met hers with a steady, gathered look. She stood—she was taller than he, and larger, though she was as slender as any maiden. It did not matter. She took him by one thin hand and led him to her bed, and there he did as he was bid.

Nor did he disappoint her. His touch—she had never been touched so softly, so gently, so deftly, with such power. Nor was he lacking in manhood, for all that he was as thin and hairless as a boy. And his lips, after all, knew how to move, and his tongue. But it was the touch of his thin hands that she hungered for, the gentle, tender, potent touch that thrilled her almost as if—she were loved. . . .

He smiled at her afterward, slightly, softly, a whisper of a smile in the muted half-light of her curtained bed, and his lips moved.

"You are swine," he said, "all of you nobles."

And he got up, put on his plain, coarse clothing and left her without a backward glance.

It terrified Lady Aelynn, that he was not truly a mute. Terrified her even more than what he had said, though she burned with mortified wrath whenever she thought of the latter. He, of all people, a mute, to speak such words to her and leave her helpless to avenge herself. . . . Perhaps for that reason he would not betray her. She had thought it would be safe to take a mute as her lover. . . . Perhaps he would not betray her.

In fact, it was not he who betrayed her to her lord, but Wald.

Her tiring-women suspected, perhaps because she had sent them on such a long errand. She had not thought they would suspect—who would think that such a wisp of a beardless boy could be a bedfellow? But perhaps they also had seen the wild glow deep in his gray-green eyes. They whispered among themselves and with the kitchen maids, and the bold kitchen maid giggled with the grooms, and Wald heard.

Even though the boy who plaited manes did it all, Wald considered the constant plaiting and adorning of manes and tails a great bother. The whole fussy business offended him, he had decided, and he had long since forgotten the few words of praise it had garnered from the lord at first. Moreover, he disliked the boy so vehemently that he was not thinking clearly. It seemed to him that he could be rid of the boy and the wretched onus of braids and rosettes all in one stroke. The day the lord returned from his journey, Wald hurried to him, begged private audience, bowed low and made his humble report.

Lord Robley heard him in icy silence, for he knew pettiness when he saw it; it had served him often in the past, and he would punish it if it misled him. He summoned his wife to question her. But the Lady Aelynn's hair hung lank, and her guilt and shame could be seen plainly in her face from the moment she came before him.

Lord Robley's roar could be heard even to the stables.

He strode over to her where she lay crumpled and weeping on his chamber floor, lifted her head by its honey-gold hair and slashed her across the face with his sword. Then he left her screaming and stinging her wound with fresh tears, and he strode to the stable with his bloody sword still drawn, Wald fleeing before him all the way; when the lord burst in all the grooms were scattered but one. The boy Wald had accused stood plaiting the white palfrey's mane.

Lord Robley hacked the palfrey's head from its braid-bedecked neck with his sword, and the boy who plaited manes stood by with something smoldering deep in his unblinking gray-green eyes, stood calmly waiting. If he had screamed and turned to flee, Lord Robley would with great satisfaction have given him a coward's death from the back. But it unnerved the lord that the boy awaited his pleasure with such mute—what? Defiance? There was no servant's boy in this one, no falling to the soiled straw, no groveling. If he had groveled he could have been kicked, stabbed, killed out of hand, also. . . . But this silent, watchful waiting, like the alertness of a wild thing—on the hunt or being hunted? It gave Lord Robley pause, like the pause of the wolf before the standing stag or the pause of the huntsman before the thicketed boar. He held the boy at the point of his sword—though no such holding was necessary, for the prisoner had not moved even to tremble—and roared for his men-at-arms to come take the boy to the dungeon.

There the nameless stranger stayed without water or food, and aside from starving him Lord Robley could not decide what to do with him.

At first the boy who plaited manes paced in his prison restlessly —he had that freedom, for he was so thin and small that the shackles were too large to hold him. Later he lay in a scant bed of short straw and stared narrow-eyed at the darkness. And yet later, seeing the thin cascades of moonlight flow down through the high, iron-barred window and puddle in moon-glades on the stone floor, he got up and began to plait the moonbeams.

They were far finer than any horsehair, moonbeams, finer even than the lady's honey-colored locks, and his eyes grew wide with wonder and pleasure as he felt them. He made them into braids as fine as silk threads, flowing together into a lacework as close as woven cloth, and when he had reached as high as he could, plaiting, he stroked as if combing a long mane with his fingers and pulled more moonlight down out of the sky—for this stuff was not like any other stuff he had ever worked with, it slipped and slid worse than any hair, there seemed to be no beginning or end to it except the barriers that men put in its way. He stood plaiting the fine, thin plaits until he had raised a shimmering heap on the floor, and then he stepped back and allowed the moon to move on. His handiwork he laid carefully aside in a corner.

The boy who plaited moonbeams did not sleep, but sat watching for the dawn, his eyes glowing greenly in the darkened cell. He saw the sky lighten beyond the high window and waited stolidly, as the wolf waits for the gathering of the pack, as a wildcat waits for the game to pass along the trail below the rock where it lies. Not until the day had neared its mid did the sun's rays, thrust through the narrow spaces between the high bars, wheel their shafts down to where he could reach them. Then he got up and began to plait the sunlight.

Guards were about, or more alert, in the daytime, and they gathered at the heavy door of his prison, peering in between the iron bars of its small window, gawking and quarreling with each other for turns. They watched his unwavering eyes, saw the slight smile come on his face as he worked, though his thin hands glowed red as if seen through fire. They saw the shining mound he raised on the floor, and whispered among themselves and did not know what to do, for none of them dared to touch it or him. One of them requested a captain to come look. And the captain summoned the steward, and the steward went to report to the lord. And from outside the cries began to sound that the sun was standing still.

After the boy had finished, he stood back and let the sun move on, then sat resting on his filthy straw. Within minutes the dungeon door burst open and Lord Robley himself strode in.

Lord Robley had grown weary of mutilating his wife, and he had not yet decided what to do with his other prisoner. Annoyed by the reports from the prison, he expected that an idea would come to him when he saw the boy. He entered with drawn sword. But all thoughts of the thin young body before him were sent whirling away from his mind by what he saw laid out on the stone floor at his feet.

A mantle, a kingly cloak—but no king had ever owned such a cloak. All shining, the outside of it silver and the inside gold—but no, to call it silver and gold was to insult it. More like water and fire, flow and flame, shimmering as if it moved, as if it were alive, and yet it had been made by hands, he could see the workmanship, so fine that every thread was worth a gasp of pleasure, the outside of it somehow braided and plaited to the lining, and all around the edge a fringe of threads like bright fur so fine that it wavered in the air like flame. Lord Robley had no thought but to settle the fiery gleaming thing on his shoulders, to wear that glory and be finer than any king. He seized it and flung it on. . . .

And screamed as he had not yet made his wife scream, with the shriek of mortal agony. His whole hard body glowed as if it had been placed in a furnace. His face contorted, and he fell dead.

The boy who plaited sunbeams got up in a quiet, alert way and walked forward, as noiseless on his feet as a lynx. He reached down and took the cloak off the body of the lord, twirled it and placed it on his own shoulders, and it did not harm him. But in that cloak he seemed insubstantial, like something moving in moonlight and shadow, something nameless roaming in the night. He walked out of the open dungeon door, between the guards clustered there, past the lord's retinue and the steward, and they all shrank back from him, flattened themselves against the stone walls of the corridor so as not to come near him. No one dared take hold of him or try to stop him. He walked out through the courtyard, past the stable, and out the manor gates with the settled air of one whose business is done. The men-at-arms gathered atop the wall and watched him go.

Wald the master groom lived to old age sweating every night with terror, and died of a weakened heart in the midst of a nightmare. Nothing else but his own fear harmed him. The boy who plaited— mane of sun, mane of moon—was never seen again in that place, except that children sometimes told the tale of having glimpsed him in the wild heart of a storm, plaiting the long lashes of wind and rain.

Out of All Them Bright Stars

✲   ✲   ✲

Nancy Kress

*Nancy Kress was primarily known as a fantasy novelist, until the pub-
lication of* An Alien Light *in 1987 proved she was equally at home with
science fiction. She has contributed only two stories to F&SF, but both
have been notable: "Explanations, Inc" (1984) and "Out of All Them
Bright Stars," which won a Nebula award in 1986.*

✲   ✲   ✲

SO I'm filling the catsup bottles at the end of the night, and I'm
listening to the radio Charlie has stuck up on top of the movable
panel in the ceiling, when the door opens and one of them walks
in. I know right away it's one of them—no chance to make a mistake
about *that*—even though it's got on a nice-cut suit and a brim hat like
Humphrey Bogart used to wear in *Casablanca*. But there's nobody with
it, no professor from the college or government men like on the TV
show from the college or even any students. It's all alone. And we're
a long way out the highway from the college.

It stands in the doorway, blinking a little, with rain dripping off
its hat. Kathy, who's supposed to be cleaning the coffee machine behind
the counter, freezes and stares with one hand still holding the used
filter up in the air like she's never going to move again. Just then Charlie

285

calls out from the kitchen, "Hey, Kathy, you ask anybody who won the trifecta?" and she doesn't even answer him. Just goes on staring with her mouth open like she's thinking of screaming but forgot how. And the old couple in the corner booth, the only ones left from the crowd after the movie got out, stop chewing their chocolate cream pie and stare, too. Kathy closes her mouth and opens it again, and a noise comes out like "Uh—errrgh. . . ."

Well, that made me annoyed. Maybe she tried to say "ugh" and maybe she didn't, but here it is standing in the doorway with rain falling around it in little drops, and we're staring like it's a clothes dummy and not a customer. So I think that's not right and maybe we're even making it feel a little bad, I wouldn't like Kathy staring at me like that, and I dry my hands on my towel and go over.

"Yes, sir, can I help you?" I say.

"Table for one," it says, like Charlie's was some nice steak house in town. But I suppose that's the kind of place the government people mostly take them to. And besides, its voice is polite and easy to understand, with a sort of accent but not as bad as some we get from the college. I can tell what it's saying. I lead him to a booth in the corner opposite the old couple, who come in every Friday night and haven't left a tip yet.

He sits down slowly. I notice he keeps his hands on his lap, but I can't tell if that's because he doesn't know what to do with them or because he thinks I won't want to see them. But I've seen the close-ups on TV—they don't look so weird to me like they do to some. Charlie says they make his stomach turn, but I can't see it. You'd think he'd of seen worse meat in Vietnam. He talks enough like he did, on and on and on, and sometimes we even believe him.

I say, "Coffee, sir?"

He makes a sort of movement with his eyes. I can't tell what the movement means, but he says in that polite voice, "No, thank you. I am unable to drink coffee," and I think that's a good thing, because I suddenly remember that Kathy's got the filter out. But then he says, "May I have a green salad, please? With no dressing, please."

The rain is still dripping off his hat. I figure the government people never told him to take off his hat in a restaurant, and for some reason that tickles me and makes me feel real bold. This polite blue guy isn't going to bother anybody, and that fool Charlie was just spouting off his mouth again.

"The salad's not too fresh, sir," I say, experimental-like, just to see what he'll say next. And it's the truth—the salad is left over from yesterday. But the guy answers like I asked something else.

"What is your name?" he says, so polite I know he's curious and not starting anything. And what could he start anyway, blue and with those hands? Still, you never know.

"Sally," I say. "Sally Gourley."

"I am John," he says, and makes that movement with his eyes again. All of a sudden it tickles me—"John!" For this blue guy! So I laugh, and right away I feel sorry, like I might have hurt his feelings or something. How could you tell?

"Hey, I'm sorry," I say, and he takes off his hat. He does it real slow, like taking off the hat is important and means something, but all there is underneath is a bald blue head. Nothing weird like with the hands.

"Do not apologize," John says. "I have another name, of course, but in my own language."

"What is it?" I say, bold as brass, because all of a sudden I picture myself telling all this to my sister Mary Ellen and her listening real hard.

John makes some noise with his mouth, and I feel my own mouth open because it's not a word he says at all, it's a beautiful sound—like a birdcall, only sadder. It's just that I wasn't expecting it, that beautiful sound right here in Charlie's diner. It surprised me, coming out of that bald blue head. That's all it was: surprise.

I don't say anything. John looks at me and says, "It has a meaning that can be translated. It means—" But before he can say what it means, Charlie comes charging out of the kitchen, Kathy right behind him. He's still got the racing form in one hand, like he's been studying the trifecta, and he pushes right up against the booth and looks red and furious. Then I see the old couple scuttling out the door, their jackets clutched to their fronts, and the chocolate cream pie not half-eaten on their plates. I see they're going to stiff me for the check, but before I can stop them, Charlie grabs my arm and squeezes so hard his nails slice into my skin.

"What the hell do you think you're doing?" he says right to me. Not so much as a look at John, but Kathy can't stop looking and her fist is pushed up to her mouth.

I drag my arm away and rub it. Once I saw Charlie push his wife so hard she went down and hit her head and had to have four stitches. It was me that drove her to the emergency room.

Charlie says again, "What the hell do you think you're doing?"

"I'm serving my table. He wants a salad. Large." I can't remember if John'd said a large or a small salad, but I figure a large order would make Charlie feel better. But Charlie doesn't want to feel better.

"You get him out of here," Charlie hisses. He still doesn't look at John. "You hear me, Sally? You get him *out*. The government says I gotta serve spiks and niggers, but it don't say I gotta serve *him!*"

I look at John. He's putting on his hat, ramming it onto his bald head, and half-standing in the booth. He can't get out because Charlie and me are both in the way. I expect John to look mad or upset, but except that he's holding the muscles in his face in some different way, I can't see any change of expression. But I figure he's got to feel something bad, and all of a sudden I'm mad at Charlie, who's a bully and who's got the feelings of a scumbag. I open my mouth to tell him so, plus one or two other little things I been saving up, when the door flies open and in burst four men, and damn if they aren't *all* wearing hats like Humphrey Bogart in *Casablanca*. As soon as the first guy sees John, his walk changes and he comes over slower but more purposeful-like, and he's talking to John and to Charlie in a sincere voice like a TV anchorman giving out the news.

I see the situation now belongs to him, so I go back to the catsup bottles. I'm still plenty burned, though, about Charlie manhandling me and about Kathy rushing so stupid into the kitchen to get Charlie. She's a flake and always has been.

Charlie is scowling and nodding. The harder he scowls, the nicer the government guy's voice gets. Pretty soon the government guy is smiling sweet as pie. Charlie slinks back into the kitchen, and the four men move toward the door with John in the middle of them like some high school football huddle. Next to the real men, he looks stranger than he did before, and I see how really flat his face is. But then when the huddle's right opposite the table with my catsup bottles, John breaks away and comes over to me.

"I am sorry, Sally Gourley," he says. And then: "I seldom have the chance to show our friendliness to an ordinary Earth person. I make so little difference!"

Well, that throws me. His voice sounds so sad, and besides, I never thought of myself as an ordinary Earth person. Who would? So I just shrug and wipe off a catsup bottle with my towel. But then John does a weird thing. He just touches my arm where Charlie squeezed it, just touches it with the palm of those hands. And the palm's not slimy at all—dry, and sort of cool, and I don't jump or anything. Instead, I remember that beautiful noise when he said his other name. Then he goes out with three of the men, and the door bangs behind them on a gust of rain because Charlie never fixed the air-stop from when some kids horsing around broke it last spring.

The fourth man stays and questions me: What did the alien say, what did I say. I tell him, but then he starts asking the exact same questions all over again, like he didn't believe me the first time, and that gets me mad. Also, he has this snotty voice, and I see how his eyebrows move when I slip once and accidently say, "he don't." I might not know what John's muscles mean, but I sure the hell can read those eyebrows. So I get miffed, and pretty soon he leaves and the door bangs behind him.

I finish the catsup and mustard bottles, and Kathy finishes the coffee machine. The radio in the ceiling plays something instrumental, no words, real sad. Kathy and me start to wash down the booths with disinfectant, and because we're doing the same work together and nobody comes in, I finally say to her, "It's funny."

She says, "What's funny?"

"Charlie called that guy 'him' right off. 'I don't got to serve him,' he said. And I thought of him as 'it' at first, least until I had a name to use. But Charlie's the one who threw him out."

Kathy swipes at the back of her booth. "And Charlie's right. That thing scared me half to death, coming in here like that. And where there's food being served, too." She snorts and sprays on more disinfectant.

Well, she's a flake. Always has been.

"The *National Enquirer*," Kathy goes on, "told how they have all this firepower up there in the big ship that hasn't landed yet. My husband says they could blow us all to smithereens, they're so powerful. I don't know why they even came here. *We* don't want them. I don't even know why they came, all that way."

"They want to make a difference," I say, but Kathy barrels on ahead, not listening.

"The Pentagon will hold them off, it doesn't matter what weapons they got up there or how much they insist on seeing about our defenses, the Pentagon won't let them get any toeholds on Earth. That's what my husband says. Blue bastards."

I say, "Will you please shut up?"

She gives me a dirty look and flounces off. I don't care. None of it is anything to me. Only, standing there with the disinfectant in my hand, looking at the dark windows and listening to the music wordless and slow on the radio, I remember that touch on my arm, so light and cool. And I think, they didn't come here with any firepower to blow us all to smithereens. I just don't believe it. But then why did they come? Why come all that way from another star to walk into Charlie's diner and order a green salad with no dressing from an ordinary Earth person?

Charlie comes out with his keys to unlock the cash register and go over the tapes. I remember the old couple who stiffed me and I curse to myself. Only pie and coffee, but it still comes off my salary. The radio in the ceiling starts playing something else, not the sad song, but nothing snappy neither. It's a love song, about some guy giving and giving and getting treated like dirt. I don't like it.

"Charlie," I say, "what did those government men say to you?"

He looks up from his tapes and scowls, "What do you care?"

"I just want to know."

"And maybe I don't want you to know," he says, and smiles nasty-like. Me asking him has put him in a better mood, the creep. All of sudden I remember what his wife said when she got the stitches, "The only way to get something from Charlie is to let him smack me around a little, and then ask him when I'm down. He'll give me anything when I'm down. He gives me shit if he thinks I'm on top."

I do the rest of the cleanup without saying anything. Charlie swears at the night's take—I know from my tips that it's not much. Kathy teases her hair in front of the mirror behind the doughnuts and pies, and I put down the breakfast menus. But all the time I'm thinking, and I don't much like my thoughts.

Charlie locks up and we all leave. Outside it's stopped raining, but it's still misty and soft, real pretty but too cold. I pull my sweater around myself and in the parking lot, after Kathy's gone, I say, "Charlie."

He stops walking toward his truck. "Yeah?"

I lick my lips. They're all of a sudden dry. It's an experiment, like, what I'm going to say. It's an experiment.

"Charlie. What if those government men hadn't come just then and the . . . blue guy hadn't been willing to leave? What would you have done?"

"What do you care?"

I shrug. "I don't care. Just curious. It's *your* place."

"Damn right it's my place!" I could see him scowl, through the mist. "I'd of squashed him flat!"

"And then what? After you squashed him flat, what if the men came then and made a stink?"

"Too bad. It'd be too late by then, huh?" He laughs, and I can see how he's seeing it: the blue guy bleeding on the linoleum, and Charlie standing over him, dusting his hands together.

Charlie laughs again and goes off to his truck, whistling. He has a little bounce to his step. He's still seeing it all, almost like it really *had* happened. Over his shoulder he calls to me, "They're built like wimps. Or girls. All bone, no muscle. Even *you* must of seen that," and his voice is cheerful. It doesn't have any more anger in it, or hatred, or anything but a sort of friendliness. I hear him whistle some more, until the truck engine starts up and he peels out of the parking lot, laying rubber like a kid.

I unlock my Chevy. But before I get in, I look up at the sky. Which is really stupid because of course I can't see anything, with all the mists and clouds. No stars.

Maybe Kathy's husband is right. Maybe they do want to blow us all to smithereens. I don't think so, but what the hell difference does it ever make what I think? And all at once I'm furious at John, furiously mad, as furious as I've ever been in my life.

Why does he have to come here, with his birdcalls and his politeness? Why can't they all go someplace else besides here? There must be lots of other places they can go, out of all them bright stars up there behind the clouds. They don't need to come here, here where I need this job and so that means I need Charlie. He's a bully, but I want to look at him and see nothing else but a bully. Nothing else but that. That's all I want to see in Charlie, in the government men—just small-time bullies, nothing special, not a mirror of anything, not a future of anything. Just Charlie. That's all. I won't see nothing else.

I won't.

"I make so little difference," he says.

Yeah. Sure.

Salvador

✻ ✻ ✻

Lucius Shepard

Many of Lucius Shepard's hard-edged, compelling stories are about strange happenings in war zones like Vietnam and Central America. "Salvador," from our April 1984 issue, is an example. It is from powerful stories like this and novels like Green Eyes *and* Life During Wartime *that Shepard has earned his acclaim as one of our most provocative new writers.*

✻ ✻ ✻

THREE weeks before they wasted Tecolutla, Dantzler had his baptism of fire. The platoon was crossing a meadow at the foot of an emerald-green volcano, and being a dreamy sort, he was idling along, swatting tall grasses with his rifle barrel and thinking how it might have been a first-grader with crayons who had devised this elementary landscape of a perfect cone rising into a cloudless sky, when cap-pistol noises sounded on the slope. Someone screamed for the medic, and Dantzler dove into the grass, fumbling for his ampules. He slipped one from the dispenser and popped it under his nose, inhaling frantically; then, to be on the safe side, he popped another—"A double helpin' of martial arts," as DT would say—and lay with his head down

293

until the drugs had worked their magic. There was dirt in his mouth, and he was very afraid.

Gradually his arms and legs lost their heaviness, and his heart rate slowed. His vision sharpened to the point that he could see not only the pinpricks of fire blooming on the slope, but also the figures behind them, half-obscured by brush. A bubble of grim anger welled up in his brain, hardened by a fierce resolve, and he started moving toward the volcano. By the time he reached the base of the cone, he was all rage and reflexes. He spent the next forty minutes spinning acrobatically through the thickets, spraying shadows with bursts of his M-18; yet part of his mind remained distant from the action, marveling at his efficiency, at the comic-strip enthusiasm he felt for the task of killing. He shouted at the men he shot, and he shot them many more times than was necessary, like a child playing soldier.

"Playin' my ass!" DT would say. "You just actin' natural."

DT was a firm believer in the ampules; though the official line was that they contained tailored RNA compounds and pseudoendorphins modified to an inhalant form, he held the opinion that they opened a man up to his inner nature. He was big, black, with heavily muscled arms and crudely stamped features, and he had come to the Special Forces direct from prison, where he had done a stretch for attempted murder; the palms of his hands were covered by jail tattoos —a pentagram and a horned monster. The words DIE HIGH were painted on his helmet. This was his second tour in Salvador, and Moody— who was Dantzler's buddy—said the drugs had addled DT's brains, that he was crazy and gone to hell.

"He collects trophies," Moody had said. "And not just ears like they done in 'Nam."

When Dantzler had finally gotten a glimpse of the trophies, he had been appalled. They were kept in a tin box in DT's pack and were nearly unrecognizable; they looked like withered brown orchids. But despite his revulsion, despite the fact that he was afraid of DT, he admired the man's capacity for survival and had taken to heart his advice to rely on the drugs.

On the way back down the slope, they discovered a live casualty, an Indian kid about Dantzler's age, nineteen or twenty. Black hair, adobe skin, and heavy-lidded brown eyes. Dantzler, whose father was an anthropologist and had done field work in Salvador, figured him for a Santa Ana tribesman; before leaving the States, Dantzler had pored over his father's notes, hoping this would give him an edge, and had learned to identify the various regional types. The kid had a minor leg wound and was wearing fatigue pants and a faded COKE ADDS LIFE T-shirt. This T-shirt irritated DT no end.

"What the hell you know 'bout Coke?" he asked the kid as they headed for the chopper that was to carry them deeper into Morazan Province. "You think it's funny or somethin'?" He whacked the kid in the back with his rifle butt, and when they reached the chopper, he slung him inside and had him sit by the door. He sat beside him, tapped out a joint from a pack of Kools, and asked, "Where's Infante?"

"Dead," said the medic.

"Shit!" DT licked the joint so it would burn evenly. "Goddamn beaner ain't no use 'cept somebody else know Spanish."

"I know a little," Dantzler volunteered.

Staring at Dantzler, DT's eyes went empty and unfocused. "Naw," he said. "You don't know no Spanish."

Dantzler ducked his head to avoid DT's stare and said nothing; he thought he understood what DT meant, but he ducked away from the understanding as well. The chopper bore them aloft, and DT lit the joint. He let the smoke out his nostrils and passed the joint to the kid, who accepted gratefully.

"*Que sabor!*" he said, exhaling a billow; he smiled and nodded, wanting to be friends.

Dantzler turned his gaze to the open door. They were flying low between the hills, and looking at the deep bays of shadow in their folds acted to drain away the residue of the drugs, leaving him weary and frazzled. Sunlight poured in, dazzling the oil-smeared floor.

"Hey, Dantzler!" DT had to shout over the noise of the rotors. "Ask him whass his name!"

The kid's eyelids were drooping from the joint, but on hearing Spanish he perked up; he shook his head, though, refusing to answer. Dantzler smiled and told him not to be afraid.

"Ricardo Quu," said the kid.

"Kool!" said DT with false heartiness. "Thass my brand!" He offered his pack to the kid.

"*Gracias, no.*" The kid waved the joint and grinned.

"Dude's named for a godamn cigarette," said DT disparagingly, as if this were the height of insanity.

Dantzler asked the kid if there were more soldiers nearby, and once again received no reply; but, apparently sensing in Dantzler a kindred soul, the kid leaned forward and spoke rapidly, saying that his village was Santander Jimenez, that his father was—he hesitated—a man of power. He asked where they were taking him. Dantzler returned a stony glare. He found it easy to reject the kid, and he realized later this was because he had already given up on him.

Latching his hands behind his head, DT began to sing—a wordless melody. His voice was discordant, barely audible above the rotors; but the tune had a familiar ring, and Dantzler soon placed it. The theme from "Star Trek." It brought back memories of watching TV with his sister, laughing at the low-budget aliens and Scotty's Actors' Equity accent. He gazed out the door again. The sun was behind the hills, and the hillsides were unfeatured blurs of dark green smoke. Oh, God, he wanted to be home, to be anywhere but Salvador! A couple of the guys joined in the singing at DT's urging, and as the volume swelled, Dantzler's emotion peaked. He was on the verge of tears, remembering tastes and sights, the way his girl Jeanine had smelled, so clean and fresh, not reeking of sweat and perfume like the whores around Ilopango—finding all this substance in the banal touchstone of his culture and the illusions of the hillsides rushing past. Then Moody tensed beside him, and he glanced up to learn the reason why.

In the gloom of the chopper's belly, DT was as unfeatured as the hills—a black presence ruling them, more the leader of a coven than a platoon. The other two guys were singing their lungs out, and even the kid was getting into the spirit of things. "*Musical!*" he said at one point, smiling at everybody, trying to fan the flame of good feeling. He swayed to the rhythm and essayed a "la-la" now and again. But no one else was responding.

The singing stopped, and Dantzler saw that the whole platoon was staring at the kid, their expressions slack and dispirited.

"Space!" shouted DT, giving the kid a little shove. "The final frontier!"

The smile had not yet left the kid's face when he toppled out the door. DT peered after him; a few seconds later, he smacked his hand against the floor and sat back, grinning. Dantzler felt like screaming, the stupid horror of the joke was so at odds with the languor of his homesickness. He looked to the others for reaction. They were sitting with their heads down, fiddling with trigger guards and pack straps, studying their bootlaces, and seeing this, he quickly imitated them.

Morazan Province was spook country. Santa Ana spooks. Flights of birds had been reported to attack pistols; animals appeared at the perimeters of campsites and vanished when you shot at them; dreams afflicted everyone who ventured there. Dantzler could not testify to the birds and animals, but he did have a recurring dream. In it the kid DT had killed was pinwheeling down through a golden fog, his T-shirt visible against the roiling backdrop, and sometimes a voice would boom out of the fog, saying, "You are killing my son." No, no, Dantzler would reply; it wasn't me, and besides, he's already dead. Then he would wake covered with sweat, groping for his rifle, his heart racing.

But the dream was not an important terror, and he assigned it no significance. The land was far more terrifying. Pine-forested ridges that stood out against the sky like fringes of electrified hair; little trails winding off into thickets and petering out, as if what they led to had been magicked away; gray rock faces along which they were forced to walk, hopelessly exposed to ambush. There were innumerable booby traps set by the guerrillas, and they lost several men to rockfalls. It was the emptiest place of Dantzler's experience. No people, no animals, just a few hawks circling the solitudes between the ridges. Once in a while they found tunnels, and these they blew with the new gas grenades; the gas ignited the rich concentrations of hydrocarbons and sent flame sweeping through the entire system. DT would praise whoever had discovered the tunnel and would estimate in a loud voice how many beaners they had "refried." But Dantzler knew they were traversing pure emptiness and burning empty holes. Days, under debilitating heat, they humped the mountains, traveling seven, eight, even ten klicks up trails so steep that frequently the feet of the guy ahead of you would be on a level with your face; nights, it was cold, the darkness absolute, the silence so profound that Dantzler imagined he could hear the great humming vibration of the earth. They might have been anywhere or nowhere. Their fear was nourished by the isolation, and the only remedy was "martial arts."

Dantzler took to popping the pills without the excuse of combat. Moody cautioned him against abusing the drugs, citing rumors of bad side effects and DT's madness; but even he was using them more and more often. During basic training, Dantzler's D.I. had told the boots that the drugs were available only to the Special Forces, that their use was optional; but there had been too many instances of lackluster battlefield performance in the last war, and this was to prevent a reoccurrence.

"The chickenshit infantry should take 'em," the D.I. had said. "You bastards are brave already. You're born killers, right?"

"Right, sir!" they had shouted.

"What are you?"

"Born killers, sir!"

But Dantzler was not a born killer; he was not even clear as to how he had been drafted, less clear as to how he had been manipulated into the Special Forces, and he had learned that nothing was optional in Salvador, with the possible exception of life itself.

The platoon's mission was reconnaissance and mop-up. Along with other Special Forces platoons, they were to secure Morazan prior to the invasion of Nicaragua; specifically, they were to proceed to the village of Tecolutla, where a Sandinista patrol had recently been spotted, and following that, they were to join up with the First Infantry and take part in the offensive against León, a provincial capital just across the Nicaraguan border. As Dantzler and Moody walked together, they frequently talked about the offensive, how it would be good to get down into flat country; occasionally they talked about the possibility of reporting DT, and once, after he had led them on a forced night march, they toyed with the idea of killing him. But most often they discussed the ways of the Indians and the land, since this was what had caused them to become buddies.

Moody was slightly built, freckled, and red-haired; his eyes had the "thousand-yard stare" that came from too much war. Dantzler had seen winos with such vacant, lusterless stares. Moody's father had been in 'Nam, and Moody said it had been worse than Salvador because there had been no real commitment to win; but he thought Nicaragua and Guatemala might be the worst of all, especially if the Cubans sent in troops as they had threatened. He was adept at locating tunnels and detecting booby traps, and it was for this reason Dantzler had cultivated his friendship. Essentially a loner, Moody had resisted all advances until learning of Dantzler's father; thereafter he had buddied up, eager to hear about the field notes, believing they might give him an edge.

"They think the land has animal traits," said Dantzler one day as they climbed along a ridgetop. "Just like some kinds of fish look like plants or sea bottom, parts of the land look like plain ground, jungle . . . whatever. But when you enter them, you find you've entered the spirit world, the world of the *Sukias*."

"What's *Sukias*?" asked Moody.

"Magicians." A twig snapped behind Dantzler, and he spun around, twitching off the safety of his rifle. It was only Hodge—a lanky kid with the beginnings of a beer gut. He stared hollow-eyed at Dantzler and popped an ampule.

Moody made a noise of disbelief. "If they got magicians, why ain't they winnin'? Why ain't they zappin' us off the cliffs?"

"It's not their business," said Dantzler. "They don't believe in messing with worldly affairs unless it concerns them directly. Anyway, these places—the ones that look like normal land but aren't—they're called. . . ." He drew a blank on the name. "*Aya*-something. I can't remember. But they have different laws. They're where your spirit goes to die after your body dies."

"Don't they got no Heaven?"

"Nope. It just takes longer for your spirit to die, and so it goes to one of these places that's between everything and nothing."

"Nothin'," said Moody disconsolately, as if all his hopes for an afterlife had been dashed. "Don't make no sense to have spirits and not have no Heaven."

"Hey," said Dantzler, tensing as wind rustled the pine boughs. "They're just a bunch of damn primitives. You know what their sacred drink is? Hot chocolate! My old man was a guest at one of their funerals, and he said they carried cups of hot chocolate balanced on these little red towers and acted like drinking it was going to wake them to the secrets of the universe." He laughed, and the laughter sounded tinny and psychotic to his own ears. "So you're going to worry about fools who think hot chocolate's holy water?"

"Maybe they just like it," said Moody. "Maybe somebody dyin' just give 'em an excuse to drink it."

But Dantzler was no longer listening. A moment before, as they emerged from pine cover onto the highest point of the ridge, a stony scarp open to the winds and providing a view of rumpled mountains and valleys extending to the horizon, he had popped an ampule. He felt so strong, so full of righteous purpose and controlled fury, it seemed only the sky was around him, that he was still ascending, preparing to do battle with the gods themselves.

Tecolutla was a village of whitewashed stone tucked into a notch between two hills. From above, the houses—with their black windows and doorways—looked like an unlucky throw of dice. The streets ran uphill and down, diverging around boulders. Bougainvilleas and hibiscuses speckled the hillsides, and there were tilled fields on the gentler slopes. It was a sweet, peaceful place when they arrived, and after they had gone it was once again peaceful; but its sweetness had been permanently banished. The reports of Sandinistas had proved accurate, and though they were causalties left behind to recuperate, DT had decided their presence called for extreme measures. Fu gas, frag grenades, and such. He had fired an M-60 until the barrel melted down, and then had manned the flamethrower. Afterward, as they rested atop the next ridge, exhausted and begrimed, having radioed in a chopper for resupply, he could not get over how one of the houses he had torched had resembled a toasted marshmallow.

"Ain't that how it was, man?" he asked, striding up and down the line. He did not care if they agreed about the house; it was a deeper question he was asking, one concerning the ethics of their actions.

"Yeah," said Dantzler, forcing a smile. "Sure did."

DT grunted with laughter. "You *know* I'm right, don'tcha man?"

The sun hung directly behind his head, a golden corona rimming a black oval, and Dantzler could not turn his eyes away. He felt weak and weakening, as if threads of himself were being spun loose and sucked into the blackness. He popped three ampules prior to the firefight, and his experience of Tecolutla had been a kind of mad whirling dance through the streets, spraying erratic bursts that appeared to be writing weird names on the walls. The leader of the Sandinistas had worn a mask—a gray face with a surprised hole of a mouth and pink circles around the eyes. A ghost face. Dantzler had been afraid of the mask and had poured round after round into it. Then, leaving the village, he had seen a small girl standing beside the shell of the last house, watching them, her colorless rag of a dress tattering in the breeze. She had been a victim of that malnutrition disease, the one that paled your skin and whitened your hair and left you retarded. He could not recall the name of the disease—things like names were slipping away from him—nor could he believe anyone had survived, and for a moment he had thought the spirit of the village had come out to mark their trail.

That was all he could remember of Tecolutla, all he wanted to remember. But he knew he had been brave.

Four days later, they headed up into a cloud forest. It was the dry season, but dry season or not, blackish gray clouds always shrouded these peaks. They were shot through by ugly glimmers of lightning, making it seem that malfunctioning neon signs were hidden beneath them, advertisements for evil. Everyone was jittery, and Jerry LeDoux—a slim, dark-haired Cajun kid—flat-out refused to go.

"It ain't reasonable," he said. "Be easier to go through the passes."

"We're on recon, man! You think the beaners be waitin' in the passes, wavin' their white flags?" DT whipped his rifle into firing position and pointed it at LeDoux. "C'mon, Louisiana man. Pop a few, and you feel different."

As LeDoux popped the ampules, DT talked to him.

"Look at it this way, man. This is your big adventure. Up there it be like all them animals shows on the tube. The savage kingdom, the unknown. Could be like Mars or somethin'. Monsters and shit, with big red eyes and tentacles. You wanna miss that, man? You wanna miss bein' the first grunt on Mars?"

Soon LeDoux was raring to go, giggling at DT's rap.

Moody kept his mouth shut, but he fingered the safety of his rifle and glared at DT's back. When DT turned to him, however, he relaxed. Since Tecolutla he had grown taciturn, and there seemed to be a shifting of lights and darks in his eyes, as if something were scurrying back and forth behind them. He had taken to wearing banana leaves on his head, arranging them under his helmet so the frayed ends stuck out the sides like strange green hair. He said this was camouflage, but Dantzler was certain it bespoke some secretive, irrational purpose. Of course DT had noticed Moody's spiritual erosion, and as they prepared to move out, he called Dantzler aside.

"He done found someplace inside his head that feel good to him," said DT. "He's tryin' to curl up into it, and once he do that he ain't gon' be responsible. Keep an eye on him."

Dantzler mumbled his assent, but was not enthused.

"I know he your fren', man, but that don't mean shit. Not the way things are. Now me, I don't give a damn 'bout you personally. But I'm your brother-in-arms, and thass somethin' you can count on . . . y'understand."

To Dantzler's shame, he did understand.

They had planned on negotiating the cloud forest by nightfall, but they had underestimated the difficulty. The vegetation beneath the clouds was lush—thick, juicy leaves that mashed underfoot, tangles of vines, trees with slick, pale bark and waxy leaves—and the visibility was only about fifteen feet. They were gray wraiths passing through grayness. The vague shapes of the foliage reminded Dantzler of fancifully engraved letters, and for a while he entertained himself with the notion that they were walking among the half-formed phrases of a constitution not yet manifest in the land. They barged off the trail, losing it completely, becoming veiled in spider webs and drenched by spills of water; their voices were oddly muffled, the tag ends of words swallowed up. After seven hours of this, DT reluctantly gave the order to pitch camp. They set electric lamps around the perimeter so they could see to string the jungle hammocks; the beam of light illuminated the moisture in the air, piercing the murk with jeweled blades. They talked in hushed tones, alarmed by the eerie atmosphere. When they had done with the hammocks, DT posted four sentries—Moody, LeDoux, Dantzler, and himself. Then they switched off the lamps.

It grew pitch-dark, and the darkness was picked out by plips and plops, the entire spectrum of dripping sounds. To Dantzler's ears they blended into a gabbling speech. He imagined tiny Santa Ana demons talking about him, and to stave off paranoia he popped two ampules. He continued to pop them, trying to limit himself to one every half hour; but he was uneasy, unsure where to train his rifle in the dark, and he exceeded his limit. Soon it began to grow light again, and he assumed that more time had passed than he had thought. That often happened with the ampules—it was easy to lose yourself in being alert, in the wealth of perceptual detail available to your sharpened senses.

Yet on checking his watch, he saw it was only a few minutes after two o'clock. His system was too inundated with the drugs to allow panic, but he twitched his head from side-to-side in tight little arcs to determine the source of the brightness. There did not appear to be a single source; it was simply that filaments of the cloud were gleaming, casting a diffuse golden glow, as if they were elements of a nervous system coming to life. He started to call out, then held back. The others must have seen the light, and they had given no cry; they probably had a good reason for their silence. He scrunched down flat, pointing his rifle out from the campsite.

Bathed in the golden mist, the forest had acquired an alchemic beauty. Beads of water glittered with gemmy brilliance; the leaves and vines and bark were gilded. Every surface shimmered with light . . . everything except a fleck of blackness hovering between two of the trunks, its size gradually increasing. As it swelled in his vision, he saw it had the shape of a bird, its wings beating, flying toward him from an inconceivable distance—inconceivable, because the dense vegetation did not permit you to see very far in a straight line, and yet the bird was growing larger with such slowness that it must have been coming from a long way off. It was not really flying, he realized; rather, it was as if the forest were painted on a piece of paper, as if someone were holding a lit match behind it and burning a hole, a hole that maintained the shape of a bird as it spread. He was transfixed, unable to react. Even when it had blotted out half the light, when he lay before it no bigger than a mote in relation to its huge span, he could not move or squeeze the trigger. And then the blackness swept over him. He had the sensation of being borne along at incredible speed, and he could no longer hear the dripping of the forest.

"Moody!" he shouted. "DT!"

But the voice that answered belonged to neither of them. It was hoarse, issuing from every part of the surrounding blackness, and he recognized it as the voice of his recurring dream.

"You are killing my son," it said. "I have led you here, to this *ayahuamaco*, so he may judge you."

Dantzler knew to his bones the voice was that of the *Sukia* of the village of Santander Jimenez. He wanted to offer a denial, to explain his innocence, but all he could manage was, "No." He said it tearfully, hopelessly, his forehead resting on his rifle barrel. Then his mind gave a savage twist, and his soldiery self regained control. He ejected an ampule from his dispenser and popped it.

The voice laughed—malefic, damning laughter whose vibrations shuddered Dantzler. He opened up with the rifle, spraying fire in all directions. Filigrees of golden holes appeared in the blackness, tendrils of mist coiled through them. He kept on firing until the blackness shattered and fell in jagged sections toward him. Slowly. Like shards of black glass dropping through water. He emptied the rifle and flung himself flat, shielding his head with his arms, expecting to be sliced into bits; but nothing touched him. At last he peeked between his arms; then—amazed, because the forest was now a uniform lustrous yellow —he rose to his knees. He scraped his hand on one of the crushed leaves beneath him, and blood welled from the cut. The broken fibers of the leaf were as stiff as wires. He stood, a giddy trickle of hysteria leaking up from the bottom of his soul. It was no forest, but a building of solid gold worked to resemble a forest—the sort of conceit that might have been fabricated for the child of an emperor. Canopied by golden leaves, columned by slender golden trunks, carpeted by golden grasses. The water beads were diamonds. All the gleam and glitter soothed his apprehension; here was something out of a myth, a habitat for princesses and wizards and dragons. Almost gleeful, he turned to the campsite to see how the others were reacting.

Once, when he was nine years old, he had sneaked into the attic to rummage through the boxes and trunks, and he had run across an old morocco-bound copy of *Gulliver's Travels*. He had been taught to treasure old books, and so he had opened it eagerly to look at the illustrations, only to find that the centers of the pages had been eaten away, and there, right in the heart of the fiction, was a nest of larvae. Pulpy, horrid things. It had been an awful sight, but one unique in his experience, and he might have studied those crawling scraps of life for a very long time if his father had not interrupted. Such a sight was now before him, and he was numb with it.

They were all dead. He should have guessed they would be; he had given no thought to them while firing his rifle. They had been struggling out of their hammocks when the bullets hit, and as a result, they were hanging half-in, half-out, their limbs dangling, blood pooled beneath them. The veils of golden mist made them look dark and mysterious and malformed, like monsters killed as they emerged from their cocoons. Dantzler could not stop staring, but he was shrinking inside himself. It was not his fault. That thought kept swooping in and out of a flock of less-acceptable thoughts; he wanted to stay put, to be true, to alleviate the sick horror he was beginning to feel.

"What's your name?" asked a girl's voice behind him.

She was sitting on a stone about twenty feet away. Her hair was a tawny shade of gold, her skin a half-tone lighter, and her dress was cunningly formed out of the mist. Only her eyes were real. Brown, heavy-lidded eyes—they were at variance with the rest of her face, which had the fresh, unaffected beauty of an American teenager.

"Don't be afraid," she said, and patted the ground, inviting him to sit beside her.

He recognized the eyes, but it was no matter. He badly needed the consolation she could offer; he walked over and sat down. She let him lean his head against her thigh.

"What's your name?" she repeated.

"Dantzler," he said. "John Dantzler." And then he added, "I'm from Boston. My father's. . . ." It would be too difficult to explain about anthropology. "He's a teacher."

"Are there many soldiers in Boston?" She stroked his cheek with a golden finger.

The caress made Dantzler happy. "Oh, no," he said. "They hardly know there's a war going on."

"This is true?" she said, incredulous.

"Well, they *do* know about it, but it's just news on the TV to them. They've got more pressing problems. Their jobs, families."

"Will you let them know about the war when you return home?" she asked. "Will you do that for me?"

Dantzler had given up hope of returning home, of surviving, and her assumption that he would do both acted to awaken his gratitude. "Yes," he said fervently. "I will."

"You must hurry," she said. "If you stay in the *ayahuamaco* too long, you will never leave. You must find the way out. It is a way not of directions or trails, but of events."

"Where is this place?" he asked, suddenly aware of how much he had taken it for granted.

She shifted her leg away, and if he had not caught himself on the stone, he would have fallen. When he looked up, she had vanished. He was surprised that her disappearance did not alarm him; in reflex he slipped out a couple of ampules, but after a moment's reflection he decided not to use them. It was impossible to slip them back into the dispenser, so he tucked them into the interior webbing of his helmet for later. He doubted he would need them, though. He felt strong, competent, and unafraid.

Dantzler stepped carefully between the hammocks, not wanting to brush against them; it might have been his imagination, but they seemed to be bulged down lower than before, as if death had weighed out heavier than life. That heaviness was in the air, pressuring him. Mist rose like golden steam from the corpses, but the sight no longer affected him— perhaps because the mist gave the illusion of being their souls. He picked up a rifle with a full magazine and headed off into the forest.

The tips of the golden leaves were sharp, and he had to ease past them to avoid being cut; but he was at the top of his form, moving gracefully, and the obstacles barely slowed his pace. He was not even anxious about the girl's warning to hurry; he was certain the way out would soon present itself. After a minute or so, he heard voices, and after another few seconds, he came to a clearing divided by a stream, one so perfectly reflecting that its banks appeared to enclose a wedge of golden mist. Moody was squatting to the left of the stream, staring at the blade of his survival knife and singing under his breath—a wordless melody that had the erratic rhythm of a trapped fly. Beside him lay Jerry LeDoux, his throat slashed from ear to ear. DT was sitting on the other side of the stream; he had been shot just above the knee, and though he had ripped up his shirt for bandages and tied off the leg with a tourniquet, he was not in good shape. He was sweating, and the gray chalky pallor infused his skin. The entire scene had the weird vitality of something that had materialized in a magic mirror, a bubble of reality enclosed within a gilt frame.

DT heard Dantzler's footfalls and glanced up. "Waste him!" he shouted, pointing at Moody.

Moody did not turn from contemplation of the knife. "No," he said, as if speaking to someone whose image was held in the blade.

"Waste him, man!" screamed DT. "He killed LeDoux!"

"Please," said Moody to the knife. "I don't want to."

There was blood clotted on his face, more blood on the banana leaves sticking out of his helmet.

"Did you kill Jerry?" asked Dantzler; while he addressed the question to Moody, he did not relate to him as an individual, only as part of a design whose message he had to unravel.

"Jesus Christ! Waste him!" DT smashed his fist against the ground in frustration.

"O.K.," said Moody. With an apologetic look, he sprang to his feet and charged Dantzler, swinging the knife.

Emotionless, Dantzler stitched a line of fire across Moody's chest; he went sideways into the bushes and down.

"What the hell was you waitin' for!" DT tried to rise, but winced and fell back. "Damn! Don't know if I can walk."

"Pop a few," Dantzler suggested mildly.

"Yeah. Good thinkin', man." DT fumbled for his dispenser.

Dantzler peered into the bushes to see where Moody had fallen. He felt nothing, and this pleased him. He was weary of feeling.

DT popped an ampule with a flourish, as if making a toast, and inhaled. "Ain't you gon' to do some, man?"

"I don't need them," said Dantzler. "I'm fine."

The stream interested him; it did not reflect the mist, as he had supposed, but was itself a seam of the mist.

"How many you think they was?" asked DT.

"How many what?"

"Beaners, man! I wasted three or four after they hit us, but I couldn't tell how many they was."

Dantzler considered this in light of his own interpretation of events and Moody's conversation with the knife. It made sense. A Santa Ana kind of sense.

"Beats me," he said. "But I guess there's less than there used to be."

DT snorted. "You got *that* right." He heaved to his feet and limped to the edge of the stream. "Gimme a hand across."

Dantzler reached out to him, but instead of taking his hand, he grabbed his wrist and pulled him off-balance. DT teetered on his good leg, then toppled and vanished beneath the mist. Dantzler had expected him to fall, but he surfaced instantly, mist clinging to his skin. Of course, thought Dantzler, his body would have to die before his spirit would fall.

"What you doin', man?" DT was more disbelieving than enraged. Dantzler planted a foot in the middle of his back and pushed him down until his head was submerged. DT bucked and clawed at the foot and managed to come to his hands and knees. Mist slithered from his eyes, his nose, and he choked out the words ". . . kill you. . . ." Dantzler pushed him down again; he got into pushing him down and letting him up, over and over. Not so as to torture him. Not really. It was because he had suddenly understood the nature of the *ayahuamaco's* laws, that they were approximations of normal laws, and he further understood that his actions had to approximate those of someone jiggling a key in a lock. DT was the key to the way out, and Dantzler was jiggling him, making sure all the tumblers were engaged.

Some of the vessels in DT's eyes had burst, and the whites were occluded by films of blood. When he tried to speak, mist curled from his mouth. Gradually his struggles subsided; he clawed runnels in the gleaming yellow dirt of the bank and shuddered. His shoulders were knobs of black land floundering in a mystic sea.

For a long time after DT sank from view, Dantzler stood beside the stream, uncertain of what was left to do and unable to remember a lesson he had been taught. Finally, he shouldered his rifle and walked away from the clearing. Morning had broken, the mist had thinned, and the forest had regained its usual coloration. But he scarcely noticed these changes, still troubled by his faulty memory. Eventually, he let it slide—it would all come clearer sooner or later. He was just happy to be alive. After a while he began to kick the stones as he went, and to swing his rifle in a carefree fashion against the weeds.

When the First Infantry poured across the Nicaraguan border and wasted León, Dantzler was having a quiet time at the VA hospital in Ann Arbor, Michigan; and at the precise moment the bulletin was flashed nationwide, he was sitting in the lounge, watching the American League play-offs between Detroit and Texas. Some of the patients ranted at the interruption, while others shouted them down, wanting to hear the details. Dantzler expressed no reaction whatsoever. He was solely concerned with being a model patient; however, noticing that one of the staff was giving him a clinical stare, he added his weight on the side of the baseball fans. He did not want to appear too controlled. The doctors were as suspicious of that sort of behavior as they were of its contrary. But the funny thing was—at least it was funny to Dantzler—that his feigned annoyance at the bulletin was an exemplary proof of his control, his expertise at moving through life the way he had moved through the golden leaves of the cloud forest. Cautiously, gracefully, efficiently. Touching nothing, and being touched by nothing. That was the lesson he had learned—to be as perfect a counterfeit of a man as the *aya-huamaco* had been of the land; to adopt the various stances of a man, and yet, by virtue of his distance from things human, to be all the more prepared for the onset of crisis or a call to action. He saw nothing aberrant in this; even the doctors would admit that men were little more than organized pretense. If he was different from other men, it was only that he had a deeper awareness of the principles on which his personality was founded.

When the battle of Managua was joined, Dantzler was living at home. His parents had urged him to go easy in readjusting to civilian life, but he had immediately gotten a job as a management trainee in a bank. Each morning he would drive to work and spend a controlled, quiet eight hours; each night he would watch TV with his mother, and before going to bed, he would climb to the attic and inspect the trunk containing his souvenirs of war—helmet, fatigues, knife, boots. The doctors had insisted he face his experiences, and this ritual was his way of following their instructions. All in all, he was quite pleased with his progress, but he still had problems. He had not been able to force himself to venture out at night, remembering too well the darkness in the cloud forest, and he had rejected his friends, refusing to see them or answer their calls—he was not secure with the idea of friendship. Further, despite his methodical approach to life, he was prone to a nagging restlessness, the feeling of a chore left undone.

One night his mother came into his room and told him that an old friend, Phil Curry, was on the phone. "Please talk to him, Johnny," she said. "He's been drafted, and I think he's a little scared."

The word "drafted" struck a responsive chord in Dantzler's soul, and after brief deliberation, he went downstairs and picked up the receiver.

"Hey," said Phil. "What's the story, man? Three months, and you don't even give me a call."

"I'm sorry," said Dantzler. "I haven't been feeling so hot."

"Yeah, I understand." Phil was silent a moment. "Listen, man. I'm leavin', y'know, and we're havin' a big send-off at Sparky's. It's goin' on right now. Why don't you come down?"

"I don't know."

"Jeanine's here, man. Y'know, she's still crazy 'bout you, talks 'bout you alla time. She don't go out with nobody."

Dantzler was unable to think of anything to say.

"Look," said Phil, "I'm pretty weirded out by this soldier shit. I hear it's pretty bad down there. If you got anything you can tell me 'bout what it's like, man, I'd 'preciate it."

Dantzler could relate to Phil's concern, his desire for an edge, and besides, it felt right to go. Very right. He would take some precautions against the darkness.

"I'll be there," he said.

It was a foul night, spitting snow, but Sparky's parking lot was jammed. Dantzler's mind was flurried like the snow, crowded like the lot—thoughts whirling in, jockeying for position, melting away. He hoped his mother would not wait up, he wondered if Jeanine still wore her hair long, he was worried because the palms of his hands were unnaturally warm. Even with the car windows rolled up, he could hear loud music coming from inside the club. Above the door the words SPARKY'S ROCK CITY were being spelled out a letter at a time in red neon, and when the spelling was complete, the letter flashed off and on and a golden neon explosion bloomed around them. After the explosion, the entire sign went dark for a split second, and the big ramshackle building seemed to grow large and merge with the black sky. He had an idea it was watching him, and he shuddered—one of those sudden lurches downward of the kind that take you just before you fall asleep. He knew the people inside did not intend him any harm, but he also knew that places have a way of changing people's intent, and he did not want to be caught off guard. Sparky's might be such a place, might be a huge black presence camouflaged by neon, its true substance one with the abyss of the sky, the phosphorescent snowflakes jittering in his headlights, the wind keening through the side vent. He would have liked very much to drive home and forget about his promise to Phil;

however, he felt a responsibility to explain about the war. More than a responsibility, an evangelistic urge. He would tell them about the kid falling out of the chopper, the white-haired girl in Tecolutla, the emptiness. God, yes! How you went down chock-full of ordinary American thoughts and dreams, memories of smoking weed and chasing tail and hanging out and freeway flying with a case of something cold, and how you smuggled back a human-shaped container of pure Salvadorian emptiness. Primo grade. Smuggled it back to the land of silk and money, of mindfuck video games and topless tennis matches and fast-food solutions to the nutritional problem. Just a taste of Salvador would banish all those trivial obsessions. Just a taste. It would be easy to explain.

Of course, some things beggared explanation.

He bent down and adjusted the survival knife in his boot so the hilt would not rub against his calf. From his coat pocket he withdrew the two ampules he had secreted in his helmet that long-ago night in the cloud forest. As the neon explosion flashed once more, glimmers of gold coursed along their shiny surfaces. He did not think he would need them; his hand was steady, and his purpose was clear. But to be on the safe side, he popped them both.

State of the Art

✳   ✳   ✳

Robert Charles Wilson

*Robert Charles Wilson is one of the best new writers of SF. F&SF began
publishing his work in 1985, and he has since published two novels, A
Hidden Place and Memory Wire. His fiction has been compared to
Bradbury's and Sturgeon's for its clean prose and memorable characters.
Here is a first-rate sample, a pointed story about the ultimate in artificial
transplants.*

✳   ✳   ✳

I T was the eyes that attracted him first. They sat in the window of
the ocular shop, nestled on velvet, protein-compatible nerve con-
duits dangling behind. The eyes were a polished silver so reflective
that they seemed to contain the world; and the irises were icy blue disks.

Rogan thought about the eyes during the long drive home. They
were Bausch & Lomb Full Spectrum Day-and-Nighters. The price,
printed on a discreet white tag, was outrageous.

"More than outrageous," Margaret said when, tentatively, he raised
the subject. "You don't need such a thing. You do O.K."

Once she had been beautiful. Rogan knew that many men, the
fortunate ones, think their wives are beautiful; but of Margaret it was
an objective, demonstrable truth. Because she was shy she had refused

to enter the Queen of Classics Department competition when they were in college; but she would have won, everybody said so. Her hair had been long and full and blonde. Her skin was china pale, her features fine, her eyes a delicate brown. Her smile had been like flashbulbs going off.

And the truth was that she was still good-looking, Rogan thought, but time had fretted at her as it had fretted at him, and they were both looking a little worn. "I'm tired of the contact lenses," he said.

"So get new ones. But not this."

Really, it *didn't* make any sense. He said, a last, hopeless salvo, "If we put off the new car for a while—"

"Ben, you want that car. You said so."

So he put the Day-and-Nighters out of his mind. In the morning he walked past the ocular shop—between the parking lot and the office where he worked—with a stern and willful disinterest. The eyes gazed back at him from the window, balefully.

Rogan was a Databloc Ordinator. He sat at a terminal all day monitoring the flow and exchange of information between his employer's corporate mainframe and all the other mainframes and databanks it accessed. These were displayed on his CRT as building blocks of various sizes and color. Rogan's job was to make sure they meshed and separated in the right sequence. He was something like an air traffic controller. Usually everything was O.K. When it wasn't, he had to investigate and sort things out, tapping madly at his keyboard while the terminal howled and blinked. This happened maybe once a day.

Today, however, there was nothing, and Rogan grew bored watching the colored blocks stack and unstack themselves on the screen. He was pleased when his afternoon relief, a tall and athletic man named Forster, came in and hung his coat on the peg. Rogan wanted desperately to get away.

"Whenever you're ready," Forster said.

"It's all yours," Rogan said. "Thank God." He stood up. He stretched. He turned. The breath seemed to catch in his throat.

"Something wrong?" Forster asked.

"No," Rogan said. "No, nothing at all."

Forster stared at him, the silvery orbs of his eyes catching the fluorescent light, and for a moment Rogan saw his own reflection there.

*   *   *

"The physical attachment takes only a short time," the ocularist explained. "The nerve glues, the muscle sealants, are very fast-acting. You'll be operational twenty minutes after you come out of surgery. No: the time for taking time is now. While you have the choice."

The sheer number of eyes in the shop daunted him. The display occupied an entire wall. Some of the Japanese-manufactured units were mounted in pale mannequin faces, where they twitched back and forth as if in the throes of a mute and terrible panic. Some were silver, like Forster's; some were tinted a deep compelling blue; several were translucent, and he could see the tiny machinery inside, like camera lenses in aspic. Rogan felt dizzy; he began to perspire. Maybe this wasn't such a wise idea after all. Maybe Margaret was right.

"The best ones," Rogan said helplessly. "Which are the best ones?"

"Depends," the ocularist said. "Do you have a special application in mind? Do you scuba dive? Hunt animals at night? Practice astronomy as a hobby?"

"No," Rogan said. "I just want—"

"A good all-rounder," the ocularist supplied.

"The *best* all-rounder." He tried to sound firm.

The ocularist went to the window display and lifted the velvet-lined pedestal with the Bausch & Lombs on it. He put them on a glass-topped counter for Rogan to admire, stepping back as Rogan bent closer, smiling distantly.

"Shake them," he suggested. "No telltale rattle of cheap machinery there."

"Should I? I'm not sure—"

"They don't take fingerprints," the ocularist sniffed. "And they're not fragile."

Rogan picked one up. It was firm and cool to the touch. The embedded iris glittered like an exotic gem.

"But the price," he said regretfully.

"Ah," the ocularist said. His manner became stiff, formal. He drew away the Bausch & Lombs. "We do of course carry other lines."

He took a blank box from beneath the counter. Inside, two fishy white eyes lay on a bed of tissue paper. Rogan reached halfheartedly to touch one.

"Careful, now," the ocularist said.

Rogan sighed. "It's all right. I'll take the Bausch & Lombs."

"The intelligent choice, I think. We can arrange financing. And we offer a generous trade-in value on your unwanted biologicals."

"My what?"

"Your eyes," the ocularist said.

He left work early on the day that had been arranged. The entire process, including the time spent blindfolded while muscles knitted and the anesthetic wore off, took less than three hours. The first thing Rogan noticed when his new eyes were unbandaged was that the winter light beyond the window had failed.

"But I can see," he marveled. "I can read—my God, I can read the billboard at Bay Street!" Five city blocks away: it was an ad for synthetic meat. "At night!"

The ocularist sat impassive in his surgical whites, making notations on a clipboard. He had a Medical Technician's degree framed and hung on the wall of his inner office; Rogan amused himself by deciphering the Latinate fine print.

"Everything moves?" the ocularist said. "Up, down, side to side?"

"Yes."

He pried up Rogan's eyelids and pressed an ophthalmoscope against his orbits. "No blind spots? Everything seems lucid?"

"Yes." He added, "They feel a bit raw. A kind of pressure—"

"It fades in time."

It had faded, in fact, by the time Rogan arrived home. He had not told Margaret about the Bausch & Lombs; he wanted to present her with a *fait accompli*. Now, riding the elevator up to their condo, he felt a knot of anxiety in his stomach. How would she react?

The surprising thing was she did *not* react. Oh, there was a moment, after he had kissed her, when she looked at him seriously for a time, and he knew she *must* have noticed; his eyes were silvery bright and touched with cornflower blue where, before, they had been merely bloodshot and watery. But she didn't remark on it. She tied back her apron and said dinner would be ready in a minute. Synthetic chicken, she said.

Rogan went into the bathroom to admire his new eyes. What he saw was gratifying. His face had always seemed somehow weak when he was forced to confront it in the mornings, frothing with toothpaste.

Now—although his chin had not been noticeably firmed nor his sagging jowls tightened—he saw a face that was cool, aloof, almost threatening. A thrill ran through him.

She didn't react, Rogan thought, because she loves me. She had accepted his decision. Anyway, it was too late to fight it. His old eyes had probably been auctioned off to some charity hospital in equatorial Africa. He respected her choice by making no comment of his own, except about the chicken, which he said was good.

The real test came later. They made love.

It was awkward at first. Rogan felt embarrassed by his eyes, or rather was afraid they would embarrass Margaret; he kept them closed. Then, when her passion had begun to build, he allowed himself to look closely at her. There was none of the revulsion he had expected to see. He was pleased. The pace picked up. He began to stare—boldly.

She said she loved him. Rogan murmured that he loved her too, but now his new eyes were having an unsettling effect: he saw Margaret's face (although the room was dark) with an almost hallucinogenic clarity, saw the wrinkles that had begun to creep out from her eyelids, the faintly cracked skin of her mouth. The flesh between the ear and her collarbone was pale and finely skeined; the Bausch & Lombs made it a topography of ancient river valleys.

He closed his eyes and thought about the way she used to look.

He went to work in the morning eager for his next encounter with the relief man, Forster. It was a difficult day. There were three consecutive data collisions, each requiring an extensive and elaborate debugging. But the time passed. He stood up promptly when he heard Forster come.

The younger man gazed impassively at Rogan's new eyes.

"B&L's," he said finally. "Very impressive."

Rogan was pleased. Forster's eyes had come from one of the big Sino-Japanese cartels; Rogan was able to discern the trademark characters incised into the silver. Take that, he thought, you son of a bitch.

"Thanks," he said modestly.

"Hearts," Forster said. His smile was enigmatic.

Rogan said, "What?"

"Hearts! Kidneys! Lungs! The vital organs!" He nudged Rogan painfully in the ribs. "That's where the real action is."

* * *

"A complete internal revision is a complex procedure. It takes time. The price, naturally, reflects this fact."

Rogan had gone, not to a sidewalk ocularist this time, but to Hills and Rutherford, the most prestigious of the city's replacement agencies. The showroom was a shag-carpeted and wood-paneled chamber high in an office tower. The salesman was poised and tailored and his glittering eyes bore down on Rogan's own. Rogan felt inadequate in this setting, almost shabby. But he was captivated by the stock.

An artificial heart in a glass case flushed rose-tinted water through translucent tubing: the motion was smooth, effortless, and quiet as a whisper. Kidneys were racked against one wall like colorful coral growths. Boa-like ropes of intestine reclined on pegs. The effect, Rogan thought, was somehow tropical.

"Too," the salesman was saying, "one inevitably pays a premium for quality. What we sell here"—he passed Rogan a stainless-steel thighbone—"is state of the art in prosthetic technology."

He did not doubt it. "I assume there'll be a reasonable exchange value on my—uh, parts?"

"Well." The salesman cocked one eyebrow in the attitude of the connoisseur or the careful shopper. "We'll do what we *can*, of course."

Rogan figured he could take out a second mortgage.

Margaret accepted the change graciously. And she was resigned to the financial reversal—after all, he still had his job. She took day work at a software store. But Rogan could not convince her that she, too, should make the change.

"Take a good look," he said. "Am I any different? Really, am I?"

"Not on the outside," she said. They had argued, she had cried; her eyes were still puffy and red.

"But it's better," Rogan said. "It really is. I don't wake up in the middle of the night thinking, Jesus, I'm not a kid anymore, what about a coronary, what about kidney disease, what about my lungs? I could smoke if I wanted to. Tobacco! I can eat anything. I could eat a goddamn chair."

"Is that so important?"

"You bet it is!"

She seemed to soften. "It's all right for you, Ben. I understand. It's how you are. But I don't want to—to change in that way. And I don't understand why you want me to."

It was a tricky question. A part of him wanted to say: because you'd feel better, you'll feel younger, and we'll be together in this thing. That would have been O.K. But another part of him wanted to say: because you've aged, because you're not young and good-looking any more and because I'm increasingly disgusted at how primitive and biological you are. He hated the idea of her blood gushing through fleshy arteries clogged with the debris of a high-cholesterol diet, of the webwork of nerve and muscle, the pulsating animal processes. He had been like that once. Now he was cleaner, sleeker—better. He had replaced almost all his internal organs. And the replacements, though regrettably hidden, carried all the best trademarks.

"Consider doing it for me," Rogan said. "You still love me, don't you?"

"Of course I do!" She had become very serious. "Ben, I loved you *before* any of this. I loved you when you were a fat middle-aged man with ordinary eyes."

It was flattering, of course, but he couldn't bring himself to believe it.

How unfair it was! He had given her, finally, something *worthy* of love. Why couldn't she hold up her end of the bargain?

"I used to put my head on your chest," she said mournfully, "when you were sleeping. I'd listen to your heart beating. It was reassuring. A good sound. Now—" She sighed. "All I hear is a sound like the wind in the trees."

His new body and his new eyes made him feel hyperconfident at work. It was as if he could see the data collisions stacking up before they happened. By the time the red light started to flash, he'd be all the way into the mainframe, ready, troubleshooting like crazy. He got a special commendation on the winter efficiency report.

Forster came in one dark afternoon shaking snow off his topcoat. "It's a bitch out there."

"I'll bet," Rogan said. But his eyes were on the screen. He was finishing off a heavy bug route. The datablocs were gliding now, slick as ice.

"Brought you coffee," Forster said. He placed the cup on Rogan's desk.

Rogan stared.

Forster's arm was sleek burnished aluminum. The fingers were slim and agile. Servomotors hummed, like the sound of distant cicadas. There was the heady aroma of warm machine oil.

"Thanks," Rogan said faintly.

"What you have in mind," the sales rep at Hills and Rutherford said, "is possible. Yes. It's even been done—to a few people, a few places. But the cost—!"

"I don't care," Rogan said.

He felt at home in the showroom now, at ease. He felt worthy of the fine things displayed around him. He felt—in an important way— part of them.

"You don't understand," the salesman said. "We're not talking about a price that's merely high. 'High' is inadequate. We're talking—" He spread his hands. "*Exalted.*"

"I realize that."

"We know a little bit about you, Mr. Rogan. We make it a policy to be informed about our customers. And your credit rating is good. But not that good. Even if you disposed of your property . . . liquidated your assets . . . even with the trade-in on what you've already purchased from us. . . ."

"There must be a way."

The salesman looked at him for a time.

Finally he said, "Perhaps."

"Good," Rogan said.

"*Perhaps.* You don't understand the strictures. It would mean leaving your job. It would mean—shall we say—a radically altered life-style. Are you prepared to deal with that?"

"Yes," Rogan said. "I don't care."

"Ah. Well, then." There was the shadow of a smile. He's working on commission, Rogan thought. "Hills and Rutherford, you see, is a wholly owned subsidiary of Loomis Technology and Resources. Our parent corporation has a model contract it offers in situations such as this. It's basically a question of reciprocity. . . ."

He did not accept at once. He felt he owed that much, at least, to Margaret.

She stared at him. He saw, involuntarily, the yellow residue that had accumulated at the inner angles of her eyes. Her skin was pale and porous; she was sweating.

"You'll hardly be human!"

He blinked. "That's a phylocentric attitude. I'll be the same old Ben."

"It's me, isn't it? It's because I've changed."

"No," he said. "This is what I want." He added, "You could have it too."

"There was a time when I was what you wanted. Me. *Just* me. I guess it was because I was young. Pretty. The best you could get. Now I'm—what? Obsolete. God, I feel so old."

She began to weep.

Rogan turned away. None of this mattered. He felt hard, cold, shiny. He knew what he wanted.

He had perhaps overlooked certain clauses and considerations in the contract. Duration, obligation, and matters of configuration. But all in all he was pleased with the results. The parts of himself he could see were sleek, efficient, and ruthlessly functional.

They shipped him to an island called Nunivak, and he descended under his own power to the Loomis T&R mines along the steep submerged slope of the Bering Sea. It was a strange, lifeless place, and the job he did was repetitive: manipulating slabs of ore-bearing rock (which reminded him of enormous chunks of incoming data) in his beryllium claws. But there were others like him there, with whom he could communicate by means of sonar signals and flashing lights, and he reminded himself that he was the newest and shiniest of them all. Some—the older ones—had tarnish crawling across their carapaces like a strange disease.

Not him. He was functional. He was clean.

The years passed, however, and Rogan was as susceptible to the vulgar work of entropy as the rest. There came a time when he was slow and barnacled and his joints were prone to seizure, when he began to doubt the wisdom of the enterprise, to think with some nostalgia of the way he had been before . . . all this.

It was a temporary malaise. It ended when the new Dredger was introduced to the mines. Her name was inscribed across her prow; Rogan's eyes, though they were failing, deciphered it through the frigid gloom. He scuttled forward, crablike, wanting to weep (although he could not), crying out her name across the sonar frequencies: "Margaret, Margaret!"

She was lovely, all gleaming silver and sealed ball joints. She was state of the art. And she was his.

Black Air

✳   ✳   ✳

Kim Stanley Robinson

This unusual and moving fantasy about a 17-year-old boy who sails with the Spanish Armada was one of Kim Stanley Robinson's first stories for F&SF. It won a World Fantasy Award in 1984. Since then, Mr. Robinson has published many more stories, won more awards and written several novels, most recently The Gold Coast.

✳   ✳   ✳

THEY sailed out of Lisbon harbor with the flags snapping and the brass culverins gleaming under a high white sun—priests proclaiming in sonorous Latin the blessing of the Pope, soldiers in armor jammed on the castles fore and aft, and sailors spider-like in the rigging, waving at the citizens of the town who had left their work to come out on the hills and watch the ships crowd out the sunbeaten roads—for this was the Armada, the Most Fortunate Invincible Armada, off to subjugate the heretic English to the will of God. There would never be another departure like it.

Unfortunately, the wind blew out of the northeast for a month after they left without shifting even a point on the compass, and at the end of that month the Armada was no closer to England than Iberia itself. Not only that, but the hard-pressed coopers of Portugal had made many of the Armada's casks of green wood, and when the ship's cooks opened them the meat was rotten and the water stank. So they trailed into the port of Corunna, where several hundred soldiers and sailors swam to the shores of Spain and were never seen again. A few hundred more had already died of disease, so from his sickbed on the flagship Don Alonso Perez de Guzman el Bueno, seventh Duke of Medina Sidonia and Admiral of the Armada, interrupted the composition of his daily complaint to Phillip II, and instructed his soldiers to go out into the countryside and collect peasants to help man the ships.

One of the squads of these soldiers stopped at a Franciscan monastery on the outskirts of Corunna, to impress all the boys who lived there and helped the monks, waiting to join the order themselves. Although they did not like it the monks could not object to the proposal, and off the boys went to join the fleet.

Among these boys, who were each taken to a different ship, was Manuel Carlos Agadir Tetuán. He was seventeen years old; he had been born in Morocco, the son of West Africans who had been captured and enslaved by Arabs. In his short life he had already lived in the Moroccan coastal town of Tetuán, in Gibraltar, the Balearics, Sicily, and Lisbon. He had worked in fields and cleaned stables, he had helped make rope and and later cloth, and he had served food in inns. After his mother died of the pox and his father drowned, he begged in the streets and alleys of Corunna, the last port his father had sailed out of, until in his fifteenth year a Franciscan had tripped over him sleeping in an alley, inquired after him, and taken him to the refuge of the monastery.

Manuel was still weeping when the soldiers took him aboard *La Lavia*, a Levantine galleon of nearly a thousand tons. The sailing master of the ship, one Laeghr, took him in charge and led him below decks. Laeghr was an Irishman, who had left his country principally to practice his trade, but also out of hatred of the English who ruled Ireland. He was a huge man with a torso like a boar's, and arms as thick as the yardarms of their ship. When he saw Manuel's distress he showed that he was not without kindness; clapping a calloused hand to the back of Manuel's neck he said, in accented but fluent Spanish, "Stop your sniveling boy, we're off to conquer the damned English, and when we do your fathers at the monastery will make you their abbot. And before that happens a dozen English girls will fall at your feet and ask for the touch of those black hands, no doubt. Come on, stop it. I'll show you your berth first, and wait till we're at sea to show you your station. I'm going to put you in the maintop; all our blacks are good topmen."

Laeghr slipped through a door half his height with the ease of a weasel ducking into one of its tiny holes in the earth. A hand half as wide as the doorway re-emerged and pulled Manuel into the gloom. The terrified boy nearly fell down a broad-stepped ladder, but caught himself before falling onto Laeghr. Far below several soldiers laughed at him. Manuel had never been on anything larger than a Sicilian pataches, and most of his fairly extensive seagoing experience was of coastal carracks; so the broad deck under him, cut by bands of yellow sunlight that flowed in at open ports big as church windows, crowded with barrels and bales of hay and tubs of rope, and a hundred busy men, was a marvel. "Saint Anna, save me," he said, scarcely able to believe he was on a ship. Why, the monastery itself had no room as large as the one he descended into now. "Get down here," Laeghr said in an encouraging way.

Once on the deck of that giant room they descended again, to a stuffy chamber a quarter the size, illuminated by narrow fans of sunlight that were let in by ports that were mere slits in the hull. "Here's where you sleep," Laeghr said, pointing at a dark corner of the deck, against one massive oak wall of the ship. Forms there shifted; eyes appeared as lids lifted; a dull voice said; "Another one you'll never find again in this dark, eh, master?"

"Shut up, Juan. See boy, there are beams dividing your berth from the rest, that will keep you from rolling around when we get to sea."

"Just like a coffin, with the lid up there."

"Shut up, Juan."

After the sailing master had made clear which slot in particular was Manuel's, Manuel collapsed in it and began to cry again. The slot was shorter than he was, and the dividing boards set in the deck were cracked and splintered. The men around him slept, or talked among themselves, ignoring Manuel's presence. His medallion chord choked him, and he shifted it on his neck and remembered to pray.

His guardian saint, the monks had decided, was Anne, mother of the Virgin Mary and grandmother of Jesus. Manuel owned a small wooden medallion with her face painted on it, which Abbot Alonso had given him. Now he took the medallion between his fingers, and looked in the tiny brown dots that were the face's eyes. "Please, Mother Anna," he prayed silently, "take me from this ship to my home. Take me home." He clenched the tag in his fist so tightly that the back of it, carved so that a cross of wood stood out from its surface, left an imprinted red cross in his palm. Many hours passed before he fell asleep.

Two days later the Most Fortunate Invincible Armada left Corunna, this time without the flags, or the crowds of spectators, or the clouds of priestly incense trailing downwind. This time God favored them with a westerly wind, and they sailed north at good speed. The ships were arranged in a formation devised by the soldiers, orderly phalanxes rising and falling on the swells: the galleasses in front, the supply hulks in the center, and the big galleons on either flank. The thousands of sails stacked on hundreds of masts made a grand and startling sight, like a copse of white trees on a broad blue plain.

Manuel was as impressed by the sight as the rest of the men. There were four hundred men on *La Lavia*, and only thirty were needed at any one time to sail the ship, so all of the three hundred soldiers stood on the sterncastle observing the fleet, and the sailors who were not on duty or sleeping did the same on the slightly lower forecastle.

Manuel's duties as a sailor were simple. He was stationed at the port midships taffrail, to which were tied the sheets for the port side of the mainmast's sails, and the sheets for the big lateen-rigged sail of the foremast. Manuel helped five other men pull these ropes in or let them out, following Laeghr's instructions; the other men took care of the belaying knots, so Manuel's job came down to pulling a rope when told to. It could have been more difficult, but Laeghr's plan to make him a topman like the other Africans aboard had come to grief. Not that Laeghr hadn't tried. "God made you Africans with a better head for heights, so you can climb trees to keep from being eaten by lions, isn't that right?" But when Manuel had followed a Moroccan named Habedeen up the halyard ladder to the maintop, he found himself plunging about space, nearly scraping low foggy clouds, and the sea, embroidered with the wakes of the ship ahead, was more often than not *directly below him*. He had clamped arms and legs around a stanchion of the maintop, and it had taken five men, laughing and cursing, to pry him loose and pull him down.

With rich disgust, but no real physical force, Laeghr had pounded him with his cane and shoved him to the port taffrail. "You must be a Sicilian with a sunburn." And so Manuel had been assigned his station.

Despite this incident he got on well with the rest of the crew. Not with the soldiers; they were rude and arrogant to the sailors, who stayed out of their way to avoid a curse or a blow. So three-quarters of the men aboard were of a different class, and remained strangers. The sailors therefore hung together. They were a mongrel lot, drawn from all over the Mediterranean, and Manuel was not unusual because of his recent arrival. They were united only in their dislike and resentment of the soldiers. "Those heroes wouldn't be able to conquer the Isle of Wight if we didn't sail them there," Juan said.

Manuel became acquainted first with the men at his post, and then with the men in his berth. As he spoke Spanish and Portuguese, and fair amounts of Arabic, Sicilian, Latin, and a Moroccan dialect, he could converse with everyone in his corner of the lower foredeck. Occasionally he was asked to translate for the Moroccans; more than once this meant he was the arbiter of a dispute, and he thought fast and mistranslated when it would help make peace.

Juan, the one who made the bitter comments to Laeghr on Manuel's arrival, was the only pure Spaniard in the berth. He loved to talk, and complained to Manuel and the others continuously. "I've fought El Draco before, in the Indies," he boasted. "We'll be lucky to get past that devil. You mark my words, we'll never do it."

Manuel's mates at the main taffrail were more cheerful, and he enjoyed his watches with them and the drills under Laeghr's demanding instruction. These men called him Topman or Climber, and made jokes about his knots around the belaying pins, which defied quick untying. This inability earned Manuel quite a few swats from Laeghr's cane, but there were worse sailors aboard, and the sailing master seemed to bear him no ill will.

A life of perpetual change had made Manuel adaptable, and shipboard routine became for him the natural course of existence. Laeghr or Pietro, the leader at Manuel's station, would wake him with a shout. Up to the gun deck, which was the domain of the soldiers, and from there up the big ladder that led to fresh air. Only then could Manuel be sure of the time of day. For the first few weeks it was an inexpressible delight to get out of the gloom of the lower decks and under the sky, in the wind and clean salt air; but as they proceeded north, it began to get too cold for comfort.

After their watches were over, Manuel and his mates would retire to the galley and be given their biscuits, water, and wine. Sometimes the cooks would have killed some of the goats and chickens and made soup. Usually, though, it was just biscuits, biscuits that had not yet hardened in their barrels. The men complained grievously about this.

"The biscuits are best when they're hard as wood, and bored through by worms," Habedeen told Manuel.

"How do you eat it, then?" Manuel asked.

"You bang pieces of biscuit against the table until the worms fall out. You can eat the worms if you want." The men laughed, and Manuel assumed Habedeen was joking, but he wasn't certain.

"I despise this doughy shit," Pietro said in Portuguese. Manuel translated into Moroccan Arabic for the two silent Africans, and agreed in Spanish that it was hard to stomach. "The worst part," he offered, "is that some parts are stale while others are still fresh."

"The fresh part was never cooked."

"No, that's the worms."

As the voyage progressed, Manuel's berthmates became more intimate. Farther north the Moroccans suffered terribly from the cold. They came belowdecks after a watch with their dark skins completely goose-pimpled, like little fields of stubble after a harvest. Their lips and fingernails were blue, and they shivered an hour before falling asleep, teeth chattering like the castanets in a fiesta band. Not only that, but the swells of the Atlantic were getting bigger, and the men, since they were forced to wear every scrap of clothing they owned, rolled in their wooden berths unpadded and unprotected.

So the Moroccans, and then everyone in the lower foredeck, slept three to a berth, taking turns in the middle, huddling together like spoons. Crowded together like that the pitching of the ship could press them against the beams, but it couldn't roll them around. Manuel's willingness to join these bundlings, and to lie against the beams, made him well-liked. Everyone agreed he made a good cushion.

Perhaps it was because of his hands that he fell ill. Though his spirit had been reconciled to the crusade north, his flesh was slower. Hauling on the coarse hemp ropes every day had ripped the skin from his palms, and salt, splinters, belaying pins, and the odd boot had all left their marks as well, so that after the first week he had wrapped his hands in strips of cloth torn from the bottom of his shirt. When he became feverish, his hands pulsed painfully at every nudge from his heart, and he assumed that the fever had entered him through the wounds in his palms.

Then his stomach rebelled, and he could keep nothing down. The sight of biscuits or soup revolted him; his fever worsened, and he became parched and weak; he spent a lot of time in the head, racked by dysentery.

"You've been poisoned by the biscuits," Juan told him. "Just like I was in the Indies. That's what comes of boxing fresh biscuits. They might as well have put fresh dough in those barrels."

Manuel's berthmates told Laeghr of his condition, and Laeghr had him moved to the hospital, which was at the stern of the ship on a lower deck, in a wide room that the sick shared with the rudder post, a large smoothed tree trunk thrusting through floor and ceiling. All of the other men were gravely ill. Manuel was miserable as they laid him down on his pallet, wretched with nausea and in great fear of the hospital, which smelled of putrefaction. The man on the pallet next to his was insensible, and rolled with the sway of the ship. Three candle-lanterns lit the low chamber and filled it with shadows.

One of the Dominican friars, a Friar Lucien, gave him hot water and wiped his face. They talked for a while, and the friar heard Manuel's confession, which only a proper priest should have done. Neither of them cared. The priests on board avoided the hospital, and tended to serve only the officers and the soldiers. Friar Lucien was known to be willing to minister to the sailors, and he was popular among them.

Manuel's fever got worse, and he could not eat. Days passed, and when he woke up the men around him were not the same men who had been there when he fell asleep. He became convinced he was going to die, and once again he felt despair that he had been made a member of the Most Fortunate Invincible Armada.

"Why are we here?" he demanded of the friar in a cracked voice. "Why shouldn't we let the English go to hell if they please?"

"The purpose of the Armada is not only to smite the heretic English," said Lucien. He held a candle closer to his book, which was not the Bible, but a slender little thing which he kept hidden in his robes. Shadows leaped on the blackened beams and planks over them, and the rudder post squeaked as it turned against the leather collar in the floor. "God also sent us as a test. Listen:

I assume the appearance of a refiner's fire, purging the dross of forms outworn. This is mine aspect of severity; I am as one who testeth gold in a furnace. Yet when thou hast been tried as by fire, the gold of thy soul shall be cleansed, and visible as fire: then the vision of the Lord shall be granted unto thee, and seeing Him shall thou behold the shining one, who is thine own true self.

"Remember that, and be strong. Drink this water here—come on, do you want to fail your God? This is part of the test."

Manuel drank, threw up. His body was no more than a tongue of flame contained by his skin, except where it burst out of his palms. He lost track of the days, and forgot the existence of anyone beyond himself and Friar Lucien. "I never wanted to leave the monastery," he told the friar, "yet I never thought I would stay there long. I've never stayed long anyplace yet. It was my home but I knew it wasn't. I haven't found my home yet. They say there is ice in England—I saw the snow in the Catalonian mountains once. Father, will we go home? I only want to return to the monastery and be a father like you."

"We will go home. What you will become, only God knows. He has a place for you. Sleep now. Sleep now."

By the time his fever broke his ribs stood out from his chest as clearly as the fingers of a fist. He could barely walk. Lucien's narrow face appeared out of the gloom clear as a memory.

"Try this soup. Apparently God has seen fit to keep you here."

"Thank you, Saint Anne, for your intercession," Manuel croaked. He drank the soup eagerly. "I want to return to my berth."

"Soon."

They took him up to the deck. Walking was like floating, as long as he held on to railings and stanchions. Laeghr greeted him with pleasure, as did his station mates. The world was a riot of blues; waves hissed past, low clouds jostled together in their rush east, tumbling between them shafts of sunlight that spilled onto the water. He was excused from active duty, but he spent as many hours as he could at his station. He found it hard to believe that he had survived his illness.

Of course, he was not entirely recovered; he could not yet eat any solids, particularly biscuit, so that his diet consisted of soup and wine. He felt weak, and perpetually light-headed. But when he was on deck in the wind he was sure that he was getting better, so he stayed there as much as possible. He was on deck, in fact, when they first caught sight of England. The soldiers pointed and shouted in great excitement, as the point Laeghr called the Lizard bounced over the horizon. Manuel had grown so used to the sea that the low headland rising off their port bow seemed unnatural, an intrusion into a marine world, as if the deluge were just now receding and these drowned hillsides were just now shouldering up out of the waves, soaking wet and covered by green seaweed that had not yet died. And that was England.

A few days after that they met the first English ships—faster than the Spanish galleons, but much smaller. They could no more impede the progress of the Armada than flies could slow a herd of cows. The swells became steeper and followed each other more closely, and the changed pitching of La Lavia made it difficult for Manuel to stand. He banged his head once, and another time ripped away a palmful of scabs, trying to keep his balance in the violent yawing caused by the chop. Unable to stand one morning, he lay in the dark of his berth, and his mates brought him cups of soup. That went on for a long time. Again he worried that he was going to die. Finally Laeghr and Lucien came below together.

"You must get up now," Laeghr declared. "We fight within the hour, and you're needed. We've arranged easy work for you."

"You have only to provide the gunners with slow match," said Friar Lucien as he helped Manuel to his feet. "God will help you."

"God will have to help me," Manuel said. He could see the two men's souls flickering above their heads: little triple knots of transparent flame, that flew up out of their hair and lit the features of their faces. "The gold of thy soul shall be cleansed, and visible as fire," Manuel recalled.

"Hush," said Lucien with a frown, and Manuel realized that what Lucien had read to him was a secret.

Amidships, Manuel noticed that now he was also able to see the air, which was tinged red. They were on the bottom of an ocean of red air, just as they were on top of an ocean of blue water. When they breathed they turned the air a darker red; men expelled plumes of air like horses breathing out clouds of steam on a frosty morning, only the steam was red. Manuel stared and stared, marveling at the new abilities God had given his sight.

"Here," Laeghr said, roughly directing him across the deck. "This tub of punk is yours. This is slow match, understand?" Against the bulkhead was a tub full of coils of closely braided cord. One end of the cord was hanging over the edge of the tub burning, fizzing the air around it to deep crimson.

Manuel nodded: "Slow match."

"Here's your knife. Cut sections about this long, and light them with a piece of it that you keep beside you. Then give sections of it to the gunners who come by, or take it to them if they call for it. But don't give away all your lit pieces. Understand?"

Manuel nodded that he understood and sat down dizzily beside the tub. One of the largest cannons poked through a port in the bulwarks just a few feet from him. Its crew greeted him. Across the deck his stationmates stood at their taffrail. The soldiers were ranked on the fore- and stern-castles, shouting with excitement, gleaming like shellfish in the sun. Through the port Manuel could see some of the English coast.

Laeghr came over to see how he was doing. "Hey, don't you lop your fingers off there, boy. See out there? That's the Isle of Wight. We're going to circle and conquer it, I've no doubt, and use it as our base for our attack on the mainland. With these soldiers and ships they'll *never* get us off that island. It's a good plan."

But things did not progress according to Laeghr's plan. The Armada swung around the east shore of the Isle of Wight, in a large crescent made of five distinct phalanxes of ships. Rounding the island, however, the forward galleasses encountered the stiffest English resistance they had met so far. White puffs of smoke appeared out of the ships and were quickly stained red, and the noise was tremendous.

Then the ships of El Draco swept around the southern point of the island onto their flank, and suddenly *La Lavia* was in the action. The soldiers roared and shot off their arquebuses, and the big cannon beside Manuel leaped back in its truck with a bang that knocked him into the bulkhead. After that he could barely hear. His slow match was suddenly in demand; he cut the cord and held the lit tip to unlit tips, igniting them with his red breath. Cannonballs passing overhead left rippling wakes in the blood air. Grimy men snatched the slow match and dashed to their guns, dodging tackle blocks that thumped to the deck. Manuel could see the cannonballs, big as grapefruit, flying at them from the English ships and passing with a whistle. And he could see the transparent knots of flame, swirling higher than ever about men's heads.

Then a cannonball burst through the porthole and knocked the cannon off its truck, the men to the deck. Manuel rose to his feet and noticed with horror that the knots of flame on the scattered gunners were gone; he could see their heads clearly now, and they were just men, just broken flesh draped over the plowed surface of the deck. He tried, sobbing, to lift a gunner who was bleeding only from the ears. Laeghr's cane lashed across his shoulders: "Keep cutting match! There's others to tend to these men!" So Manuel cut lengths of cord and lit them with desperate puffs and shaking hands, while the guns roared, and the exposed soldiers on the castles shrieked under a hail of iron, and the red air was ripped by passing shot.

The next few days saw several battles like that, as the Armada was forced past the Isle of Wight and up the Channel. His fever kept him from sleeping, and at night, Manuel helped the wounded on his deck, holding them down and wiping sweat from their faces, nearly as delirious as they were. At dawn he ate biscuits and drank from his cup of wine, and went to his tub of slow match to await the next engagement. *La Lavia*, being the largest ship on the left flank, always took the brunt of the English attack.

It was on the third day that *La Lavia*'s mainmast topgallant yard fell on his old taffrail crew, crushing Hanan and Pietro. Manuel rushed across the deck to help them, shouting his anguish. He got a dazed Juan down to their berth and returned amidships. Around him men were being dashed to the decks but he didn't care. He hopped through red mist that nearly obscured his sight, carrying lengths of match to the gun crews, who were now so depleted that they couldn't afford to send men to him. He helped the wounded below to the hospital, which had truly become an antechamber of hell; he helped toss the dead over the side, croaking a short prayer in every case; he ministered to the soldiers hiding behind the bulwarks, waiting vainly for the English to get within range of their arquebuses.

Now the cry amidships was "Manuel, match here! Manuel, some water! Help, Manuel!" In a dry fever of energy Manuel hurried to their aid.

He was in such perpetual haste that in the middle of a furious engagement he nearly ran into his patroness, Saint Anne, who was suddenly standing there in the corner by his tub. He was startled to see her.

"Grandmother!" he cried. "You shouldn't be here, it's dangerous."

"As you have helped others, I am here to help you," she replied. She pointed across the purplish chop to one of the English ships. Manuel saw a puff of smoke appear from its side, and out of the puff came a cannonball, floating in an arc over the water. He could see it as clearly as he could have seen an olive tossed at him from across a room: a round black ball, spinning lazily, growing bigger as it got closer. Now Manuel could tell that it was coming at him, *directly* at him, so that its trajectory would intersect his heart. "Um, blessed Anna," he said, hoping to bring this to his saint's attention. But she had already seen it, and with a brief touch to his forehead she floated up into the maintop, among the unseeing soldiers. Manuel watched her, eyeing the approaching cannonball's flight, knocking the ball downward into the hull where it stuck, half-embedded in the thick wood. Manuel stared at the black half-sphere, mouth open. He waved up at Saint Anna, who waved back and flew up into the red clouds towards heaven. Manuel kneeled and said a prayer of thanks to her, and to Jesus for sending her, and went back to cutting match.

A night or two later—Manuel himself was not sure, as the passage of time had become for him something pliable and elusive and, more than anything else, meaningless—the Armada anchored at Calais Roads, just off the Flemish coast. For the first time since they had left Corunna, *La Lavia* lay still, and listening at night Manuel realized how much the constant chorus of wooden squeaks and groans was the voice of the crew, and not the ship. He drank his ration of wine and water quickly, and walked the length of the lower deck, talking with the wounded and helping when he could to remove splinters. Many of the men wanted him to touch them, for his safe passage through some of the worst scenes of carnage had not gone unnoticed. He touched them and, when they wanted, said a prayer.

Afterwards he went up on deck. There was a fair breeze from the southwest, and the ship rocked ever so gently on the tide. For the first time in a week the air was not suffused red: Manuel could see stars, and distant bonfires on the Flemish shore, like stars that had fallen and now burnt out their life on the land.

Laeghr was limping up and down amidship, detouring from his usual path to avoid a bit of shattered decking.

"Are you hurt, Laeghr?" Manuel inquired.

For answer Laeghr growled. Manuel walked beside him. After a bit Laeghr stopped and said, "They're saying you're a holy man now because you were running all over the deck these last few days, acting like the shot we were taking was hail and never getting hit for it. But I say you're just too foolish to know any better. Fools dance where angels would hide. It's part of the curse laid on us. Those who learn the rules and play things right end up getting hurt—sometimes from doing just the things that will protect them the most. While the blind fools who wander right into the thick of things are never touched."

Manuel watched Laeghr's stride. "Your foot?"

Laeghr shrugged. "I don't know what will happen to it."

Under a lantern Manuel stopped and looked Laeghr in the eye. "Saint Anna appeared and plucked a cannonball that was heading for me right out of the sky. She saved my life for a purpose."

"No." Laeghr thumped his cane on the deck. "Your fever has made you mad, boy."

"I can show you the shot!" Manuel said. "It stuck in the hull!" Laeghr stumped away.

Manuel looked across the water at Flanders, distressed by Laeghr's words, and by his hobbled walk. He saw something he didn't comprehend.

"Laeghr?"

"What?" came Laeghr's voice from across midships.

"Something bright . . . the souls of all the English at once, maybe. . . ." his voice shook.

"*What?*"

"Something coming at us. Come here, master."

Thump, thump, thump. Manuel heard the hiss of Laeghr's indrawn breath, the muttered curse.

"*Fireships*," Laeghr bellowed at the top of his lungs. "Fireships! Awake!"

In a minute the ship was bedlam, soldiers running everywhere. "Come with me," Laeghr told Manuel, who followed the sailing master to the forecastle, where the anchor hawser descended into the water. Somewhere along the way Laeghr had gotten a halberd, and he gave it to Manuel. "Cut the line."

"But master, we'll lose the anchor."

"Those fireships are too big to stop, and if they're hellburners they explode and kill us all. Cut it."

Manuel began chopping at the thick hawser, which was very like the trunk of a small tree. He chopped and chopped, but only one strand of the huge rope was cut when Laeghr seized the halberd and began chopping himself, awkwardly to avoid putting his weight on his bad foot. They heard the voice of the ship's captain—"Cut the anchor cable!"—and Laeghr laughed.

The rope snapped, and they were floating free. But the fireships were right behind them. In the hellish light Manuel could see English sailors walking on their burning decks, passing through the flames like salamanders or demons. No doubt they were devils. The fires towering above the eight fireships shared the demonic life of the English; each tongue of yellow flame contained an English demon eye looking for the Armada, and some of these leaped free of the blaze that twisted above the fireships, in vain attempts to float onto *La Lavia* and incinerate it.

Manuel held off these embers with his wooden medallion, and the gesture that in his boyhood in Sicily had warded off the evil eye. Meanwhile the ships of the fleet were cut loose and drifting on the tide, colliding in the rush to avoid the fireships. Captains and officers screamed furiously at their colleagues on other ships, but to no avail. In the dark and without anchors, the ships could not be regathered, and as the night progressed most were blown out into the North Sea. For the first time the neat phalanxes of the Armada were broken, and they were never to be reformed again.

* * *

When it was all over *La Lavia* held its position in the North Sea by sail, while the officers attempted to identify the ships around them, and to find out what Medina Sidonia's orders were. Manuel and Juan stood amidships with the rest of their berthmates. Juan shook his head. "I used to make corks in Portugal. We were like a cork back there in the Channel, being pushed into the neck of a bottle. As long as we were stuck in the neck we were all right—the neck got narrower and narrower, and they might never have gotten us out. Now the English have pushed us right down into the bottle itself. We're floating about in our own dregs. And we'll never get out of the bottle again."

"Not through the neck, anyway," one of the others agreed.

"Not any way."

"God will see us home," Manuel said.

Juan shook his head.

Rather than try to force the Channel, Admiral Medina Sidonia decided that the Armada should sail around Scotland, and then home. Laeghr was taken to the flagship for a day to help chart a course, for he was familiar with the north as none of the Spanish pilots were.

The battered fleet headed away from the sun, ever higher into the cold North Sea. After the night of the fireships Medina Sidonia had restored discipline with a vengeance. One day the survivors of the many Channel battles were witness to the hanging from the yardarm of a captain who let his ship get ahead of the admiral's flagship, a position which was now forbidden. A carrack sailed through the fleet again and again so every crew could see the corpse of the disobedient captain, swinging freely from its spar.

Manuel observed the sight with distaste. Once dead, a man was only a bag of bones; nowhere in the clouds overhead could he spot the captain's soul. Perhaps it had plummeted into the sea, on its way to hell. It was an odd transition, death. Curious that God did not make more explicit the aftermath.

So *La Lavia* faithfully trailed the admiral's flagship, as did the rest of the fleet. They were led farther and farther north, into the domain of cold. Some mornings when they came on deck in the raw yellow of dawn the riggings would be rimed with icicles, so that they seemed strings of diamonds. Some days it seemed they sailed across a sea of milk, under a silver sky. Other days the ocean was the color of a bruise, and the sky a fresh pale blue so clear that Manuel gasped with the desire to survive this voyage and live. Yet he was as cold as death. He remembered the burning nights of his fever as fondly as if he were remembering his first home on the coast of North Africa.

All the men were suffering from the cold. The livestock was dead, so the galley closed down: no hot soup. The admiral imposed rationing on everyone, including himself; the deprivation kept him in his bed for the rest of the voyage. For the sailors, who had to haul wet or frozen rope, it was worse. Manuel watched the grim faces, in line for their two biscuits and one large cup of wine and water—their daily ration —and concluded that they would continue sailing north until the sun was under the horizon and they were in the icy realm of death, the north pole where God's dominion was weak, and there they would give up and die all at once. Indeed, the winds drove them nearly to Norway, and it was with great difficulty that they brought the shot-peppered hulks around to a westerly heading.

When they did, they discovered a score of new leaks in La Lavia's hull, and the men, already exhausted by the effort of bringing the ship about, were forced to man the pumps around the clock. A pint of wine and a pint of water a day were not enough. Men died. Dysentery, colds, the slightest injury: all were quickly fatal.

Once again Manuel could see the air. Now it was a thick blue, distinctly darker where men breathed it out, so that they all were shrouded in dark blue air that obscured the burning crowns of their souls. All of the wounded men in the hospital had died. Many of them had called for Manuel in their last moments; he held their hands or touched their heads, and as their souls had flickered away from their heads like the last pops of flame out of coals of a dying fire, he had prayed for them. Now other men too weak to leave their berths called for him, and he went and stood by them in their distress. Two of these men recovered from dysentery, so his presence was requested even more frequently. The captain himself asked for Manuel's touch when he fell sick; but he died anyway, like most of the rest.

One morning Manuel was standing with Laeghr at the midships bulkhead. It was chill and cloudy, the sea the color of flint. The soldiers were bringing their horses up and forcing them over the side, to save water.

"That should have been done as soon as we were forced out of the Sleeve," Laeghr said. "Waste of water."

"I didn't even know we had horses aboard," Manuel said.

Laeghr laughed briefly. "Boy, you are a prize of a fool. One surprise after another."

They watched the horses' awkward falls, their rolling eyes, their flared nostrils expelling clouds of blue air. Their brief attempts to swim.

"On the other hand, we should probably be eating some of those," Laeghr said.

"Horsemeat?"

"It can't be that bad."

The horses all disappeared, exchanging blue air for flint water. "It's cruel," Manuel said.

"In the horse latitudes they swim for an hour," Laeghr said. "This is better." He pointed to the west. "See those tall clouds?"

"Yes."

"They stand over the Orkneys. The Orkneys or the Shetlands, I can't be sure any more. It will be interesting to see if these fools can get this wreck through the islands safely." Looking around, Manuel could spot only a dozen or so ships; presumably, the rest of the Armada lay over the horizon ahead of them. He stopped to wonder about what Laeghr had just said, for it would naturally be Laeghr's task to navigate them through the northernmost of the British Isles; at that very moment Laeghr's eyes rolled like the horses' had, and he collapsed on the deck. Manuel and some other sailors carried him down to the hospital.

"It's his foot," said Friar Lucien. "His foot is crushed and his leg has putrefied. He should have let me amputate."

Around noon Laeghr regained consciousness. Manuel, who had not left his side, held his hand, but Laeghr frowned and pulled it away.

"Listen," Laeghr said with difficulty. His soul was no more than a blue cap covering his tangled salt-and-pepper hair. "I'm going to teach you some words that may be useful to you later." Slowly he said, *"Tor conaloc an dhia,"* and Manuel repeated it. "Say it again." Manuel repeated the syllables over and over, like a Latin prayer. Laeghr nodded. *"Tor conaloc an naom dhia.* Good. Remember the words always." After that he stared at the deckbeams above, and would answer none of

Manuel's questions. Emotions played over his face like shadows, one after another. Finally he took his gaze from the infinite and looked at Manuel. "Touch me, boy."

Manuel touched his forehead, and with a sardonic smile Laeghr closed his eyes: his blue crown of flames flickered up through the deck above and disappeared.

They buried him that evening, in a smoky, hellish brown sunset. Friar Lucien said the shortened Mass, mumbling in a voice that no one could hear, and Manuel pressed the back of his medallion against the cold flesh of Laeghr's arm, until the impression of the cross remained. Then they tossed him overboard. Manuel watched with a serenity that surprised him. Just weeks ago he had shouted with rage and pain as his companions had been torn apart; now he watched with a peace he did not understand as the man who had taught him and protected him sank into the iron water and disappeared.

A couple of nights after that Manuel sat apart from his remaining berthmates, who slept in one pile like a litter of kittens. He watched the blue flames wandering over the exhausted flesh, watched without reason or feeling. He was tired.

Friar Lucien looked in the narrow doorway and hissed. "Manuel! Are you there?"

"I'm here."

"Come with me."

Manuel got up and followed him. "Where are we going?"

Friar Lucien shook his head. "It's time." Everything else he said was in Greek. He had a little candle lantern with three sides shuttered, and by its illumination they made their way to the hatch that led to the lower decks.

Manuel's berth, though it was below the gun deck, was not on the lowest deck of the ship. La Lavia was very much bigger than that. Below the berth deck were three more decks that had no ports, as they were beneath the waterline. Here in perpetual gloom were stored the barrels of water and biscuit, the cannonballs and rope and other supplies. They passed by the powder room, where the armorer wore felt slippers so that a spark from his boots might not blow up the ship. They found a hatchway that held a ladder leading to an even lower deck. At each level the passages became narrower, and they were forced to stoop.

Manuel was astounded when they descended yet again, for he would have imagined them already on the keel, or in some strange chamber suspended beneath it; but Lucien knew better. Down they went, through a labyrinth of dank black wooden passageways. Manuel was long lost, and held Lucien's arm for fear of being separated from him, and becoming hopelessly trapped in the bowels of the ship. Finally they came to a door that made their narrow hallway a dead end. Lucien rapped on the door and hissed something, and the door opened, letting out enough light to dazzle Manuel.

After the passageways, the chamber they entered seemed very large. It was the cable tier, located in the bow of the ship just over the keel. Since the encounter with the fireships, La Lavia had little cable, and what was left lay in the corners of the room. Now it was lit by candles, set in small iron candelabra that had been nailed to the side beams. The floor was covered by an inch of water, which reflected each of the candle flames as a small spot of white light. The curving walls dripped and gleamed. In the center of the room a box had been set on end, and covered with a bit of cloth. Around the box stood several men: a soldier, one of the petty officers, and some sailors Manuel knew only by sight. The transparent knots of cobalt flame on their heads added a bluish cast to the light in the room.

"We're ready, Father," one of the men said to Lucien. The friar led Manuel to a spot near the upturned box, and the others arranged themselves in a circle around him. Against the aft wall, near gaps where floor met wall imperfectly, Manuel spotted two big rats with shiny brown fur, all ablink and twitch-whiskered at the unusual activity. Manuel frowned and one of the rats plopped into the water covering the floor and swam under the wall, its tail swishing back and forth like a small snake, revealing to Manuel its true nature. The other rat stood its ground and blinked its bright little round eyes as it brazenly returned Manuel's unwelcoming gaze.

From behind the box Lucien looked at each man in turn, and read in Latin. Manuel understood the first part: "I believe in God the Father Almighty, maker of heaven and earth, and of all things visible and invisible. . . ." From there Lucien read on, in a voice powerful yet soothing, entreatful yet proud. After finishing the creed he took up another book, the little one he always carried with him, and read in Spanish:

Know ye, O Ísrael, that what men call life and death are as
beads of white and black strung upon a thread; and this thread
of perpetual change is mine own changeless life, which bindeth
together the unending string of little lives and little deaths.

The wind turns a ship from its course upon the deep: the
wandering winds of the senses cast man's mind adrift on the
deep.

But lo! That day shall come when the light that *is* shall still
all winds, and bind every hideous liquid darkness; and all thy
habitations shall be blest by the white brilliance which
descendeth from the crown.

While Lucien read this, the soldier moved slowly about the chamber. First he set on the top of the box a plate of sliced biscuit; the bread
was hard, as it became after months at sea, and someone had taken the
trouble to cut slices, and then polish them into wafers so thin that they
were translucent, and the color of honey. Occasional wormholes gave
them the look of old coins that had been beaten flat and holed for use
as jewelry.

Next the soldier brought forth from behind the box an empty glass
bottle, with its top cut off so that it was a sort of bowl. Taking the flask
in his other hand, he filled the bowl to the midway point with *La
Lavia*'s awful wine. Putting the flask down, he circled the group while
the friar finished reading. Every man there had cuts on his hands that
more or less continuously leaked blood, and each man pulled a cut
open over the bottle held to him, allowing a drop to splash in, until
the wine was so dark that to Manuel, aware of the blue light, it was a
deep violet.

The soldier replaced the bottle beside the plate of wafers on the
box. Friar Lucien finished his reading, looked at the box, and recited
one final sentence: "O, lamps of fire! make bright the deep caverns of
sense; with strange brightness give heat and light together to your beloved, that we may be one with you." Taking the plate in hand, he
circled the chamber, putting a wafer in the mouths of the men. "The
body of Christ, given for you. The body of Christ, given for you."

Manuel snapped the wafer of biscuit between his teeth and chewed
it. At last he understood what they were doing. This was a communion
for the dead: a service for Laeghr, a service for all of them, for they

were all doomed. Beyond the damp curved wall of their chamber was the deep sea, pressing against the timbers, pressing in on them. Eventually they would all be swallowed, and would sink down to become food for the fishes, after which their bones would decorate the floor of the ocean, where God seldom visited. Manuel could scarcely get the chewed biscuit past the lump in his throat. When Friar Lucien lifted the half-bottle and put it to his lips, saying first, "The blood of Christ, shed for you," Manuel stopped him. He took the friar's hand. The soldier stepped forward, but Lucien waved him away. The friar kneeled before Manuel and crossed himself, but backwards as Greeks did, left to right rather than the proper way.

Manuel said, "You are the blood of Christ," and held the half-bottle to Lucien's lips, tilting it so he could drink.

He did the same for each of the men, the soldier included. "You are the Christ." This was the first time any of them had partaken of this part of the communion, and some of them could barely swallow. When they had all drunk, Manuel put the bottle to his lips and drained it to the dregs. "Friar Lucien's book says, all thy habitations shall be blest by the white brilliance that is the crown of fire, and we shall all be made the Christ. And so it is. We drank, and now we are the Christ. See"—he pointed at the remaining rat, which was now on its hind legs, washing its forepaws so that it appeared to pray, its bright round eyes fixed on Manuel—"even the beasts know it." He broke off a piece of biscuit wafer, and leaned down to offer it to the rat. The rat accepted the fragment in its paws, and ate it. It submitted to Manuel's touch.

Standing back up, Manuel felt the blood rush to his head. The crowns of fire blazed on every head, reaching far above them to lick the beams of the ceiling, filling the room with light—"He is here!" Manuel cried, "He has touched us with light, see it!" He touched each of their foreheads in turn, and saw their eyes widen as they perceived the others' burning souls in wonder, pointing at each other's heads; then they were all embracing in the clear white light, hugging one another with the tears running down their cheeks and giant grins splitting their beards. Reflected candlelight danced in a thousand parts on the watery floor. The rat, startled, splashed under the gap in the wall, and they laughed and laughed and laughed.

Manuel put his arm around the friar, whose eyes shone with joy.

"It is good," Manuel said when they were all quiet again. "God will see us home."

They made their way back to the upper decks like boys playing in a cave they know very well.

The Armada made it through the Orkneys without Laeghr, though it was a close thing for some ships. Then they were out in the North Atlantic, where the swells were broader, their troughs deeper, and their tops as high as the castles of *La Lavia*, and then higher than that.

Winds came out of the southwest, bitter gales that never ceased, and three weeks later they were no closer to Spain than they had been when they slipped through the Orkneys. The situation on *La Lavia* was desperate, as it was all through the fleet. Men on *La Lavia* died every day, and were thrown overboard with no ceremony except the impression of Manuel's medallion into their arms. The deaths made the food and water shortage less acute, but it was still serious. *La Lavia* was now manned by a ghost crew, composed mostly of soldiers. There weren't enough of them to properly man the pumps, and the Atlantic was springing new leaks every day in the already broken hull. The ship began taking on water in such quantities that the acting captain of the ship—who had started the voyage as third mate—decided that they must make straight for Spain, making no spare leeway for the imperfectly known west coast of Ireland.

This decision was shared by the captains of several other damaged ships, and they conveyed their decision to the main body of the fleet, which was reaching farther west before turning south to Spain. From his sickbed Medina Sidonia gave his consent, and *La Lavia* sailed due south.

Unfortunately, a storm struck from just north of west soon after they had turned homeward. They were helpless before it. *La Lavia* wallowed in the troughs and was slammed by crest after crest, until the poor hulk lay just off the lee shore, Ireland.

It was the end, and everyone knew it. Manuel knew it because the air had turned black. The clouds were like thousands of black English cannonballs, rolling ten deep over a clear floor set just above the masts, and spitting lightning into the sea whenever two of them banged together hard enough. The air beneath them was black as well, just less thick: the wind as tangible as the waves, and swirling around the masts with smoky fury. Other men caught glimpses of the lee shore, but Manuel couldn't see it for the blackness. These men called out in fear; apparently the western coast of Ireland was sheer cliff. It was the end.

Manuel had nothing but admiration for the third-mate-now-captain, who took the helm and shouted to the lookout in the top to find a bay in the cliffs they were drifting towards. But Manuel, like many of the men, ignored the mate's commands to stay at post, as they were clearly pointless. Men embraced each other on the castles, saying their farewells; others cowered in fear against the bulkheads. Many of them approached Manuel and asked for a touch, and Manuel brushed their foreheads as he angrily marched about the forecastle. As soon as Manuel touched them, some of the men flew directly up toward heaven while others dove over the side of the ship and became porpoises the moment they struck the water. But Manuel scarcely noticed these occurrences, as he was busy praying, praying at the top of his lungs.

"*Why* this storm, Lord, *why*? First there were winds from the north holding us back, which is the only reason I'm here in the first place. So you wanted me here, but why why why? Juan is dead and Laeghr is dead and Pietro is dead and Habedeen is dead and soon we will all be dead, and why? It isn't just. You promised you would take us home." In a fury, he took his slow-match knife, climbed down to the swamped midships, and went to the mainmast. He thrust the knife deep into the wood, stabbing with the grain. "There! I say *that* to your storm!"

"Now, that's blasphemy," Laeghr said as he pulled the knife from the mast and threw it over the side. "You know what stabbing the mast means. To do it in a storm like this—you'll offend gods a lot older than Jesus, and more powerful, too."

"Talk about blasphemy," Manuel replied. "And you wonder why you're still wandering the seas a ghost, when you say things like that. You should take more care." He looked up and saw Saint Anne, in the maintop giving directions to the third mate. "Did you hear what Laeghr said?" he shouted up to her. She didn't hear him.

"Do you remember the words I taught you?" Laeghr inquired.

"Of course. Don't bother me now. Laeghr; I'll be a ghost with you soon enough." Laeghr stepped back, but Manuel changed his mind, and said, "Laeghr, why are we being punished like this? We were on a crusade for God, weren't we? I don't understand."

Laeghr smiled and turned around, and Manuel saw then that he had wings, wings with feathers intensely white in the black murk of the air. He clasped Manuel's arm. "You know all that I know." With some hard flaps he was off, tumbling east swiftly in the black air, like a gull.

With the help of Saint Anne the third mate had actually found a break in the cliffs, a quite considerable bay. Other ships of the Armada had found it as well, and they were already cracking up on a wide beach as *La Lavia* limped near shore. The keel grounded and immediately things began breaking. Soupy waves crashed over the canted midships, and Manuel leaped up the ladder to the forecastle, which was now under a tangle of rigging from the broken foremast. The mainmast went over the side, and the lee flank of the ship splintered like a match tub and flooded, right before their eyes.

Among the floating timbers Manuel saw one that held a black cannonball embedded in it, undoubtedly the very one that Saint Anne had deflected from its course toward him. Reminded that she had saved his life before, Manuel grew calmer and waited for her to appear. The beach was only a few ship-lengths away, scarcely visible in the thick air; like most of the men, Manuel could not swim, and he was searching with some urgency for a sight of Saint Anne when Friar Lucien appeared at his side, in his black robes. Over the shriek of the dark wind Lucien shouted, "If we hold on to a plank we'll float ashore."

"You go ahead," Manuel shouted back. "I'm waiting for Saint Anna." The friar shrugged. The wind caught his robes and Manuel saw that Lucien was attempting to save the ship's liturgical gold, which was in the form of chains that were now wrapped around the friar's middle. Lucien made his way to the rail and jumped over it, onto a spar that a wave was carrying away from the ship. He missed his hold on the rounded spar, however, and sank instantly.

The forecastle was now awash, and soon the foaming breakers would tear it loose from the keel. Most of the men had already left the wreck, trusting to one bit of flotsam or other. But Manuel still waited. Just as he was beginning to worry he saw the blessed grandmother of God, standing among figures on the beach that he perceived but dimly, gesturing to him. She walked out onto the white water, and he understood. "We are the Christ, of course! I will walk to shore as He once did." He tested the surface with one shoe; it seemed a little, well, infirm, but surely it would serve—it would be like the floor of their now-demolished chapel, a sheet of water covering one of God's good solids. So Manuel walked out onto the next wave that passed at the level of the forecastle, and plunged deep into the brine.

"Hey!" he spluttered as he struggled back to the surface. "Hey!" No answer from Saint Anne this time; just cold salt water. He began the laborious process of drowning, remembering as he struggled a time when he was a child, and his father had taken him down to the beach in Morocco, to see the galley of the pilgrims to Mecca rowing away. Nothing could have been less like the Irish coast than that serene, hot, tawny beach, and he and his father had gone out into the shallows to splash around in the warm water, chasing lemons. His father would toss the lemons out into the deeper water, where they bobbed just under the surface, and then Manuel would paddle out to retrieve them, laughing and choking on water.

Manuel could picture those lemons perfectly, as he snorted and coughed and thrashed to get his head back above the freezing soup one more time. Lemons bobbing in the green sea, lemons oblong and bumpy, the color of the sun when the sun is its own width above the horizon at dawn . . . bobbing gently just under the surface, with a knob showing here and there. Manuel pretended he was a lemon, at the same time that he tried to remember the primitive dogpaddle that had gotten him around the shallows. Arms, pushing downward. It wasn't working. Waves tumbled him, lemonlike, in towards the strand. He bumped on the bottom and stood up. The water was only waist deep. Another wave smashed him from behind and he couldn't find the bottom again. Not fair! he thought. His elbow ran into sand, and he twisted around and stood. Knee deep, this time. He kept an eye on the treacherous waves as they came out of the black, and trudged through them up to a beach made of coarse sand, covered by a mat of loose seaweed.

Down on the beach a distance were sailors, companions, survivors of the wrecks offshore. But there among them—soldiers on horses. English soldiers, on horses and on foot—Manuel groaned to see it— wielding swords and clubs on exhausted men strewn across the seaweed. "No!" Manuel cried, "No!" But it was true. "Ah, God," he said, and sank till he was sitting. Down the strand soldiers clubbed his brothers, splitting their fragile eggshell skulls so that the yolk of their brains ran into the kelp.

Manuel beat his insensible fists against the sand. Filled with horror at the sight, he watched horses rear in the murk, giant and shadowy. They were coming down the beach towards him. "I'll make myself invisible," he decided. "Saint Anna will make me invisible." But remembering his plan to walk on the water, he determined to help the miracle, by staggering up the beach and burrowing under a particularly tall pile of seaweed. He was invisible without it, of course, but the cover of kelp would help keep him warm. Thinking such thoughts, he shivered and shivered and on the still land fell insensible as his hands.

When he woke up, the soldiers were gone. His fellows lay up and down the beach like white driftwood; ravens and wolves already converged on them. He couldn't move very well. It took him half an hour to move his head to survey the beach, and another half hour to free himself from his pile of seaweed. And then he had to lie down again.

When he regained consciousness, he found himself behind a large log, an old piece of driftwood that had been polished silver by its years of rolling in the sand. The air was clear again. He could feel it filling him and leaving him, but he could no longer see it. The sun was out; it was morning, and the storm was over. Each movement of Manuel's body was a complete effort, a complete experience. He could see quite deeply into his skin, which appeared pickled. He had lost all of his clothes, except for a tattered shred of trousers around his middle. With all his will he made his arm move his hand, and with his stiff forefinger he touched the driftwood. He could feel it. He was still alive.

His hand fell away in the sand. The wood touched by his finger was changing, becoming a bright green spot in the surrounding silver. A thin green sprig bulged from the spot, and grew up toward the sun; leaves unfolded from this sprout as it thickened, and beneath Manuel's fascinated gaze a bud appeared and burst open: a white rose, gleaming wetly in the white morning light.

He had managed to stand, and cover himself with kelp, and walk a full quarter of a mile inland, when he came upon people. Three of them, to be exact, two men and a woman. Wilder-looking people Manuel couldn't imagine: the men had beards that had never been cut, and arms like Laeghr's. The woman looked exactly like his miniature portrait of Saint Anne, until she got closer and he saw that she was dirty and her teeth were broken and her skin was brindled like a dog's belly. He had never seen such freckling before, and he stared at it, and her, every bit as much as she and her companions stared at him. He was afraid of them.

"Hide me from the English, please," he said. At the word *English* the men frowned and cocked their heads. They jabbered at him in a tongue he did not know. "Help me," he said. "I don't know what you're saying. Help me." He tried Spanish and Portuguese and Sicilian and Arabic. The men were looking angry. He tried Latin, and they stepped back. "I believe in God the Father Almighty, Maker of Heaven and Earth, and in all things visible and invisible." He laughed, a bit hysterically. "Especially invisible." He grabbed his medallion and showed them the cross. They studied him, clearly at a loss.

"*Tor conaloc an dhia,*" he said without thinking. All four of them jumped. Then the two men moved to his sides to hold him steady. They chattered at him, waving their free arms. The woman smiled, and Manuel saw that she was young. He said the syllables again, and they chattered some more. "Thank you, Laeghr," he said. "Thank you, Anna. Anna," he said to the girl, and reached for her. She squealed and stepped back. He said the phrase again. The men lifted him, for he could no longer walk, and carried him across the heather. He smiled and kissed both men on the cheek, which made them laugh, and he said the magic phrase again and started to fall asleep and said the phrase. *Tor conaloc an dhia.* The girl brushed his wet hair out of his eyes; Manuel recognized the touch, and he could feel the flowering begin inside him.

Give mercy for God's sake.

Uncle Tuggs

✳   ✳   ✳

Michael Shea

True devotees of horror fiction know that its best length is the short story (since most horror tales wear thin over the novel length) and that one of its best practitioners is Michael Shea (who writes mostly short stories and may not be familiar to readers who never get past the drug store paperback racks). Only Michael Shea could have written "Uncle Tuggs," a tale of backwoods terror that is also one of the funniest stories you will ever read.

✳   ✳   ✳

1

NOW you should understand that when Gabe Tuggs offered me this job, I didn't like the idea of working for him. I didn't like getting into any kind of deal with any of those three Tuggs brothers, but right then my bank account was hurtin' for certain. I'd had like a great burst of energy take hold of me when I made so much money landscaping that spring. I started building that cabin Barbara's always bitching about—and with the kids getting so big now, the trailer does seem small, even with all the little rooms I've tacked onto it. Anyway, I'd poured the slab and had the packets of two-by-fours delivered. So right then, early that fall, there was a little freak rain, and the job calls stopped dead. A lot of people are just looking for any excuse to put off having work done till next spring. I'd been two weeks without a nibble. I still owed on the two-by-fours, and we had big dentist bills, and both my stakebed and my pickup needed new sets of tires.

So. When Gabe Tuggs came and found me in the Eight Ball off Courthouse Square and offered me this job, I said, "Hmmm." I said to him, "Gabe, why don't we have another beer while I weigh it in my mind?"

Gabe used the cast on his left hand for a hammer on the bar. He ordered two beers. "And a shooter of bourbon with mine, Lloyd," I told Lloyd. Gabe didn't say anything, just paid. He was tightfisted, so I could see now he really meant to talk business. The job was cutting fifty or sixty trees on Uncle Tuggs's place to firewood, and I liked the deal. But I took my time drinking. I didn't want to answer too fast. I sat there a bit like I was just relaxing and savoring Lloyd's god-awful house bourbon.

Of course the truth was, I never could feel very relaxed sitting next to Gabe Tuggs. It's true he was the smallest of the three brothers. He stood not a hair over six feet two and was scarcely a yard wide. And if he weighed an ounce over 240, I'd eat the difference—and a nasty meal it would be. The thing was that what Gabe lacked in size he made up in meanness. His cast covered up one of his gaudier tattoos, but he had plenty of others showing—three-color tattoos with lots of teeth and tails and claws in them. A kind of burnt-leather-and-motor-oil smell came off of Gabe—his ponytail even had a kind of motor-oily look, and he always wore shades that were as black as a bug's eyes. He was the kind of guy that sitting next to him made you uneasy, like sitting next to a bear.

But anyway, I did like the deal. I could take one cord out for every cord I left to them. In October I could already get 140 for a cord that was only half splitters. If I pushed it, I could truck out two of those a day.

I also *trusted* the deal. I didn't trust the brothers, you understand—I trusted their situation, which was plain to anyone who thought about it. Since moving onto their Uncle Tuggs's place to caretake after he disappeared, they would have planted every shed and barn on it cram-full of prime skunkweed. No doubt of it. It'd be safe indoors from theft and law, and it'd be the readiest big cash they could make off the property. So. Waiting for harvest, with the grow-lights working over-time, they'd need cash in the short term for gas, drugs, booze, and food. What to do? Chop up and sell old Uncle's oaks and madronas. The boys would be living off all that wood all through the winter and spring. They'd have to play straight with their cutters and customers. And this was twice as true just now, with both Grant Tuggs, the oldest—and now Gabe, too—injured like they had been, and within a week of each other. Knowing Gabe from high school wouldn't have counted for anything if they'd wanted to cheat me, but their having to depend on that firewood for their octanes and their Jack Daniels and their elephant tranquilizers—that was what made me say to Gabe:

"Well, Gabe, I believe I could take on that job. Do I understand rightly that you've cut some kind of road so I can get my stakebed down into the draw?"

I knew Uncle's place since high school, from having my cars up there to be fixed from time to time, like a lot of people. It was six or seven acres, with the house and barn and sheds on about a half acre of fairly level ground, not far off the highway. Behind that the land dropped away to hilly ground with several draws winding through it with plenty of trees growing in them with lots of midsized scraggly stuff perfect for weeding out for firewood.

Gabe looked pissed at my question. He hammered the bar with his cast again. He said, "We got a roadcut down into the first draw. Goddamn dozer broke down right at the bottom. Still sittin' there, but you can get around it. Same," he told Lloyd.

I was impressed—I mean that he bought me another drink like that. I could see the boys really wanted someone they could trust on this job. I said:

"Boy, that's too bad. You guys really seem to be having some bad luck lately. How's Grant doin'?" I didn't quite dare ask about *his* break, but I looked at his cast when I asked about Grant's. He gave me that black bugeye like he was considering how it would be to twist my scalp off like a beer bottle cap. Though I'm kind of short, my cap's on pretty tight and might give him some trouble. It would sure hurt like hell to have him trying it out, though. Finally, not moving his lips much, Gabe says:

"They're changing his cast tomorrow."

Gabe had actually thought Grunt's accident was pretty funny when he had it—back before Gabe was hurt himself. He described it to Billy Vale, who he'd sometimes drink with, and Billy Vale described it to me. Old Grunt (Grunt was what we all called Grant behind his back)—Grunt decided to split up a heap of rollers they had by the house, so their own stoves would be taken care of.

Now Grunt had plenty of back for labor, but he didn't like it any better than his brothers did, so when he got inspired to some kind of work, he liked to jump on it, power through it, and get it over with. So Grunt honked up a couple foot-long rails of crank, and had five or six shooters of Cuervo Gold, and munched down some salt and lime slices, and fired up the splitter that old Uncle Tuggs had left behind, like he'd left behind almost all his other gear when he disappeared. Grunt starts plunking those rollers into the splitter and gets such a rhythm going that in no time he finishes the pile.

Grunt's breathing fire by now. He jumps into Uncle's old stakebed (which the front brakes are just about shot on, but what the hell) and goes jouncing down their little roadcut and into the draw. He lays about him with the chain saw and drives up another heap of rollers. He does some more shooters, munches a bunch more salt and lime slices, honks a couple more rails of crank, and fires the splitter back up. He starts feeding it rollers from off the truckbed, turning back and forth between the bed and the splitter. Well, the splitter's wheels are locked, but you know how they can creep sometimes? Except this one practically jumps—swings one end all the way around behind Grunt's legs so that he trips and falls backward across it as he turns from the truck with another roller. To top it off, just then the wedge goes into drive! And Grunt swore he never touched the drive lever when he fell, and it's hard to see how he *could* have. If he hadn't had so much crank in him, he'd never have hoisted his legs out of the way in time, and as it was, one of his feet snagged and the wedge nipped him just hard enough to crack his shinbone.

Anyway, I just shook my head sympathetically, about Grunt's cast and all. "Well, Gabe," I said, "I like your offer. I'll want to leave early enough each day to take my buyers their wood straight off my truck so I don't have to stockpile."

"Long as you leave the same amount you leave with every day, I *give* a shit. I want to start tomorrow morning. I'll be out to mark the trees for you."

I wanted to ask him what he was going to do, take a bite out of each one he wanted cut? "What about trucking *your* cords for you?" I asked him. "Will you want to hire me for that—I mean, since your truck's out?"

I thought this might make Gabe mad again because that was how he got hurt, you see, trying to change the front brake shoes on that truck, but he surprised me. He kind of looked off into the air. "Who knows?" he said. "Maybe we won't want to sweat the work ourselves. Let's just get some cut first. And remember, you're making two cords of splitters for us, too."

"No problem. I can use your splitter?"

Gabe shrugged. "If you want."

I wasn't sure I *did* want. I worked on my drink, thinking how it was no wonder the brothers seemed ready to hire out all the work, even selling their own cords. First you had their trouble with that splitter. Then you had Gabe's accident. He'd got that truck's front end up on Uncle's roll-under hydraulic pump-jack, laid under there and started hammering off the front left drum with a blunt chisel and a hand sledge. (He'd told Billy Vale this one, too, but he didn't laugh as much telling it as he did about Grunt's.) All of a sudden, *whoosh*, the pressure blows out of the jack and the truck sits on Gabe's face. He was lying on thick grass and he had the wheel lying under the axle, so his head wasn't mashed, but one of his hands got caught half-raised and he cracked two of the bones in it. And then, on top of all this, there was their grader breaking down, which I hadn't heard about. Put it all together, it was starting to seem like everything old Uncle Tuggs had left on the place was giving the brothers trouble. When Uncle and Cherry (his little honey) and Ralph (his big, mean, smelly old dog) disappeared early last summer, he took nothing but his old black repair van with him. Every vehicle, tool, or component known to man, or pieces of it, was left on his place, though a lot of it was scattered or rusted or hidden in a pile of parts. And none of it seemed to be doing the boys any good. I got up.

"Well, O.K., Gabe," I told him. "I'll see you in the morning. You guys hear anything from the sheriff yet?"

This question actually seemed to shock Gabe for a minute. I guess since him and his brothers had got the official search for Uncle and Cherry started in the first place—since they'd been waiting two months now with no results, and since it was actually three more months before that since Grunt had been the last person to see Uncle alive—why, the boys must just have given up any hope of ever seeing Uncle again, and must not even be thinking about it anymore.

"Hell," Gabe said after a minute. "They haven't found jack-shit."

As I drove home I thought about the job, and got more and more pleased with it. There were mucho cords in those draws. Once I got home I hadn't been on the phone fifteen minutes before I'd sold three cords, C.O.D., as soon as I could deliver.

2

A little after sunrise I drove my stakebed up to Tuggs's yard. I knew that place pretty well, as I say, and right then, in that early sunlight, it seemed like a lot of years since I'd started bringing my first car up here—an old Plymouth. Hell, twenty years at least, in plain fact. In those days the brothers might be around, but it was Uncle everyone came up here to see. The boys had never lived here before now. When you thought about it, it was kind of funny, actually, that being called Uncle was the old man's own joke, from his kid sister having three such big sons. He'd sure stuck by the joke—*I* couldn't recall any other name for him—but the thing was, he was just the opposite of a family-minded man. He'd let his nephews hang around his place, but even though their mother did a lot of moving and drinking and remarrying, and they got shuffled around a lot, he'd never take them in even temporarily. He probably figured she'd try to scrape them off on him, and he probably was right, but even so, I could remember thinking it was funny how he didn't even seem to feel like an uncle toward them, even though he'd let them use his tools and fix their heaps at his place. For instance, there was that accident with Ronnie Partlett that had made Gabe Tuggs kind of famous when we were back in high school. He and Ronnie stole a bottle of bourbon from Gabe's stepdad, and took Ronnie's mom's car, and were driving all around one Friday night smashing mailboxes with a baseball bat they'd stolen from the school gym. Well, Gabe was driving, and Ronnie was leaning way out with the bat to smash a bunch of boxes that they were just coming up on, and all of a sudden a cat shoots across the road, and Gabe swerves to mash it, and poor Ronnie's head is jammed into those mailboxes. Gabe got a year on the youth farm, and I remembered being up here a couple days later and hearing Uncle talking about it with some other old fart that he was fixing his tractor for. The other guy said that Ronnie was no better than a vegetable now, for all intents and purposes, and Uncle laughed and said, yeah, but you had to be fair to Gabe, because Ronnie hadn't had that far to go in the first place. Which was God's truth. What struck me just then was how Uncle said it, like he saw Ronnie and Gabe on a par, and didn't feel any more involved with one than the other.

What Uncle did—even more than working here at his place— was ride a kind of circuit mechanic's route in an old black van jammed with tools. Back when I was a kid, he was already a strange, tall, skinny old guy that everybody's grandfather liked to joke and cackle with and everybody's grandmother disapproved of as being foulmouthed but was also a little secretly tickled by. He was kind of like an old-time circuit preacher that prayed over cars and graders and trucks. He'd stand talking over an engine, jawing with the owner, as long as he ever spent touching it. But then, finally, just here and there, he'd give a little dab with a wrench, a little poke with the screwdriver, and ba-*room!*, the thing would be humming. Like a laying on of hands.

Also, the old goat always had some much younger woman (or chippy, as some people's mothers called them) living up here with him. He was a greasy, gangly, bump-throated old guy. He had a big, spade-shaped nose that came all the way down past his mouth, or seemed to. His mouth was wide, without all its teeth, and when he wasn't talking—when he was looking at an engine and thinking, his eyes far away—he had this sort of secret, lemon-sucking smile that always, as long as I could remember, set my teeth a little on edge. As I got older, and *he* got older, it surprised and irritated me more and more that he always had these younger women living with him. If after a while one of them stopped showing up around his place, no more than a week or so would pass and he'd have another one out there with the same nice big advantages on her as the one before her'd had. What sort of rubbed it all in, you might say, was that he loved to talk about what he did in bed with them. Or talk about what he'd *like* to do in bed with them, or talk about what he'd like to do in bed with any *other* woman who came to mind, or came in sight, at any moment. Old Uncle Tuggs liked to talk about screwing, or possible screwing, or even impossible screwing, in any way, shape, or form. The thing was, he had a *talent* for it. He had such a humorous, greedy, descriptive way of talking about it that you just had to listen, and laugh.

But it sort of hit me just then, looking at his old place, that I'd never really liked Uncle Tuggs. It surprised me. I mean, I guess I always knew I didn't like him, but the fact never stood out for me to notice it like it did now. There was something about him that I always thought was just like Ralph, his dog—dirty, bony, sneaky . . . *hungry* in some kind of strange way you couldn't put your finger on, with his eyes like they were circling you, hanging back, spying at you and laughing.

Gabe came out of the barn. He had two chain saws by their grip bars in one hand and a can of gas under the arm with the cast. As I pulled up to let him in, I could see that they had walled off a back part of the barn, and so were probably growing dope back there, too, as well as in all the sheds (you could hear a generator going somewhere—Walter had been into town to buy a new one, so the one Uncle'd left must have broken down). Gabe got in, and I drove us down past the old stakebed sitting nose to the grass where the jack gave out, and down to the edge of the nearest draw.

The roadcut down into it *was* rough, and that little John Deere was right bang at the bottom of it, its skip-loader shoved halfway into the dirt for another bite when it died. You had to admit it was bizarre. The last time it had been used before that it had worked fine. Grant had come up to grade off some old weedy dirt piles from a cellar and septic tank dug years before—I guess Uncle just didn't feel like doing it himself for some reason—and that in fact was the last time anyone had seen Uncle, because when Grunt came back the next day to finish up, he said he found Uncle, Cherry, Ralph, and the van all gone. Anyway, three months later, after the brothers decided it was time the law looked into this (and a lot of people by this time were wondering), and after the sheriff O.K.'d their caretaking the place, they no sooner fire the John Deere up again to develop the property's cash potential a little, and *bam* it breaks down. I was just able to edge my truck out around it and onto the draw bottom.

"Well, Gabe," I told him, "this gravel feels pretty firm—I shouldn't have any trouble getting down-draw a ways."

"Forget it. You're cuttin' up here. Just get all these fuckers at the head of the draw here."

Old Gabe sure had a friendly, winning way about him. Why the hell did he need to mark the trees at all if that was what he wanted? Turned out—as I was breaking out my twelve-pack of Buckhorn, rolling up my sleeves, and firing up the bigger chain saw—that he didn't bother with marking trees, just took one of my beers and sat on a rock and started watching, like I was free TV.

I went to work. I dropped a half dozen smaller trees that would be in the way of falling the bigger ones later on. I trimmed the lettuce off them and dragged it out of the way and started cutting them into rollers. All this time Gabe was watching me, looking broody. After a while I see it's the chain saw he's actually watching. After a half hour or so, he gets up, pins the other saw with his foot, and starts it with his good hand.

"Hey!" he tells me, "use this awhile! I don't like that one to overheat."

Well, this is bullshit, the saw was fine. But I didn't want to lose my stride, so I just put the one down, took the other, and kept going. Gabe took another one of my beers, sat down on a madrona I'd cut, and started watching *that* saw. After a while I stopped for a rest.

"Mind if I switch back to the big one now, Gabe?" I asked him. "It goes faster."

Sullen, like it hurt his mouth to ask it, Gabe said, "Seem to you like either one of them pulls?"

"Pulls? Left or right?"

"Left *or* right!" he shouts—I'm surprised how suddenly worked up he was. "Up *or* down! Pulls *any* direction!"

I waited a minute. "Why, no, Gabe," I said very calmly. "I've got to say I haven't felt either one of these saws pull particularly in any direction at all whatsoever."

He just grunted, but I could've sworn he looked relieved. I went back to work with the bigger saw, and he didn't mention overheating anymore. Gabe watched and drank my beer. I had figured a twelve-pack would last me till lunch, but the cheap bastard drank three of my beers, and by eleven I'd run dry. I made a big deal about emptying the last can, but hints are wasted on any Tuggs. Just then from up at the house came the sound of someone firing up a car, and I said to Gabe:

"Is that Walter? Going out? Could you get him to bring back another twelve-pack?"

"Walter's not here. That's Grant. He won't be back till late, he's going to get his cast changed."

"Well, have you got any beers in the house, Gabe? It's getting kind of thirsty out, and it looks like I've just run dry."

Good old Gabe just shrugged. "Fuck if I know," he said cheerfully.

I went back to falling some more trees. I decided at noon I'd drive out for another twelver, and this one I was going to lock in my cab and take out can by can so that even a Tuggs would get the point. And then the strangest thing happened that I've ever had happen with a chain saw—and I mean including the time I lost this joint of my finger here, right? I'd started on this little oak, you see. It had two main branchings that pushed out at its neighbors so as to give it a tricky kind of torque, but it had a definite lean out over the draw bottom that should control its fall. Well, what happened was that when I touched the saw to begin the undercut, the saw had an incredible power surge, and ripped clear through the trunk with one backhanded stroke!

Now this can't happen. Certainly not on an undercut like that. The shift and pinch of the trunk as its support gets cut through would trap the biggest saw just like *that*. You have to get the weight of the tree hanging with the undercuts, but then you cut through the back of this stress and the tree snaps forward off the saw—it's the only way to do it.

Except it did happen. Can you picture the kind of acceleration I'm talking about? The blade just roared straight through the tree—I'd still swear that kind of power just physically was not *in* that saw. It sliced the trunk at a crazy angle, and the tree pitches down, flips off the hang-up of one of its boughs on the next tree, and twists sideways as it whops down the rest of the way, bang-square on the tree that Gabe was perched on.

Gabe had lots of fast in him, like all the Tuggs. He'd just jumped off when the oak came down and clamped him facedown across the madrona, chest and right arm pinned, head and left arm poking out on the other side. And as if things weren't strange already, the impact itself was strange. The oak fell on one of its two branchings, which snapped off but didn't break off, and acted like a kind of hinge, letting the oak down just enough to pinch Gabe solid, but also giving just enough support so that no more than two or three of his ribs were cracked at most. When his head cleared and his eyes focused again, he started to swear something terrible.

"God*damn*, Gabe," I told him. "You weren't just woofin' when you asked about it pulling! Did you *see* how this thing yawed on me?"

Gabe kept on swearing, and it sounded weird because what he was saying was so fierce and yet his voice was almost quiet at the same time, because it hurt him too much to fill his lungs and roar. I was really sorry a thing like this had happened to a guy like Gabe with me *involved* in its happening. Of course he himself had seemed to suspect his chain saws were acting up, but he was the kind of guy that if you broke a couple of his ribs, he was going to hold it against you no matter what. He'd just spent too many of his years running elephant tranquilizers and crystal meth with other crazy bikers, and *doing* them, to have much sense of the fine point of a case left in him. I studied how to cut him free.

"Look here, Gabe," I told him. "A lot of the weight's from this other side branch here. I'll lop it off and maybe the oak will rise off you some."

"Cut me the fuck outa here, you fuckin' clown! Ow!" Gabe said —he'd shouted too loud. I laid the blade to that side branch, and the saw sank through it smooth and normal as you please. A good three hundred pounds' weight dropped free. But goddamn if that oak didn't lift at all. By some freak twist in it, the trunk actually seemed to press a shade harder on poor Gabe.

"Well, at least this saw's behaving O.K. now, Gabe," I told him. "I guess I'll try cutting that branch above you, and maybe then I'll be able to—"

"GET—THIS—THING—OFF—ME!" Gabe screeched, and then had to groan, it hurt so much to do it. The branch wasn't a main one but was hefty, and I might be able to push up the oak with it off and just lift it enough for Gabe to pull himself out. His head stuck out just below and to one side of the branch, so I got on its opposite side and reached the blade up.

"Keep your eyes shut," I advised him, "because this sawdust is going to be coming down around your head." Gabe just groaned again and ground his teeth. I gunned the saw and set it to the branch.

Right there—right then—things started to go bad in a big way. It was like when I touched the saw to that branch, a kind of nightmare started, and kept on, getting worse and worse, until—well, I'm going to describe it all to you in just the order it happened in.

I touch the saw to the bough, right? It sinks maybe halfway in, lulling me, getting me off guard—and then it has another one of those unreal power surges! It whips—I mean *whips*—through the rest of the branch in a second. I can't unsqueeze the trigger! I can't let go the grip! *Zip* through the bough and on down—*chonk*-zoom—clean through poor Gabe Tuggs's neck. That saw moved so fast that Gabe's head and the bough hit the ground at just about the same second, and I just had time to free my hands and pull back before the branch hit my arms—and it did hit the chain saw right where I dropped it and smashed it dead.

I stood cursing, but I was in kind of a trance, too. I walked around the trees, and on the other side of them I walked up and down, helpless, shaking my head and swearing. I was using my voice to drown out the awful noise of Gabe's bleeding on the other side of that tree sandwich. From this side he might just be some guy peacefully bent over a fence or something that you were seeing from behind—except for that oak tree on him, of course. But I could still see in my mind the horrible way he was cut off short on the other side. I made myself stand still. I took a deep breath and blew it out.

"Brother," I told myself out loud, "this is the worst luck you've ever had in a long and distinguished *career* of bad luck, and you better get a grip on yourself because now you have really got your ass in a crack."

I never talk to myself out loud like that, and the fact that I was doing it just shows how blown away my mind was, but somehow it helped me, and so I went on:

"You're going to have to hide poor Gabe. Bury him. Because there's no way Walter or Grunt Tuggs is going to accept a reasonable explanation of how this tragic mishap happened. So you're going to have to come in tomorrow, and tell them that after Grunt left for the hospital, Gabe took off somewhere and still hadn't showed up before you left with your wood."

I sounded reasonable to myself, and it got me moving. I went back around the trees. But I was still like in shock. All I could do for a while was stare at those remains and the horrible mess of blood they had sprayed on the ground and a lot of the wood. And then when I made myself move again, all I could think of to do was pick up poor Gabe's head by the ponytail and hide it in a manzanita bush—pretty ridiculous with the whole rest of him still clamped between those trees. The oak lay longwise on the madrona, almost aligned to it. To keep from binding the saw or from mangling the body any worse, the neatest way to cut him out would be to chop that oak to rollers from its crown, the nearest end.

"All right, then," I told myself, "chop it to rollers, pull him free and bury him, and use the shovel to bury the blood, too. Then get the bloody rollers on the flatbed first, cover them with the clean ones you'll have just cut, and get the hell out of here before Grunt or Walter comes back."

I felt encouraged—I was still making sense. Down the draw a little way was the mouth of a ravine that Grunt Tuggs had shoved the dirt piles into when he graded them off for Uncle. The loose heap spilled right out into the draw and should be easy to bury Gabe in.

My mind felt like it was clicking again. I fired up the smaller saw and set to the crown of that oak, dropping it roller by roller. This saw hadn't acted up yet, but you can bet I kept it well away from me while I worked.

I don't want you to think that all through this I wasn't feeling some personal regret for Gabe as a man. No matter what kind of scumbug a person might be, they have some human characteristics, too, usually, and you should try to come up with these and give them their due when they pass on. So I tried to remember Gabe's high points while I worked, though I'd never stayed in touch with him. I remember while I was still in the service hearing how him and Walter had got together as septic tank contractors. They and two guys they subbed part of their work to apparently had a knack for getting things out of the houses they worked at. Then there was a divorced lady and her daughters had a big place in the hills where these boys were setting a tank for an extra wing she was adding. Maybe the lady was too trusting, too sociable, but Gabe and the boys, who had some bottles on hand, let the day turn into a kind of wild party and all four got sent up for Rape forcible and Rape statutory and Breaking and Entering and some other things. And from what I heard afterward here and there, both Walter and Gabe used every opportunity to work on their rape techniques while they were in the joint.

Well, after that? I seemed to remember they all got out of the joint within a year of each other—Grunt was already up-country in another state for a second-degree murder—and got together on something. Yes, that would be the garage they leased near Courthouse Square in Healdsburg. Now there was an example—Gabe wasn't charged with anything on that one, though there were some Mexican car-clubbers got shot outside of town by someone, and Grunt did go up again, for receiving stolen goods. On the other hand, you couldn't really give Gabe too much credit for that, because everyone knew he would've gone up, too, if they'd been able to get enough evidence on him. Anyway, after that Gabe and Walter were running crank down around L.A. I knew that from Billy Vale, who'd met Gabe while he was in jail for it, and went in with him awhile when Gabe went back to it after he got out.

It began to sink in to me how much the brothers tended to stay together in spite of their various adventures. Would they really buy my story that Gabe had just taken off? And wouldn't I have to get rid of his chopper to make them believe it even for a little while? Could I ramp it up onto my stakebed and cover it with rollers? It made me feel a little panicky. Christ! Could I get all this done in time? I raised my saw to start a new cut, and from up near the house I heard the roar of a car pull in.

Oh, perfect! Oh, fine! That had to be Walter! I was so stupefied by this new bad luck, I just kept cutting. I dropped a roller, started another one. I heard Walter's motor cut off, his car door bang shut, then a house door bang. I just kept cutting.

3

It was like one of those nightmares where you're supposed to be hiding from these people, but your cover is just too thin and all the time you're really blatant. And somehow they keep on not seeing you, but at any second they just *have* to see you. I just kept standing there cutting my way toward poor Gabe and the big red splotch on the ground in front of him. Up at the house another door banged. Over the saw, in a pause between cuts, I could just make out the sound of someone sifting through tools near one of the sheds.

I was maybe five cuts from springing Gabe's trunk. Would my luck hold? After I hid him, I'd still have to get a shovel to cover the blood. I heard an engine fire up in the yard. It wasn't Walter's car—it was shriller. And then Walter howled and I heard him screeching and swearing.

It wouldn't be natural for me to ignore that noise—he'd expect me to come running up there to see what happened. For a minute, though, it was impossible for me to move, every ounce of me was so unwilling to leave the body so obvious like that for anyone to see who came to the edge of the yard. But at last I made myself trot on up to the yard, the chain saw idling in my hand.

There was Walter, standing by a rusty, stripped-down V-8 engine Uncle had left sitting on a block of wood in the grass. One of his hands was bloody—Walter was clutching it and cursing a blue streak. And damned if the fan blades on that derelict weren't still spinning!

"What the hell happened, Walter?"

Walter was a lot bigger than Gabe—almost as big as Grunt—but he didn't wear his hair like his older and younger brothers did. His was dude-hair, and his face was shaved, which let you see all the dings and chunks taken out of it. Right now Walter Tuggs looked amazed.

"I was takin' the fuckin' distributor cap! The fuckin' engine fired up!"

"Jesus, Walter! That is *bizarre!*"

Walter looked at me. The whites were showing all the way around his mean little gray eyes. Between each word he said, his jaw kind of sagged, like it wanted to hang. "*Bizarre?*" he said. "*Bizarre?* What the fuck do you *mean* bizarre?"

"I mean *strange,* Walter. I mean, Jesus Christ, that's *strange.*"

"Strange? *Strange?* You're fuckin'-aye-straight it's strange! That sucker's amputated! There's no *gas!*"

What could I say? He was right! That fan had mauled a lot of skin off his knuckles, but it was that kind of thing that is so surprising that it blots out pain for a while. I still didn't like to see Walter Tuggs bleeding like that. In just pure disposition, you'd have to say he was the meanest of the brothers. True, he did skunkweed and reds to such an extent that a lot of the time he seemed more amazed than mean. But he had a way of getting confused, and if he stayed confused about any one thing long enough, then he turned mean. Luckily his memory was so short he usually forgot what was confusing him pretty quick, but bleeding like he was was likely to keep the confusing fact that a dead engine had mauled him on Walter's *mind.*

But he didn't get steamed up. No! Walter surprised me. He looked at that V-8 and said, fairly quietly, "So fuck your fuckin' distributor. *Be* that way! I'll just go trim the fuckin' dope." Then he just turned and walked toward the toolshed. It was the oddest thing, like he had some running argument with that motor, or with something in it—an argument he was so involved in he didn't even notice he'd copped to their dope crop right in front of me.

I figured I should keep an eye on Walter for a few minutes to see that he settled into something. I killed off the saw and set it down, and went to the shed where he was tying a rag around his hand and got out a double-bitted ax.

"I'm gonna do some of your splits now, Walter. Then I'm gonna haul a load of rollers out of the draw for myself."

He just shrugged. I went over to the rollers piled by the back porch near the splitter—which, the way things were going, there was no way I was going to use—and started setting them on end and splitting them. I warmed up to the ax work, and my mind started moving again. How big would their dope be? Two months old, dating from the day they moved in. There'd be some spraying as well as trimming to do, and all those downers made Walter a slow worker. He'd be at it an hour. If I could just get back down to the draw for another twenty minutes, I could spring Gabe and hide him and the worst of the blood. Then I could settle to clean up in more detail, because then even if Walter did come to the edge of the yard, he'd miss anything that didn't outright kick him in the face.

So I kept splitting. I've always liked splitting madrona—it's so red the cross cuts look like steaks. It's crisp and kind of waxy and splits clean with one good stroke: *whack*-plop, *whack*-plop, *whack*-plop. The splitters fell apart rosy and mellow in the sunlight. I was just starting to feel I might get out of this mess if I stayed cool.

Meanwhile Walter had found a pair of hand shears in the shed and was working them to get the rustiness out of them. He worked them and worked them, already looking like his usual vacant self again: *eee-eee, eee-eee, eee-eee*. In the noon quiet and the fine sunshine, the two of us made a funny, peaceful kind of music: *whack*-plop, *eee-eee*, *whack*-plop, *eee-eee*.

An inspiration came to Walter. He rummaged in the shed again and got a spray can of Liquid Wrench. Holding this he wandered toward the barn, spraying the shears and still working them as he went: *eee-eee, eee-eee*. And right there, just as he got to the barn door, Walter had one of the strangest accidents I've ever seen. Not worst, but strangest, and coming from me that ought to mean something. Maybe the shears were slippery from the Liquid Wrench, but as he worked them faster they suddenly snapped open so hard they flipped out of his grip, spun end over end straight down, and sank one blade all the way through Walter's shoe and foot and it must have been another inch on into the ground.

For a minute Walter froze. He stood and gaped at his foot like it had betrayed him. Then he hoisted the foot, shears and all, off the ground and started hopping around on his other foot and roaring. He roared some things there's no need to repeat, things—and combinations of things—that I'd never even thought of. The kind of things I guess you need a pair of shears through your foot to help you think up. I ran over to him.

"Sit down, Walter. Against the barn here!"

"_____ __ _____ _____ _____ __ _____!"

"That's it, scoot back this way a little more. Lean back on the wall here! That's it!"

"_____ ___ _____ _____ _____!"

"Hold that knee straight now. Lock it!" I told him. I planted one of my feet against his toes to hold his foot rigid, and then I hauled the shears out of him. He slammed the barn wall with his head, cracking one of the planks. When his eyes had cleared a little, he said:

"In the kitchen. Counter. Jack Daniels."

"Good idea!" I told him. "Get your shoe off and we can pour some in the hole!"

"Fuck the hole!" Walter screeched. "I'm gonna drink it!"

Just the same he started working on his laces, and I hurried through the back door into the kitchen, and when I got to that JD bottle I took some of Walter's advice and had a long pull off it. I found a sixer of Buckhorn in their icebox and had one of them and half another as a chaser. I watched poor Walter from the window, loosening his shoelaces gingerly, like they were snakes that might bite him. I took another pull, finished my beer, and cracked another.

"Can you believe a day like this?" I asked myself. I felt like I was a stranger I had to give advice to and couldn't think of what to tell him. "They talk about accident-prone?" I asked. "Those aren't just empty words. It seems like every tool or gadget on this place has it in for these boys."

Just then the coldest kind of a shudder went straight through me —up from the floor I stood on and right out through my scalp, and it was like Uncle Tuggs was standing right there with me. I mean, I was still looking out the window, seeing Walter ease his shoe off and get some reds out of his vest pocket and swallow them, but what I was really seeing was Uncle Tuggs's face. I was feeling him in my guts, the smell of his dirty kitchen was the smell of Uncle himself in my nostrils. And he had this particular look on his face that I'd seen there again and again over the years, and it hit me now that it was that look that somehow summed up Old Uncle Tuggs—got right at the gist of him. It was the look he'd have when he'd just fixed some immediate problem on whatever car I had at the time. Well, that takes care of that, he'd say, but before long that X or Y of yours is going to go and then you might as well just shitcan the whole rig. And we'd stand there, both of us knowing he was right, and both knowing I'd never have the money to fix that X or Y—and his oily black eyes would be laughing in just this particular way. And now I could feel the meaning in that look like never before—that deep inside Uncle gloated more over knowing how things broke than knowing how to fix them.

It was truly scary—I could see Cherry, too, in a manner of speaking. I mean with that same feel of the smell and rub of her. A little honey about my age, ex-flower child, with the kind of advantages on her that back in high school it would have blown every zit on my face to get my hands on—but her eyes were missing! Right at the centers they were dead and gone, so that you couldn't picture them. It really went through me. Uncle's other honeys? What about them? Could I remember their eyes? Walter was bellowing for me. As I took him out the whiskey and beer, I told myself:

"Calm down now. Just stay cool. This is actually good luck. He won't go wandering around now and look in the draw."

Walter got out some more reds and washed them down with the JD. Then he drank a beer at one breath. He settled back against the barn and gave me a serious look. "This place, man," he told me, "is trying to *ambush* me. This whole fucking *place*." He looked off into space, nodding a sort of a just-you-wait nod. He chugged more JD and brooded over his thoughts. Old Walter's thoughts, few though they might be, could often occupy him for hours at a time. Things were looking up. I'd work here just until I saw his reds kick in, then get down into the draw and clean up.

"Listen, Walter," I told him. "You want a ride to the hospital? Because I'll take you down in my truck as soon as I make up a load. I'll split a few more here, and then I'll go down and make up the load." Walter nodded—he looked vague already.

I went back to splitting. This shouldn't take long—*whack*-plop. Then I'd come back here from the hospital after dropping him off—*whack*-plop. Get Gabe's keys and just *drive* his chopper off the place —*whack*-plop. Hide it somewhere nearby and run back—*whonk*.

It was just the ax handle that I hit that one with, and it made my elbows pop. The head had flown off the handle slick as snot. It *whistled*, it spun so straight. It sank its whole length into the center of Walter Tugg's chest. He'd been sitting with one hand laid sort of loose across his chest, and so two of his fingers got clipped off just as neat as you could imagine and rolled down onto his lap. Walter's eyes and mouth came wide open, he sat up, and then fell back, stone-dead.

4

It seemed like I'd never move again. Like the sun would set, the moon would rise, Grunt would come home and call the sheriff—and I'd just be standing there through it all, that ax handle in my hands, poor Walter in front of me, and poor old Gabe down in the draw, sandwiched between two trees with his head behind a manzanita bush. Except of course Grunt would just blow me away himself and bury me down in the draw—he'd make no bones about that kind of thing. And it seemed like I *did* stand there forever, and without a single idea in my head how to save myself.

And then, straight out of that like trance, I started to move—to clean things up—and it was bizarre how smoothly I started doing everything, how suddenly I was moving and wasn't wasting a move. I tossed the ax handle in the toolshed, dragged out a piece of carpet Uncle had used to lie under cars on, took it over to Walter, tucked his two fingers into his vest pocket with his reds, and laid him on the carpet. It was amazing how little he bled—I guess because his heart had stopped pumping in a split second. I dragged him over to the road. Big though he was, it still seemed impossible one man could be so heavy.

I dragged him down the road into the draw. I ran back up, got the JD and cans of beer, drained them all, and threw them on a trash heap with a lot of others of their kind. I got the chain saw and a pick and shovel and ran back down into the draw with them. I set them down near Gabe, grabbed Walter's rug again, dragged it as far as the manzanita, got poor Gabe's head by the ponytail and put it on Walter's lap, and dragged both of them still deeper into the draw.

Near where that slide was, where Grunt had dozed a gully full with Uncle's old dirt piles, was a clump of bushes, and I hid Walter and Gabe's head behind it. I ran back up the draw with the carpet, laid it near Gabe's feet, fired the chain saw back up, and started to get the rest of the oak off him.

I couldn't progress so fast in this part of the work. I forced myself to make twenty-inch cuts because I'd need lots of clean rollers to hide the bloody wood in the truck, but I had to clench my teeth to keep from bellowing out the fear that was in me now. It was like being trapped in a film that had slowed down. All the shadows in the draw looked darker and cooler, and I overdrove the chain saw to keep from hearing this bizarre, thick *quiet* that was welling like a flood out of the ground, like it might fill the draw and close over my head and snuff out even the chain saw's noise like a candle flame. Crazy? I *was* crazy! I kept seeing Uncle. With Grunt, and after him the law to be afraid of, and all the tricky moves I had to plan, it was that old goat that kept pushing himself into my mind. Just like a goat, too—the way one might push its clammy muzzle against your hand, wanting something from you? It *was* a cold, sweaty nudge—his face shoved against my mind with a scary, skin-rub feeling. And it was those months the brothers had their garage scam going that I especially remembered him from. There was that same gloating smile, but watching his nephews this time. It was only his donating some talent, dropping around to help every few days, that kept any straight customers coming after the first month or so.

And he hadn't had any part in the boys' cheats. No. What he was there to do showed in that smile if you really saw it: to enjoy the spectacle of the boys at their loser's racket. He knew that if some housewife stopped in with a nice new car, she'd drive it off with a big bill and with her carburetor and battery and what-all replaced by used junk. He knew about their rip-off contracts with those cholos that eventually got shot. *He* was hanging around for the show, giving the boys' setup a shove now and then to keep it rolling—just like he'd give an engine that finicky, kind of disdainful jab with a screwdriver or poke with a wrench. That was how Uncle had fun. People always assumed it was by tinkering things to life, but actually it was by keeping things going so that he could watch them dying longer. I dropped the piece that had Gabe pinned. He sagged down to his knees and flopped back on the carpet.

Even so tragically shortened, Gabe was like an oak stump to pull, but now I felt like the film was speeded back up and I could move ahead of my feelings again. I left Gabe behind the bushes with his head and Walter. I ran back and grabbed the shovel. I started scooping sand from where it was thick on the draw bottom and slinging it over the drag marks and the blood splotches and salting it over the bloody rollers. They looked crusty, but it killed the color. I tossed the smashed saw on the truckbed and started tossing those rollers on after it. Big sugary clots of sand drizzled off that raw-meat madrona as it bounced on the bed, and in that late light it all looked like a nightmare you might have after gorging yourself on rare roast beef and jelly doughnuts. I had to rest before starting to throw the clean rollers on to cover the mess. I looked up and was completely stunned. The sun was setting! Just one red half of it was left, all webbed over by the black branches of oak trees.

I jumped. I spun. I made those rollers rise and fly into the truck, but as fast as I could move wasn't half fast enough. The fear was truly big in me now—and still not of Grunt, or the law, but of Uncle—like he could somehow catch up with me, grab me, and stop me dead in the middle of this awful work of mine. When the clean wood I'd cut was loaded, it wasn't enough to cover the mess, so I started lopping off some more. The first roller I dropped, the sun went with it. The sky was still light, but now all the shadows ran together in the draw. I gritted my teeth and kept cutting, and remembered Uncle's eyes. His eyes as he'd been telling you where he'd like to stick his tongue and his fingers in some woman passing by just then—his little lemon-sucking smile as he told you about it, as he rubbed the balls of his mind against your ears, *tinkering* with your mind just as he tinkered with his nephews' customers' cars, smiling as he watched the boys—so blatant and so dumb—hassle, cheat, steal, and strong-arm their way back to jail. His eyes as he sat in his van, fingering the back of Cherry's neck as they drove by, tinkering with her nerves as he steered. And *her* eyes while he did it, looking empty and dismantled, like clocks with their hands stripped off. I stopped cutting. I didn't really have enough, but to hell with it. I wasn't going to be able to make myself stay down here much longer.

I killed the saw, loaded my cuts, and set in and bolted my truck's tailgate. I stood there in the quiet that had closed right back in like a pool, and in the shadows that now were also like a pool that I was sunk in way over my head, with my feet turned to lead. I didn't want to go down that draw to do my last piece of work. They lay there waiting for me to take hold of them and wrestle them into the dirt, and I had to say something, to hold their silence off at arm's length.

"O.K.," I said. "There you boys lie, and I've got to bury you now and get out of here fast. And first I'm going to have to get your scooter's key out of your pocket, Gabe. I *really* hate doing this. But you know, deep down, that all this was a tragic mishap—I mean, if you know anything, you know that it's something *he* . . . something Uncle . . ."

I knew as I said it that I shouldn't say his name, and no sooner *did* I say it than he was there. Standing right behind me.

My heart nearly sneezed a piston. I screeched and jumped and spun around—and saw the draw was empty. No one was there but me, my stakebed, and that busted John Deere. I stood down in that lagoon of shadows, my heart still thudding back into place, and listened to the cricket noise start nibbling at the edges of all that cold, creaky quiet. I shook myself. I took up the pick and shovel and ran down to where the boys were hidden.

It was eerie getting Gabe's key out of his pocket with his face staring at me from off to one side, where it sat on Walter's lap. But I got it, and stood up. I felt wired to work again, felt like with just a little more hustle I might still get my ass out of here alive. I grabbed the pick and swung it against that dirt slide.

Burying them in that slide was one of those ideas that looks good at a fast glance, but the minute you start doing it you can see why it stinks. The loose dirt kept pouring onto what I dug out, as any idiot would expect from a slide. I swung the pick like a propeller, stabbed out dirt by the bushel with that shovel, ground my teeth and grunted and sweated—and all I was doing was dragging that whole pile farther and farther out onto the draw bottom.

So I tried to put less back in it—ease the dirt out till I'd opened just enough of a notch in the slope to hide the boys in. I couldn't do it! The least little bit I moved them, the pick and shovel seemed to *jump* with it. They yanked my shoulders sore trying to hold back their lunges at the slide. I was staggering, swearing, and losing every single stroke of the battle. It was like fighting the buck of a power tool, and these were just dead wood and steel. Finally I flung that shovel down, kicked it, cursed it, and stomped on it. I stood there trying to catch my breath, and right then, up by the house, I heard a car's engine cut off and its door open.

5

I was petrified. I'd totally missed any sound it'd made coming in. I stopped breathing to listen. I heard the door thunk shut, and heavy, limping steps move toward the house. I breathed again.

Let Grunt get inside the house. Let him get inside and shut the door, I told myself. Then sling a pile on the boys just where they lie —enough to keep the flies off. Then fire up the truck and drive the hell out of here. If Grunt comes out to ask, idle just long enough to say Walt and Gabe went off with someone who came by around noon. You were in the draw, didn't see them, just heard a car and some conversation you couldn't make out, then Gabe came to the edge of the draw and said if he and Walter didn't get back here before dark, just to take your wood on out, so that's what you were doing.

All this came to me in the space of a half dozen of those steps I heard moving toward the house. That just showed how wound tight I was. I was so deep in shit I couldn't feel the new waves hit me anymore, just rolled with them. The steps got hollow, climbing and crossing the back porch. Four, three, two more and he'd reach the back door. That was when, right in front of me, the pick jumped off the ground, twirled in the air, and *chunk*—started chopping at the slide all by itself, while the shovel came up on its nose, twirled, and *chonk*—stabbed into the dirt beside the pick. The click and rasp and clank of them rose so biting clear above the cricket noise—such an age-old, unmistakable sound— it seemed you could hear it clear to Healdsburg. Up on the porch the footsteps stopped. There was a long pause while those tools worked and nothing else moved anywhere on old Uncle's acres. Then came the footsteps again—creak-*thock*, creak-*thock*—heading back off the porch and down the steps they had just climbed.

I still wasn't moving. I was *with* those god-awful tools, you see, not three yards from where they hung in midair tearing that slide apart. The terrible magic moving them was like a thickness in the air around them, and it held me fast like a bug in jelly. Not that I didn't finally understand what was happening on this place. I saw it now, I got the gist of it, and I realized that pick and shovel weren't going to bother turning on me, because they had their own row to hoe, but I couldn't move anyway. My legs just wouldn't thaw out. I watched them hack and chew, all alone in the shadowy air, and I listened to Grunt's steps coming back. He stopped, the car's trunk popped open, something clanked slightly, the trunk was shut and the steps came on.

It was dark in the draw now, but straight overhead—where I looked like a drowning man might—the sky was still blue and the first star had just showed in it. There was a little piece of my mind like that star, up there apart from me looking down on the mess I was in, and it told me that when Grunt had paused up on the porch there, that pause had lasted too long. Too long for him just to be identifying what this noise was. This noise meant something particular to old Grunt. Though his steps were nearer now, they were quieter—the little grinding noises of his 280 pounds gimping across the grass to the draw. The tools had that dirt pouring down like winter runoff onto the draw bottom. Right then as I was watching, like an island in a stream, a corner of black metal poked out of that runoff.

I moved then. I got my feet unrooted, and after that it was easy —I felt so light and small compared to the power that hummed through those tools. I was quick and quiet as a fish in that pool of darkness— I slipped up the opposite slope and behind some oaks. I didn't want to stay even that near to what those tools were uncovering, but there came Grunt Tuggs, limping down the roadcut, a twelve-gauge pump-riot in his right hand, which made that shotgun look no bigger than a bread-stick.

Dear Christ, old Grunt was big. Barrel-gutted though beer had made him, his shoulders still made his belly look small. He was balding on top, so his ponytail started from a kind of equator around the back of his head. His face had that full-moon look—puffy with little slitty crafty-mean eyes, like a samurai gone to seed on bad sake. He stopped at the foot of the roadcut and leaned against the John Deere, hoisting the leg with the cast on it so he could dangle and rest it a minute. That cast was so clean and new and white, and the bulk of Grunt was so oily-dark, bristly, and mean, that it was a little comical-looking some-how, like a party hat on a grizzly.

From where he was he couldn't see the tools past those bushes down the draw, but he knew my truck, and he bellowed out my name. The pick and shovel paused, like a man would do that was startled. It made a shiver go right through me. Then they started digging again. They made the dirt river down wider and wider off that black island. It was the tail end of a black van, tilted almost upside down in its grave. If it hadn't been for that shotgun, I would have run. Grunt called out again. His voice was like a grader blade breaking dirt:

"Step out where I can see you, sucker, or I'm gonna cut your ass in half. Willy? You hear me? Stop digging and step out!"

When the tools didn't stop, he started walking down the draw, his moonface bright in the dark, his eyes creased almost shut with his anger. And not just anger, maybe. Maybe a touch of worry, too. Yes. A touch of something I'd never seen on the face of Grunt Tuggs before. And then he stopped, and stared, seeing what made the noise he'd thought was me.

His head came back and his mouth opened a little. A shudder went through him as he watched the dirt trickling off the old black chassis lying wheels-up. Then his hands remembered the shotgun. He shook his head and heaved his shoulders like throwing off weight.

"All right, then, old man!" he shouted. His voice was sharp with a touch of a wild laugh in it. "O.K.! If that's how you want it! I've *still* got plenty of shells. Plenty left. So whatever it takes!" And he pumped off a wad of double-ought that slammed spang against that shovel's head and set it twirling like a ballerina on its toe.

But just *like* a dancer, it stayed balanced, and spun to a sudden stop. It tipped back once for some thrust and launched itself end over end through the air. That shovelhead swatted Grunt a smack upside the ear that rang like a churchbell, and that I *know* you could hear down in Healdsburg. Meanwhile the pick had swung up like a pendulum and clouted Grunt's head sideways—clubwise—knocking it half-way back to where the shovel had smacked it from, and dropping him on the ground.

Grant got up on one elbow, shaking his head. The John Deere fired up. It roared alive. Its lights came on. It clanked into gear and came chugging and grunting like a giant pig down-draw toward Grunt Tuggs.

The pick and shovel went back to working faster than ever. They looked like two pairs now with their long shadows in the headlights, and in those lights I could see Grunt still blinking the glaze from his eyes, staring at that old black van that the dirt twisted and snaked off of like something alive—that van that no one had seen for five months, along with Uncle and Cherry and Ralph, and all of them together last seen alive by Grunt Tuggs himself. Grunt pushed his chest up off the ground, but still couldn't get the rest of his body moving before the John Deere had reached him. His legs lay dead as cordwood as the John Deere stopped and set the bottom teeth of its skip-loader against the dirt a foot from Grunt.

My throat was bulging up toward my mouth, like I was going to puke my heart out. Every square inch of me wanted out of that draw, but I had no more muscle to move than a shadow does. The grader grunted, bit down, chewed loose the plug of gravel Grunt lay on, and hoisted him, its jaw drooling pebbles that drizzed down like hungry spit. The handle of the van's rear door twitched downward once, then again, and again, and again—and popped the gritty doorcatch free. The door shoved open with a noise like broken teeth grinding.

Ralph stuck his muzzle out into the headlight beams. Those beams showed all the detail of him, the fur-clumps dangling from gluey black skin. You could see through the gaps in his snout to the honeycombed bone of him, see the maggots wrestling and crowding and twisting their little tails in there like thousands of tiny flames. Ralph jumped down from the van. His tail, all busy with worms, wagged a little, like he was pleased to see old Grunt. As the dog trotted to him, you could see his left shoulder had a big, frayed blast-hole blown out of it—splintered shoulder-bone showed like chalk in the moldy muscle. The John Deere lowered Grunt, like a waiter bowing. He was struggling his shotgun to his shoulder, but when the scoop banged down he rolled out, and as he came face up, Ralph set his huge paws on his chest, jawed him by the throat, and clamped his head down hard as iron to the gravel. That was when Uncle came out—and that was when I ran.

True enough, I looked before I ran. I saw him plain enough, or most of him—how *he* had a blast-hole in the left side of his chest and how the headlights made it look black as a moon crater in the crumbly white cheese of his skin. How he had a pipe wrench in one hand and a pair of bolt-cutters in the other, and how his lizard-skinned fingers had a grip on them like roots on earth. But it was his eyes I didn't want to see. We both knew I was there—I understood that—but I just didn't want to make a personal point of it, eye to eye. So I ran. I was still slick as a shadow. I was scared hollow, and light as air. I cut across that slope to the head of the draw as Grunt's bellowing started. I fired up my truck and gunned up the roadcut. Jouncing, flinging rollers high and wide, I rocketed through Uncle Tuggs's yard, made the highway and took off for help.

I thought I'd never reach it in time—not before my brainsprings started popping out of my ears—but at last I saw that light up ahead. I swung into the lot and jumped out. I ran in and got a twelve-pack and a pint of Jack Daniels.

Behind the wheel again, breathing a little easier, I took the freeway down to River Road, which I took out to the ocean. I drove slow, and worked on the twelve-pack, and thought about it all. It seemed pretty clear to me, when I added it all up, that Uncle just had no reason to have it in for *me*, especially when I'd helped him so much.

When I got to the coast, I turned south, and I dumped the firewood and the broken saw off of several cliffs along a ten-mile stretch of Highway 1. It was a good three hundred dollars worth of firewood. Somehow, after all I'd been put through, having to do that really pissed me off.